D1267233

BONNEY'S PLACE

Books by Leon Hale

TURN SOUTH AT THE SECOND BRIDGE
ADDISON

 SHEARER PUBLISHING • BRYAN

Bonney's PLACE

by Leon Hale

Illustrated by Buck Schiwetz

Published in 1981 by
Shearer Publishing
3208 Turtle Grove, Bryan, Texas 77801

First Edition published in 1972 by Doubleday Books

Special thanks to Texas A&M Press
for use of *Buck Schiwetz Memories*.

Library of Congress Cataloging in Publication Data
  Hale, Leon 1921–
    Bonney's Place
    Reprint of the 1972 ed. Published by Doubleday
    Garden City, N.Y.
    PN 81-82753
    ISBN 0-940672-02-2 (sc)
         0-940672-01-4 (hc)
         0-940672-00-6 (le)

This book has been printed on acid free paper and sewn in
signatures. The paper will not yellow with age, the binding
will not deteriorate, and the pages will not fall out.

Manufactured in the United States of America

*All the characters in this book are ficticious
and any resemblance to actual persons, living
or dead, is purely coincidental.*

BONNEY'S PLACE

After that first day, I saw the woman Millie only one other time, several weeks later at Slat's wedding. Until then, I didn't even know who she was.

But she became an important woman to me almost immediately because of what happened just five minutes after I walked in. If she hadn't been there it wouldn't have happened and I wouldn't have made Bonney's acquaintance as quick and easy, and I might have gotten started all wrong.

She and Bonney were playing eight-ball that afternoon, and she was giving him a hard time.

Maybe you've seen women like Millie. At first sight, I disliked her. I decided she was thirty-five. That's a hobby of mine, guessing the ages of women. I'm not really certain I'm very good at it, since I seldom find out the correct ages after I've guessed. But whatever Millie's age was, she was fighting it. She had on this thin lavender blouse, and it would have looked all right except a roll of fat was bulging out just above the top of her skirt. Made her look as if she had a loaf of French bread stuck in her clothes. Her skirt was way too short, so when she leaned across the pool table to make a shot you could see her underwear. It wasn't an interesting sight, though, because she wasn't wearing hose and her legs had all these dark purple veins showing—an entire watershed of purple veins, with the main streams and all their tributaries laid out in detail.

Then she had two mouths. First she had the one she was born with, which was thin-lipped and turned down at the corners a little. The second mouth was the one she *wished* she had, and so she'd painted it over the first one with a lipstick. The two mouths didn't fit at all. The second one tried to be full and curvy and it just looked awful, with

1

the first one showing beneath it. I've never met a two-mouthed woman like that I thought was a good person.

But then I suppose Millie might have looked pretty good, maybe even sexy, to a guy of about fifty, especially if he's drinking bourbon and chasing it with beer. That's what the fellow sitting next to the pool table was doing. A pint in a brown paper sack was lying flat on the table in front of him. Every minute or two he'd take a short swig out of a bottle of beer, as a way of stoking the fire the bourbon had built. You see a lot of that in taverns in Texas, where a bar often means beer only.

The fellow with the bottle was a big, heavy-shouldered man with hardly any neck at all and maybe three days of stubble on his jaws. His sagging eyelids said he'd been at the bourbon and beer a good while, even though it was only about three o'clock in the afternoon. But he wasn't dozing. He was zeroed in on the eight-ball game, watching all the moves made by Bonney and Millie. And he wasn't pleased.

The moves were being made mainly by Millie, and all of them in Bonney's direction. That's why it was an awkward situation. Pretending to line up a shot, Millie would wiggle around the table and do her damnedest to touch Bonney in a way that tried to look accidental but didn't succeed. I mean she'd just brush against him slightly, or hit him a glancing blow with her hip, or put her hand on his shoulder while she was looking at the lay of the balls on the table. It made Bonney nervous. When Millie touched him he drew back just a tiny bit. Not much, because if he retreated it would be admitting he knew the woman was after him, and he didn't want to admit it. That was plain.

Bonney hadn't even looked up at me when I came in, and he made no move toward setting his cue aside to wait on me. So I just leaned on the bar and watched the game. I shoot better than a fair stick myself and any game of eight-ball is of interest to me, even when one of the players is a two-mouthed woman who doesn't know how to hold a cue.

Bonney was shooting the spots. So Millie had the stripes and she was three balls to the good when I started watching. The reason was that Bonney was throwing the contest, which

2

isn't unusual in such a match since it's no fun to beat a woman. Twice I watched Bonney miss the trey when it was sitting in the hole. A guy who handles a stick like he was handling it just doesn't miss such shots.

It wasn't hard to tell Bonney had served his time around a pool table. The signs were all there—the way he kept his feet under him, the way he made his bridge, the way he anticipated, and the way his cue slid through the crook of his left index finger, like it was moving on its own steam and not being propelled by a man's arm at all. It's a beautiful thing to see, and I never watched a guy handle a stick any better than Bonney was doing it, unless you want to count Shote in Houston and Tate in Albuquerque and guys like that. But then they're pros, and make a living at it.

Every time Millie made contact with Bonney, he'd glance over at the table to see if the big fellow was reacting. The woman had Bonney in a spot and she was enjoying it. She was talking in this giggly, little-girl way, about what a disadvantage she was at, playing with a big strong man who'd had so much *experience*, and then she'd look up at Bonney and smile sort of crooked. She really didn't have a bad face, but when she smiled that crooked smile the painted mouth didn't follow the natural one. I hate to see a thing like that, especially on a woman who would look real nice if she dressed right and wouldn't try to act like a kid.

Bonney still had five spots on the table when he put an end to the game. He did it by missing the six in the corner in a way that the cue ball, with an almighty amount of backspin on it, retreated and kissed the eight and sunk it in the side. It was a remarkable shot, and I had no doubt it was intentional.

Well, in any eight-ball game in this world, when you make the eight out of turn that way, you have lost. The woman knew at least that much, and when the eight fell she began to jump about like a high school cheerleader. She danced over to Bonney and before he could retreat she threw this big hug on him. Just really laid it on him, as if she was out of her wits with joy to win a game of eight-ball. And yet, the way I had it figured, she was using the game as an excuse to make trouble.

Bonney tried to draw back but he didn't make it in time. So he decided to respond to the hug in a casual manner, as a man will when he's getting a going-over by a woman that way. He grinned, and sort of ducked, and reached out his right hand to pat the woman on the back a time or two, merely as a way of returning the hug with the very smallest amount of enthusiasm.

He made a mistake. He patted Millie low. I mean right on her fanny. It was almost comical, because when he realized what he'd done, Bonney tucked his hand behind him, as if he didn't want to claim it if it was going to do things like that. I could almost hear him suck in his breath, and he looked at the big man to see when the storm would strike.

It struck immediately.

The big fellow came out of his seat and the front of his thighs bumped the table and sent it scooting.

"All right, Bonney," he growled, "by godamighty that'll be enough of that stuff." He kicked backward and turned over the chair at his heels. The stubble on his short neck seemed to bristle.

"Now hold on a minute, Henry," Bonney said. "Don't get yourself all stirred up. It was just an accident, was all it was." He stepped toward Henry with his right palm out, a gesture that asked the big man to calm down.

Henry switched the beer bottle from his left hand to his right and grasped it by the neck. "By god, you put that by god cue down or I'll lay this bottle across your skull."

Why, he *meant* that, and it was a fearsome thing to hear. Bonney looked at the cue still in his left hand, and then back at the big man, and his expression was pained. A pool cue, I suppose you know, can be a terrible weapon when it's swung like a baseball bat with the butt end out. But it was obvious Bonney had no intention of using it. He wasn't even holding it the way he'd have to if he meant to swing it.

"Aw, *Henry* . . ." He said it as if his feelings were hurt. He dropped the cue. It made a terrible racket on the bare wooden floor.

And that moment I saw something that surprised me a little. Bonney was scared. His mouth was stiff and white at the corners where the blood had drained away. It surprised me because fear on that face just didn't seem right. I mean it just wasn't the kind of face you expect to see it on.

Then I did something I just never do, and I'm not sure yet why I did it. I spoke out, loud, and tried to make it sound testy. "Is anybody waiting on trade around here? I need a cup of coffee."

Bonney looked at me then as if he hadn't even known I was in the place. But his face relaxed.

"Sit down a minute, Henry," he said. "I got a customer to wait on."

"You got one right here," Henry said, still clutching the bottle by the neck.

"Henry, I *got* to wait on *cus*tomers. Now I'm askin' you to sit down and calm out a little." Bonney circled slowly around Henry and got behind the bar. "Whatcha need?" he asked me.

"Coffee."

He turned and looked at the glass vacuum coffeepot. "It's been made since six o'clock this mornin'. It'll be pretty hairy. Make you some fresh, if you want to wait."

I said I'd take the hairy.

He sloshed a big cup two-thirds full of the stuff, about the color of crude oil. His hands were trembling a little. They weren't the hands which just minutes earlier had been wielding a pool cue as if they didn't know what it was to shake.

I tested the coffee, just a sip, and Bonney stood there and watched and seemed to have a special interest in how I'd like it.

"You use cream?" he asked. "I'll get you some cream." He disappeared through the swinging door to the kitchen. In two seconds he poked his head out again. "It's this powdered cream, is all it is. I don't get many coffee drinkers in here. You use powdered cream?"

I said I did and he set it on the counter. "Hey, you want sugar? I got a sugar jar around here somewhere."

So he was making a project out of serving the coffee, burning time, hoping the big man Henry would settle down. But it wasn't working. Henry was at the bar now, leaning, staring

5

at Bonney, and his right elbow was resting not a foot from my coffee cup. The beer bottle was still in his hand.

Bonney located one of these heavy glass sugar jars, with a small hole in the top. It had maybe an inch of sugar in it, all caked at the bottom. "I been meanin' to put some rice in this jar," Bonney said. "You put rice in the sugar it soaks up the moisture and helps the sugar pour."

"Bonney?" the big man Henry said. "Listen, Bonney, by god . . ."

"Hold on a minute, Henry," Bonney answered, and he whammed the sugar jar on the bar to break the cake in the bottom. "There. Ought to pour now. I'm gonna get me couple pounds rice next time I'm in town. Had a fellow in here from New Mexico one time, from Roswell. He said they don't have any trouble pourin' sugar out there. Pours just like sand, all the time. It's the dry weather, does that." He was mopping the counter where he'd spilled a little coffee, keeping his head down, not looking at Henry. I noticed the scar tissue over his eyes. One of his eyebrows was divided by a bare spot of colorless skin where hair wouldn't grow. Here was a guy who'd been hit a few times.

"Bonney," the big man Henry said, all low and mean, "by god, Bonney, you listen to me . . ."

Henry straightened up and bellowed. "Bonney!"

So Bonney threw the wet towel down and put both hands on the bar and spoke to Henry straight. "Now look, Henry, you want me to apologize? All right, I apologize. But that thing happened over there, it wasn't anything to get steamed up about. It wasn't anything but an accident."

"Yeah, well, you been havin' too many accidents like that around here."

Bonney drew a deep breath. He looked over at Millie and then at me and he said, "All right, let's ask this man here. He's a stranger, just came in, saw the whole thing. Let's just ask him, how it looked to him."

Then Millie was staring at me like I was some kind of a blinking judge, about to announce a verdict. So was Bonney, and even Henry turned to me and heaved a bourbon-and-beer

6

breath in my direction that almost made me gasp. Lord, he smelled like a forty-acre swamp.

I didn't care to witness a beer-joint brawl so I said, "It didn't look like anything to me. Just a friendly game of eight-ball. Tell the truth, when I came in I figured the two of them playing there were . . . well, maybe brother and sister, just having a game."

Bonney's eyes grinned at me. I picked up my coffee cup and sipped, wondering whether Henry might swing the bottle at my skull now instead of Bonney's. But the astonishing thing was that he accepted my decision, grunted, and turned away.

Millie waltzed over and took his arm. "Come on. You need some sleep." And they walked out and didn't even look back.

Then Bonney went hustling to the front door and yelled something I thought would surely start the trouble all over again.

"Henry? Henry!" he called. "Henry, if you ever come in this place and threaten me with a beer bottle again, I promise you they'll take you out this door feet first!"

He slammed the door and came grinning back to the bar. Outside I heard the woman Millie laugh, high and loud, and then there was the sound of a car driving off.

"Say," Bonney laughed, rubbing his hands, "you just did me a big favor. I owe you a beer, man." And he took one from the icebox and pulled it before I could say no thanks. When I did say it, he shrugged, and drank the beer himself.

I finished the coffee and fished some change out of my pocket. Bonney took a dime from me and rung it up on the cash register. I couldn't help thinking he might have refused the dime, seeing he'd just offered me a free beer.

"Tell you what," I said to him, "if you want to return the favor, you might satisfy my curiosity about why you yelled what you did at Henry a minute ago. I'd have sworn, when the argument started, that you were afraid of him."

He grinned again. "Well, I didn't want any trouble. You know who I thought you were when you walked in? Figured you for a Liquor Control man, or some kind of plainclothes law. They been on my tail lately. I had a little trouble out here couple weeks ago and I don't expect it'd take much more before they'd shut me down for about ninety days. You just had the look of a state man to me. It's your clothes, maybe, and the way you kept looking around and all. I just don't want any whiskey fights in here, especially on Wednesday afternoon at three o'clock. Saturday nights, it wouldn't be so bad. They expect it more, I reckon. But on Wednesday afternoon, well, you know, it might look like this is some kind of a bad place." He laughed, and presented his back to me a couple of seconds and looked through the wide serving window and into the kitchen. Evidently he didn't spot what he was looking for and turned back.

"But that's not really why I was scared," he went on. "If you think I'd be afraid to tie into Henry, you're mighty right I *would* be. That bastard's *mean*. He can be a real tush hog when he gets on that beer-and-whiskey diet, and he's been on it now two, three days. Listen, you won't find many of these cowboys and mill hands around here that cares about mixing it up with Henry, not even the young ones with tight pants. That gal, that woman with him, she's just a damn tramp and she's got to act like one and Henry he takes it personal. He's dumb, is Henry's trouble. Just hasn't read many books. But when he's sober he's real soft. What you said, about me and Millie being brother and sister, that was right down Henry's road. It was a good thing to say. You saw how it softened him." He laughed again. "Brother and sister. That was really the right thing to say."

He drained the beer bottle, took a step backward, and flipped it into a case of empties. He snapped his fingers when the bottle fell precisely into one of the cardboard compartments, butt-first, just like it was supposed to go. I'd been noticing. Every move Bonney made had a little flair, a bit of style. Even when he'd been scared earlier, this had been so. He was a mover, almost never still, and yet he was smooth. All his motions seemed to be accomplishing something, whether they did or not. He'd light up a smoke, and there was a nice even flow to the way he took the pack out and reached for the lighter he kept in his watch pocket and fired up and put the lighter back, all in one sweeping move.

"All right," I said, standing up to leave, "but if you're really

8

afraid of Henry, why did you go out there and yell at him the way you did?"

He seemed surprised at the question. "Why, man, I can't let him *know* I'm afraid of him, that's why. It wouldn't be good business."

He turned and leaned to glance through the serving window. A tall Negro boy stood in the back entrance to the place, holding the screen door open and looking outside at something drawing his attention. Bonney watched him a few seconds, then cracked the kitchen door and said, "Hodamighty, Turnip, shut the screen. You're gonna let all my flies out."

The boy stepped in and let the door close but continued to stare outside.

"You got three dirty tables in here," Bonney called to him. "And be damn sure you wash your hands, if you've been over there with that little yellow gal again."

The boy came grinning through the swinging door, took the damp towel from the bar and began wiping a table. "Naw, I ain't been over there. I been in the barn. Molly Bitch havin' her pups. Got three so far and all solid white. Not a spot on 'em. I reckon that Bill dog of Mister Brad's must be the daddy of 'em."

Bonney snorted. "If that's so you might as well heave 'em all in the tank right now, because they won't ever do nothin' but sit on a grass burr and howl when it hurts."

The boy grinned again but didn't answer.

"Turnip here's a dog breeder," Bonney said. "He breeds cow dogs. That's all his dogs ever do, is breed. They been breedin' around here for two years and haven't ever whelped a single pup that knows the difference between a steer calf and a tom-cat."

"Aw, Mister Bonney," the boy said, and giggled.

I felt I'd stayed long enough but I didn't want to go. Not quite yet. I spotted the cigarette machine to the right of the front door and asked Bonney for some change.

The machine refused to take one of the quarters and after I'd tried three times, Bonney glided over. "Wait a minute. Sometimes you got to get this machine's attention first." And he stood to the side and delivered it such a tremendous kick that I was amazed the glass in its front didn't shatter. "Now try," he said quietly.

It worked perfectly.

"I told that cigarette man last week," he said, "he doesn't bring me a new machine he's gonna find this one kicked out yonder in that culvert next time he comes to rob it." He disappeared into the kitchen.

While he was gone I eased back to the bar and read the display of state licenses, framed and hung between the swinging door and the serving window. They were issued to Bonham J. McCamey, Highway Café & Gro., Route 2, Farley, Texas.

Grocery? I turned to search and found the groceries on two shelves at the east end of the bar. The shelves had obviously been constructed more recently than the building, after the walls of cheap pine paneling had been stained. Bonham J. McCamey's grocery stock consisted of six cans of pork and beans, four of Vienna sausages, three of chili, and one loaf of thick-sliced bread that looked like it had been there for a month. The stock, all dusty and lonesome, sat on two one-by-twelve unpainted planks supported by black metal brackets.

I walked over to the pool table near the west wall, picked up the cue ball and banked it off the far cushion, as I suppose men everywhere do when they walk by a pool table.

"Hey, I thought you'd gone." It was Bonney, behind me. "How about a game of eight-ball? You got time?"

"All right." I said it too quick, I guess. *You're staying too long. Be careful, now.*

"Go ahead and break," Bonney said. "Be with you in a New York minute." He sailed around the end of the bar, back into the kitchen, and I heard him yell. "Turnip! Hod dang it, get your butt back in here and do a little work. Those beer drinkers be here in another hour and a half and you haven't even swept out."

I couldn't understand Turnip's answer. Something about the dogs.

"Well," Bonney said, a little more softly, "that ol' bitch been havin' pups all her life and she can have one more litter without any midwifin' from you."

He came curving back around the bar with a little smile.

"Tellin' you, if that kid dies and goes to heaven he's not gonna like the place if it's not full of cow dogs. Go ahead and break. I got till about five-thirty before those mill hands come flockin' in here."

I broke, and the phone rang. Bonney was on it for five minutes, talking low. I didn't catch any of the conversation. I leaned on my cue and inspected the interior of the Highway Café & Gro. It was a colorless, almost bleak place. Walls that tried to be knotty pine but didn't do a very good job of it. The building was a perfect rectangle, large and roomy, its wide dimension running east and west, facing the road. A space I took for a dance floor was left clear between the front door and the bar. Maybe two dozen tables were loosely arranged on the east side. Each had a salt shaker on it and two or three empty aluminum plates, the flimsy kind that frozen pies come in. They did duty as ash trays.

There was a vague balance about the interior of the place that appealed to me. The pool table in the west end, with chairs spaced along the wall for the sweaters. The small bar across the back, with six stools. The cheap metal folding chairs at the beer-drinking tables. One long table, with chairs for eight, near the east end of the bar. Four small tables on the west side, and a big butane heater between the pool table and the dance floor. Not a window was curtained and the sun bore in and produced a glare and, in the harsh light, dust particles were hovering, glinting, stirring lazily from the wash of two ancient ceiling fans. The fans bolted onto ceiling joists. But there was no ceiling. Joists and rafters and braces were exposed. Some of the lumber in the roof structure was still oozing resin, so the building wasn't old. But it was built economy-style. Here and there, used lumber was mixed in with the new. One of the ceiling fans hung almost directly above the butane heater. And it wobbled. Appeared almost ready to fall, hanging there by what amounted to only one bolt. I moved out from under it.

Through the serving window I could read a crude sign above a Dutch door, apparently leading into a back room east of the kitchen. The upper half of the door was open. The bottom half had a one-by-twelve plank nailed across its top to make a sort of serving bar. The sign said, THE DARK ROOM. What

11

could that mean? Surely not a photographic dark room. I had time to decide it was related in some way to another sign, outside, by the entrance. The one that read, WHITES ONLY. COLORED ENTRANCE AT THE SIDE. And then an arrow pointing east. You still see such signs in the Southwest. Not many, but a few. In the rural regions, mainly.

Waiting for Bonney to get off the phone, I imagined the tavern with curtains and pictures—the walls were totally bare —and I thought it would be really a nice place then, with a little decoration. The only touch of color was provided by the skimpy stock of groceries. And then a vase of slightly droopy flowers on the bar. Zinnias, loosely arranged with ferns. I walked over to see if they were genuine. They were, but they had a sick-sweet fragrance I've never associated with zinnias.

"Special occasion?" I asked when Bonney hung up the phone.

"How you mean?"

"The vase of flowers here. Thought maybe they were left over from a party or something."

"Naw. A lady, a customer of mine, brings flowers in here every afternoon and sets 'em up there. She claims the place needs a little sprucin' up." He got his cue from the floor, sighted down it carefully, examined the tip to see if dropping it had done any damage. "Now then, did you leave me anything to shoot?"

An hour later he'd beaten me four straight games. We played two more and I finally got my eye—I was a little rusty— and lucked out and won two straight. I made a pair of pretty wicked shots and he bragged on them. Seemed impressed.

A pickup truck skidded on the gravel out front. Bonney looked at the big electric clock behind the bar, a clock hard to read because of all the advertising splattered across its face by the beer distributor who furnished it.

"Well, here comes my suds guzzlers," he said. "I gotta get to work. Say, whyn't you hang around? I get a little quiet spot long about six-thirty or seven. You sort of hurt my feelings. I don't get many guys come in here and beat me two straight." But he was walking away, toward the bar, and didn't wait for a reply.

Six men came clodding in. Men who'd done a day's work.

Dirty men, dressed mostly in khaki pants and shirts that showed big arcs of sweat and salt below the armpits. They took their hats off and plopped down in the chairs at the long table nearest the bar and leaned back and spraddled their legs and heaved long sighs. Tired men, anywhere from twenty-one to fifty-five, with snow-white, sweat-bleached foreheads and red-rusty-tan faces where their hats didn't protect them from the sun.

Behind the bar Bonney's hands and arms were moving in that fluid style, doing four things at once. He was pulling quarts of beer, and nobody had placed an order. Six, eight more men came in, shouting, cursing, laughing. Bonney made the rounds, bamming the quarts on the bare tables, flipping paper cups off his forearm where he carried them, balanced.

"Hey, Bonney," a skinny fellow yelled, while five more hands from the sawmill entered, "I hear Millie's come back. How much she chargin' now?" And it brought an explosion of laughter.

"Haven't seen her," Bonney said, grinning and moving fast. "Me and Turnip been out in the barn all afternoon. We been havin' pups again." More laughter.

"Hey, Bonney, you don't happen have a beer back there been on ice, have you, and might be a little cool?"

"Hell, no. Drink it warm or go into town where it'll cost you a nickel more. Any of you guys got any money?"

"Not a red damn cent," said a young man standing near the door. But he dug in his pocket, fed a quarter into the jukebox, and then some cowboy was singing about going home to Montana with the volume at the top peg, and after that the place was filled with a roaring, a buzzing, a noise made only by working men temporarily energized by alcohol poured into empty stomachs.

I sat on a stool at the west end of the bar, next to the vase of flowers, and watched. Must have been thirty-five or forty men in the place now and Bonney hadn't yet taken an order. He knew what every one of them wanted. So they were all regulars. Once he glanced my way as he made the U-turn around the far end of the bar and next trip he set a cold can of beer in front of me, without a word, but he did it in a way that said it was on the house. It was a premium beer. Or out-of-state beer, as they call it in Texas, to distinguish it from local and cheaper brands. I supposed it was Bonney's way of favoring a newcomer, assuming a guy wearing a business suit would drink better beer than the sawmill men. I didn't have the chance to tell him I don't care for beer, local, premium, or imported. But he'd already popped the can so I found a plastic cup and nursed the beer down.

A woman in black slacks came in (I guessed her at thirty-eight) with a long-legged young girl wearing shorts. They both had sharp noses and I put them down as mother and daughter. They sat on stools at the east end of the bar. Bonney stopped in front of them, smiled at the woman and said, "Hello, Charlotte. Hear anything new at the beauty shop?"

"I haven't *been* to the beauty shop," Charlotte said.

"Well, you *look* like you've been to the beauty shop." That just melted Charlotte. She looked at Bonney the way a woman looks at a man when she'd like to hug his neck. I remembered the big fellow Henry's remark about Bonney patting the women. Yes, he would be good with the ladies, all right.

Not that he was Hollywood handsome. He had this narrow face that should have had delicate features, but instead his nose was a little broad and his eyes were too small and his chin too long. Yet when he grinned, a transformation took place. His face became an entirely different proposition from what it was when solemn and composed. His grin made things happen. I've known guys like that. Well, women too, who when they smile they seem to throw a mellow spotlight on the person they're smiling at, and it's impossible not to smile back. I noticed the young girl there at the bar. She watched Bonney work with a certain softness in her eyes, the same as her mother did, and she couldn't have been past fifteen.

"You need a haircut, Bonney," the young girl said. He rubbed his hand over his scalp and down the back of his neck and nodded and kept moving. The girl was right. His short brown hair was creeping down his neck and crowding his ears at the sides but I'd have bet a buck that haircuts weren't important to him. Here he was serving his customers and he was dressed in gray jeans and tennis shoes without socks and a T-shirt that looked as if it had been worn two days.

14

I watched him reach up and jerk a cord hanging from a light fixture over the serving window. It was a short cord and I wouldn't have thought he could reach it without straining. But he had these extra long arms that you didn't notice ordinarily because they were forever moving, seldom down at his sides.

A young fellow with a blond mustache slipped onto the stool beside me. Bonney had gone to the tables and Turnip materialized from somewhere in back to wait on the bar.

"Gimme a Pearl," the young man said.

Turnip set the bottle of beer before him but before it had time to make a ring on the bar, Bonney was back. He reached over Turnip's shoulder, grabbed the bottle and said to the boy, "No beer for you, little buddy. Come back in a couple of years."

"Aw, Bonney, I been buyin' beer now for a whole year."

"Not in here, you haven't. Look, you see this man here?" He jerked a thumb at me. "This man's with Liquor Control, just sittin' here, waitin' for me to sell beer to somebody that don't shave yet."

The boy looked at me. "He don't know how old I am."

"But I do. Now how about a red soda pop?"

The boy was embarrassed now but wouldn't back down. "It ain't right, Bonney. How come I can be old enough to be in the Guard, and stand a chance goin' to Vietnam and get my gut shot, and I can't come in and buy one lousy beer?"

Bonney faked a sigh. "Look, I'm gonna do you a favor." He reached under the bar and came up with an old campaign poster which one Ray L. Mertz had used in a race for the State Legislature. "You see this guy? He's your representative in Austin. Now you go home and get you a pencil and paper and sit down and write to him. Here's his address, zip code and everything. You tell Ray Mertz, 'Bonney don't make the liquor laws, but you do, and I want you to pass me a bill says I can buy a beer at age nineteen.' Now that's the only thing you can do about it, and you might as well tell the same thing to all those other fuzzy-cheeks you've been runnin' with."

The boy said, "I can buy beer in Farley."

"Then go to Farley."

The boy growled, the deepest he could manage, and walked out.

"Hodamighty, Turnip," Bonney said, "I swear I believe you'd set a beer in front of a wet baby. Now get on the stick, dammit, or I'm gonna run your black tail back out yonder and put you to diggin' postholes again."

Turnip didn't giggle or grin.

Bonney looked up at the clock. "Buck? Oh, Buck!"

"Ho!" came an answer from one of the tables.

"You better drag it out of here. It's nearly six o'clock. I don't want your old lady on my back again."

"Right. Thanks, Bonney." The man stood, drained a beer bottle and headed for the door.

"Hey, Buck," called a rancher-dressed, middle-aged fellow at the pool table. "Eat you a little peanut butter and tell 'er you been to a Sunday school picnic." There was scattered laughter.

"Look who's singin' *that* tune," Bonney said, razzing the cowman. "When his preacher wandered in here last week, Howard there was over by the window with a beer in his hand and tried to hide it in the hip kick of them tight britches of his and spilled it all over the seat of his pants. I had to tell the preacher Howard's got kidney trouble, and shows up with wet pants that way, all the time." The house exploded with laughter and Howard grinned and turned a little redder beneath his sun-scorched face.

When Bonney scored a simple victory like that and made the house laugh, he'd stand still a few seconds, which I'd already decided was a rare thing for him. He'd spread his feet a little and put his hands in his back pockets and stretch to his full height. I suppose he was just savoring the accomplishment, until the laughter subsided. Then he'd be off and running again. But in the few seconds he stood still, I pegged him to be six feet or better. He was generally slender and trim except for the slight stomach bulge under his T-shirt that most men develop in their middle thirties.

Well, middle thirties is what I figured, although I seldom waste any time trying to guess the ages of men the way I do women. It doesn't seem as important and isn't near as interesting a hobby, anyway.

A yellow school bus stopped out front. It was empty except for the driver. Black lettering on its side read, FARLEY INDEPENDENT SCHOOL DISTRICT. The driver came in, looking a bit out of place because he wore dark slacks and a pale blue shirt with a necktie, loose and flapping. I figured him for a young teacher, doubling as a school-bus driver. That's not uncommon in Texas, where schoolteachers are always moonlighting.

Bonney came out from behind the bar to greet the driver. "Hey, Hank." He looked at the bus as if he expected somebody else to get out of it.

"They're not with me, Bonney," the young man said. "That's what I came in to tell you."

"What happened?"

"They took off, about the middle of the morning. Mr. Acheson told me they went out for recess and just kept walking. I looked for them on the road, but didn't see any sign. I talked with Edna Hamlin, she has both of 'em in her remedial reading class, and she said they just won't respond. Said they just sit there and stare at her when she speaks to them. I don't know, Bonney. It looks like a pretty long shot to me. They're just Flynns, you know. We've never kept a Flynn in that school more than two weeks since it was built."

"Yeah." Bonney had the saddest expression on his face, like somebody had died.

"I suppose they're all right. I expect you'd find them back up the creek somewhere."

"Oh, they're all *right*," Bonney said, his face still solemn. "They've spent more nights off in the woods than under a roof. Listen, Hank, thanks. Thanks for stoppin' by. I think I know about where they are. They don't come in tomorrow, I'll go take a look. And you might watch for 'em at the bus stop, say about Monday morning. I'll send the little bastards again if I can catch 'em."

Hank looked doubtful. "I don't know, Bonney. I don't know whether they'll go or not."

"They'll *go*. Question is will they stay. But it's worth a try."

17

The young man nodded and walked out. "I'll look for them Monday."

Bonney came back to the bar, slower than I'd seen him move all afternoon.

"What's up?" asked the woman Charlotte. "Anything the matter?"

"Naw," said Bonney.

By seven o'clock, the mass of the mill hands had cleared out and Bonney had the quiet spell he'd predicted. Turnip was keeping his head down and doing his work, apparently still smarting from the scolding about serving the beer to a minor. Bonney put one foot up on the cooler, crossed his arms over a knee and looked thoughtful. He didn't move for a full minute.

"How far is it on into Farley?" I asked him.

"Seven miles, little better."

"Got a decent hotel there?"

"Got a ho*tel*. It's not exactly the Farley Hilton, though. There's a pretty nice little *mo*tel out on the west side of town. You stayin' in Farley tonight?"

"Yeah. I expect I'll be there six, maybe eight weeks. I got some work to do around there for a while."

I watched his face to see if he was going to ask me what kind of work. But I saw nothing. And he didn't ask.

"Well," he said, "don't know how you'd like it, but we got several women around here take in roomers. Fact, there's a lady just up the road here, Mrs. Whitaker, takes a roomer sometimes. Got a nice house, and she's a good woman, except she talks an awful hell of a lot. Course you'd have the seven miles to drive into Farley every day."

I said that wouldn't bother me and got off the stool and offered to pay for the beer. He refused the money and I went out to my car, a little disappointed he'd forgotten about continuing the eight-ball match.

I'd started up my engine when he popped out of the front door and hustled out to the car.

"Say," he said, "if you want to stop at Mrs. Whitaker's, it'll be that first house up yonder on the left, right there at the top of the slope. And listen, tell her Bonney sent you. Bonney McCamey. That's my name."

He stuck his hand in the window to shake.

The hotel in Farley was an old two-story white frame job. There was one window air conditioner poking out of it. I knew that cooler would be in the living quarters of the manager. It was the first week of September and it'd be six weeks, maybe more, before the weather cooled off. If I had to stay two months, I didn't intend to sleep in a puddle of my own sweat.

The motel was all right, but the old bird at the desk was raised without any manners and I am past the point of putting up with sour-faced motel managers. I drove back out to Mrs. Whitaker's. The sun was down when I got there.

She was in the front yard, watering flowers. The entire yard was devoted to flower beds. Mostly zinnias, with ferns growing in big clay pots on the front porch.

"Would you be the lady who takes a vase of flowers down to Bonney McCamey's every day?" I asked her, just to see if I was guessing right.

"That's right. I'm Grace Whitaker. Did Bonney send you?"

"He did, yes ma'am."

"Well, then he's had his beak stuck in his own beer box all afternoon, because I won't be ready until eight-thirty and Bonney would know that if he's sober."

She saw the question on my face, I guess. She said, "You didn't come to get me?"

"I came about a room. A place to stay."

She threw back her head and bellowed with laughter. "My god, you must think I'm a real pine nut. No, I don't have a car, see, and sometimes when Bonney's busy he sends one of his customers up here to get me and the flowers. I thought . . . oh well, hell's jingle bells, what's it matter? You say you want a place to stay. Did Bonney really send you?"

"Yes, he did. He said, 'Tell her Bonney sent you.' "

"Then that's good enough. How long you known Bonney?"

I looked at my watch. "About five hours."

19

"Well, it never takes Bonney long. Did you play eight-ball with him?"

"Six games."

"Did you win one?"

"Won two."

"Not two straight."

"Yes ma'am, two straight."

"Ha. That's why he wants you to stay here. Well, you look harmless."

"Mrs. Whitaker, my name's John Lancaster. I'm forty-five years old and a widower. I make an honest living and pay my bills. I smoke two packs of filter tips a day and sometimes burn holes in bedspreads. I drink bourbon and rain water, about three good stiff ones before supper. I haven't been drunk in twenty years, I don't bring home stray women, you can't hear me snore if you're half a mile away, and I like dogs."

She gave me a stern stare. "I have a cat," she said. "Sleeps in the house."

"Like cats too."

Her face spread a smile I wouldn't have thought it could manage. "Come on in," she said.

I liked her immediately. Guessed her at sixty-three. She was a tall, long-shanked, rawboned woman, with a heavy jaw, a big mouthful of teeth, and a voice about like one of the sawmill hands.

She led the way inside. "Come look at the room. It was my son's. I lost him in Korea in '55 and his daddy died in '56. I'm a lonesome woman but I'm sixty-five and I'm over the hill and I won't bother you." She turned to face me. "It's all right about the bourbon. Keep it in my kitchen if you want to, except I may tap it myself now and then, when I get the droops. I go down there to Bonney's every night, and sometimes I drink his beer. But you know what I think of it? Think of beer?"

She waited, and I said, "No, what?"

"It's slop. It gives me gas." She walked on and the house echoed her laughter.

I hoped the room had an air conditioner in it, because I'd already decided to rent it.

20

"You might as well know," Mrs. Whitaker said, "this room's hot as seven kinds of hell. It used to have a cooler in the window, but one night while I was down at Bonney's some of these nesters around here came and walked off with it. If you want to buy one and stick it in there, that's up to you. I can't afford one. I get thirty a month for the room. For six bits a day extra, I'll serve you breakfast. Eggs and bacon and sourdough biscuits and cane syrup and all the coffee you're man enough to drink. For four bits more I'll fix you a lunch, two baloney sandwiches and a thermos of iced tea. I don't cook at night."

I said I'd pass the lunch but I might take the breakfast.

"Now look here. You've got a private bathroom. Jim, he was my husband, he put it in. He was a plumber, and a carpenter, the best between here and Houston. When our boy turned sixteen and his comb was gettin' a little red and he started runnin' around at night, Jim put him in this bathroom and cut him a door here to come and go. But you can just use the front door, if you want. Joe always did." Her voice softened when she spoke of the boy. "Joe always said he was the only boy in Kirby County ever got an indoor john for a birthday present."

The room was all right but the temperature in it was probably knocking around ninety degrees so I'd have to buy the window air conditioner. I went back through the living room to go out and get my gear. It was the sort of living room you expect to see in a rural home with a front yard planted entirely in flowers. Old, overstuffed furniture, whatnot shelves in the corners, clean but worn rugs with big floral designs, wavy brown stains on the ceiling where the roof had leaked on the wallpaper. Four photographs in dime-store frames sat on the mantle. There was the boy, Joe, all solemn-faced in a Marine uniform, showing his mother's heavy jaw. There was his father, looking uncomfortable in a suit of clothes. Even in the photograph I could see his bleached forehead, same as the mill hands had. The third photo showed father, mother, and son together, standing among the flowers in the yard. Then the fourth was a smaller picture of a young man who looked vaguely familiar. I read the scribbling down in the corner. "Love and kisses to Rose-Mama from Bonney."

Mrs. Whitaker caught me looking at the picture.

"I didn't recognize him at first," I said. "It's Bonney. A lot younger."

She came and stood beside me. "Yes."

I thought she was about to say more but instead she asked, "Was anybody in Bonney's this afternoon when you got there?"

I said No, and wondered why I told that little lie. I supposed it was because Bonney had denied, when the beer drinkers asked him earlier, that he'd seen the woman Millie. "Who is Rose-Mama?" I asked.

"Aw, that's what Bonney calls me. He's got to hang a name on everybody and everything. Back when Joe and Bonney commenced messin' around together, I had a lot of roses. Twice as many as now. Every time Bonney came I'd be out there foolin' with all my roses, always foolin' with roses, so he started callin' me that. He was a lovable little old thing then. But mean? Hell's jingle bells but he was mean. Always in hot water."

"What sort of mean? Like picking fights?"

"No-o-o, not Bonney. He never picked a fight in his life. He's been *in* a good many, but not by his own choice. He was just always a mess." She fished a man's handkerchief out of her dress pocket and blew her nose. And kept talking:

"Reason I go down there all the time, I walk in and Bonney comes sailin' out from behind that bar and grabs me like he hasn't seen me in a year and puts a big hug on me. Mister, he pretty near pops the pants off me, and gives me a big kiss, and he'll say, 'Rose-Mama, you're the prettiest thing that's walked through that door since you left last night.' He does that to *me*, an old dried-up, lantern-jawed, sixty-five-year-old mare like me, and I don't mind tellin' you it does me good. Like I said, I'm a lonesome old woman. But Bonney . . ." Her tone softened. "Well, Bonney gives me a reason to take a bath every day, and put on a fresh dress. Wasn't for him, I'd just mope around here and dry up and die."

Then I made my first error. "Mrs. Whitaker, what sort of

22

reputation does Bonney have? I mean, would you say he's an honest man?"

Before I got the question out, I wished I had it back. It was a stupid thing to ask. Mrs. Whitaker didn't react to it in a spectacular way, but I could tell she thought it was a strange question. She was looking at me closely, with what I felt was distrust, maybe suspicion. I cursed myself, because I'd been doing real well, just the way I'd planned, and I was sure she'd liked me from the start, and here I had to go and big-mouth and risk lousing up the works.

She was about to say something when I hurriedly explained that I was just interested in Bonney because he'd impressed me as a very unusual kind of a man, and I didn't mean to *imply* anything, of course. It sounded mighty weak, but it helped. Mrs. Whitaker sat down on the big sofa. She smiled at me, but not a warm smile as before.

"Look," she said, "I don't know what your business is. But I can guess that you mean to hang around down there at Bonney's and try to beat him playin' eight-ball. If that's so, you ought to know you're not the first one that's been through here tryin' it. But before you pay your first month's rent *here*, I'll tell you that my roomers don't go around askin' whether people are honest, and especially not Bonney. He'll pay his bets, if you happen to beat him another game or two."

I apologized for the question, said I didn't even know why I asked it, and suggested we forget it.

"All right," she said, "but before we do, there's a thing or two you ought to know about Bonney." I sat down, hoping now that she'd go ahead and answer the question that had made her bristle. Bonney was right. Mrs. Whitaker talked an awful hell of a lot.

"There's mighty few folks around here in these woods that don't owe Bonney McCamey, one way or another, and that includes the nesters, maybe the very ones that lifted my window cooler. But now whether he's honest or not, hell's jingle bells, that just never has come up. But you get the chance, ask Buck Thornton about Bonney sometime, or ask Ben Ashley, or Charlotte Ord, they all hang out down there. Ask that colored boy Bonney keeps. He's . . ."

23

"You mean Turnip?"

"Yes. You saw him, then. Well, now, Turnip's a fair sample. That bunch of high muckety-muck women in town have been tryin' to get Turnip away from Bonney and put him in that school they've built for boys like that. Built it so they could get their name in the paper. They've got about as much interest in colored boys as I've got in the welfare of a jackass." She snorted. But the little storm I'd created in her by asking the wrong question had abated. I was relieved, and sat listening while she talked about what was plainly her favorite topic.

"That Turnip boy's daddy is up in Huntsville, doing twenty years for stickin' a knife in a constable, and his mama . . . well, godamighty himself may know where she is, and if he doesn't then the devil damn well does. Turnip wanders up to Bonney's back door. So what does Bonney do? He takes him in. I mean *in*. Builds him a room, on his own house. Puts him to work, and gets a pair of those cow dogs for him to raise. Why, before then, that boy never had a roof over his head you couldn't throw a cat through, and now Bonney's got him workin' and makin' change and learnin' something.

"Then those little Flynn boys that I expect you'll meet. They're just a couple of woods colts. Run up and down the creek like a pair of coons. May not come home for three days, and their old man layin' up drunk on that poison whiskey he makes. Those kids must be eight, one of 'em maybe ten years old, and they can't even read. All right, Bonney loads 'em in his pickup and takes 'em into Farley and gets their hair cut and buys 'em new clothes and puts shoes on 'em and then the next morning he kicks their skinny little tails on the school bus. Of course that doesn't make him an *honest* man, but you see what I mean."

The Flynn boys. They'd be the ones the bus driver stopped to talk to Bonney about. I decided against telling Mrs. Whitaker that they'd walked away from school. It was too early for me to be delivering local news.

I got my gear unloaded and took my bottle of bourbon and set it on the kitchen table. Good lord, the table had oilcloth on it, and a fruit jar with silverware stuck in it, just the way we used to do it at home when I was a kid. Mrs. Whitaker

24

came in from the back bedroom, smelling of body powder, decked out in a fresh-ironed housedress. She had a bourbon with me, and went out and cut two dozen zinnias. She arranged them with fern in a cheap yellow vase, looked at the kitchen clock, and picked up the phone.

"Get me Bonney's, Ada," she told the phone. And while the call was being placed, she took up a spray can with a label that said Lavender Bloom and squirted each one of the zinnias square in the face. "Zinnias," she told me, "are about the only thing I got with a bloom on it this time of year, and Bonney says they stink. So I put a little of this spray on 'em. Makes 'em smell real sweet." She brought the phone back to her mouth. "Turnip? Tell Bonney not to bother sendin' after me. Tell him I got me a man here in my kitchen, a pool player, and he's gonna bring me down."

And so I went to Bonney's Place that first night, accompanied by a dried-up, lantern-jawed, sixty-five-year-old mare, carrying two dozen zinnias sprayed with Lavender Bloom.

2.

Within two days I was almost certain that Bonney was my man. I felt pretty smug about it, because so far I'd handled everything well. Bonney turned out to be a talker, one who rivaled even Mrs. Whitaker. I figured I'd have him nailed within a month.

Finding him was easy. In the beginning I imagined the search might take weeks, maybe a year, because the only clue I had was the strange note the Old Man wrote before he died. Midge and I—Midge, she's my daughter, twenty-one years old and a senior in college and engaged—we found the note together, two days after his funeral when we were going through his things. That was when we knew the money was gone. Fifteen thousand dollars—all gone.

25

It was the insurance money on the house I bought for my mother and the Old Man, when he quit work. He loved to fish so I put them up in this sturdy little place at Salt Cedar Cut down on the coast. And they were comfortable, as long as it lasted.

It lasted until Hurricane Carla blew in and hit the shore just fifteen miles below the Cut. When the storm was over they found Mom's body buried under two feet of sand and silt, not a hundred yards from where the house had stood. The Coast Guard found the Old Man, two miles inland, half alive, lying in the bottom of a skiff. Mom had fallen out of the skiff, he said, when they tried to leave the house after it finally became clear to him that the storm wasn't going to let them stay.

I know why they didn't get out ahead of the storm, as all the others did. The Old Man was just too damned stubborn. Thought he knew more about hurricanes than the Weather Bureau.

I fought the insurance people for three months after that storm. Finally they came across with the fifteen thousand settlement and the Old Man came to live with us. He put the money in the bank and never spent anything but the interest. He'd always say, "When I go on to glory, that money belongs to Midge, for her college education." He said that almost every day. Even after Midge graduated from high school and finished her first year of college, he kept saying it. The day we found the letter he wrote, Midge was getting ready to go back to school for her senior year.

It was in a plain business envelope and had my name on the outside in the Old Man's cramped scrawl.

Son, you wont read this untill I go onto glory. Son I have to tell you about the insurence money. The 15000 dollars ought to be your's and Midge because you bought the house at The Cut. But I am sorry the money is gone. I loaned it to the Bonnie boy so we could go partners, he has not come back and I dont know where he is. Son I ask you one last thing, when you go looking for the boy, before you jump him find out what he did with the money first. I don't think he is crooked, learn what you can about him, then do what you think is right. Remember this is your Dads last request before going onto glory. Dad.

I read the letter twice and I felt exactly nothing. That "last request" business sounded entirely phony to me, I suppose because I'd heard the Old Man deliver so many of his fake pronouncements. But the letter had a different effect on Midge. "You know," she said, "I think that's the only letter of Granddad's I ever saw. He sure wasn't much of a speller." And she buried her head in my lap and cried.

It was strange to me that Midge felt that sort of grief about her grandfather. In the years he lived with us, he didn't give Midge anything but a hard time. He was a bothersome, nosy, troublesome old man. I suppose I hated him, at least for a while.

Not because his stubbornness helped kill Mom. When I really began to hate him was the day he spoke the two words to me. The two words were, "Eva's dead."

You have to know a little about Eva. She was my wife for eighteen years.

For a long time after I married her, I couldn't quite believe that Eva was true. She was a miracle that happened to me a long time ago in Baton Rouge, Louisiana.

The first time I ever touched her, my knees threatened to buckle. I walked into the lobby of that law office and she was standing there waiting to see Sid Terrell. She was some kind of a young woman. Twenty years old. Five feet seven. A hundred and thirty-six pounds. And all that jet-black hair parted in back and braided and coiled on top of her head so that it made a sort of hat, a hat no designer could duplicate because it was that beautiful. She had on this pale green sweater-suit outfit. I stood there staring and grinning at her and then Sid came out of the office and said, "This is my little sister Eva." I waited to see if she'd hold out her hand. When she did and I took it—well, that's when the horse kicked me, as we used to say.

We got married three months after I first touched her. She

27

wasn't in that big a hurry but she gave in after I threatened to quit my job and just follow her around Louisiana.

She had this little joke, about Midge being born "nine months and ten minutes" after our wedding. I sat by her narrow bed in the maternity ward and cried and had as many labor pains as she did. It seemed a raw deal to me, that Eva had to suffer like that just to bring into the world a little knot-headed baby. She saw my anguish and reached out from that hospital bed and took my hand and smiled through her pains and comforted me. Eva's Cajun magic. She could put anything into that smile. Love, sex, understanding, sympathy, anything.

It took me a long time to learn how to share Eva even with Midge. I never did learn to share her with the Old Man, after he came to stay with us. He and I almost never talked and Eva carried the load. She put up with his meddling in her kitchen and made all his favorite dishes and she even got up in the middle of the night and put the heating pad on his hairy old leg, the one that got hurt in the hurricane and never quite healed.

There toward the end it got so bad Eva and I couldn't even make love. I'd get her in the bedroom and shut the door and in ten minutes here he'd come, rapping on the floor with that goddamned cane of his and asking Eva where in hell the aspirin was.

The last night I saw her alive, she executed one of her Beautiful Ideas. The Old Man had been following us around the house for about a week and she knew it was raveling my nerves. Well, about eight o'clock I was sitting in the living room and I heard this "psst, psst." I turned around and saw Eva beckoning. I went back to the kitchen and, my god, she was dressed up like the national debt and she had an overnight bag in her hand. She smiled at me in a way that would heat up a statue and she said, "Hiya, stranger, how'd you like to take me to a motel?"

How about that? And us married for eighteen years. She had a hip cocked the way a woman stands when she wants to look seductive and one foot turned so the light caught the nylon on her ankle.

"Let me get my wallet," I told her, and she laughed.

28

So we drove just a dozen blocks from home and I paid twenty-five bucks for a motel room with low ceilings and deep carpets and about half an acre of bed. Eva went in the bathroom and stayed fifteen minutes. She came out in a shorty see-through nightgown and stood there being thirty-eight years old and I promise you I wouldn't have traded her for anything I ever saw in the *Playboy* center fold-out. We stayed until long past midnight. The next day I had to go to Albuquerque. Flying across Texas I sat and looked out at the clouds and thought about Eva in that motel room, and smiled like a silly damn high school boy. And I kept smiling all the way to New Mexico.

You see? You see what I mean?

I got back from Albuquerque four days later. I walked into the house at eleven o'clock at night and right away I knew—something was wrong. Lights were on in every room. The sheets on our bed were rumpled, the pillows wadded. Nobody answered my calls. The door to the Old Man's room was open. He was sitting on the edge of his bed. He looked at me over the top of his glasses. And he spoke the two words.

"Eva's dead."

It made no sense for me to blame the Old Man. But for a while I did blame him. Couldn't escape the feeling that if he hadn't said the words, they wouldn't be true. And I resented that it had been him, not me, at home with Eva that night. He wasn't responsible. He hadn't contributed to Eva's death in the same way his stubbornness had helped kill Mom. But I wasn't thinking quite straight, and for two weeks after we buried Eva I really hated that man. Loathed the sight of him. Ugly, old, whining. So I put him in a rest home. He didn't want to go.

Lakecrest was the name of the place. He called it "the bone yard." It was ninety miles from home, and that distance appealed to me. At least a dozen such homes were within ten miles of us, but Lakecrest was the only one he'd ever shown an interest in. A year earlier I'd taken him along on a trip to Beaumont, mainly to get him out of Eva's hair for a day. And he had spotted this rest home by the highway, in the Beaumont suburbs. When he commented on it I turned around and went back and we took a look at the place. Met the manager, a fellow named Bailey. He had waxy skin and looked to me like an undertaker.

I was encouraged, at first. The Old Man bragged on the home. He went out on the grounds and visited. He stuck his cane under his arm, Fred Astaire-style, and pranced around among the old gents and the white-haired women sitting on the benches. He pulled himself up straight and walked on the balls of his feet. He called the nice old ladies honey and he slapped the old men on the back and asked how they were doin', ol' buddy. *He* wasn't old. He was a savior, come to comfort the sick and the sorrowful, to cure the lame and the halt. Before we left he returned to Bailey and gave him a playful tap on the thigh with his cane and said, "Tell you what, podna, save me a stall here. I might need it one of these days." When we got back in the car he almost collapsed, exhausted from the effort of trying to be young for half an hour. I had to help him in the house when we got home. So I knew, after that day, he'd never go to a rest home voluntarily.

But after Eva's funeral, I couldn't stand having him underfoot, talking constantly about her, saying over and over those two words about her being dead. So I just called Bailey at Lakecrest and said we were coming. When I told the Old Man, he nodded slowly. He didn't say a word. The next morning he was up early. At six o'clock he was sitting in the living room with his hat on. He spoke maybe half a dozen words to me in the two hours it took to drive to Lakecrest.

It didn't take long to check him into the home, and then we were standing out front, for the good-bye.

"Son," he said—I don't think he ever called me by my first name in his life—"Son, it's mighty good of you, to fix me up in this place."

Oh god, now he's going to stick the knife in me. "You'll be all right," I said.

"Sure, sure." He looked down and traced a pattern with his cane on the asphalt of the parking lot. "I could come back, I guess, like on weekends. Bailey says there's a bus."

"Sure you can. Any time you want. We'll come get you."

"And Christmas. I could come Christmas."

30

"Of course."

"Tell Midge . . ." His voice faltered. *If he cries I just won't be able to stand it.* "Tell Midge . . . tell her to come."

I nodded, not trusting myself to say anything. He looked so awful old and pitiful. He let his head hang, the way he did when he was feeling sorry for himself, and his lower eyelids drooped and showed their ugly inner redness. I almost felt sorry for him; almost took him back home.

He cleared his throat and blew his nose. "About Eva, son. I want you to know, I loved that girl."

I nodded again. *Why doesn't he shut up?*

He spoke once more. "It's hard for me to realize . . . that Eva's dead."

Well, that made it easier. When he said those two words, again, I was able to drive off and leave him without looking back.

He lived at Lakecrest about four years. The first year, I went to see him five times, and Midge perhaps six. After that our visits became less frequent. It was an unpleasant chore to go. The last time I saw him we seemed total strangers. We couldn't talk. Then finally, the hot August night that Bailey called me. The Old Man was dead. I hadn't been to see him in ten months.

It took me three days after we found his letter to work up any anger, any feeling at all, about the missing money. Midge confessed to me later she was afraid I wasn't going to do anything at all about it. She'd reread the letter a dozen times a day, and once she underlined that sentence, "Remember this is your Dads last request . . ."

After Eva died, nothing much was important to me for a long while. I had enough money to get Midge through school, and beyond that I just didn't think much about money. And I never did resent the disappearance of the fifteen thousand as much as I did the *way* it disappeared. "I loaned it to the Bonnie boy . . . he has not come back . . ."

I started at the bank in Beaumont, where the Old Man moved his savings when I put him in the home. The money was gone, all right. He had withdrawn every dollar of it, about

31

three years before his death! Less than a year after he went to Lakecrest.

I went to the home and saw Bailey, who put on his undertaker's mask and succeeded in making me feel like a criminal. His manner expressed what his tongue didn't say: that it sure took plenty of guts, for me to come back there looking for my dead father's money when I'd neglected him so shamefully when he was alive.

No, Bailey said, he knew of no money my father might have had. No, he'd never heard of a young man called Bonnie. No, my father never had any visitors "except for yourself and your daughter" and the waxy grin added "and those were precious few." Yes, my father *would* have had the opportunity to make friends away from the home, because he often went into town, seldom associated with the other guests.

"At night," Bailey said, "he kept to his room, especially after he got his color television."

That surprised me. "I didn't know . . ."

When I caught myself, Bailey gave me his palest mortician's smile. "How *could* you know?" it said. "You were never here." He said my father never quite became "one *of* us," that he suffered terribly from loneliness.

"Incidentally," Bailey told me, "when your father became ill, toward the end, he presented the TV set to the guests here, as a gift, and they enjoy it immensely. But I owe you an apology. I forgot to tell you about the TV. I expect you'll want to take it."

That was about all I could stand of Mr. Bailey. I told him I'd leave the TV where it was. I also told him to turn right at the next corner and go straight to hell. And I left.

I went to the business office of the telephone company in Beaumont and spent two hours going through the directories of every city within a reasonable distance. I knew the Old Man's spelling wasn't to be trusted so I also listed similar names, such as Boney, Bonney, Burney, and others. I found few Bonnies but a multitude of Bonneys, literally scores in Houston and Dallas and New Orleans alone.

I checked police records in Beaumont and Houston. I suffered through the city directories and tax rolls and utility connections.

32

Then I went home and studied my list and began to feel frustration. In less than half a dozen cities I had two hundred three people named Bonnie or Bonney. If the one I was looking for had taken that money three years before, he could be in Tasmania by now and the money long since spent. I pictured myself playing private eye, knocking on the door of a family named Bonnie and asking, "Did anybody here ever take fifteen thousand dollars from my father?" Or I could report the missing money to the police, and hope. It seemed a mighty long shot, maybe not worth the trouble. And I might have been willing to forget it all if the Old Man's letter hadn't been lying there on the coffee table, under my right hand. Where, I don't doubt, Midge had been careful to leave it.

"Son . . . I ask you one last thing, when you go looking for the boy . . ." Not *if* you go, but *when*. ". . . I don't think he is crooked . . ."

Not crooked!

I helped Midge pack her car, and before she drove away to go back to school, I told her.

"Listen, I'm not going to be here at home the next few weeks. I'll be traveling. If you want anything, need anything, call the office and Dan will see that you get it. I'll tell him. I'm going to look for that Bonnie, Midge, like your granddad asked. I'll find him, if he's alive, and I'll see him behind bars and I'll get that money, if it's possible. If I do, it'll be yours. A wedding present for you and Arch. So I'm doing it for you, and for your granddad."

She hugged my neck and got in the car. "No, Pop. Not for me. You're doing it for yourself. And I'm glad."

I telephoned Dan. Dan Arledge, my friend since we were fifteen, and my boss since the year Eva and I were married. "Something's come up," I said. "I need a leave of absence. Six months. Maybe a year. It's important."

Silence, for three seconds. Then, "What'll you do if I say no?"

"I'll quit."

"That's what I thought. All right, but you can't take a leave without coming by the office first."

I hadn't intended to unload the details on Dan but when I got to the office he asked if he could read the Old Man's letter and so I just laid the whole story on him. My search for "the Bonnie boy" sounded like windmill-jousting when I talked about it. But Dan didn't blink. Just asked, "What's this about your dad going partners with the boy? Got any idea what kind of partnership?"

"No, not a prayer."

"Did your dad ever talk about going into business?"

"Talk, sure. He was always *going* to start a business."

"What kind?"

"Any kind. Grocery, furniture, beer joint, pool hall. Pool hall, mostly. He always talked about getting him a little place and putting in a couple of tables. He used to hang out a lot at pool halls."

"Then maybe," Dan said, "that's what he did at Beaumont. Maybe he met that boy at a pool hall. Be a place to start looking."

"You mean hit every joint around Beaumont that's got a pool table and ask if they know anybody named Bonnie?"

"Have you got a better place to begin?"

Which was a point, at that. And I had to admit this much: if the Old Man had agreed to go into a business partnership, I couldn't think of anything it was more likely to be than a pool hall.

Dan tapped me on the wrist with his index finger. "Wait a second," he said. "Let's assume this guy took your dad's money with the agreement that they'd open a pool hall. But he decides to take the cash and cut your dad out. So, if he does open a place, it won't be at Beaumont, right? Because he damn sure doesn't want to be operating where your dad can walk in and find him. So he's gone somewhere. Maybe even here in town. So what I'd do, I'd begin looking for a man named Bonnie who's running a pool hall somewhere other than in Beaumont. All right, surely you've got to have some kind of a license for a pool hall . . . so if he is running a hall, he shouldn't be hard to find. Somebody has got to have a list of people who buy pool hall licenses."

"What sort of license would it be? City? State?"

Dan slapped his desk. "I don't know, but I know somebody who could damn sure tell us." He laughed before he spoke the name. "Jack Hawk."

"Mr. Jack," is what Dan and I called him, back when we hung around his pool hall that first summer. We were fifteen. My folks had just moved into town off the prairie and Mr. Jack's place was where I first picked up a cue stick and learned the rules. And he was still there, in the same crummy little corner he used for an office. He said he remembered me. I doubt he did.

"Well," he said, when I told him why I came, "if the fella you're huntin' is runnin' tables anywheres close around here, it's likely I'd know him. What's his name?"

"That's one of my problems. I don't have a full name. Just the last. Bonnie."

At the sound of the name, Mr. Jack's eyes quit wandering around his cluttered desk, settled onto my face, and held. "You sure that's a last name?"

"Well, no. I've been assuming it was." Assuming it, because of my father's habit of saying "the Smith boy," or "the Watkins boy."

"If it's a first name," Mr. Jack said, "I thought maybe you meant Bonney McCamey."

"Bonney McCamey. That's a boy? A man?"

"Yeah, a man. Pretty good one, too. Just about anybody that's hung out around pool halls in this state the last ten years knows Bonney . . . or anyway *about* him. He played in here for about a year. Made a livin' at it too. He's a stick. But he ain't runnin' no tables, I don't think. Last I heard, he went back up into Kirby County, where he was raised, and opened him a little beer joint . . . out in the country . . . close to Farley."

"How old," I asked, "would you say this Bonney is?"

A shrug. "Thirties. Thirty-four, five."

That much fit all right. A man in his mid-thirties would be a boy to the Old Man. Still, just the name and the age didn't add up to a very solid lead.

But then there was Mr. Jack, talking voluntarily about Bonney McCamey, while a small grin nipped at the corners of his mouth and a certain fondness showed in his eye. ". . . then even when

35

he beat you, you still *liked* him, no way to keep from it. But I hadn't seen Bonney . . . oh, I reckon it's been four years. One day he just showed up missin'. . . . They said he went over around Port Arthur for awhile . . . and Beaumont. . . ."

Beaumont. Now that made it different. If this Bonney McCamey was the man I wanted, and if he was still at Farley, he was within sixty miles of Mr. Jack Hawk's cluttered desk.

Two days later I walked into Bonney's Place and found him playing eight-ball with the woman Millie.

3.

No one's imagination could stretch quite far enough to see Bonney's Place as an attractive building. The outside was even plainer than the inside. Just a long frame rectangle, resting on sawed-off telegraph poles set into the ground as pilings. So the floor was about a foot and a half off the ground and under the west end of the building was a jumbled mass of used lumber and old corrugated sheet metal, evidently left over from the tavern's construction or stowed there to await use in some forgotten project. The siding of the building had ended up a sort of patchwork-quilt design of planks ranging in width from four to ten inches. I supposed the original plan had been to disguise all that inconsistency with paint, but the only color showing was a ragged section of dull gray one-by-sixes near the front door, secondhand planks, their paint peeling and fading. Four windows looked out at the narrow two-lane asphalt road, which all hands around Bonney's called "the blacktop." The building sat about fifty feet back from the pavement and the space between was a parking lot—dull gray-red sand and clay. Near the front door the surface was packed to the density of concrete, the hardened soil reinforced by thousands of half-buried beer-bottle caps.

So the building itself was not a thing of beauty. But the

setting. That's something else. There was no way to fault the setting, because of the trees.

A magnificent cottonwood rose up just to the west of the front door, so close to the building its branches rested on the roof and its trunk almost touched the eaves. Two more cottonwoods, not quite so tall as the first, grew in the back between Bonney's little house and his barn. Then a pine, surely a hundred feet tall, shot up at the east end of the tavern near the side door, the door with the sign over it: COLORED ENTRANCE. But the most impressive tree of all was the live oak. Its ancient and gnarled trunk came bulging and curling from the earth and sent out horizontal branches greater in girth than the base of the big pine. Its foliage must have shaded half an acre or more, there toward the rear and to the east of the tavern. Then more pines by the barn, and elms to the west, and an assortment of lower-growing trees I couldn't identify. Somehow those trees softened the tavern's ugliness and made it seem at home among them.

And the surrounding countryside, though dry from a withering summer, was still beautiful in September. A sandy-bottom creek branch curved through a half circle near the live oak, to feed its great roots and then disappear into a culvert under the blacktop. Behind the tavern the land swept gradually upward. Part clear pasture, part brushy woods. It had been a long time since I'd stood and looked at the countryside, and smelled it, and listened to its sounds.

I had the feeling, after I'd hung around Bonney's for a week without going into town, that somebody was about to ask me why. But nobody did. Bonney himself evidently accepted it as a perfectly natural thing that a guy would come to Kirby County just to play pool. He didn't ask me one personal question throughout the first seven days I stayed in that tavern, almost constantly, and tried to beat him at eight-ball.

The only person who did ask me a question was Colonel Ralls, an ancient little fellow who hung around the tavern as much as I did. And he wanted to know whether I'd been in Santiago, Cuba, during the Spanish-American War. When I said No he padded away and went back to sleep in a cane chair he kept propped against the wall near the ladies' restroom.

37

"The Colonel gets mixed up," Bonney told me. "He thinks he's always seeing somebody he served with in Cuba." The Colonel, Bonney said, was probably ninety-seven, a bona fide Spanish-American War veteran who lived nearby with a grand-daughter. "He's a pain in the butt to everybody around here, but there's not much you can do about him."

The best break I got was that the girl, Slat, arrived at Bonney's just a week behind me. Because she absorbed all the attention and she also gave me the chance to sleep in Bonney's house for ten nights.

The day she came, Bonney and I were hooked up in probably the hundredth game we'd played, when Turnip came quietly through the kitchen and stood at Bonney's elbow and an-nounced, "Mister Bonney, there's a dead lady in the barn."

Bonney laid his cue on the table and led us all out the back door. On the dirt floor of the barn, lying near Turnip's mama dog and her boxful of seven nursing pups, was the motionless form of a woman. Or a girl? She didn't appear to be sleeping normally. Her neck was twisted, as if she might have fallen.

"She's dead," Turnip said.

"She's *not* dead," Bonney said, his head down on her chest. "I think she's sick. Let's get her inside." He scooped her up and the girl stirred. She put her hand over her eyes but didn't speak.

"Hodamighty," Bonney said, "she hasn't got as much meat on her as a bed slat."

"It's Mary Eloise, Mister Bonney," Turnip said, following along and looking at the girl's face.

"Who?"

"Mary Eloise Rankin. It's Joe Rankin's girl."

"Well I'll be damned," Bonney said, studying the girl's face when he put her down in the kitchen of the tavern. He turned to me. "Would you run get Rose-Mama?"

I drove up and found Rose-Mama fooling with a new calf in her cow lot. She was dressed in a sunbonnet and a pair of her dead husband's blue suspender overalls and some black rubber kneeboots. She jumped in the car just that way when I said Bonney wanted her.

When we got back to the tavern, Bonney and Turnip and

Colonel Ralls and Charlotte Ord were standing over the girl and the Colonel was saying, "She ain't got much of a chest on her."

"Colonel," Bonney said, "how about you going out and watch the front, and call me if anybody comes in, all right?"

The Colonel shuffled out, glad to have an assignment.

The girl's eyes were open. She was on a worn black leather couch that stood against the rear wall of the kitchen. Barney's Couch, it was called. Barney was Bonney's cook. He'd worked two days in the week I'd been there, then disappeared.

Bonney was telling Rose-Mama, "She says she reckons she passed out, in the barn. Says she's sick."

Rose-Mama was down on her knees beside the couch, with a hand on the girl's forehead. "She looks bilious."

When she began to show a little life, I guessed the girl's age at eighteen. She was a tiny thing, hardly five feet tall, with large brown eyes in such a narrow face that she seemed to consist, for the moment, solely of those two big eyes.

"I'm not going home," she told Bonney. "I'm looking for work, if you've got any work." I was surprised at the tonal quality of that voice. It was weak but it had depth, resonance, music. *Yes, like Eva's voice.*

Bonney glanced at Rose-Mama. "Well, I reckon she could sleep right here tonight. Barney won't be back."

"She's not gonna sleep on this stinkin' couch," Rose-Mama returned. "We'll take her up to my place. I'll put her up in Joe's room and . . ." She looked my way and grinned, a little embarrassed she'd forgotten for the moment that I'd rented her son's room. "Well, I've got a cot. We'll work it out."

"It's all right," I said. "I'll sleep here on the couch tonight."

So we took her up the slope. The girl fell asleep almost immediately, after Rose-Mama put her into one of her own long nightgowns and laughed and said there was "enough room left over in there to throw a dance."

Then we discovered that Rose-Mama's "condemned, bladder-spated, noggin-headed old cow" had disappeared. Just walked off, with the new calf, after we'd rushed down to Bonney's and forgotten to latch the gate. So we went hunting for the cow. Found her two miles up the road toward Farley.

"God give us grace," Rose-Mama said. "That little squirt of

a calf has sucked his mama pretty near dry. If he hasn't popped his belly, by mornin' he'll be scowerin' the fence a yard high and a foot to the right." We drove home slowly, Rose-Mama sitting on the front fender of my car holding the calf in her lap, and the cow hurrying along behind, nervous and worried and bawling every step.

By the time I got cleaned up, Rose-Mama had almost murdered my bottle of bourbon by fixing us each a huge branch-water highball, so strong it was the color of weak coffee. We sipped the bourbon and ate rattrap cheese and baloney. And talked about the girl.

"Sure, I know her," Rose-Mama said. "She's a nester, or her daddy is. Joe Rankin. He used to be a good farmer, back when you could make a livin' with thirty acres in cotton and twenty in corn on this old sand. Just no way, now. But pretty much the same thing happened to Joe Rankin, happened to all those farmers in the Blackjack. They got to makin' whiskey, and tryin' to drink it all up theirselves and then they got to thievin' around. Just went bad, most of 'em. This girl here's mother, she was a real pretty little woman when she was young. But she went sour. Finally just left home."

"How long ago?"

"Six, seven years. This Mary Eloise, she stayed in school, oh, way up there I guess to the ninth or tenth grade, but then she had two little brothers to take care of after her mama left, so she stayed home, and raised 'em."

"How old do you suppose the girl is?"

"Twenty-one, twenty-two."

"That old? She seems younger."

"Well, it's just she's so little. Not enough flesh on her right now to pad a crutch. When she wakes up I'll find out how come she took off from home. I got my idea about why already . . . that bastard of a daddy of hers, I expect."

"You think she came to Bonney's on purpose? Didn't just wander up there?"

"Sure she came on purpose. It's not the *first* time they've showed up at Bonney's like this. Look at Turnip, same way."

She produced a cavernous yawn, so I went on back down to Bonney's. He was closed. Only light in the place came from the

40

long bulb above the back bar, and the red neon glow from the beer-distributor's electric clock. But Charlotte Ord's car was still there, parked under the big pine. I walked around to the house and saw Turnip at the barn, with a flashlight, checking Molly Bitch and her pups.

"Is Bonney in the house?" I asked him.

"No, him and Miss Charlotte in the kitchen." He nodded toward the back door of the tavern. The kitchen was dark. "On Mr. Barney's Couch," he added quietly.

"Oh."

"You got a cot fixed," the boy said, moving a hand toward the house, "in the front room."

I hadn't been in Bonney's house before. It stood on concrete blocks not ten good steps from the rear door of the tavern. I walked through it, to locate the bathroom. Originally the floor plan had been a perfect square. The front half nearest the tavern was a large sparsely furnished living room. The rear half was evenly divided by a wall. Bonney's room took up the northeast quarter. The remaining quarter was the bath, a large one, for obviously it was meant in the beginning to be another bedroom. The plumbing was scattered, as if it had been added piecemeal and without planning. A commode and a washbasin seemed lonesome in one corner. A bathtub with a showerhead, but no curtain, occupied another corner. An unpainted table held Bonney's toilet articles, and a wall mirror looked down on it. A new door near the back entrance was cut in the north wall of the bathroom. It led into Turnip's room, a shed-type, built-on affair. There was no kitchen. Bonney and Turnip ate in the tavern. The house wasn't dirty but it had a bleak, not-lived-in look. Walls bare. No chairs anywhere, except in the living room.

I got into the cot and couldn't sleep. An hour later Bonney came in.

"I wake you up?" he asked.

"No."

"Well, I got that chore done."

"What chore is that?"

"Charlotte."

"Oh?"

"Yeah. Won't have to bother about *that* for a while."

"Why so?"

"Her husband's comin' home tomorrow."

I slept at Bonney's the next ten nights, because the girl was sick at Rose-Mama's. Couldn't keep anything on her stomach. Rose-Mama stayed home with her patient, and I fell naturally into the routine of driving up to the house late in the afternoon to bring back the fresh vase of flowers for the bar.

Once I drove into town, opened a small checking account at the Farley State Bank, and ordered two hundred personalized checks in the name of John E. Lancaster. Lancaster is my mother's maiden name. I also rented a post office box and wrote a short note to Midge.

I stopped at Rose-Mama's on the return trip and found a note attached to the screen door with a safety pin. It said Rose-Mama and Bonney had gone to Houston to take the girl to the doctor and might be late getting home.

They were. Elizabeth, Rose-Mama's milk cow, by sundown had her neck stuck over the fence and was bawling. I slipped on the old blue suspender overalls that always hung on the back porch and found a two-gallon milk bucket and went out and turned the calf to her mother. A sack of Qualitee Milk Ration was in the feed room, with a syrup bucket sitting beside it. I dumped two buckets of feed into Elizabeth's trough and wrestled the calf off her front teats and onto the rear ones.

I could hear my mother saying the words. "Milking is like swimming, or riding a bicycle. Once you learn you won't forget."

I hadn't milked a cow since I was fifteen. I finally found Rose-Mama's calf rope hanging on a nail inside the feed room, and tied off the calf. I couldn't locate a milking stool so I just squatted, Indian-fashion, and washed Elizabeth's udder, gently, to let her get used to a strange touch. When I felt her relax I buried my head in her flank and went at her with both hands. And I grinned, because there was something good and basic and earthy about it, hearing the tinny music of the milk hitting the bottom of the bucket and breathing in the sweet-sour cow smell, an odor I once detested.

42

I didn't even hear the car doors slam. I was in the short rows, concentrating on running the bucket over with foam, when Rose-Mama split the quiet dusk with that belly laugh of hers.

"Bonney! Come look at my new milkmaid! Hell's jingle bells, here I worry the last fifty miles that Elizabeth's gonna bust ever tit to her name, and all the time this pool player's takin' care of her. Squattin' like Pocahontas, too, and got a head of foam on his bucket."

Bonney came grinning to the fence, and the girl behind him. I felt a silly little pleasure at having done a thing that pleased them, so I raised up and performed a mock bow. And my rump hit Elizabeth's flank and she raised a manure-encrusted hind foot and stepped into the bucket, spilling a gallon and a half of warm foamy milk over my feet.

A minute later Rose-Mama was still leaning against the wash-house, trying to control her laughter. When she stopped she said, "Well, don't just stand there starin' at spilt milk. Turn the calf loose and let 'im strip 'er, and come on in. I've brought you a bottle, and this time I'll buy *you* a drink for a change." She clodded up the back steps, still laughing.

The girl looked better. She held a white slip of paper. "Look," she said to me, "I got me a health certificate. I'm going to work, at Bonney's Place."

And she did, the next day. It was Saturday. Saturday at Bonney's was busy, from midmorning until closing time. Barney came back to work, all red-faced and clean and wearing a white T-shirt and a big apron. He was a huge man with a great round stomach. His face was equipped with a built-in scowl which I soon learned wasn't meant for anybody in particular, but just the world at large. He seemed forever angry, for reasons I couldn't figure. He took off his apron and resigned on the average of twice a week.

"One week," Bonney told me, "he quit four times. That's his record."

"Why does he keep coming back?" I wondered.

"He's afraid I'll hire somebody to take his place," Bonney grinned. "Barney's a pretty good kind of a cook. Used to work in town, at Spearman's, that big place on the square, but he

43

can't stand anybody tellin' him what to do. So I just let him run things the way he wants. I let him work or quit, doesn't matter to me. Fact is I don't really need a cook except on Saturdays and Sundays, and Barney's generally here on weekends. He quits mostly during the week when he hasn't got enough to do."

On Saturdays, Maudie came to work just before noon. Maudie, Bonney said, was worth twice her pay. I guessed her to be about thirty. She worked in town, Mondays through Saturday noon, at a coin-operated laundry, then helped out at Bonney's on weekends. Worked seven days a week, so Bonney said, "to support a sorry-ass husband."

She knew how to talk to the beer drinkers, and she laughed a lot, and had this nice round bottom that the men liked to watch and which Bonney liked to pat. He patted it faithfully every time Maudie got within patting distance, and unless I was misjudging, she routed herself within range of Bonney's hand at every opportunity.

The first Saturday I spent at Bonney's, a young fellow in a cowboy hat spotted Bonney patting Maudie, must have thought it looked like fun, and tried it himself. Maudie stopped, and smiled at him, and then delivered him a roundhouse slap on the jaw that I felt certain had dislocated his neck. Still smiling, Maudie wiggled on off as if nothing important had happened. So it seemed clear that nobody but Bonney was supposed to pat her.

When the girl came down from Rose-Mama's to start work, I noticed that Bonney was careful to take her straight to Maudie and say, "Maudie, I got you an assistant here. Name's Slat, and her job's gonna be to help you out, any way you want her to." Maudie was delighted.

Why Bonney called the girl Slat is beyond me, unless it was because, as he said when Turnip found her in the barn, that she hadn't any more heft to her than a bed slat. In any event, nobody expected him to call her Mary Eloise. There were certain names that refused to come off Bonney's tongue in a comfortable way, so if he didn't like a name on a person, he changed it. As he'd done with Rose-Mama, and Turnip, and now the girl. And me, to a degree. The second day I was there he started calling me Johnny.

He said he had too many Johns around the place, and made this terrible joke about having three johns on the premises already, and five if you count the two outhouses he kept for the colored folks. That got a big laugh out of the beer drinkers, who didn't need much to make them laugh after they'd had four or five.

I have to confess I liked answering to Johnny. When I was a boy I wanted to be called Johnny. But I was always John Edward to my mother and "son" or "boy" to the Old Man. I don't know, maybe Johnny made me feel younger. *Good god, a forty-five-year-old man wanting to be called Johnny.*

Turnip insisted on calling me *Mister* Johnny. Finally I jumped him about it, said it wasn't necessary to put that mister in front of my name. He looked at me as if I'd kicked him, and walked away. Bonney said I oughtn't to get on Turnip's back about something that comes natural, that the boy wouldn't be comfortable not calling me mister. So I let it go.

The first hint I had of how Slat was going to affect life around Bonney's Place came when she removed the scowl from Barney's face. She did it on a Monday, her third working day. She had gotten over the nervousness of serving strangers and she was sitting on Barney's Couch, eating one of his hamburgers. Barney was standing at the back door, scowling at the barn and the sky and the entire landscape. She polished off the hamburger and bounced up and said, "Barney, that's the best hamburger I *ever* ate."

I could see the muscles under Barney's T-shirt tighten just a little, as if he'd received a light electric shock. When he turned to look at the girl disappearing through the swinging door, his scowl wasn't quite as deep as it generally was. I wondered if anybody else had ever offered Barney a compliment on what he cooked.

He was still scowling when Slat breezed back into the kitchen. But he said to her, "You want a nuthern?"

Slat paused, not quite sure what to say. She didn't want another one. How could a tiny little thing like that eat two of Barney's hamburgers?

"Why," she said, "I just believe I *could* eat another one.

45

They're so good. . . . They're better than . . . why, than peach pie."

She ate it too, with Barney standing there watching, and forgetting to scowl. That night he made her a peach cobbler in a pan half the size of a card table and when Slat got through bragging on that, the scowl was gone. From that hour, Barney worshiped her.

Yes, and so did everybody else around Bonney's, with the exception of Charlotte Ord. The girl really wasn't quite believable. She was so almighty naïve, so gee-whizzy about everything. "Oh, *Rose-Mama*, those zinnias are plain *beautiful*, with the ferns and all." And, "Turnip, if those little old pups of Molly Bitch were any *cuter*, I swan I'd just eat 'em *up!*"

If any other female who came into Bonney's had delivered such sentiments, well, it would have been just way too much. But there wasn't any way to challenge Slat's sincerity, and she made you think of trite old saws such as "breath of spring." *My lord, breath of spring.* But you *did* think of it, when she'd walk in from Rose-Mama's with those big eyes smiling and saying hello to everybody, and even patting Colonel Ralls on the shoulder. She was, as Bonney said, damn good help.

She brought changes to Bonney's Place, without altering its plainness and the general air that the Regulars somehow loved and didn't know why. Made it cleaner, for one thing. She was forever dusting and emptying ash trays. And sweeping so often that Bonney had to make her quit, since sweeping was Turnip's job.

And she sold things.

"How much you charge for Vienna sausage?" Bonney and I were at the barn, replacing three boards that Sam Hobbs knocked out. Knocked them out because Saturday night some of the boys said he was too drunk to drive a car and he resented that and he went out and got in Bonney's pickup and started it and ran it into the barn.

"Charge for what?" Bonney asked.

"Vienna sausage." She was holding up one of the little cans, standing there all businesslike.

"Why you want to know?"

"Well, I just want to know how much to charge," she said. "There's not any price marked on any of those cans. I need to know about the pork and beans, too."

"You mean the stuff on the shelves?"

"Yes, the groceries."

Bonney seemed puzzled. "Hell, I don't know. It never has come up. Two bits, I guess, for a can of the sausage. And the beans . . ." He looked at me. "What would you say, on beans?"

I shrugged. "Fifteen cents?"

"Fifteen cents," he said to Slat.

"OK. Thanks." She smiled, and turned, and I swear I expected her to skip back to the tavern door. But she only ran.

Bonney, with a hammer in his hand, walked slowly toward the tavern, circling slightly, peering, as if something was sizzling inside that might explode.

"Hodamighty," he said, turning and dropping the hammer, "it's J.R. I better catch 'im."

He hurried around the corner of the tavern. My curiosity got to me and I followed. Bonney signaled to a gray-headed man getting in his car. Man with a large round face and a mustache.

"Hey J.R.? What in hell you doin' buyin' my groceries?"

The man grinned. "Sorry about that. I just couldn't turn that little girl down, she wanted to sell groceries so bad."

"Well, don't eat that stuff. It's been sittin' there on the shelf for three years."

"I know."

"Well, just slip it all back to me, and I'll . . ."

"Go to hell," the man said, grinning wider. "I bought this stuff, fair and square, and I may put it in the trophy case at school. Who else has got groceries from Bonney's Place?" He drove off laughing.

"I'll be damn," Bonney said. "That's first time a can of beans ever got sold out of this beer joint."

"Who is he?" I asked.

"Name's Wetzel. J. R. Wetzel. He's school superintendent."

"At Farley?"

"Yeah. Nice old guy. Squarehead, you know, and likes his suds. He takes a lot of crap, bein' a school man. Comes out here

47

and gets tanked up pretty good sometimes. Knows I keep the school kids out. Does him good, he says." Bonney laughed out loud. "That bastard, buyin' my groceries."

"Rose-Mama . . ." I'd stopped calling her Mrs. Whitaker about a week after I moved into her house. Mainly because sometimes when I addressed her formally, she wouldn't answer. "Rose-Mama, may I ask you a question?"

"Shoot," she said, "and if I haven't got the answer, I'll send for it."

"Why is it that Bonney keeps that little bunch of canned goods, and the bread, on the shelves there in the place?"

"That's his groceries. He keeps those . . . well, on account of his mama, mostly."

"His mother? I've never heard him mention her."

"Well, he's got a mother, all the same, and a good one. Lives down at Corpus, and he goes down to see her about once a month."

"Does she ever come here to visit?"

"No." She kicked the screen door of the kitchen open, stepped out on the back porch and slung a dishpan of water into a zinnia bed.

"But what do the groceries have to do with Bonney's mother?"

"Well, the name of the place is Highway Café and Grocery, you know. Bonney's mama writes him about once a week, and that's the way she addresses the letters, to the Highway Café and Grocery, and I just reckon Bonney figures a place called a grocery store ought to have groceries in it."

"But he doesn't really sell groceries, or doesn't want to. The fact is, it's not much of a café, either, is it?"

"No, Bonney's in the beer business."

"Then I wonder why he calls the place a café and a grocery store?"

Rose-Mama put a heavy mug of black coffee in front of me on the kitchen table and sat down. "He doesn't want his mama to know he's runnin' a beer joint."

Sunday night, and almost closing time. Bonney had sent Slat on home early with Rose-Mama. Barney was snoring on his couch in the kitchen. Five customers were still in the place. One was Sam Hobbs, passed out on the old wooden bench Bonney kept against the east wall. Sam's Bench, everybody called it. Barney had his couch, and Sam had his bench, to pass out on.

Maudie was still there. She and Bonney were leaning over the bar, shoulders touching, talking low sometimes. I wandered back in the kitchen for some ice water out of Barney's big refrigerator. I stood at the serving window and looked out into the tavern, over the lowered heads of Bonney and Maudie. I was almost directly behind them. Bonney was carefully tracing little loops and whorls and figure eights, with his index finger, on Maudie's plump behind. Not twenty feet away three men sat drinking beer, and one of them was Carlos Freeman, who just happened to be Maudie's husband. It did seem to me that Bonney lived mighty dangerous at times.

"You know what I'd like to have, Bonney?" Maudie was saying. "I'd sure like to have a little camp meat."

"That's not any problem," Bonney said. "Let's get some."

"Now? Tonight?"

"Why not?"

That brief exchange caused Turnip to appear. "Can I go, Mister Bonney? Can I go, and work the light?"

"Damn right you're goin'," Bonney said, "and do all the work. Get the knives, and the Thirty Aught Six, and put 'em in the truck. And a shovel." Turnip was already headed out the back door.

"Get two shovels!" Bonney called after him. "And where's the light?"

"In the barn," came Turnip's answer. He was already gone, obviously excited over the project.

"Any you guys want to go with us after some camp meat? Carlos? How about it?"

"Naw," Carlos growled.

Bonney turned to me. "Johnny?" At first I'd thought it all to be a ruse, an excuse for Bonney and Maudie to go off without company. But they were taking Turnip . . .

"Won't take half an hour," Bonney said, and I said all right.

Bonney looked at the clock and locked the front door. "You guys want another beer, just wake Barney up." Bonney was particular about customers going behind his bar for their own beer. He claimed beer had a habit of not getting paid for that way.

He moved Carlos and his friends over into a corner, away from the window, and turned out everything but the light over the bar. "If you leave," Bonney said, "be damn sure that front door's locked. And for cripe's sake, anybody comes around looks like Liquor Control, keep over there in the corner and stay quiet."

So we walked out, leaving the men to drink after legal hours.

Turnip had the hood of the truck up and was hooking a big spotlight to the battery. He slammed the hood and strung the wires back over the cab and hopped in the bed.

"You get the tubs?" Bonney asked.

"Right here in back. And the rope, too."

"All right, where you think, Turnip?"

"I been seein' a bunch of doe in that little clearin', in Mister Akers' corner, there by the burnt stump on our back fence. *Bunch* of 'em, and fat. They been eatin' with Mister Akers' calves. You want a doe, I guess."

"Yeah, I think a doe. All right, we'll see."

So in ten minutes we had stopped at a barbed-wire fence on the back side of Bonney's pasture and a fat little doe, not thirty feet from the truck, stood staring blindly at Turnip's spotlight and Bonney got out and shot her, the noise of the powerful rifle echoing, echoing, over the still night.

Turnip went through the fence. He dragged the animal under the wire, put the rope on it, strung it up on the limb of an oak, and stuck one of the tubs under it. He worked fast with the knife, and expertly. He had the doe half skinned when Bonney said, "You gonna be in all that big a hurry, I better get started diggin' us a hole." Then to me, "You want to help on that other shovel?"

So we dug a hole, and when it was finished Turnip dumped the contents of the tub into it—the hide, entrails, head, and hoofs. He'd already cut up the small carcass and had it tucked neatly into the other tub, and we headed back.

Bouncing through the pasture, and me sitting there brooding. *Well, I've just helped commit a crime against the state, killing*

50

*a doe deer out of season, and spotlighting it, at that. Me, the
one the boys around the office used to call Honest John because I wouldn't cheat on my expense account.*

We curved around the barn and the headlights of Bonney's
truck caught a tan-and-white sedan sitting at the corner of the
tavern. A cherry on top and a tall antenna and a stencil on its
front door, plain as the alphabet in Bonney's headlights: KIRBY
COUNTY SHERIFF'S DEPARTMENT.

Bonney hit the brakes and the lights. "Go see who it is,"
he said quietly out the window. Turnip catfooted out of the
truck bed and circled the tavern on the side opposite where
the sheriff's car was. He came trotting back in thirty seconds.

"It ain't nobody but Mister Scott."

Bonney started up again and drove right up to the sedan.
A skinny law officer appeared. Had on a broad-brimmed hat
and cowboy boots and a big pistol.

"Howdy, Wiley," Bonney said. "What in hell you doin'
snoopin' around my place this late? Tryin' to rob me?"

"Howdy, Bonney. Why, *howdy* there, Maudie. Naw, I just
come out here to buy me a cold fresh bottle of beer."

"Why, now, Wiley, you know it's after hours and I can't
sell beer this time of night."

"Well, my watch has stopped, I guess. It don't say but 'leven.
Say, was that you fired off that shot while ago? You wouldn't
be spotlightin' no deer back in there, I don't guess."

"No," Bonney said. "Me and Turnip and Maudie and—you
didn't meet our friend Johnny here. Johnny, this is Wiley
Scott, our deputy sheriff that protects us from criminals and
all—we been over on the back side of the place, gettin' us
some meat. One of my calves. Little ol' thing got all messed
up in the fence, and had to shoot 'im, and Turnip's dressed
him out already. Turnip? Switch on your torch there, and show
Mister Scott our meat we got."

Turnip turned on the spotlight and Deputy Scott peered into
the tub of meat and said, "Well, I'll swan, it was just a little
bitty ol' thing, wasn't it? Don't look no biggern a doe deer,
and just a whole lot *like* one."

"Well, they're similar animals, you might say. Four legs
apiece, and one head and hide. We buried its guts and other

51

parts good, so it wouldn't draw wolves into ol' Norman Akers' fancy calves back there."

"You know, Bonney," the deputy said, hitching his cartridge belt, "this here's the *deer*-smellin'est *calf* carcass I *ever* run across."

"Well," Bonney said—he'd lapsed his grammar and his tone to match exactly the deputy's; Bonney could speak an acceptable brand of English when he cared to—"I expect the reason for that, Turnip's been seein' them deer and them calves of ol' Akers' eatin' right alongside each other, belly to belly, right out of that grain in them creep feeders. So I expect it figures, you know, if a calf eats the same thing a deer does, he's apt to *smell* like a deer."

"Why, that does figure," Scott said, and then, "Listen, Bonney, seein' it's past hours and you can't *sell* me no beer, how 'bout if you just *give* me a couple?"

"Come on round to the back," Bonney said. And they both laughed.

So we all went in the kitchen, and Turnip and I stood around and listened and watched while Scott and Bonney and Maudie put away three cold ones apiece.

Scott's physical appearance both fascinated and repelled me. In profile his body was shaped like a question mark. Two thirds of his height seemed to be long skinny legs. Then his chest suddenly sank in a ridiculous backward curve and left a little potbelly sticking up, rather than out, and his long neck protruded and left four or five inches of space between his shirt collar and the top of his spine. A physical-fitness instructor would have fainted at the sight of him.

Toward the end of his second beer, Scott was moved to start reminiscing, about his and Bonney's earlier years, some of which they'd spent together. Bonney didn't seem too interested. Tolerant, was more like it.

Scott would want to know if Bonney remembered that night they were over there on the Chickenhawk—right there at the horseshoe bend on the old York place—and they had a telephone rig in that little ol' square-ended jon boat, and the wires in the water, and crankin' away, and them ol' yellas and blues just ajumpin', why, even floppin' right out on the *sand* bars when that 'lectristy hit 'em, and then there's this light ashinin' on the boat and who is it yellin' from the bank but ol' Joe Nabors, the *game* warden, and he hollers *Bonney McCamey whatta you think you're adoin' out there with that telephone?* and Bonney he says—you 'member what you said, Bonney?—he says *Why Mister Joe I ain't doin' nothin' but tryin' to put in a phone call to my Aunt Addie McCamey that got drownded right here at this bend in nineteen and twenty-six!* 'Member that, Bonney? Hoo-o-o *wee!* Mad? Ol' man Nabors so goddamn mad you could see slobber on his whiskers and he taken Bonney and Wiley into the J.P. and they got soaked fifty apiece and fifteen dollars and sixty cents costs and had to listen to that friggin' *sermon* again, 'bout how it's a sin, and a *crime*, to telephone them fish up that way. Then when they'd gone and scraped up the money and paid off, why ol' Autis Avery, he was J.P. then, ol' Autis leant out over his desk just as serious and he said *Say Bonney about your Aunt Addie when you was out there acrankin' that phone did you happen to GITTER?* Then laugh? God-oh-mighty ol' Autis damn near bent double laughin' and he musta told that story in the café a thousand times, 'bout what ol' Bonney said that time.

Bonney stood grinning, nodding, not commenting.

Wiley drained his beer bottle and said, "Well, I reckon I better go take me a turn or two. He gets one of them spells he can't sleep, the high sheriff's liable to come roamin' around checkin' on me."

He stopped at the back door. "Maudie, I think I seen Carlos drivin' into town. Looks like you got left again. You want me to drive you home?"

Maudie looked at Bonney, who shook his head. "Naw, we got a little cleanin' up to do around here yet. Thanks, Wiley. I'll run her on home, we get through."

Scott opened the door but paused and turned again. "Bonney, you wouldn't have couple more cool ones you'd like to get shed of."

Without a word Bonney went to the beer box and returned with a cold six-pack and handed it to the deputy.

"Much obliged," Scott said. "Man, it gets lonesome on this night duty."

Turnip and I went on to bed. Ten minutes later I heard Bonney and Maudie drive away in the truck. And Bonney woke me when he returned, just before dawn.

The next Wednesday I found two items of special interest on the front page of Harvey Wilks' Farley *Weekly Rocket*. Both written, as every word in the *Rocket* was, by Harvey himself—publisher, editor, reporter, printer, and advertising and circulation manager. I subscribed to the *Rocket* because Rose-Mama asked me to. Said Harvey was the best friend her dead husband had, and anyway he needed the business. Harvey grew up in that weekly newspaper shop, as a printer. Never wrote a sentence of news in his life until one day Mr. Peters who published and edited the *Rocket* for forty-two years slumped over dead at his desk, and in the upper left-hand drawer they found a handwritten will saying Mr. Peters had left the *Rocket* to Harvey. Just willed the whole works to Harvey—building, equipment, what little cash the *Rocket* had in the bank, and all its good will and unpaid bills. So one day Harvey was a printer, and the next he was a newspaper publisher and editor.

"What Harvey writes," Rose-Mama said, "it doesn't sound like what your usual editor writes. It's sort of like, well, like Harvey *talkin'* to you. He says that's because he doesn't know anything about being a newspaper reporter."

After I'd read two issues of the *Rocket* I found myself looking forward to Wednesdays, to see what Harvey would have to say next. Everything in the paper was The News According to Harvey Wilks, who seldom printed a fact without commenting on it and saying just exactly what he pleased. The result was that half the people around Farley hated Harvey Wilks and the other half loved him, and those who loved him one week were often the same ones who hated him the next, depending on what he printed.

One item that caught my eye had a two-column headline:

WILEY DOES IT AGAIN

Late Sunday night, well it was really early Monday AM about 3:30, Ada Hicks phoned me and said Dr. Reynolds had got called to the hospital on emergency to sew up a big cut in Wiley Scott's head. I went down to the hospital to check and Wiley was full of beer, it was easy to tell. He is getting worse at that drinking, and on the job too. He ran the patrol car into the culvert on Tilden Creek and messed the front of it all up and his head hit the windshield and broke it out. Dr. Reynolds said Wiley would be all right but this is the third time he has wrecked the patrol car and Bobby Wells says he can't carry the insurance on it any more if Wiley is goin to keep wrecking it. Wiley is all right except when he drinks that beer on the job. If Sheriff Overton wants to hire his brother-in-law for a deputy he ought to at least keep him sober. Wiley wasn't chasing any robbers or anything when he hit the bridge, I bet he was just weaving around on the roads about six sheets to the wind. How would you like it if you needed some help from the law in the middle of the night and called Wiley and here he'd come, pulling his pistol and so full of beer he wouldn't know who to shoot? Come on Wiley lets sober up or turn in your gun. How does your head feel Wiley? A hangover and six stitches ought to teach you something.

In that same issue Harvey also tore into Farley Lumber Mills, the town's only industrial payroll, for not providing group hospitalization insurance for its employees. But Harvey could hand out flowers too. This item surprised me:

BONNEY HIRES A JEWEL
There's a sweet little new waitress out at Bonney's Place, they call her Slat. You ought to go out there just to let her wait on you, you'll see. Bonney says she is Joe Rankin's girl, the one that her mother ran off from home several years ago. Its hard to believe a sweet little thing like that came out of the Blackjack. Its a pleasure to get waited on by somebody nice. I'm tired of going into cafes, like at Spearmans, and the help makes you think they're the queen of the may and expect a dime tip for bringing out a cup of coffee. This little girl at Bonneys is staying right now at my old dead friend Jim Whitaker widow's house, but Bonney says he's planning this week

55

to build the girl a room of her own onto his house, and put her into school as she had to quit when her mother ran off.

That night, Bonney said, he had the biggest Wednesday business in two years. Barney ran out of hamburger meat and Rose-Mama and I went up and brought back the two pounds of ground beef she was going to make a meat loaf with the next day. "Power of the press," Bonney said. "Man, I owe ol' Harvey a case of beer, givin' me a plug like that."

Then there was Colonel Ralls standing out in the middle of the dance floor, watching Slat sail by with an armload of hamburgers and beer. And the Colonel saying, "She's sure gainin' in the chest, folks."

The statement was lost to most of the audience, because of the racket of the beer drinkers and the jukebox. But the Colonel was right. Slat had gained not only in the chest but everywhere else. She had bloomed in the short time she'd been at Bonney's. Her face had taken on flesh and the sallowness was gone and she had this marvel of a complexion, just flawless. And now her dark eyes didn't look as large in that narrow face, and she had started putting her black hair up on top of her head, which made her look taller. And older. *Eva, Eva. It looks like Eva's hair.*

"She's just so *fresh.*" That was Maudie saying that. It was true. Maudie had given Slat two of her white uniforms and Rose-Mama had altered them to fit. Somehow Slat had been born knowing how to move, to walk. She didn't wiggle the way Maudie did; she sailed, and glided, and skimmed, and darted, her head never bobbing. It was something to watch, and all of us devoted much of our time to watching it. Slat had a natural sense of modesty. Maudie could have learned something by watching Slat. But of course it wasn't Maudie's job to be modest. The way Maudie dressed and moved was a fringe benefit a male customer received for coming to Bonney's on weekends. She kept the top two buttons of her uniform loose, because she had what Colonel Ralls called "a goddamn good chest on her." When she picked something up off the floor she was careful to provide the men with a good look down her dress and she also knew it was important that they get a view up the inside of her thigh, well, as far as possible, and so she provided that too. "The floor show," Bonney called it. One of the beer drinkers invented it on a Saturday night. Walked out in the middle of the dance floor with a salt shaker and announced, "Ladies and gents, we now present the 'leven o'clock floor show at Bonney's Place. And first on the pro-grum, I now place this salt shaker on the floor, and Maudie's gonna come pick it up for us." Cheers, whistles, foot stompings. Then here came Maudie to perform, all slinky and smiling, to pick up the shaker, and it pleased everybody except the men sitting on the east side of the house, who booed, so Maudie turned around and picked up the salt shaker facing in *that* direction. Floor show big success. Well received. Much applause.

But Slat. When she picked something up off the floor, she did it like they taught Midge in that course Eva made her take one summer when Midge was fourteen and her mother thought she ought to quit standing on her head in the front yard and letting her dress fall down to her waist. And Midge did learn, how to stoop down and pick something up by bending at the knees and keeping her legs together. But she did it only when she thought about it. And here was Slat, out of a farmhouse in Kirby County, doing graceful things like that, well, as if she'd been to a blinking charm school. She had natural class. If you tried to fault her, you'd say it was her speech, and all that gee-whizziness. "If a *pole* cat walked in here," Charlotte Ord growled, "that girl'd say it's the *cutest* thing she *ever* met." Probably so. But what saved Slat is that she didn't whine. She used whiney expressions, yes, the ones you hear coming out of these baby-talking backwoods girls on television dramas about the South. *Law me, Bonney!* and *My nerves!* and *Lordy, Colonel Ralls!* But she didn't whine. Couldn't. Because of that pure miracle of a speaking voice. Low, throaty. If she had broken into a song, she'd have sung contralto.

"You mean to high school?"
"Sure to high school," Bonney said. "Where else?"

I sat on the cot in Bonney's living room holding the copy of the Farley *Rocket* that had the little piece about Slat in it.

"What about this building her a room on the house?"

"We'll get that done Sunday," he said.

"You mean start Sunday?"

"I mean *do* it Sunday. You want to help?"

"Just you and me and Turnip and Barney?"

"Hell, no. We'll get everybody. We built Turnip's room in about six hours one afternoon, and outside of materials it didn't cost me anything except about four cases of beer."

"Oh."

He went into his room, and I reread Harvey's comments in the *Rocket*. Then I walked over and stood in Bonney's door and watched him shed his sneakers. I almost didn't say anything, because the matter wasn't any of my business. *You're just passing through, remember? You're just going to be here a few weeks, to do some work around Farley. What kind of work?* But Bonney had never questioned me. Didn't even seem curious. And on the nights I'd slept in his house, we'd sometimes sat and discussed Slat as if . . . well, discussed her just the way I used to talk with Dan Arledge about Midge.

"Do you think Slat would be happy going back to public school?"

"Why not?" he asked.

"Well, for one thing, she's twenty years old."

"She's twenty-two."

"All right, and what would she be? A sophomore?"

"I guess."

"Well, a twenty-two-year-old sophomore is apt to be a little conspicuous, wouldn't you say?"

"I don't know."

"And you'd probably have to pay tuition, since she's overage." He glanced up quickly. "How much?"

"I don't know. Maybe a hundred dollars."

"A month?"

"No, no. A year, I guess. Or a semester."

He relaxed. "Be all right."

58

"But how about Slat's father, this Rankin? Won't he be coming around here, to get her?"

"Hell, no. Joe Rankin's sorry-ass. He don't care a damn about that girl. I *know* him."

"How about her mother?"

"I know her, too. Know her *too* damn well."

I didn't ask what that meant.

I said, "Well, I was just thinking. I mean taking on a girl like that, bringing her in your house, sending her to school, it's pretty much of a responsibility." *My god, man, who do you think you are, coming in here, just walking in, and setting up some kind of counseling service. He's going to resent that remark.*

He didn't resent it, though.

"Rose-Mama said you had a daughter once." So there it was, the very first reference he'd made to my personal life. And it wasn't really a question.

"I still do have a daughter. Name's Midge. Margaret."

"How old?" Ah, the question, at last. And about Midge's age, of all the things he could have asked.

"Twenty-one. Twenty-two before long."

"What's she doing?"

"Senior in college. And engaged." *Midge. I wonder how Midge is getting along.*

"I bet you're glad she's not poppin' caps in a beer joint."

"Yes."

"This girl's something special, Johnny. She needs to finish school, and get the hell away from here."

"Well."

"How about if you go with me, to talk about it?" he said.

"You mean to school, to talk about Slat?"

"Yeah."

"All right, if you want me."

"You have a daughter. You know about schools."

"Why don't you see your friend, the superintendent? What's his name?"

"Wetzel. Naw, I don't want to bother J.R. He comes out here to drink my pivo and risks his job every time he walks in.

He sure doesn't need to be associatin' with me in town. Might hurt him some way. That school board's a bunch of Hard-shells, man. We'll go see the principal, not J.R."

So on the next Sunday morning, we built the room for Slat. Fifty people worked on it. On Monday we went to see the principal. Slat popped caps in the tavern until closing time that night. And early Tuesday morning, she stood with Bonney and me in the deep sand by the blacktop out front. She wore one of the flowered school dresses that Maudie had bought for her in town and a new pair of brown loafers. Her hair was down and had a bandeau on it like Midge used to wear. She looked sixteen.

The yellow school bus came around the curve a quarter mile away, and Bonney said to Slat, "Now listen, hoddamit, you pay attention, you hear me?"

"I will," she said. She kissed us both on the cheek, and then gave Bonney such a hug you'd have thought she was leaving for a year. Bonney waved the bus down and Slat stepped smoothly aboard.

The bus pulled away and suddenly there she was, sticking her head out the window and yelling at us in that strong voice. You could have heard her a mile away.

"Hey, I almost forgot! Turnip said tell you he's gone to help Mister Brad today and don't forget to feed Molly Bitch!"

4.

Dear Midge:

I received your letter at the P.O. box, so communications are working OK. I know you are happy to have Arch home safe and sound. Tell him I said he ought to try loafing around for a couple of weeks before he goes to work. I've discovered I have a special talent for taking things easy. I find myself enjoying it and am feeling first rate.—In emergencies, if you can't locate me at either of the two phone numbers I sent, call Dan at the office and he'll find me.—By all means, go ahead and order the stone for your Granddad's grave. I should have done that before I left. Have it fixed up as you wish and send the bill to Dan. Your mother would not forgive me for neglecting that duty.—I am ninety per cent certain I'm on the right track here.

Love from your
Pop

Back in my room at Rose-Mama's. The Cardui calendar safety-pinned to the wallpaper indicated October first. Women like Rose-Mama always have safety pins around the house. A month now, since I'd driven up to Bonney's Place.

The time was 2 A.M. and I couldn't get to sleep. I reread the last line of the note to Midge.

Ninety per cent certain I'm on the right track:

Well, isn't that about right? To begin with, how many men are you going to meet with the nickname Bonney?

The Old Man, in the note he left, spelled the name Bonnie but that means exactly nothing. He'd never have seen the name written out and even if he had he'd have paid no attention to the spelling. That name Bonney, that's 25 per cent of the 90, right there.

And is he the sort who'd steal fifteen thousand dollars from an old man? Well, *isn't* he? He's certainly no scoutmaster. Runs a beer joint. Sells beer after hours. Violates the game laws of this state by spotlighting deer (and female deer at that) two months before the season opens, and teaches a boy to dress the carcasses. He bribes, or what amounts to bribing, a weak deputy sheriff with a few bottles of beer. He's sleeping with at least two women, both married to somebody else. At one time (this shows he went bad early, you know) he caught fish with one of those old hand-crank telephone rigs, which shocks the fish insensible so they can be picked up, and that's illegal.

61

Ten per cent doubtful:

Of course he has credits. "There's not anybody around here doesn't owe Bonney, one way or another." Yes, but Rose-Mama's prejudiced. She loves Bonney. And you know why? Because he snows her, that's why. But is that a bad thing? Is it wrong to hug a homely old woman and tell her she's beautiful when she's lost the only two men in her life and needs love so awful much?

Then the little Flynn boys. He bought clothes for them and sent them to school. All right so they didn't stay, but he tried, didn't he? And Turnip . . . should Turnip be listed under the defense or the prosecution? Sure, Bonney has provided him a home and taught him things, most of which aren't so good. He's sent Slat to school in new clothes, but you don't see him sending that black boy to school, do you?

Next we have Colonel Ralls. Who else in all hell would put up with that old bastard, and be kind to him? Slat, that's who else. Yes, she's something else. How about Slat? Right this minute she's sleeping down there in her new room in Bonney's house that all of us built in seven hours and thirty-five minutes and six cases of free beer. She's got a closetful of new clothes and a job and friends and a *chance*, when a month ago she had nothing. Did Bonney give her all that for reasons that ought to be questioned? Remember what Charlotte Ord said, the day we were building the room. "Beats hell outta me why that girl needs a room to herself. Bonney'll have her between his own sheets inside a week." Oh, I don't know about that. Don't think so. You have to discount Charlotte. Jealous.

The thing that makes Bonney so tough to put the pencil on, to judge, is he's got this absolutely ridiculous capacity to *love* everybody. Yes, and to *be* loved too. All those sawmill hands and cowboys who come in, they don't just like Bonney, they flat love him. I never saw a man so blamed loved. Why, even Henry, the mean one, the tough old guy who threatened Bonney with a beer bottle that first day, last night he was back in the place, sober, and he and Bonney sat over there in the corner for two hours and talked and laughed and decided to buy some steers together—partners!—when a month ago Henry was threatening to lay Bonney's skull open.

And how about me, the detective, Captain Vengeance, come to right the wrong, to see justice done? Let's see now, what you've done since you came. Well, you've played Bonney a jillion games of eight-ball; you slept in his house for ten nights and even swept the place out; helped him get the girl in school; tended bar one night for him when he went to see his mother; worked like a yellow dog on the new room for Slat; drove Turnip into Farley to the dentist because Bonney couldn't go; carried flowers from Rose-Mama's for the bar; yes, and milked that condemned cow of hers, not just once but several times and now she's beginning to expect it.

Why do you want to milk that cow? You hate milking cows.

Well, it's all right. Gives me something to do, and Rose-Mama's sort of old to be out milking twice a day.

It pleases Bonney, too, doesn't it?

Yes, it does please him.

Ha. Maybe that's why you do it. He's already hooked you, just the same way he's got everybody else hooked.

No, wait, if I'm going to nail him I've got to find out a few things first. I've got to associate with him, haven't I?

All right, but why don't you get cracking? Start probing. Dig into his background. You don't even know if he ever stayed as much as a week around Beaumont when the Old Man was there.

What's the hurry? Besides, it's not easy asking questions. Nobody asks *me* any. They just accept me around here. This is going to take time.

Oh good. That's grand. Stick around and be one of the boys. Maybe you'll get to go spotlighting again, and this time Bonney will let you be the one to shoot the deer instead of just digging a hole to bury the guts.

At 3 A.M. I turned out the light and went to bed. But before I did, I changed the last line in the note to Midge. Marked out the "ninety per cent" and made it read, "I'm fifty per cent certain I'm on the right track here."

5.

He clomped in wearing those ridiculous boots with the silver inlays and the cow heads hand-tooled on the tops. They must have cost him a bundle. When he came to Bonney's he'd always have the legs of his new khaki pants stuck down in his boot tops. That irritated all the Regulars.

He stopped in the middle of the dance floor and spread his legs a little and drew himself up, like he was trying to be Matt Dillon just before the draw. He said, "Bonney? I'll buy a round. Beer for everybody."

Norman Akers, millionaire, ordering drinks for the house. He did it at least once a week.

All the Regulars at Bonney's nursed a thorough contempt for Akers. He wasn't one of the crowd. That in itself was all right, but his problem was that he tried to be a Regular and didn't know how.

Besides that, he was a phony. He owned a string of furniture stores—Houston, Galveston, Dallas, Baton Rouge and other places I forget—and had made his pile, and then he decided to be a rancher. He sent a real estate man into Kirby County and blocked up about seven old farms and established a ranch.

"Maybe it wouldn't be so bad," Bonney told me, "if he hadn't let his wife name that place Akers Acres."

Their dislike for him didn't keep Bonney's customers from drinking the beer Akers bought. In fact they'd all order premium beer, instead of the Texas brands they drank normally. It cost a nickel more, and they enjoyed seeing Akers get separated from his money.

About twenty customers were in the place the first time I watched Akers buy beer for the house. Slat was back in her room, studying for a history test. Bonney called to me. "Johnny, you want to give me a hand?" I was playing eight-ball with

J. W. Bradley. Brad was everything Akers tried to be. A genuine cowman, practically born aboard a horse. He owned a place that bordered on Akers'. Brad seldom talked about his business around the tavern. In fact he seldom talked at all. So what he said surprised me. I racked my cue and walked toward the bar to help Bonney with the round of beer, and Brad looked at Akers standing spraddled-legged on the dance floor and muttered, almost too loud, "Cowboy Bob rides again."

We passed out a dozen bottles of premium beer at thirty-five cents per. Akers handed me a twenty-dollar bill. I went back to the register and rang up the tab and started to deliver the change.

"Hold it a minute," Bonney said quietly. "I forgot to tell you, Norman always gives me a nice tip." He returned the change to the register and counted out ten ones, wadded them up with about eighty cents in silver, glided over and slapped the wad in Akers' hand. Akers jammed it in his pocket without looking at it. Never knew he'd been shortchanged exactly five dollars.

Bonney winked at me and muttered, "Ol' Norman's a real heavy tipper that way."

That night after he locked up we played ten games of eight-ball.

"Doesn't Akers ever notice when you take out for those—what do you call 'em?—tips?" I asked him. It was much easier to question Bonney now. He just didn't seem to know how to resent a question, even one that probed into his most private business.

"Naw, Akers wouldn't ever count change out of anything little as a twenty. He's too proud. Besides, five bucks to him is about like a dime to you and me."

"Do you hit him with those tips like that, all the time?"

"Ever chance I get, I promise you that."

"Why?"

"Well, hell, it's just the way things work. Akers he screws all those people who buy in his furniture stores and so I screw him when he comes in here. It's the system, Johnny. You take turns."

"But you wouldn't shortchange Brad, or Colonel Ralls, or

even Henry, after he's stood right there and threatened to hit you with a beer bottle."

"No."

"Then what's the difference?"

"Well, Akers can *afford* to be screwed, for one thing."

"All right, let's say you start shortchanging Brad just two cents a day. He can afford two cents a day. Would you do that?"

"No."

"Why not? Because it wouldn't be right?"

"OK, it wouldn't be right."

"What's the difference, then, between cheating Brad two cents and shortchanging Akers five bucks?"

"Difference is," Bonney said, rolling the eight-ball in the corner, "difference is that Akers *asks* to be screwed. He *needs* to be. There's just certain people in this world need to be screwed. It keeps everything on even keel."

"But does that make it right?"

"Hodamighty, Johnny, your trouble is you think if a thing's not right, then it's got to be wrong. It's not that simple. You find half-right things, and half-wrongs, and in-betweens. You can't keep score, man. You're not smart enough."

You can't keep score. But that's just what I'd been doing. It's why I'd come. I pictured myself driving back up to my room at Rose-Mama's that night and getting out my notebook and filling in, under a column labeled Wrong, Bonnie's habit of cheating Norman Akers.

I didn't have a notebook, but I kept score just the same. And if I'd actually been writing the score down I'd have spent an hour scribbling on the Wrong side of the ledger.

The business of Bonney's bookkeeping, for example.

One night he was doing "bookwork" and asked me to read off a sheet of figures while he totaled them on his rickety adding machine. I noticed the receipts on his beer seemed to indicate he sold local beer for twenty-five cents, although nowhere on the books was the price recorded. I asked about that, since he actually sold local beer for thirty cents a bottle.

"Well, two bits is what I charged for beer when I first went

66

in business. Then I went up to thirty and I just never have changed it, here on the books."

"How long ago did you go up?"

"About two years, I reckon."

Bonney sold a lot of beer. About a hundred cases a week. And his books showed he was retailing it for a nickel a bottle less than he actually charged. Which meant that every time he sold a case he pocketed a dollar and twenty cents on which he never paid income tax. Which meant nearly five hundred bucks a month in tax-free income.

"But, my god, Bonney," I told him, "it'd take an Internal Revenue man about five minutes on your books to spot that."

He shrugged. "Maybe so, but they got to come look at me first. They haven't been around here in three years. They don't pay attention to little fellas like me."

I noticed his books also showed his jukebox had taken in thirty dollars in the last week. Just sitting and watching the customers feed that machine, I guessed it took in almost that much on a good Saturday.

"That juke," Bonney said, just as if he were lecturing to an economics class, "takes in around seventy, even eighty bucks in a good week. Well, you know I don't own that box. The guy who comes to rob it, he puts the machine in here and we split sixty-forty. Sixty for him, forty for me. So when he comes round here to rob he says to me, all right, nobody's looking over our shoulder, we'll just say the juke took in thirty dollars this week. Well, it really took in seventy, but who's gonna know? How can they check? No way. So that's forty dollars me and that juke robber split for the week and we don't have to show it as income or pay tax on it. And it helps, I tell you that."

Helps! I guess it does. "But don't you know they're going to catch you at it?"

"How? Are they gonna sit here and count every quarter drops in that juke? Look, it works the same way on my pool table. Strictly a cash proposition, that table. If it makes forty bucks this week, I can damn well put it on my sheet that it didn't make but twenty and there's not a bookkeeper in Kansas City can catch it. It's the way this business works, Johnny. It's the way you have to do, to make a living in a place like this. If

they ever come stick me in a federal jug for doing it, I sure won't be lonesome."

I walked out the back door to my car, to go home. Turnip was squatting back there in the dust, with a case of empty beer bottles. He had a small hammer and he was taking empties out of the case and giving each a few light taps, on the top where the cap fits. He'd tap carefully until he chipped off a bit of glass from the mouth of the bottle. I asked him what he was doing.

"Just chippin' bottles."

"Why?"

"It's Mister Bonney's orders."

The next day I asked about it and Bonney explained willingly. When the trucks came to deliver beer, the distributors gave the retailer credit for chipped bottles—those which customers refused to drink from because of a chip or a crack or a flaw in the glass. Bonney always returned one case of chipped bottles a week. If not that many showed up in the normal course of business, he put Turnip to work, chipping, to make sure he had a full case. The distributors, Bonney said, knew what he was doing but ignored it because he was a good customer. If Turnip was obliged to chip an entire case of bottles, well and good. Because that meant Bonney had sold twenty-four bottles of beer that the distributor didn't charge him a cent for.

"It mounts up," Bonney said, "over a year's time. Helps pay expenses around here."

Bonney did have expenses you wouldn't expect him to have. Five, maybe six times a year, he tossed a gigantic supper under the trees beside the tavern, and he fed everybody who walked up, free of charge. He had two such feeds while I was there.

The first one was in early October. The heat of the Texas summer was still with us, but autumn had taken the edge off it and the beer business suffered a bit.

Bonney always said selling beer is simply a matter of "temperature and salt." He talked about it often, to the very people who drank his beer.

"Now these young guys, I mean the cowboys twenty-five years old and the swampers on the pulpwood trucks, they're suckers for salt. They do a hot day's work and come in here, they got a terrible thirst for about thirty minutes, but then they get gut-full and for an hour they won't do nothin' but nurse down one beer and spend half the time goin' to the toilet. You got to nudge 'em off high center. Barney and me, we go back in there to the freezer and get out all them leftover shoestring spuds and Barney heats up his grease and refries 'em and then just *covers* 'em with salt. And I bring 'em out here by the platter and set 'em on the table in front of them cowboys and tell 'em it's on the house, eat up, boys. And they think, man, what a nice guy ol' Bonney is, givin' away fried spuds that way. But when they get into that salt, mister, they begin yellin' for beer, more beer. Why, Barney and me figure a gallon of them ol' leftover spuds is worth a whole extra case of beer if we got two, three tables of cowboys in here. . . ."

He'd talk that way for an hour, maybe longer, surrounded by people who loved him, who'd sit and watch his face even if what he said didn't interest them. The women would look at him smiling, almost dewey-eyed. Maudie and Charlotte and Slat and Rose-Mama and even Aunt Kate, who was old as Rose-Mama and maybe older. And sometimes, as he did that night in early October, he would appear to bubble up and spill over with well-being, and suddenly he'd just have to jump up and do something *good!*

"Uncle Batey," he burst out, "hoddamn, Uncle Batey, let's us fire up them ol' pots tomorrow and *feed* us a bunch of folks. Are you with me? These nesters and colored folks walkin' past out there in the road been lookin' a little pore lately. How 'bout it, Uncle Batey, because if you ain't here to see it's done right I won't put a fire under the first pot."

Uncle Batey stood up. "Why, you name the time, Bonney, and we'll give it a go."

"I say tomorrow. No, wait. Make it Tuesday, because I got to get meat. I'll get us four hundred pounds of the best stew meat in Kirby County. How many pots do we fire, Uncle Batey? Three?"

"Three'll do it. Three of them big pots'll stuff ever gut in these woods, you got plenty spuds."

Bonney stood up. "Turnip? Turnip! Get your butt in here and listen to me." Turnip appeared from out of the kitchen and

Bonney said, "First thing in the morning, and I don't give a damn if ever one of your cow-dog bitches is havin' pups, you take that truck and make you a wide circle, all the way to the Chickenhawk like last time, and tell everbody we're gonna have the pots boilin' around here on Tuesday. Say about five o'clock. Tell 'em just to bring their empty bellies and somethin' to eat out of and a spoon to scoop it up with, and if you miss anybody I'll spread your black hide on the back fence. Hoddamn, we gonna have us a feed!"

Turnip grinned, a yard wide. With the possible exception of his dogs, what he loved most was to drive that truck and do something Bonney ordered him to do.

The next morning early I saw him pass Rose-Mama's, with a dog in the cab beside him and three more riding in the back, their noses stuck to the wind.

In business, in military service, in a few civic ventures, I've seen some remarkable examples of organized effort. I've never seen one, though, that approached the efficiency of Bonney's big feed.

I was assigned to help Uncle Batey, to meet him at Bonney's around eleven o'clock Tuesday morning. At one-thirty he hadn't showed up yet.

Neither had Bonney. At two o'clock he rolled in, the bed of his pickup loaded and covered with a tarp. He and Turnip unloaded two hundred pounds of potatoes and a hundred pounds of big white onions. Then Rose-Mama came in, with her women. Buck Thornton's wife, and Charlotte, and three or four younger women I'd seen around Bonney's but didn't know. Slat had pleaded with Bonney for permission to stay home from school. He refused and sent her, crying, off on the bus. "Getting on about report card time," he told her, "and you don't need to be playing any hooky. Because if you don't bring home good grades I'll dislocate that little tail of yours with a fence paling." Maudie came too, and along with Barney she took care of the regular business in the tavern. Rose-Mama told me Bonney had gone into Farley and personally hired a woman to take Maudie's place at the washateria, so she could have Tuesday off.

Uncle Batey and Aunt Kate came about two-thirty. Aunt Kate

joined the women, chattering and peeling those potatoes and onions in Barney's kitchen. Uncle Batey sat down in the shade and looked important. He brought with him a brown paper sack, and nothing more.

For half an hour all he did was talk. I'd already heard a great deal of what Uncle Batey had to say, for he did a lot of talking in the tavern at night. Often about himself and Aunt Kate. They were sixty-six years old and married for fifty years. They growed up together, he'd say, on joinin' farms, just right down the road here a ways on what's now the Bascom Place, and when they were sixteen they gotten aholt of a real inter-restin' book that told all about how to make love in twelve different ways. Well, they'd read it to each other up in her daddy's hay-loft. They'd look at the pictures a while and then they'd make love a while, accordin' to the directions, and it was just a whole *bunch* of fun, except it wasn't but just a few months after they'd got holt of the book, why Katey her stomach commenced to swellin' up like she'd swallowed a punkin and her daddy taken 'em to Tatum Bentley's and got 'em hitched up and it wasn't long till Katey she popped out a little ol' bitty baby girl no biggern a suckin' pig, which it wasn't healthy and died. And Katey she cried and taken on over it a good while, and wanted it back, and ever since that time they been atryin' to fetch up another youngun without any luck. Not a nibble, after fifty years of goin' at it strong and hard. *Still* try, too, you bet, when the notion strikes 'em in frosty weather, but it ain't no go. Still got the book? Why, you damn *right* they still got it, and got ever line in it memerized and they've thought of a few ways to do it that wasn't even in there to begin with. Wasn't but just last week Aunt Kate said to Uncle Batey, "Honey, we gonna have to get holt of us a new book because we done wore this old one out," and Uncle Batey said, "Katey girl, it ain't the book we've wore out. What *I* need is new tools because the 'quipment I started out with up there in that hayloft has got the *bone* broke in it some way."

"Uncle Batey!" It was Bonney, sticking his head out the kitchen door. "You better get your pots fired. We got stew to make, man. Look at the sun."

Uncle Batey squinted at the sun and checked it against the

big gold watch in the pocket of his blue overalls. He got up and meandered out toward Bonney's barn.

"No," he said, "I don't reckon me and Katey could raise a youngun now if somebody give us one, and the milk along with it. But we don't grieve. That book, it's got things in it besides twelve different ways. It's got advice, on how to argue in proper ways, and one page has got a place where it says a man and a wife ought to sing a song or dance a waltz together ever day they live, and me and Katey has done that. Never missed a day in near about fifty years. Now, let's see wher'n hell Bonney has hid them pots."

That was so, about the dancing. Almost nightly Aunt Kate and Uncle Batey came to Bonney's and played a waltz on the jukebox and danced together. If they couldn't make it to Bonney's they danced at least one waltz at Farley, or over at Sullivan, wherever Uncle Batey happened to have a fence-building job going.

We carried three big cast-iron pots out of the barn. Washpots, really. Capacity about thirty gallons each.

We set the pots on the flat rocks which stayed in place, always, beneath the big live oak east of the tavern. Uncle Batey insisted on building the fires himself. When the flames licked around the pot bottoms he went in the kitchen and came out carrying two five-pound packages of lard. He dumped a great hunk of it, about three pounds, into each pot.

"Why do you make stew, Uncle Batey, at a feed like this?" I asked him. "Why not barbecue?"

Uncle Batey ignored the question, so Bonney answered. "Well, when you're trying to feed a bunch of hungry folks, a stew beats barbecue any day. Uncle Batey taught me that. He says when you barbecue meat, it shrinks. When you stew it, it expands. This bunch we're feeding just needs their bellies full, is all they need. So we give 'em stew."

I almost asked why, just to see what he'd say. Why give them anything at all?

"Look yonder," Bonney said, pointing east, "and yonder," jerking his thumb to the north.

They were coming.

Not by way of the road. They were cutting through the

woods, across the rolling meadows and pastures. They came in singles, in pairs, in loose groups of three and four. Walking slow. Not shy, not tentative, and yet not in an aggressive way. Not like schoolboys charging a cafeteria line. They came as if they knew the food wasn't ready, as if they wanted to be there while it was being prepared.

Most of the early arrivals were black people. A few whites, the nesters. They weren't a raggedy-taggedy bunch. Some of the Negro men were dressed in clean white shirts and dark pants; the women in print dresses. Every one carried a plate, or a saucer, or a tin pan, or a deep cup. Some brought shiny syrup buckets. A few had tin cans, the label peeled, the metal glistening in the orange October sunlight.

I'd never seen any of them before, or hadn't paid attention if I had. They weren't Bonney's customers.

"Who are they?" I asked him.

"They're just folks that live out there in the woods," he said quietly.

Said it almost reverently.

Turnip came out of the tavern and got up in the bed of the pickup and looked out over the woods and through the clearings to see them coming. His expression said there was something almost holy, biblical, prophetic, about the Coming. He had invited them, and here they were. *And lo, the multitude came, even as I commanded.*

I felt someone standing close behind me, and turned. It was J. R. Wetzel, smiling, a beer in his hand. He nodded hello and stepped forward and stood beside me and we watched the people coming. There was a sort of organization, a ceremony about it.

Presently Wetzel said quietly, "You know, Bonney always invites me to these feeds of his because he thinks I enjoy drinking his beer. And he's right. But the main reason I come is that it's not often a man has the opportunity to witness a completely unselfish act."

Wetzel went back in the tavern. His little speech struck me as strange, delivered as it was to a man he'd met only once or twice before. I decided it was something he needed to hear himself say, that he'd never have said it to Bonney or to one of the

75

Regulars. But he could say it to me because, the same as he, I was an Outsider.

"All righty," Uncle Batey said to Bonney, "let's have your meat."

Bonney and Turnip brought three boxes of meat, fresh red beef cut into hunks ranging up to the size of a man's fist. Each pot got about a hundred and twenty-five pounds. Uncle Batey opened his paper sack and brought out salt and threw five handfuls into every pot. Then black pepper, two handfuls. And a bottle of chili powder.

I tried to think of something useful to do and asked, "You want me to bring some water, Uncle Batey?"

"Nossir," he snapped. "This meat's gonna make its own gravy. Ain't gonna catch me puttin' water in my stew. I'd sooner water good whiskey. But you can get me them two paddles in yonder in Bonney's kitchen. We got to turn this meat."

I found the paddles—full-sized boat paddles—and helped Uncle Batey turn the meat with them in the pots. It was bubbling now, producing gravy in the pot bottoms. Uncle Batey made some spice bags. He tied up caraway seed and pickling spice and cloves in little white pieces of cloth and threw them in. And followed with garlic powder, and within half an hour the gravy was rising, the meat boiling in its own juice.

"Now," Uncle Batey said, "all we gotta do is keep the heat under 'em and keep 'em stirred. Gravy's comin' up real nice."

"How about vegetables?"

"No vegetable's goin' in this here stew. Cookin' vegetables is for women. They're boilin' potatoes in yonder in the kitchen but they won't get into my stew. Only other thing goes in here, I'll drop in a few onions later on. Put 'em in now, all the onion flavor'll boil away before the meat's done. Then toward the end we'll put some vinegar in these pots. Tenderizes the meat. Whyn't you go get us a beer?"

Slat came in from school about five, and a little later the hands from the sawmill showed up, and the cowboys. They all came and stood around the pots. They didn't mix with Bonney's guests, whose numbers must have built up now to more than two hundred. They milled about under the trees and around the barn.

76

Bonney shaved and cleaned up and put on fresh jeans and socks, with his old dirty sneakers. He came out and walked a while among the Negroes, calling some by name, shaking hands, asking about families.

"Where's Calladium?" he asked, loudly, looking over the crowd. "Is Calladium here?"

Presently a remarkably aged black woman emerged from the crowd. Her hair solid white. Her face a perfect marvel of deep lines.

"Calladium," Bonney said, "how old are you now?"

"It ain't no tellin', Mister Bonney. I might be a hunnert and I might be more, but I can still chop a row of cotton and fetch in my firewood."

"Tell us who your mama was, Calladium, and your daddy."

"Why, Mister Bonney, I never did have no mama or no daddy. I was laid by the buzzards, and hatched by the sun."

The guests laughed, politely, at what I decided was a line they'd heard many times before. But Bonney was obviously fond of hearing the old woman say it. He took Calladium by the arm and steered her into the kitchen. Through the window I saw him pour her a generous drink of bourbon, which she downed in two gulps.

At sundown we set up serving lines and fed two hundred fifty people. Fed 'em boiled potatoes and sliced onions and Uncle Batey's stew. By dark, they'd all gone, back over the fields and the pastures and through the woods.

No, not all. About a dozen of the Negro men stayed and gathered in the Dark Room. I went in to visit with them. Went in, I guess, under the influence of two bowls of Uncle Batey's stew and three large bourbons. I pulled open the screen door at the side entrance and stuck my head in and said hello. Four of them were playing dominoes, keeping score with a piece of chalk on the corner of the table, and the others were sweating.

"Come in, come in."

That was Lincoln Hill, large and white-haired and smiling, showing two gold teeth. I hadn't met him but Bonney had pointed him out, explained him. "Lincoln, he's a kind of overseer back there in the Dark Room. He keeps everything straight."

"Just visiting," I told Lincoln. "Don't want to interrupt anything."

"Glad to have you," he said. "Come take you a chair here."

I thought maybe he would introduce me around, but he didn't.

"I've been hearing about the Dark Room," I said. "I thought I'd come back here and see it."

"Well, it's just a room," Lincoln smiled. "We like it. Did Mister Bonney tell you how this room got named?"

"No, when I first saw the sign I thought maybe it had something to do with photography, you know. Taking pictures."

"Well, it did, in a way. When Mister Bonney put up this buildin' and had his openin' day, he had that pictureman in town come out and snap Kodaks all around. That night the pictureman drank him a pretty good lot of beer, seems like, and he's the one painted that Dark Room sign over the door. It was like a joke, at first, you know, about this bein' a room for colored folks. Mister Bonney used to tell us he'd paint the sign out, but we sort of got used to it, I guess, and it stayed."

The subject wasn't a delicate one then, so I said, "You don't find many rooms like this now, in public places. Separate rooms, I mean, for the colored." That word, colored, seemed to be the accepted term for Negroes around Bonney's, when Negroes were within hearing range. Sometimes it was "you folks" or "you people." When no Negroes were around it was niggers, of course. But not from Bonney. I never heard him use the word, not once, which was almost unique for a rural tavern operator in Texas.

Lincoln received my comment, about places like the Dark Room being scarce now, with raised brows. "Is that so?"

Why, he was being honest. He *was* surprised to hear that.

"Lincoln," I said, "tell me this, if you don't mind my asking. Do you and your friends like it back here? I mean does it bother you, being separated from the whites?" I probably wouldn't have asked that if I hadn't had the three big bourbons.

"Bother us?" he said. "Why, no. This here's the only place we can come and play dominoes and have us some beer. If Mister Bonney didn't keep this room for us, we wouldn't have *no* place. We'd have to go all the way into Farley, or over to Sullivan."

"But there's not any law says you can't come into Bonney's. In fact there's a law that says you can."

He was shaking his head. "We wouldn't want to go in there."

"Why? Has Bonney ever told you not to?"

"No, but we come here, well, for fun. We couldn't have no fun in there, with the white people. We like it here, just the way it is."

"You know, of course," I said, "that a great many colored people, all over the country, are struggling now against just this sort of thing, about having Dark Rooms and being segregated, separated."

He smiled, in a very dignified way. "I know. I hear. But that's somewhere else. That's for our young folks, mostly. It's not for us, here in the Blackjack. For us, it only just makes trouble."

Then Turnip came to the Dutch door, grinning, and said Mister Brad was out yonder at the pool table wanting to bet two dollars he could whip me in an eight-ball game.

Lying in bed that night, I tried to figure how much that feed had cost Bonney. The meat, of course, would be the biggest item. Nearly four hundred pounds of boneless stew meat must have cost plenty.

When I got the chance I asked Uncle Batey.

"Well, wasn't but about half that meat Bonney's. Rest of it come offa that big red heifer used to belong to Big Belly Akers."

"Norman Akers?"

"Yeah."

"What do you mean the heifer *used* to belong to Akers?"

"Well, she growed up over there on his place, and *seemed* to belong to Akers. But she come through the fence into Bonney's pasture about six weeks ago and didn't never find her way back home."

"Bonney slaughtered her."

"You might say."

"But won't Akers miss that heifer?"

"I doubt it. I doubt Akers'd miss his *wife*, if *she* went through the fence."

79

"But slaughtering another man's livestock," I said, "that's slightly illegal, wouldn't you say? Cattle theft?"

"I wouldn't hardly say that. That heifer grazed in Bonney's pasture for six weeks. Big heifer that age'll eat just a bunch of grass. A man's got to protect his grazin'. The heifer refused to go home where she belonged, so Bonney's got to do somethin' to get back the grass she ate. Grass is money to a man in the cow business." Uncle Batey walked away, turning to say, "Besides, Bonney didn't eat none of that heifer's meat. He don't like stew."

I wondered what J. R. Wetzel would say, if he knew. *A completely unselfish act. Performed with stolen beef.*

I also thought about where, on my imaginary Right and Wrong ledger, I'd enter Bonney's Feeding of the Poor. Maybe that would be one of his Half-Rights. Or a Half-Wrong. Or an In-Between. I didn't think about it long. I was getting bored with the ledger, anyhow. What the hell. Maybe he was right. You can't keep score. You're not smart enough.

"You want to have a what?"

"A date," she said.

"You mean with a man, a boy?"

"Yes."

"Why?"

Bonney didn't like the idea. He stood behind the bar, his hands clutching the front of his T-shirt the way he did when he was perplexed. Suddenly I remembered Charlotte's remark: "He'll have that girl between his own sheets inside a week." I didn't believe it but I thought of the remark all the same.

"Why?" Slat returned. "Well, I don't know. Law, Bonney, girls just have dates. I haven't ever had one, and I got asked."

Twenty-two years old, an angel of a girl, and she hasn't ever had a date.

"Who asked you?" Bonney demanded.

"Hank did. Hank Mills."

"You mean Hank that drives the bus? Why, hell, Slat, he's a teacher. He can't have dates with high school girls."

"He asked the principal, and he checked with Mr. Wetzel, and Mr. Wetzel said he didn't see a goddamn thing wrong with it."

80

"Quit saying goddamn."

"Well, that's just what Hank said Mr. Wetzel said. I wasn't saying goddamn myself. Besides, *you* say it, all the time."

"No, I don't." (He didn't, at that. One of his favorite expletives was *hoddamn*. Rose-Mama explained to me that when Bonney was twelve years old he promised his mother he'd never take the Lord's name in vain, and he hadn't, ever.)

"What would you do," Bonney demanded, "on this date?"

"Just go to the football game."

He seemed relieved. "Well, that's out. Football game's Friday. You know what a riot we get around here Friday nights. I need you here, to work."

"Maudie said she'd get Gertrude to work for me." Gertrude, a friend of Maudie's, had filled in at Bonney's in the past.

I said, "Why don't you let her go, Bonney?"

That was an error. He fired a stare at me, his eyes gray and narrow, the veins distended in his temple. "I'll handle this," he snapped. It was the first time he'd ever hit me with a look like that. It said I was out of line, to mind my own affairs. I shut up.

He didn't speak for a while. I guessed he was hoping Slat would turn away and forget the matter. But she just kept standing there, waiting.

"Well," Bonney said at last, "you tell Hank to come round here and see me. I'll talk to him. Then we'll decide."

"All right. Thanks."

If Charlotte Ord had heard that conversation she'd have nudged me and said, "See? What'd I tell you? He's already got that girl in the sack. Doesn't want anybody else even to hold her hand. Mighty convenient arrangement, her sleeping back there in his own house." But I still didn't buy it. Bonney's attitude toward Slat, from what I'd seen, was just very, very protective. More protective than possessive. Not like a lover. More like a father, or a big brother.

The young men who came to the tavern had learned about it. There was the night one of the cowboys, full of beer, had reached out and touched Slat—well, all right, *goosed* her—and Bonney saw it. In a split second he had the cowboy by the front of the shirt and was telling him, "Big buddy, you do that again and I'll tear you a new rectum, you hear? You want to

81

drink in my place you keep your hands off that girl, and you tell the same thing to those other horny drugstore cowboys come in here." My, my. That sure did quiet things down around that table.

Hank came to see Bonney the next afternoon, after he finished his school-bus run. I was standing beside Bonney behind the bar when Hank walked up and I started to go back in the kitchen and Bonney said, "No, no. Come on. I might need you on this."

We sat down over in the corner, with nobody near us except Sam Hobbs sleeping on his bench.

"Slat said you wanted to see me."

Bonney was nervous. "Yeah. Well, she told me you wanted to have a date with her and . . . well, I just wanted to ask you about your . . . well . . ." He looked at me.

"About his intentions?" I offered, and almost laughed.

"About your intentions," Bonney said, nodding. *My god, he's serious about this.*

"My intentions are," Hank said, staring Bonney straight between the eyes, "to take Slat to the football game."

"And then what?"

"And then nothing. Get a drink, I suppose. Then bring her home."

"What kind of drink? I don't want anybody feeding her booze."

"A Coke, then."

"And no parking on these country roads," Bonney said. "I don't want you taking her pants off."

Hank bristled a little. "Aw, come on now, Bonney. Look, all we'd do is just have a date, for crying out loud. I like Slat. I'm not going to rape her, I just want to date her. If it'll make you feel any better, soon's the game's over I'll bring her right on back out here, and we can have a Coke here in your place."

Bonney was shaking his head. "No, if you take her anywhere, I want it to be a nice place. Take her to Spearman's, or to the Kingfish over at Sullivan. I don't want her having dates here in this beer joint."

"All right. Whatever you say."

82

Bonney had softened now. He'd relented. Seemed satisfied. "How about a beer?" he asked Hank.

Hank studied the offer a couple of seconds. I'd seen him drink beer in Bonney's a few times. But he said, "No, I believe not. I'll take a Coke, though."

Bonney got up and went to the bar. Hank looked at me and grinned. "You think I passed?" he asked.

I told him I thought he did.

That Wednesday, Slat brought home her first report cards. One B, four C's, and a D.

"What's this Social Studies," Bonney asked, "where you got the D?"

"It's like geography," Slat said, hanging over his shoulder as he studied the cards.

"You mean like what's the capital of Minnesota, and the principal products of North Dakota?"

"Sort of like that. And some history, and other stuff."

"I'll be damn. I didn't know they still taught crap like that."

Slat giggled. "It's a lot of crap, all right."

"Quit saying crap."

"You just said it yourself."

"That doesn't make it right."

"Well, it's not a cuss word."

"It's not ladylike," Bonney said. "How come you got this D?"

"I would have got a B," Slat said, "except I had to do this report about Cuba and I used Rose-Mama's Book of Knowledge. It had all about Cuba the way it was before Castro came and that made my report wrong."

Colonel Ralls had been nodding, half-asleep, over by the pool table but suddenly he came shuffling into the conversation. "Were you in Cuba?" he asked.

Slat smiled and patted the old gent on the cheek. "No, Colonel, I wasn't in Cuba, ever. I just did a paper about it for school."

"I didn't *think* you were in Cuba," the Colonel said, "be-cause——"

"Colonel," Bonney interrupted, "whyn't you go back in the kitchen and get Barney to make you a nice toddy." Turning back to the report cards. "I don't like this D."

"Well," Slat said, "I just put in my paper what the book said. I didn't know Castro had changed Cuba all up that way."

Buck Thornton, who had silently nursed a beer through the report card conference, came and peered at the D and cleared his throat and said, "Damn Communists mess up everything they touch."

The following noon I heard Bonney on the phone, talking to J. R. Wetzel.

"Just go ahead and order 'em, J.R.," he was saying. "Right, and the bookcase to put 'em in. Just be sure they're up-to-date. I want 'em to have Castro living in Cuba, and Hitler dead and buried and everything just like it is, right now. . . . Well, that's all right. . . . Three hundred and *how* much? . . . Great hod-oh-mighty. . . . No, no, go ahead and order 'em. But I may have to go up a nickel on beer."

Friday night, all the Regulars showed up early to see Slat go forth on her first date. She didn't come home on Hank's bus that afternoon. I rode in with Bonney to pick her up and take her to the beauty shop.

About seven o'clock Maudie suggested, "When she gets ready, Bonney, tell her to come in here so we can all see her."

"No," Bonney said, and he picked up Wednesday's copy of the Farley *Rocket* and went out and sat in his living room, to wait for Hank. I'd never known him to sit in that living room before. Or to put on patent leather shoes. He'd issued a lot of instructions. Hank was not to come through the tavern; he was to drive up in the back and knock on the front door of the house "just like white folks"; he was to sit there and wait until Slat got ready; the waiting period somehow seemed important to Bonney. Hank, a perceptive young man, showed up a quarter of an hour early to be certain there'd *be* a waiting period.

When they came out of the house, Bonney came too. *I hope he doesn't try to go with 'em.* He watched while Hank opened

84

the car door and handed Slat in, and that pleased him, you could tell. We all crowded back in the kitchen—all right, sure, I was there too, on the front row—to get a look at Slat. She was something. That tone-black hair was put up high on her head. She had on nylons and heels and one of the new dresses she'd not had occasion to wear. She didn't look like any high school girl, I promise you that.

"Don't she look nice?" Barney said.

Bonney watched them drive away, standing out there in the dust with five of Turnip's cow dogs.

When he came in he asked me, "What'd you think?"

"I think she looked like a million bucks. She's a beautiful girl. She's something special."

"Yeah. Well, let's see if we can get in a couple games before the crowd gets too thick."

I beat him two straight again, the first time I'd done it since the day I came. His concentration was off. We quit playing and went over and sat down with Sam Hobbs, who didn't look quite as drunk as usual.

"What you been drinkin', Sam?" Bonney asked.

"Little beer, this mornin'."

"And a little of that rotgut too?"

"Well, a little."

"Tell you what, I picked up couple bottles bourbon in Houston other day. Let's us break a seal on one and see how it goes down."

"All right," Sam said. "I'd like that."

Bonney got a little drunk that night, and Sam got magnificently loaded and danced with Rose-Mama and passed out on his bench at nine-thirty. I'd never seen Bonney tight. He moved slower, talked less, didn't take care of business the way he normally did. I ended up on the cash register because Maudie and Gertrude had their hands full with the Friday-night business.

Bonney danced three numbers with Charlotte Ord, and once he went back in the Dark Room and sang songs with the Negroes. Barney got mad and quit at ten o'clock. Second time he'd quit that week. Said Bonney was "too friggin' hard to get along with."

Once Bonney looked at the clock behind the bar and asked me, "What time does a football game get over with?" I said I didn't know for sure.

At eleven Hank brought Slat home. She didn't come into the tavern. Bonney's orders again. She was to go on to bed, or stay in the house.

Just before midnight I took Rose-Mama home. Bonney had put about four good bourbons into her and a minute after she went in her bedroom I could hear her snoring. I sat down and read the *Rocket* for about the fourth time. Even got into the classified ads. Here was an interesting one:

LOST, STRAYED OR STOLEN—$50 reward
for one 2-yr-old heifer of mixed breeding missing
since Sept 7, red with white splash on left flank.
Contact Norman Akers, Akers Acres, Tel 146.

At one o'clock I didn't feel like going to bed so I drove back down to the tavern, to see if Bonney was still up. The place was dark except for the night lights. One car was parked under the big pine. Charlotte Ord's young daughter sat behind the steering wheel, and her father was sleeping on the back seat.

"Anything wrong?" I asked her.

"No, we're just waiting for mama. She's helping Gertrude and Maudie and Bonney clean up the kitchen. She said Barney quit again. Daddy got pretty beered up so I got him out here in the car, and we're just sitting here waiting. Are you going in? If you do, would you tell mama to hurry?"

"All right, sure."

I walked round to the back and looked in the window. The light Barney usually left burning in the kitchen was switched off. No sign of anybody. I almost went in, but the mumble of voices stopped me. They were coming from Barney's Couch. I walked away when I recognized, in the dim light from the bar, a red-flowered dress hanging on the handle of the big refrigerator door. It was Charlotte's dress.

I went back to the front and told the girl, "They're almost through. She'll be along in a minute or so."

"Thanks."

"Oh, say. How'd the football game come out?"

"We got beat."

"That's too bad."

"Yes, sir."

"Well, good night."

"Good night."

Good night, little miss. Just you be patient a little while longer. Your daddy's safely sleeping and your mama's inside getting banged on Barney's Couch and all's right with the world. Don't you fret.

6.

We stood in the door and watched Sam Hobbs roll off the end of the flatbed truck and hit the sand and come up spitting. The truck didn't quite stop, only slowed down, and when Sam bailed out he landed flat on his belly. He took a pretty good jolt.

Instinctively I started out to help him, but Bonney grabbed my arm. "No, wait. Let him get up by himself. He'll be all right. He's just hung over. He's hitchhiked out here to see if he can find anything to drink. I expect he's broke."

Sam came up slow, testing his knees to see if they were going to work. His khaki pants hung loose from his hipbones. I marveled they stayed up. He was a god-awful thin person. He made his way toward the front door. Bonney glided back to the cash register and returned to the juke and dropped two quarters in the coin slot but didn't punch any selector buttons. "Now watch this," he said, and we went behind the bar.

Sam entered and walked straight to the jukebox and stuck a shaky index finger into the coin-return receptacle. This was his ritual, always, on entering Bonney's Place. He'd look in the coin return to see if by some kind miracle any change had fallen there, forgotten. Enough, maybe, for a beer.

He found no coins so he completed the ritual. He reached around and punched the coin reject button and of course Bonney's two quarters came clattering down. Sam reacted slowly. He fished the quarters out and stared at them a while. Just a clue of a grin showed in his eyes as he approached the bar.

"Mornin', Sam," Bonney greeted him. "What'll you have?"

"Beer," Sam croaked, weak and hoarse. It was ten o'clock in the morning and obviously this was the first time he'd used his voice. He cleared his throat and said louder. "Quart." He put the two quarters on the bar. Sam was accustomed to showing his money before he was served.

Bonney sold quarts for sixty cents but he fished one out of the box and pulled it. Sam downed about a third of it, sat and waited for the belch. When it came he grinned. And said, "My lucky day. I found two quarters in the juke."

"Son of a gun," Bonney said.

"I was at the bank yesterday," said Sam.

"What you doin' at the bank?" Bonney asked him. "Puttin' in or takin' out?"

"I went to borrow a hundred dollars."

"But you didn't get it."

"No."

"Who'd you talk to? Coleman?"

"Yeah. He said he'd let me have the hundred if you'd sign my note. I told him I'd get you to call him."

Bonney growled. He looked up at the clock and grabbed the phone. "Ada, get me the bank, will you?" He took his pencil from behind his ear and made little figure eights on the bar. Then into the phone again, "Well, good morning, Lucille. How's my gal? Has any of that money down there rubbed off on you lately? . . . Well, maybe you haven't been *rubbin'* it right. Say, Lucille, I got business down there. Let me talk to Mr. Milk-of-Human-Kindness."

The grin came off his face when Lucille switched him over to the banker.

"Hello, Mr. Coleman? Bonney McCamey. . . . All right, doing all right. Say, Mr. Coleman, Sam Hobbs is out here at my place. Sitting right here, yeah. Sam says you'll let him have a hundred if I'll sign his note. . . . Right. . . . Uh-huh. . . .

Well, I just wanted to tell you, Mr. Coleman, if *you'll* sign Sam's note, *I'll* let him have the hundred." And he hung up, grinning again.

Then he opened the register and took ten dollars out and handed it to Sam. "That's all, Sam. Not another buck. And you're gonna work that out, you hear? When I ship my calves you're gonna be out there, sober, and you're gonna work it out."

"Sure, sure. I'll be there." Sam stuck the ten in his pocket and left.

"Will he be there? To work?" I wondered.

"He might, might not."

"What'll he do with the money?"

"Buy squirrel whiskey."

"Why did you give it to him?"

Bonney sighed. "Well, it's sort of damned if you do and damned if you don't. If he hasn't got money, he'll go buy whiskey on credit from one of those nesters and they'll charge him three prices and when he can't pay they'll beat hell out of him and I'll have to pay off for him anyway. This way at least I got a *chance* of getting some work out of him for my money, and he won't get killed. Least not till that rotgut kills him."

Before noon Brad came in and drank a cup of Bonney's coffee, which I'd learned to avoid.

"Say, Brad," Bonney said, "you still got that little white-nosed jackass your kids used to ride around here?"

"Yeah, he's still over yonder on the place."

"Is he still gentle? Could you bring him inside, without he got nervous and tore everything up?"

"That jack hasn't got any nerves to get nervous *with*. You could take him to church and he'd go to sleep."

"How about bringing him over here, around five o'clock this afternoon. Sam's gonna be in here, drunk, and I want to see if we can shake him up a little bit."

"All right."

Sam came in at five-thirty weaving and grinning. He stopped at the jukebox and stuck a finger in the coin return. But no disappointment registered on his face when he found no change there. He patted his pocket. He still had some of the ten dollars.

He walked out on the dance floor, waved at the mill hands at the tables, hello'd the cowboys, and offered to buy Brad a beer. When the number on the jukebox stopped, he started singing. He always sang when he carried a load.

> *When I was in O'Riley's Store*
> *Listenin' to the tales of blood and*
> *   slaughter,*
> *Came an idea to my mind,*
> *That I should shag O'Riley's daughter ...*

Then the jukebox started up again, and he quit.

Every customer in the place had been carefully briefed by Bonney, about how to react to the donkey. Colonel Ralls was sent off on an errand, since he couldn't possibly co-operate and might spoil the plot. Bonney nodded at Brad, sitting at the bar, and Brad went out in the back. Presently he came in the rear door leading a drowsy-eyed donkey. It was saddled, and riding stiffly backward in the saddle was a tall plastic red rooster with Early Call Coffee Co. in yellow letters across its chest. An advertising gimmick that stayed normally in Turnip's bedroom in the house. Some drummer had given it to him.

"I think it's a shame, to do poor Sam this way," Slat said to me quietly. I felt somewhat the same, but Bonney was hung on doing it. "It might help him, you can't tell," he argued. "It might scare him into sobering up."

Brad and the donkey came through the kitchen slowly, out the swinging door, turned to pass in front of the bar. Brad maintained a perfectly dead-pan expression. The donkey raised his muzzle and sniffed at the vase of Rose-Mama's flowers. Brad waited until the little animal satisfied his curiosity, then led him on over toward the pool table.

The eight-ball players didn't even look up. Neither did the cowboys or the mill hands or any of the Regulars. They went right on talking, laughing, just as they always did. Bonney almost brushed the donkey's rump as he sailed across the floor

90

carrying a round of beer, but paid it no heed, as if it didn't exist.

Slat and I watched from the serving window. Sam's eyes were zero'd in on the donkey as it meandered past the pool table and stopped to inspect the cigarette machine. Sam's eyes left the donkey occasionally, to look around him, to see how the crowd was reacting to this donkey in the house. Was everybody crazy? Couldn't they *see*? Couldn't they see a donkey was in here, with a red rooster riding on its back?

I saw Sam elbow Buck Thornton, sitting beside him, and point. Buck looked in the direction Sam indicated, but shook his head, and turned back to listen to something one of the mill hands was saying.

Uncle Batey got up and fed the jukebox and a waltz began playing. He and Aunt Kate swept out on the dance floor to do their daily duty. They circled smoothly around Brad and the donkey, standing half-asleep in the middle of the floor.

Then Brad tugged gently on the lead rope and he and the donkey went out the front door, negotiated the two front steps, and disappeared.

For a minute Sam apparently tried to act as if nothing had happened. But he was nervous. He kept wiping his mouth with his hand. Then he rose and, stumbling once, went to the bar and took Bonney by the arm.

"A donkey," he said.

"A what?" Bonney looked at him, blank-faced.

"What was that donkey doin' in here, with Brad?"

"What you talkin' about?"

"Brad brought a donkey in here with a rooster on it."

"Look, Sam, I'm busy. It's my rush hour. Don't pester me now." He took off for one of the tables.

Sam went to the pool table and collared Ben Ashley.

"You saw that donkey," Sam commanded.

"When was that?" Ben asked.

"Just a minute ago. It came in here with Brad and had a rooster on it."

"What in hell you been drinkin', Sam? Ain't been no donkey through here. Now get out of my way."

While Sam was at the pool table, Brad came back through the kitchen and sat at the bar.

"Brad!" Sam said, relieved to see him. "How come you brought that donkey through here?"

"What's all this crap about a donkey?" Brad said.

"But I *saw* you. You came through the kitchen, and you had a donkey with you and a rooster on its back and you went right by here, and then over there to the table, and you went out the front door, and you were leadin' that donkey. Just a *minute* ago!"

"Sam, you better quit drinkin' that rotgut," Brad said quietly. "I been sittin' right here, ever since you came in."

That's when things got out of hand.

Sam charged drunkenly out in the middle of the floor. "*I saw it! Goddamn you all I saw it! I saw it I saw it I saw it . . . I . . . saw . . . that . . . don-key. . . .*"

Then he was down, on the floor, like a little baby, his bony old rear end sticking up in the air and his face buried in his hands and his shoulder blades shaking with the awfulest, awfulest sobs. The jukebox stopped and the pool players stood motionless, looking down their cues, and the place was suddenly like a funeral parlor with nobody saying a word or shuffling a foot and Bonney stood at the cash register with the saddest face. Then Slat, tears gushing, came out of the kitchen and put her arms around Bonney's waist and buried her head under his arm and pleaded with him. "Tell him, Bonney. Please. Please tell him."

He nodded. "All right."

He went out on the floor and kneeled down and took Sam by the shoulders and said, "Come on, Sam. Come on, boy. Now you quit, hear? Come on, we'll go see the donkey. It's out back."

Bonney pulled him up and half-carried him out through the kitchen, and still nobody said a word, even after they were gone.

Barney and I stood at the window and watched. Bonney had his arm around Sam's thin shoulder, which still shook, in sharp sob-spasms. The donkey was under the live oak, nuzzling at a

92

block of hay. Sam reached out, to touch it, to rub it between the ears, to know it was real.

Bonney looked at Turnip. "Get the rooster."

Turnip brought the rooster and put it on the donkey's back, just the way it was in the tavern. We could see Sam nodding. But the sobs wouldn't stop. His shoulders kept jerking.

So Bonney did a thing I didn't think he could do. He pulled Sam to him, and wrapped his arms around him, and patted his shoulders. A father, comforting a little child who's had a bad dream. They stood that way a long while out there in the yard. Barney coughed, and turned back to his stove. Turnip hung his head, and looked out toward the barn.

Then finally Sam pushed away, broke away, and we heard him say, "A drink. I gotta have a drink." He tried to run, out there toward the blacktop where he had his rotgut stashed away in a culvert. He fell, and Bonney was there to pick him up.

"Come on, Sam. Come on, boy," he said. "Let's go in the kitchen. You don't have to drink that rotgut. I got us a good bottle of bourbon in here. Green-stamp whiskey. Just me and you. We'll drink it ever damn bit, just me and you."

They did, too.

Slat got Barney to fix Sam some poached eggs and a bowl of soup. But he wouldn't eat. He passed out at nine o'clock. On his bench. With a smile on his face.

October had been a dry month and November wasn't doing any better. By the tenth of the month only one wet norther had managed to struggle down off the Rockies and push all the way across Texas, and it hadn't dumped more than half an inch of rain. Gray-red dust boiled up behind Brad's Jeep.

"Look at those cracks," Bonney said, jerking a thumb at the dry ground. "Couple more weeks and you could lose a pig down 'em. You know, Brad, I measured just exactly thirty-five hundredths in my gauge, out here at the pens, since the first of October."

Brad nodded. "Pretty dry."

"I hate like hell to take these old cows into the winter without any grass," Bonney said. He turned to look at Sam and

93

me, riding in the back of the Jeep, sitting on top of a tool box. "Sam, I'm gonna send you to church Sunday to pray for rain."

Bonney had permitted Sam only one drink that morning, and not even that until after he'd eaten some breakfast. The prospect of being out most of the day without a drink wasn't lifting Sam's spirit. But he promised to help when Bonney shipped calves, and here he was, sober. Or almost.

He leaned forward and said, with considerable effort, "Ain't no use prayin' for rain. Pray instead for an east wind. You get the wind out of the east for five days and all hell can't keep it from rainin'."

Brad and Bonney both grinned, and Brad stopped the Jeep at a set of rickety cattle pens in a clearing.

"How many calves can we put in that trailer of yours?" Bonney asked. "You reckon twelve?"

"More like ten," Brad said, "unless they're mighty light."

"Well, I doubt there's one in the bunch that'll go four hundred. Most about three-fifty. Maybe we can pack 'em a little and take twelve at a time. I don't want to make but two trips if we can help it."

Now Turnip came up in a cloud of dust, driving Bonney's pickup and pulling a long gooseneck cattle trailer borrowed from Brad. He got out and said, "Mister Bonney, Miz Whitaker telephoned down to the place after you left." Turnip had never been able to call Rose-Mama anything but Mrs. Whitaker. "You don't have to call me Mrs. Whitaker, Turnip. Hell's jingle bells, call me Rose-Mama." But Turnip couldn't do it.

"Her milk cow's bullin'," the boy said, "and she wants to know can we take her to Sullivan and breed her to that Jersey."

Bonney spat. "Shoot, that's just a waste, puttin' that cow under that Jersey bull. We get time we'll bring her over here and let ol' Eddie bull ease *her* pain. Then she might have a calf with a little meat on it, be worth carryin' to town. Well, let it go now. We got calves to ship. If that milk cow just came in heat last night there's not any hurry about it. Where you think our cattle'll be, Turnip?"

"Down yonder in the creek bottom," he said. "They hadn't come out of there in two weeks."

"All right, let's see if we can honk 'em up. Better drive that truck around yonder on the far side of the pens, where they can see it from the creek." He looked my way. "All right, Johnny, we're gonna show you an East Texas cow roundup."

What that meant, that East Texas cow roundup, it meant he wasn't going to start saddling horses and riding off across the range and driving up cattle, the way they do on those TV shows.

Turnip moved the truck and Bonney stood by the cab with his hand on the horn. He honked, and honked, and honked, looking off down at the creek. And suddenly one of Turnip's cow dogs, which he'd brought in the cab of the truck, stuck his muzzle out the window and gave Bonney a big happy lick on the side of the jaw. Brad nudged me, as if to say, "Watch the explosion."

"*Hoddammit, Turnip,*" the explosion came, "who in the purple-splattered hell told you to bring this hoddamn ol' long-tongue *dawg* out here!"

"He needs to work, Mister Bonney. Lemme send him down there. He'll bring them cows out, you'll see, in a minute. Lemme work him, please."

Bonney calmed a little but he wouldn't relent. "Now look, boy, that dog won't do a damn thing but go down in there and scatter those cows all over hell, and run about five pounds apiece off ever calf I'm tryin' to sell. Now when all my cows get loose and run off over yonder on the Chickenhawk and get back in that brush, *then's* when I'll use your dogs. Hell, these cows here don't need dogs. We've been feedin' 'em out of a sack since the fifteenth day of last August. It's a damn wonder they don't all wear napkins and carry knives and forks. Look yonder, comin' out of the creek. Why, they come up here to this truck like a bunch of cotton pickers to a dinner bell."

About half a mile away, a string of cows and calves was emerging from the brushy timber along the creek. They headed up the slope, straight toward the truck, walking slowly but steadily. The sound of the horn meant a truck, and a truck meant feed.

Turnip went to the rear of the pickup, sulking, as he always did when he earned Bonney's disfavor.

"Bonney," Brad said quietly, "you know what you oughta do with this place? You oughta give it to me, and ever cow on it. It's the only way you'll ever make any money out of it. I ain't sure I'd take it, but I might."

"You'd take it, all right," Bonney said, "even if it was solid in concrete. You'd take it just to get more ground. You're just like Norman Akers. You don't want any more land, except just what joins you."

"How much you got in here, three hundred acres?"

"Three twenty-five, and it's not for sale. One of these days I'm gonna finish clearin' up that creek bottom and get all this brush and timber off and fertilize it and sprig that fancy grass on it and that's what I'm gonna do in my old age, is sit right here on my butt and watch them cows make me a livin'."

"Sounds nice," Brad said. "It might work, too. All you need to do is bring those Elkins boys in here with their bulldozers and clear this place. They wouldn't charge you but ever dollar you've got."

"I know what land-clearing costs," Bonney said.

"How many mother cows you got? Thirty-five, forty?"

"Fifty."

"Fifty! Why, hell, Bonney, that's a cow and a calf to six acres. Ain't no native pasture in Kirby County gonna carry a cow to six acres. No wonder you been feedin' 'em since middle of August."

"Well, what you want me to do?"

"Get out of the cow business, is what you ought to do. I can sit right here on my butt without a pencil and show you, you're losin' money. I bet after you sell your calves and pay your feed bill you won't have enough left to cover the interest on what you had to borrow to buy this place. You'd do better givin' your land to me, and takin' your money off Johnny here, beatin' him at eight-ball for two bucks a game."

Bonney smiled. "I just wonder what you'll have to say, Mister

96

Smart, when I tell you I don't *pay* no interest on any land loan because I own this place free and clear."

"The hell you do," Brad said.

"The hell I don't. I wrote Mrs. Eloise Covington a check for twelve thousand dollars to get this place. It's all mine, and I got the papers to prove it."

"That's one of the awfulest lies I ever heard," Brad said amiably. "Because twelve thousand would be just forty dollars an acre and as sorry as this place is, even ten years ago it'd bring a hundred and twenty."

"It's no lie," Bonney said.

"Why, hell, Bonney, before you showed up around here I camped on that widow woman's doorstep for a whole year, tryin' to get her to sell me this place for a hundred an acre."

Bonney brought out his most triumphant grin. "You camped in the wrong place, Brad. You should have moved on inside, into her house."

Brad stared into Bonney's face, hoping to make him laugh, to admit he was kidding. "You son of a bitch," he said, and got to his feet.

"That widow woman didn't need *money*, Brad. All she needed was attention. I'm surprised at you, Brad. Man like you, knows so much about bulls and cows. All that widow woman needed was breedin' a little bit. She was in *heat*, just the same as Rose-Mama's old milk cow."

"You son of a bitch," Brad said, grinning. He put a boot on the rear bumper of the pickup and said, "Still, even without payin' interest, you're not gonna make money out of runnin' cows on this place, and if you think you are, you're a damn fool."

Bonney accepted the friendly insult. "Well, a man don't need a license to be a damn fool, does he?"

"No. I reckon not." Brad walked to the front of the truck. "Well, here's your thunderin' herd. Let's get them calves loaded, so you can carry 'em into town and see how much money you can lose."

The cattle had arrived at the pens. They all stood in a loose bunch, tails switching, ears at attention, watching the truck like a bunch of Turnip's cow dogs waiting to be fed.

The "roundup" was ridiculously easy. Turnip filled a battered two-gallon bucket with range nuggets from the truck and walked into the main lot of the cattle pens. Bonney opened the gate and every animal in the bunch tried to push inside. He let about twenty-five head in, and shut the others out. Then he and Turnip, armed with long slender sticks, moved through the cattle, cut out the calves Bonney indicated, and waved them through an inside gate that led into a loading chute. Brad worked the cutting gate. When he got a calf into the chute he shut the gate and, using an electric cattle prod from the tool box in the Jeep, he'd move the calf on up the loading chute and into the waiting trailer.

Within ten minutes Brad yelled, "All right, just gimme one more. Gimme the biggest one you got."

Then the trailer was loaded and Brad was latching the endgate and Turnip was starting the truck. "All right," Bonney told him, "take 'em on in and tell Riley I got another load comin', just about like this one. And get your tail right straight back. We can't stay out here playin' cowboy all day. We got a beer joint to run."

The truck and trailer disappeared into the brush and we sat down to smoke and to wait. Presently something drew Brad's attention and he got up and walked out among the cattle. The object of his interest was a young white-faced male calf, sturdy-built, a handsome little animal with a certain regal presence.

"Hey, Bonney," Brad called, "who's bull calf is this?"

Bonney winked at me and said to Brad, "Ain't he a sweetheart? Built like a brick crapper, wouldn't you say?"

"He's all right, but that's not what I asked. I asked who's he was."

"He's mine, who's do you think? That calf's name is Saint Nick. He was born last Christmas Day, and he's gonna be my herd bull one of these days. What you think of him?"

Brad didn't answer but it was obvious he thought highly of the little bull. He asked, "Where'd he come from?"

"He came right out from under his mama's tail, same as all the rest of 'em. That's his mama right there behind you, that Miss Lucy cow with the bald face and the high horns."

98

Brad inspected Miss Lucy, and grunted. "He may be out of this cow but your Eddie bull damn sure ain't his daddy."

"No, that's right," Bonney admitted. "That calf's daddy is the best Hereford bull in this county. He's got a set of papers long as a mail route, and cost twenty thousand dollars."

Brad's glance moved from Bonney over to the west, toward Norman Akers' place. "Belly Akers' bull?"

Bonney nodded. "Yep. That fancy one he got out in Mills County. That bull——"

"I know the bull, but how come he got on a cow of yours? I know damn well Norman didn't loan him to you."

"No, the way that happened, not long after Norman brought that bull in from West Texas he was keepin' him in a little trap on the back side of his place. Well, it's that trap right yonder, you can see it from here. Me and Turnip was back here one day and this Miss Lucy cow was bullin', walkin' up and down the fence, you know, talkin' romance with that pretty bull and she got him all excited and he commenced pawin' at them six strands of new bob wire, and tossin' his shaggy old head, and Turnip he said, 'That bull's gonna come through the fence, and tight as them new wires is strung he's gonna hurt himself.' Well, I could see Turnip was right, so I told him to get the cutters and clip a few of those wires, and he did, and the bull stepped right across, without gettin' a scratch, and he mounted Miss Lucy and fixed her up real proper. Then we hazed him back through the hole in the fence and patched it up. While we were at it, why here came Norman, jumpin' stumps in that Cadillac the way he does, and he wants to know how come we're messin' with his fence. So I just told him the truth. Told him we'd just got through savin' that fancy bull of his some terrible bad cuts from the bob wire."

"I reckon he appreciated that," Brad said dryly.

"Not too much," Bonney went on. "He wanted to know if we'd bred his bull to that common old cow, meanin' Miss Lucy, which she was still standin' around there with a smile on her face. And I told him, why no, *we* didn't do any of the breedin', it was all a private agreement between the bull and Miss Lucy, and they didn't ask us a question or make a comment, just went right at it, all by themselves."

99

Brad said, "Well, you got a calf out of his bull, and except for them free beers he buys at your place, that's about the only thing anybody ever got out of Akers. You got a pretty nice bull calf, too. *Damn* good, I'd say, seein' his mama's just an old grade cow."

Bonney grinned. "Well, I got a price on him, just like his daddy had. I wonder if you'd like to buy him, for twenty thousand."

"I wonder if you'd like to go to hell," Brad answered.

Turnip was back within an hour, since it was a drive of less than ten miles to the auction barn. They loaded nine more calves and one aged cow that Brad said was so old she must have come over on the *Mayflower*, or had a calf by Noah's bull on the ark that time.

When the loading was done, Sam stirred and latched the end-gate on the trailer and I believe that was the first lick of work he'd done since we'd arrived at the pens. He'd sat on the fence the whole time and hadn't moved or spoken.

"Sam," Bonney said, as we were leaving, "you're so sweaty from all that work you've done, you might catch a chill if you ride in this Jeep in the open air. I tell you what, just so you can earn about fifty cents of that ten bucks you owe me, how about you gettin' in behind Eddie bull and push him up toward the barn? Rose-Mama's milk cow has got a date with him, and it seems a shame to make a nice old cow walk near a mile to get made love to. Just drive him on up and put him in the lot, will you?"

Sam nodded. "You got the whiskey on the truck?"

"No, no whiskey. Soon's you get Eddie in the lot, you go in and tell Barney I said let you have a beer."

"A quart?"

"All right, a quart, but then you lay off until I get back from the auction barn. No use you going in the house and tearing up my mattress looking for the bottle because there's not a shot of whiskey on the place. You just take it easy, and maybe I'll bring us a little something when I come back."

Sam picked up a switch and started Eddie moving. "Come on, Eddie," he mumbled, "let's go to the house. You gonna get you a piece of tail and I'm gonna get me a cold beer."

100

Bonney swung into the truck with Turnip and said to Brad, "You gonna come on in to the auction and watch me lose money on these calves?"

"Naw, I've seen that so many times it's not any fun to watch. But listen, before you go, I'll make you an offer. Serious one, too. I mean it. When you come to your senses and get ready to quit playin' around in the cow business, I'll buy this place from you. I'll give you a hundred and a quarter an acre for it, and buy all your cattle at the market. Won't take me anything but a phone call to get the financin'. Now that'll give you a real sweet profit, seein' you didn't pay but forty for it."

Bonney kept a solemn face. "Brad, that's nice. That's a real nice offer. It's so damn generous it's a wonder your halo ain't burnin' your hat and your wings flappin' in the breeze. Why hell, Brad, Akers just last week offered me three hundred an acre for my creek bottom, about seventy acres of it that runs along his east fence."

Brad nodded. "You gonna let him have it?"

"Hell no. They're not makin' any more creek bottom anywhere."

Brad nodded again. "I'm gonna tell you something. This place here of yours, it's not real good dirt except for the creek, but I been wantin' this place myself for a long time. Long time before *you* ever showed up. And then you come pirootin' in here and jump in the sheets with Miz Covington and get it off her for forty damn dollars. Now, is that a fact?"

"It's a fact."

"Well, you know what you oughta do? When you pull off your pants tonight you oughta reach down and give that thing a pat on the head, because it made you the best land deal that's been made around here in fifty years."

"I'll remember that," Bonney grinned.

"Listen, it's none of my business, I know, but I'll ask you anyway. Where in hell did you ever get twelve thousand cash to pay for land? Which bank did you rob?"

I, too, had wanted to ask that, but couldn't. And now here was J. W. Bradley, being able to ask it because he and Bonney were the kind of friends who could ask such questions.

"You're right," Bonney answered, "it's none of your business.

But I got that money playin' pool. I won it shootin' eight-ball on Capitol Avenue in Houston and over there in Jefferson County. Most of it I took off those sailors at Port Arthur and all those tin hats out of the refineries at Orange and Beaumont. Thanks for your trailer. If we don't tear it up, we'll get it back to you tomorrow."

"No hurry," Brad waved them off. "Just when you get done with it."

Beaumont. Bonney McCamey had come pirootin' in here from Beaumont, with twelve thousand in cash. And how much more? About three thousand more? He'd come from Beaumont, where Lakecrest Home is. Where the Old Man was. Where that fifteen thousand was, before it disappeared.

Deer season opened November fifteenth. At dusk on the fourteenth, before it was legal to do so, Bonney killed a twelve-point buck.

He never did get to tell the truth about how he shot that buck, which must have been painful to him because a requirement for membership in the Regulars seemed to be that you have a good deer story to tell. Around the tavern, the stories began about mid-October and became increasingly hairy until opening day. Even Rose-Mama generally got her buck, and one of the more popular stories concerned the way she killed a deer in 1967. Harvey Wilks retold it in the *Rocket,* before the season opened:

DEER DEER DEER

You cant hardly get any business done in town now because everybody is talking about deer season. I never heard any better lies than this year. Still the best story is Grace Whitaker's that lives 7 miles east of town. In 67 she didn't get her buck until the last day. All during the season she sat up in that deer stand which was built by her dead husband and never got a shot. Well she was out in her back yard about sundown and looked around and there was this nice buck eating in her milk cows trough. She got a double bit ax off the back porch and slipped up and cleeved that deers skull. Its the first time a buck was

killed in Kirby County as far as I know with an ax.—
Interest in hunting this season is improved on account
of Bakers Hardware Contest. Bakers is offering 50 dollars
for the first buck brought in to the store on opening day.
Also two Remington Thirty Aught Six deer rifles, one
for the heaviest buck, field dress, and one for the biggest
rack. Arty Baker says a hunter must sign a affadavet that
he shot the deer in Kirby County and he needs to have
a witness sign with him.—Anyway back to Mrs. Whitaker
just remember she is a widow woman and stays all alone
out there except for a roomer but if any of you criminals
or robbers get an idea about messin around her place, just
ask that deer about what your liable to get, he'll tell you
a split skull.

When Bonney read Harvey's report aloud in the tavern, Rose-
Mama said Harvey didn't get the story quite right but it was
close. She said the yarn got a little better every year, but
what's a deer story good for if you can't stretch it, hell's
jingle bells.

"Hey, Buck," Bonney said, "tell Johnny here about your
deer hunt out there in the Hill Country that time. Slat, bring
Buck a fresh one. He can't tell a deer story over an empty."

"Wasn't much to it," he said. "About ten, twelve years ago
I hadn't ever shot a deer in my life, or even *at* one, and didn't
care nothin' about it. That was back when Old Man Farley
himself was still livin', and still president of the Mills. He
come up with this idea that he'd have a drawin' for everbody
on the payroll and the winner would get to go along on the
airplane out to the deer lease the Mills had out in the Hill
Country, out there west of San Antone. Well, my name come
up winners in the drawin'. I didn't care nothin' about shootin'
a deer, but I never had been on an airplane ride so I went.
About ten of us went, and everbody but me was an officer,
like a vice-president or a department head, and they'd try to
be nice to you, you know, show they didn't mind associatin'
with a hired hand, but it wasn't much fun. Ridin' out there
I sat in a back seat with that dog belonged to Old Man
Farley. *Big* dog, white and spotted. What kind of dog, Bonney?"

"Dalmatian."

"Dalmatian," Buck went on. "You remember that dog, Rose-Mama. Old Man set a terrible store by that dog. Wouldn't go anywhere without he took that damn dog, and I swear to god they had a seat set aside for him on that company plane.

"Anyway, we got out there, and it was nice. Big lodgehouse, with servants, and a long bar and poker tables. Well, about four o'clock the next mornin' they got us up and loaded us in cars and taken us out to these deerstands. They gave me a deer rifle, which I never had shot anything at that time except a twenty-two target or a twelve-gauge bird gun. And they gave me a little sack of feed, sort of like cottonseed cake, and they told me to scatter that feed out there in front of my stand and get inside and when the deer came to eat the feed, why just shoot whatever had horns on it. Then they drove on off and left me.

"Well, I scattered the feed and went in that stand. It was about on the size of a outdoor toilet but it was fixed up inside. Had a little rug on the floor and a swivel seat to sit in and even a gasoline heater that you lit up to keep warm. I lit the heater and sat there, and sat, and nothin' ever showed up, and I commenced to get warm and I'd drowse off a while, and wake up and look out, and drowse off again. It wasn't much in the way of excitement. I got to rummagin' around in that stand and found some cans of stuff, like little sausages and meat that they'd put in there for you to eat. I ate some of that a while. Once I opened a can of meat and it didn't taste right to me, so I just chunked it out on the ground in front of the stand, and then I went on back to sleep.

"Next time I woke up, hell, the sun was way high and I looked out and musta been a dozen damn deer standin' around out there in front of me, eatin' on that feed like a bunch of calves. Well, I come down with the damndest case of buck fever. I didn't know what was happenin' to me, but I had a *case*. Fact, after that's when they commenced callin' me Buck at the Mills, which my real name is Claude.

"I'd stick that rifle out the port and I'd get sighted in with that scope, and then I'd get to shakin', just tremblin' all over. So I'd put the gun down, and get aholt of myself, and put it out again and sight, and then my glasses would get to foggin'. So I'd bring in the rifle and I'd sit there and wipe my glasses, and shake, and I thought once I was havin' a damn heart attack. I musta sat in there for quarter of an hour, tryin' to hold that gun and get off a shot.

"The last time I sighted I couldn't see nothin' in that scope except just a gray kind of blur, and I said, well, my eyes has just gone flat bad so it ain't no use me tryin to sight, I'll just shoot and holler fall. So that's what I done. I turned my head to one side and shut my eyes and pulled the trigger—blooey! Man, that rifle like to killed me. I had it maybe an inch away from my shoulder and I ain't sure but what it didn't turn me a back flip. It took my glasses off, which I can't see the sun come up without 'em. I reckon it was a couple minutes before I collected myself and looked out. I couldn't see much without my specs, just mostly blurs, but there was somethin' alayin' out there in front of my stand. I 'member it didn't seem exactly the right color for a dead deer, and it seemed terrible close to the stand, too, so I commenced fumblin' around after my glasses when I heard this voice. It was Old Man Farley himself, come up behind my stand. He yelled, 'Thornton, is that you? Did you fire that shot?' I told him Yes, and he hollered, 'Did you hit anything?' I told him I believed so but I couldn't make out what it was just yet. And he said, 'Come on out, then, and we'll go take a look.' Well, I located my specs and come out of the stand, and me and Mr. Farley walked out toward the clearin' and damn near stumbled over what I'd shot. Mr. Farley he stood there alookin' down with his false teeth aclackin' and when I seen what it was, it all come to me. It come to me why I couldn't see nothin' in my scope just before I shot except that gray blur, because what I'd shot was the Old Man's big spotted dog, which it had come up there to my stand to eat that meat I tossed out.

"I blowed a hole in that dog," Buck said, "which you could set a pie plate in it."

He sat down. The Regulars applauded his story, and Bonney personally brought him another beer.

"Tell 'em, Buck," Bonney said. "Tell 'em what happened then."

"Well," Buck continued, "next thing I know, why up come Junior Farley, the Old Man's boy that's president of the Mills now. When he seen what happened, he taken us back to the lodge and he got his daddy to bed, and then he put me in a station wagon and drove into Kerrville to the bus station and bought me a ticket home. He didn't say a word to me until I was fixin' to get on the bus and then he put his hand on my shoulder and he said, 'Thornton, I'm gonna do my best to keep the Old Man from firin' you. I may not be able to do it, so I want you to have this. It ain't much,' he said, 'but it's all I got in my wallet.' And he stuck some bills in my hand, two twenties and four tens and a little wad of ones. I counted it, which it come to eighty-four dollars, and I asked him whatever it was for. And he told me, 'Why, it's for makin' the finest rifle shot ever squeezed off in these hills. I feel like you just shot a snake off my back. My daddy has thought more of that goddamn spotted dog than he has of me, and I hated that animal since the first day he crapped on the kitchen floor in our house.' So I rode on home, and went back to work the next mornin' and never heard a word about gettin' fired. Since I blowed a hole in that dog I ain't been able to do no wrong around the Mills when Junior Farley is anywheres close, and I'm satisfied it's the reason I'm foreman of Number Two crew right today."

A deer story, no matter how simple or how involved, commanded stern attention from almost anybody in the Farley neighborhood as opening day neared. The men, including Bonney, showed a boyish enthusiasm about the season. This excitement, anticipation, was something I hadn't seen in Bonney before. He put his deer rifle in the gunrack, in the rear window of his pickup, a month before the season opened. Nearly every pickup truck owner did that. Some left their rifles on exhibit this way the year round.

"See that big elm yonder?" Bonney asked me. "The one just the other side of that palmetto flat? Last year, no, year before last, I sat right down yonder on the bank of thát slough and dropped an eight-point buck standing under the elm. I stepped off the distance. Two hundred yards. Real nice buck.

Field-dressed a hundred and ten pounds. I put a slug right through the point of his shoulder and he never took a step. Just folded up."

We were driving, in his pickup, over to Sullivan and then across the Chickenhawk into Burton County, to attend a barbecue the afternoon before the deer season would open the following morning.

"Come on, Johnny, go with me," he'd urged. "Ol' Jake's the Pearl distributor. I sell a hell of a lot of his beer, and he always invites me. Just a bunch of guys. They play poker and drink green-stamp whiskey, and Jake serves steaks thick as your wrist. You'll like it."

So I went with him.

"We won't stay late," he said. "Hank's taking Slat to the show and I promised her I'd be in when she gets home."

Warned her, was more like it. The dating game between Hank and Slat had become more of a habit than Bonney liked. It seemed to worry him. He was always home, looking at the clock, when Hank brought Slat in. He'd set her a time she was supposed to be home and if she was going to be even ten minutes late she'd call and explain why. Barney would tell him, "Bonney, you're treatin' that girl like she's a kid. She's twenty-two years old." And Bonney would say, "Barney, your job around here is to cook hamburgers."

I did enjoy the affair at the deer camp on the Chickenhawk. At least I enjoyed the bonded bourbon, but then not long before we were due to eat, Bonney pulled me inside. He was excited. "Listen, I was just down yonder on the creek, lookin' around, and there's the biggest damn buck down there I *ever* saw. I bet you he'll dress a hundred and forty, maybe fifty, and a *rack?* Hod-oh-mighty, he must be fourteen points. I got to have that buck, Johnny, but I need help."

"You mean you're gonna shoot him?"

"Hell yes."

"You mean now?"

"Hell yes now."

"You can't do that."

"Hell yes I can."

"The day before the season opens?"

107

"Hell with that. But listen, to get him out of that creek he's got to be lugged up a damn claybank, steep, and about thirty feet high. That bastard's gonna be big, and I can't get him out of there by myself. You got to help me."

"I don't want to get mixed——"

"You got to, Johnny. Wait here a second. Yonder's Jake." He hustled over toward his host, who was overseeing the barbecue pit.

"Hey, Jake," Bonney said. "Man, them steaks sure smellin' good. Say, Jake, I wanted to ask you. If it's all right, I'd like to take my rifle off down yonder on the creek and sight it in. I been so busy I flat forgot to, and here's the season openin' tomorrow and that gun hadn't been fired since last Christmas Day."

Jake waved his cooking fork up the lane. "We've got a range up against that old sand hill, about half a mile from here. It's got targets and the distances marked, if you'd like to go back up there."

"Yeah, I saw that, but I'm afraid it'd be dark before I could get there. I see a pretty good clearing right off down in yonder a little way and I'll just do it there, if you don't care."

Jake looked doubtful. Without any enthusiasm at all he said, "Well, it'll be all right, I guess."

"Thanks, Jake," and Bonney started back toward me.

"Bonney," Jake called, "I hope you won't shoot any more than you have to. We've got a couple of real nice trophies on this lease and these guys sure would hate it if those bucks got spooked off across that creek tonight."

"Don't worry," Bonney said. "I won't shoot but just a couple of times. Just to check, is all." Then to me, loudly, so Jake would hear, "Johnny, would you grab one of those target cards there in the truck, behind the seat, and come give me a hand?"

So he trapped me. I got the card and we went off into the bottom.

He didn't shoot but once. The buck had moved, but not but about twenty-five yards from where Bonney had spotted him. I never did see the deer until the slug laid it kicking in a yaupon thicket, and Bonney was on him in five seconds with his knife.

"No time to gut him now," he said quietly, looking back toward camp to see if the shot was going to bring anybody running. "Let's just get him up this bank. We got to go up the bank or they can see us from camp. *Hod*amighty but this is some kind of a buck. Look at that rack. He may dress one fifty-five."

He felt like three hundred when we were dragging him up the claybank. "Now then," Bonney said, at the rim of the bank, "just help me get under him and I can handle him by myself. Then you get on back. Tell 'em I'm foolin' with my rifle. Say I got a casing that won't eject, and that's why I didn't shoot but once. Tell 'em anything. I'll stick this buster in the bushes over yonder by the road and then we'll eat and pick him up on the way out. Now go on. And for Lord sake, Johnny, get that stupid look off your face. You seem like you're about to cry." He moved off silently through the timber, the antlers of the buck bumping against his buttocks.

On the way home. The buck in the bed of the truck, covered with a tarp. Bonney was elated. He whistled, sang, laughed. I felt as if I'd just helped rob a bank.

"Cheer up, Johnny," he grinned. "You worry too much. It's gonna cut your life short, you don't quit that."

"You're not worried?"

"Hell no."

"You're riding along on a public highway with a deer in this truck the night before the season opens and the game warden very likely waiting up yonder around the next curve and you're not worried?"

He shook his head, grinning widely. "Naw, man. No game warden's anywhere near here. Ol' Hico Gates always goes out to Junior Farley's ranch the night before the season opens, and gets about three-quarters drunk. Him and Wiley Scott, not that Wiley would give a damn, and the high sheriff and pretty near all the pistol toters in the county, out there drinkin' Junior's whiskey. Man, it's a pretty night. Clear as a bell and cold as hell. Gonna be good and frosty in the mornin'. We're gonna win us that prize, Johnny, and maybe all three of 'em."

109

"What prize?"

"Why, the contest, that the hardware store has got on."

"But Harvey said in the paper a deer had to be killed in Kirby County to win the contest. Said you have to sign an affidavit."

"So we'll sign it. And I got you as a witness."

"Whoa, now, hold on. That'd be swearing a lie. I'm not going to swear any lie."

"It's not *much* of a lie. That buck was standin' on the bank of Chickenhawk Creek, which is the county line. You might be swearin' a lie but it wouldn't be but about fifty feet from the truth, and that's mighty close. County line's layin' right out there on the bottom of that creek, in the middle, down there with the gars and the polywogs."

"Just the same . . ."

"All right. You don't have to sign it. I'll get Rose-Mama to do it." Nothing was going to dampen his spirits.

He sang. A line or two of Sam's old drinking song.

> *When I was in O'Riley's Store,*
> *Listenin' to the tales of blood and*
> *slaughter . . .*

Rose-Mama signed the affidavit, all right. Signed it with a flourish and a special pleasure, swearing that she witnessed Bonney kill that deer, at dawn on opening day, near the cattle pens in his own pasture. And I know if he'd asked her to swear that he killed it with a slingshot, she'd have done that too.

The buck won all three of the hardware store prizes.

Fifty dollars for the first deer brought to town. (Bonney was waiting for Arty Baker when he unlocked the store.) The Remington rifle for the heaviest deer of the day. (It field-dressed a hundred and forty-eight pounds.) And the second rifle for the biggest rack. (Twelve points.)

And then this:

Bonney gave one of the rifles to Barney.

He gave the other to Turnip.

The meat, the deer carcass, he donated to the Farley School

for Boys, favorite charity of the women who passed for high society in town.

With the fifty dollars cash, he bought Sam Hobbs a new overcoat.

A Monday in late November. Monday nights were always slow at Bonney's. The week's activity at the tavern peaked on Saturday night. On Sunday afternoon it picked up where it left off, but slowed early Sunday night in observance of the coming Monday. Late Tuesday it began building again. On Wednesday there was a surge. Bonney called Wednesday his Little Saturday, when the place was sometimes jammed by people who seemed to be celebrating the fact that they'd made it through half a week. Thursday was better than Tuesday, but not much. Thursday was the calm before the Friday storm which introduced the weekend.

Bonney was gone to Corpus Christi on the monthly visit to see his mother. He always went on a Monday and returned Tuesday afternoon. Barney too was absent. He had quit again, on Sunday night, for a reason I never did hear. He wadded up his apron and threw it on top of the big refrigerator, as he always did when he quit. It was still there, where it would remain until he returned to work to take care of the rush on Wednesday. He was especially angry when he walked out Sunday night. He invited Bonney to go to hell and take the stove and the whole damn place and he gave him back the gift rifle and said by god Bonney could cook his *own* friggin' hamburgers and see how he liked it. And Bonney said, "OK, see you Wednesday."

The lights were low in the tavern. Outside, only one bulb, too weak, tried to illuminate the entrance, its efforts almost hidden by the huge limbs of the cottonwood. That cotton-

111

wood . . . Bonney's favorite tree. He called it his "talkin' tree," because of the noise its broad leaves made when the wind came through them. When the leaves shed in the fall he refused to rake them up and burn them, and now the parking area was almost cushioned by a carpet of cottonwood leaves. Bonney had a special feeling for all the trees near the tavern. He even fought for them. The white scar in his left eyebrow, I learned, he acquired defending the big pine that Charlotte always parked under. One night a couple of hard hats from over in Burton County, all beered-and-whiskey'd up, decided to cut the pine down, "just for the hell of it." They found an ax and began, and Bonney plowed into them, fists whirling, windmilling, all amateurish and sincere, and one of the hard hats caught him above the eye with a ring and laid him out. Six stitches. But the hard hats didn't cut the pine down.

The tavern's only customers this quiet night were the Regulars, at the long table. Uncle Batey and Aunt Kate. Buck and his wife. Colonel Ralls, Maudie and Carlos, Ben Ashley, Brad, and Sam, on his bench but not quite gone yet. Slat at the bar, studying. Beside her, reading, were the two little Flynn boys. A week earlier Bonney had put them on the bus with Slat and told her to "watch after 'em." So she watched, and they loved it. Loved *her*. So they'd stayed at school six days and now they had come to the tavern to study with her.

"Who died?" That was Rose-Mama's comment on the quietness that greeted us when we walked in. Nobody answered. No remark was offered about Rose-Mama's bar flowers, a skinny bouquet because Bonney was gone. I doubt those present fully realized the reason for the low spirits.

I've never met another man who so completely dominated his environment. When Bonney was there, the tavern lived. When he left, it died. Nothing happened until he returned. No plans laid. No arguments settled. No decisions made.

A pair of headlights swept briefly across the windows and every head at the long table turned, to watch, until the car was parked and the lights switched off.

"That'll be J.R.," Maudie said.

And it was. Wetzel came to Bonney's every Monday night. It was his night. At first I thought this was because he knew

112

the crowd would be small, that he could sit there and enjoy his beer without much chance of meeting a school board member or one of his teachers.

But finally I decided no, it was because he enjoyed the exclusive company of the Monday night crowd, the Regulars. I'm not certain all of them understood the nature of Wetzel's job. The superintendent of schools in a large consolidated district, particularly in a rural area, is a position of considerable local influence and responsibility. Wetzel had a great deal of sensitive politicking to do in Kirby County. His duties, as he told me, often wore him pretty thin. But there at Bonney's he had nothing to do but just sit there and be one of the bunch. They all called him J.R.

One of the little curiosities that I enjoyed about life at the tavern was standing out front with Wetzel at night when Hank would bring Slat in after a date. And Hank would say, "Hello, Mr. Wetzel," as a teacher properly should to his superintendent. And Slat, one of his high school students, would say, "Why, howdy, J.R." Wetzel got a kick out of it too.

"What would happen," I asked him, "if a couple of your school trustees walked in here some night and found you nursing a beer?"

"Probably nothing," Wetzel said. There was a trace, just a hint, of German accent in his speech. I thought it made him sound scholarly. "There's no law, not even a school rule, that says the superintendent or any employee of the system can't drink in public. Of course we have the unwritten law, which states that all school people should comport themselves as ladies and gentlemen, set an example for our students. And I think we do, in the main. We practice our little vices chiefly in private. That's one reason public school people in this area hang so closely together, not only professionally but socially as well. We are careful, you know, who we invite to our New Year's Eve parties, which are always held in private homes, never in public. That way, if the principal gets a snootful and recites a few verses from an obscene poem, the vice-president of the PTA won't be on hand to hear it. It's a dishonest system, really. I don't endorse it but I condone it because it's practical.

"When I go out in public at Farley, say to Spearman's,

I don't drink beer because Farley parents don't want their school superintendent drinking before his students, no matter how much the parents drink in front of their children at home. So that's why I come to Bonney's. Or at least it's *one* reason. Another is that I have a high regard for the great majority of Bonney's regular customers.

"Not because they're what you'd call the best people in the community. They don't always go to church, though many of them do. They don't contribute to the United Fund. They don't serve as presidents of the Lions or the Rotary. They aren't scoutmasters, or Little League coaches, or den mothers, or Sunday school teachers. But they have one quality, almost all of them, which endears them to me. I wonder if you've noticed what it is. *They do not judge!* It's the one characteristic they have in common and which sets them so far apart from that Friday night crowd at Spearman's. *That* bunch ought to wear long robes and white wigs, because they sit in judgment of all they see, as if they're vice-presidents of heaven or God's lieutenants.

"Ah. I see the smile in your eye. I know, I know. In making that pronouncement against them, I am doing some judging of my own. And you're right. I share the weakness. Which makes me admire Bonney's people that much more." He turned toward the bar. "Slat? Another one, please, when you pass this way, dear."

"Comin' up, J.R.," she answered, from over her homework at the bar, "just as quick as I get finished with this question. Say, Johnny, maybe you can tell me—who in the whey was Charlemagne?"

"Who?"

"Charlemagne. It's a question here in my history workbook. It says was Charlemagne real or imaginary, and state briefly a noted Charlemagne legend."

The heads of the Regulars at the long table came up. They all took a strong interest in Slat's schoolwork.

"Charlie who?" asked Ben Ashley.

"Charlemagne."

"Maybe it means Charlie Maynard," Ben said. "Charlie Maynard was damn sure a real person. He was chief of the Volunteer

114

Fire Department for pretty near twenty-five years, and got killed by a freight at Hancock Crossin' that time."

"No, Ben, this is history, not about anybody around here," Slat said, "but thanks just the same."

"Charlemagne was an emperor," I said. "Right, J.R.?"

"Yes. He was Charles the Great, King of the Franks. As for a noted Charlemagne legend, you'll get no help from me on that."

"What exactly *is* a legend, J.R.?" Slat asked.

"A legend, my dear, is nothing but a polite term for a damn lie."

Bonney returned Tuesday noon. Around four o'clock we were having a game when a white panel truck stopped out front. "CO-OP MEAT LOCKERS," read the sign on its side. A slight middle-aged man in a dirty white smock came in. He seemed nervous.

"Hey, Smitty," Bonney greeted him. "What *you* doing way out here among us nesters?"

The man grinned. "Nothin' much. I got some meat for you on the truck."

"I didn't order meat."

"I know. This is that deer."

"What deer?"

"Your buck, that you killed openin' day."

"The buck that won the prizes?"

"Yeah."

"What *you* doing with it? I gave it to the school."

Smitty shifted his weight and rubbed the leather on the corner pocket of the pool table. "Well, we dressed it at the plant, and delivered it. But the school . . . well, they sent it back."

"Why?"

"Said they had plenty meat, and didn't need it."

"Why, hell, Smitty, they been spreading news all over the county, asking hunters to donate their meat to the school."

Smitty was silent.

Bonney asked quietly, "What's the real reason they sent it back, Smitty?"

A shake of the head. "All I know's what they told me."

"Does your wife still work at the school, in the office?"
Smitty nodded.

"And isn't Junior Farley's wife still the big-mama cheese around there?"

"Yes."

"So I reckon Mrs. Farley is the one sent the meat back, right?"

"I reckon."

"Now, Smitty, all I want to know is what Mrs. Farley said. I know good and damn well Elsie told you what Mrs. Farley said."

"But, Bonney, it ain't my place to——"

"Just tell me."

"You won't get mad?"

"I won't get mad." He was already mad. He was wearing that stiff little grin he always put on when he got mad. He wasn't mad at Smitty, but Smitty wasn't sure. Bonney said, "Maybe I can help you a little. I'd say it's got something to do with my colored boy, with Turnip."

"Well, partly that."

"All right, so tell me."

Smitty was tortured, but he got it out. "Well, Mrs. Farley, she told Elsie her school wasn't gonna take no meat from you, when you was livin' out here in the same house with that tramp girl and that nigger boy."

A throbbing silence, for about five seconds.

Then Bonney almost whispered. "All right, thanks, Smitty. Thanks for telling me."

Smitty exhaled, and shuddered a bit in relief. "Bonney, you won't tell 'em I——"

"Don't worry. I won't get you in trouble. Or Elsie either. Is that buck frozen?"

"No, it's not froze. It's a good carcass. Real pretty meat for a buck that size. Fat. Looks like he's been on corn."

"Tell you what, Smitty, you know that old colored lady, Calladium, lives in the Blackjack back in yonder behind J. W. Bradley's place?"

"I know her, right where she lives."

"Well, she's got a big old boy staying there with her, name's Chester. I wonder if you'd do me a favor and run that meat over there and tell Chester I said to cut it up and spread it around to those folks."

"Sure, sure, be glad to."

"Fine, I'm much obliged to you, and you tell Elsie I said hello."

"I sure will, Bonney. I sure will," and he went backpedaling out the door, nodding and grinning like a man who'd been unstrapped and set free from the chair just before they threw the switch.

Bonney put his cue in the rack and walked toward the bar. "You ever meet Mrs. Junior Farley?" he asked me.

"No."

"Well, you've missed our Number One Tourist Attraction around here. I'm gonna see if I can give you that pleasure."

He got the phone off the hook. "Ada, ring me that school, where Mrs. Farley keeps all her colored boys. Yeah, thanks. . . . Hello, Elsie? Bonney McCamey. How's my gal? . . . Good, real good. Say, Elsie, I need to talk to Mrs. Farley. . . . All right, fine. . . ."

He said to me, "I didn't think Her Majesty would be donating her services there this time of day, but seems she is."

Then to the phone again, "Mrs. Farley? This is Bonney McCamey, out here at the Highway Café toward Sullivan. . . . Yes ma'am, that's right. . . . Yes ma'am, that was my deer. . . . Why, that's all right, Mrs. Farley. I understand that and I know you *did* appreciate it. Smitty from the locker plant told me why you couldn't use it. Big old buck like that takes up a lot of space in a freezer. Look, Mrs. Farley, I didn't call about that buck. Reason I called, I was just wondering if you're gonna be out around this way, say the next two, three days. I'd sure appreciate it if you'd stop by my place. Being you're interested so much in the school there, and these colored boys, I got a situation out here I thought you might like to see. I got a boy out here that . . . Why, yes, that's him. You know about him then? . . . Why, sure, that'll be fine. Right now's a real good time for me. . . . All right, I'll watch for you."

He hung up and there was something—I couldn't quite make it out—showing in his eye. Victory, maybe. Revenge?

"She's coming now," he said. "All right, Johnny, if you want to see the best pair of legs in Texas and everything that goes with 'em, you'll have to follow me outside because you can bet she'll not come in this beer joint."

"Have you known Mrs. Farley long?"

"Oh, I've *known* her," he said, "since way back. Everybody knows Mrs. Junior Farley. You might say we circulated in different places, mostly. I haven't what you'd call talked to her for a good many years. Ol' Junior used to let her throw these big dances, and feeds, for all the guys coming back from Korea. I went to a couple of 'em. She wasn't interested in poverty-stricken colored boys then. She was interested in soldier boys, seeing they were more popular at that time. She's a—" He decided not to say what he was about to say. Instead he said, "She *knows* me, all right. But you watch. She won't let on she does."

She didn't, as Bonney predicted, come in the tavern. She came streaming down the slope in a long black Continental with wire wheels and a big gleaming hump on the back where the spare tire rode and she honked twice and got out and stood waiting there, on a rug of Bonney's cottonwood leaves. We went out to meet her.

"Howdy, Mrs. Farley. Real nice of you to come right on out like this. Mrs. Farley, I want you to meet my friend here, Johnny Lancaster. He's interested in this colored boy too, same as me. Would you like to come in? You might not expect it but I got me a cook back yonder in the kitchen knows how to make a real good martini."

"No thank you, Mr. McCamey. I came about the boy. Is he here?"

"Well, no ma'am, not right now. He's back in the pasture, feedin' cattle, but he ought to be along pretty quick."

Bonney was right about the legs but he'd neglected to say that what went with them was even better. Mrs. Farley was an absolutely beautiful woman. Tall and long-stemmed, with a figure that made her simple skirt and sweater look like it cost half the mint in Denver. Junior Farley must have ordered her, prepaid, from Neiman-Marcus, designed and styled according to plans and specifications, to get the kind of woman he needed to

118

be Mrs. Junior Farley, Mrs. Farley Lumber Mills, Mrs. City of Farley, Mrs. Two Thirds of Kirby County.

She had this cool, level, right-straight-through-your-brain-and-I-can-tell-what-you're-thinking way of looking at you. She finally turned that look on me, to remind me that I was staring, that I'd been at it long enough.

". . . and that's really about all I know, on his background," Bonney was saying. So he'd been talking about Turnip. I hadn't been listening. "If you'd care to, while we're waitin' we can go around to the house, in back, and you can see where he's livin'. The girl hasn't come in from school yet, so nobody's back there, but Johnny here can go with us and it'll be all right." I looked at her when he said that, but she either didn't catch the vague implication or chose to ignore it. The latter, I bet. Mrs. Junior Farley didn't appear to be a person who would fail to catch implications. A very, very intelligent face. Guessing her age was tough. I decided temporarily on thirty-two.

"Fine," she said. "I'd like that." So we went back to the house. Bonney was gigging her a little. That business, for example, about Barney fixing her a martini. *A martini for the grand lady, fixed in the back of a beer joint; why Mrs. Farley that'll give you something to talk about when you get back to the bar at the country club and a waiter named William.*

Barney was hanging out the back door, staring, when we rounded the tavern. He had three days of beard and his apron was dirty. Molly Bitch was sprawled in front of the step to the door of the house. She raised her head and whipped the dust with her tail to say hello but didn't offer to move. Bonney moved her, about ten feet, with his foot. Didn't comment. Just booted her. The first time I'd ever seen him do that. Usually he stepped over her.

I wasn't certain whether to feel a bit embarrassed for him. I paid little attention, normally, to our surroundings. But now, with Mrs. Junior Farley visiting, the place suddenly looked seedy, unkempt. A bed of ragweed by the step was yellowed and flattened by the first frost. A bottom corner of the wire on the screen door was loose, where one of Turnip's pups went through it.

"I been tellin' that boy," Bonney said, looking down at the

119

ripped screen—just as if he wanted to call attention to it—"I told him five, six times to fix that place."

Bonney now lapsed, for a reason I didn't comprehend, into his most rural speech. Talked just as he talked to the mill hands and the cowboys.

"I reckon you'll just have to excuse this house," he said to Mrs. Farley. The living room wasn't dirty but it was untidy. Newspapers on the floor. A pair of Turnip's jeans. His shoes. Two towels on the sofa. "I tell you, Miz Farley, if you've taught them boys at your school to clean up a room, I wish you'd tell me how."

The truth was I'd never been in that house, since Slat moved into it, that it wasn't clean and straight. But here was Bonney displaying the rubble in the living room as if it was the usual thing.

"Now here's that boy's room, you want to see that."

Turnip used his room to sleep and for no other purpose. It was comfortable enough but it was just a room, a cubicle, with an unmade bed and bare walls. Mrs. Farley only glanced at it.

She waved at Slat's bedroom door, closed, a new door with a copper knob. "I suppose that's the young lady's room?" she said.

"Why, yes, ma'am, it is. You want to see that? I didn't reckon you'd have any interest in the *girl*."

You phony. You liar.

Mrs. Farley stood in the center of Slat's room for quite a long while. I hadn't seen the room since the day we built it. I'd only heard Slat say that Rose-Mama and Maudie had helped her "fix it up just real nice." It wasn't the bedroom of a twenty-two-year-old woman. It was the room of a schoolgirl. Reminded me of the way Midge had her room fixed when she was about fifteen. Everything pink, and ruffles. Ruffles on the bedspread, on the fluffy tieback curtains, on the vanity chair. Over her bed was a huge triangular pennant: FARLEY WILDCATS. And photographs everywhere, made with the Polaroid that Bonney bought. Three of the pictures, on the dresser, were in cheap gilt-edged frames. One of Bonney, one of Rose-Mama, one of Hank. A cork bulletin board on the west wall was thumbtacked solid with snapshots. One of the tavern, taken earlier in November when the foliage of the hardwoods had its autumn coloring. Another of Hank's school bus. Of Farley High. Then Maudie smiling from behind the bar. Uncle Batey and Aunt Kate dancing. Brad on his quarter horse. Turnip with Molly Bitch. Charlotte and her daughter. Colonel Ralls. The Flynn boys. Even I was on the board, making a shot at the pool table with Bonney watching in the background.

"Very nice," Mrs. Farley said, and returned to the living room.

Bonney said, "Now that's *my* room, there. I don't reckon"—here came the gig, the implication again—"I don't reckon you'd like to go in there."

She ignored the remark and asked, "Do you suppose the boy is back yet?"

"Not quite yet. We'll hear him roar up in that truck. He's got a kind of a heavy foot on that truck."

"Do you suppose, Mr. McCamey, that the boy would be interested in coming to the school?"

"Why, I don't know. He's not ever said anything to me about it. Has he to you, Johnny?"

"No." *Listen, you leave me out of this shammery, this plot, this whatever-it-is-you're-doing.*

"Are you saying," Mrs. Farley asked, "that you'd let him move to the school?"

Bonney spread his arms. "Mrs. Farley, what I want is just what's best for that boy. Fact is I got no right, what you'd call *legal* right, to keep him here, or to say *where* he goes."

"Then you wouldn't object to my speaking to him, about the school?"

"No ma'am, I sure wouldn't. And you can do it right now. I can hear him comin', tryin' to throw a rod out of my pickup, seems like."

We went back outside just as Turnip came around the barn and swung out of the truck even before it fully stopped. He hit the ground with his left foot while his right was still inside on the brake.

"Well," Bonney called to him, "I can't see who you're racin' but it looks like you come in first."

"Aw, Mister Bonney," Turnip grinned.

121

"Come over here a minute, Turnip. Got somebody wants to meet you. This here's Mrs. Farley, that owns the school for colored boys like you."

"I don't *own* the school, Mr. McCamey. It's a non-profit corporation."

"Well, she *runs* it, then."

Mrs. Farley, it was clear, wasn't accustomed to having people speak for her. "I happen to be, right now, chairman of the board, Mr. McCamey."

"Anyway," Bonney said, "she wants to speak to you a minute, and I'll just sit right here and stay out of it." He plopped down on the front step of the house.

"I'm Elaine Farley," she said to Turnip. "May I ask your name?"

"Turnip."

"But your full name. Your real name."

"Well, it used to be Douglas. Douglas Henderson."

"A very nice name, too. Douglas, have you heard about our school?"

"Yessum, I heard."

"I wonder if you might be interested in coming to see us, just for a visit?"

"Nome, I don't b'lieve. But I'm much obliged." He kept looking at Bonney, who kept looking away.

"How old are you, Douglas?"

"I'll be nineteen."

"We have a number of boys at the school just your age. We have a football team now. We're going to have a game Saturday. Would you like to come, as my guest, and watch the game?"

"Nome, I can't go off Saturdays. I got to work, in the place here."

Bonney was going to stay out of it. "You want to go, Turnip," he said. "I'll get somebody to work for you."

"I don't reckon. I don't much like ball games." Now to Turnip's side came Molly Bitch, wagging, her eyes full of love, to lick the hand which automatically reached out to receive her. The dog found on the fingers the yellow-brown dust and crumbs from the feed Turnip had been handling. She licked at it eagerly and the boy, unconsciously, slowly rotated his wrist so

122

Molly Bitch could clean his hand of the morsels. Mrs. Farley watched the process in silence, as if it fascinated her. I glanced at Bonney and his eyes were smiling.

"Wouldn't you like to go back to school, Douglas, and finish?"

"I *been* to school."

"Where?"

He jerked his head out toward the pasture. "Back yonder, in the Blackjack."

"But isn't it true that the grades in the Blackjack didn't go beyond the sixth? Did you finish the sixth?"

"I reckon so. Almost."

"Well, we have boys at the school older than you who didn't finish the sixth grade. Now they're back in school, so they can get a diploma, and a job."

"I got a job. I work here for Mister Bonney, and I raise my dogs, and I got two heifers Mister Bonney give me."

"Well, some of our boys are learning trades, skills. Welding, carpentry, cabinetmaking. We have a nice shop at the school."

"Yessum."

"Wouldn't you like to come and visit, just for a day?"

"Nome."

She turned to Bonney, finally asking for help.

"Turnip," he said, "I hear they got a indoor swimmin' pool with heated water, that you can swim in it even in the winter."

"I heard," Turnip said.

"Well, prob'ly be best thing for you if you did move to that school. Get you an education, so you won't be spendin' your whole life here around a beer joint."

Turnip slumped, put a knee to the ground and took one of the dog's ears in his hands and inspected it. He wouldn't look up.

"I could *make* you go, you know," Bonney said.

My god, man, what are you trying to do to that boy? Don't you see his pain? Can't you feel it?

"What would you do," Bonney kept twisting away, "if I made you go?"

At last Turnip bristled. "I wouldn't stay," he shot back.

"Where would you go?"

"I'd come here. Back here."

123

"Why here?"

"I reckon because this here's where I live."

Bonney stood, slapped his thighs, and said, "Well, you run on in, now, and wash up. You're gonna have you some beer drinkers to take care of before long."

Turnip sailed in the house.

"Well, Mrs. Farley, I'm afraid he's just not much interested."

She smiled that cool smile. "No, I'd say you're right," she said. "But I appreciate the opportunity of talking with him. I'd better be going." She started to leave.

"Why, I appreciate you comin'," Bonney said.

I made a move to fade out of that scene and go in the back door of the tavern. But Bonney tugged slightly at my sleeve, a tug that said, "No, wait. Stick around. I'm not through."

"You have some beautiful trees here," Mrs. Farley said, walking to her car.

"I'm proud of my trees."

"That big live oak, that's really a prize. I love live oaks. We have an old one in our back yard, but I believe yours is bigger."

"I don't know about that. I'd say mine was bigger at the trunk but I believe yours and Mr. Farley's has got a wider spread. I've seen your tree."

When she got in the car Bonney stood close to the window and looked down at her legs and said, "Mrs. Farley, about that boy, there's one way you could get him away from here."

"Oh?"

"Yes ma'am. And if you'll agree to do it, why I'll see that he goes and I'll see that he stays."

"Agree to do what?"

So then he dropped his bomb. "If you'll do for him the same thing I've done, if you'll take him home with you, and give him a room in your house, and let him eat at your table with you and Mr. Farley, and take him places in this car he needs to go, and doctor him when he's sick, just the same way I do, then I'll see he goes with you."

So that was it.

And all that went before it had been the setup—the phone call, the visit to the house, the painful interview with Turnip.

Now then Miz High-Muckety-Muck Farley Lumber Mills whatta you gonna say to that?

Her eyes fixed on him, expressionless, for a long moment while it all sunk in on her.

And then she smiled. Not that cool smile, either. The warmest, yes, the most *sensuous* smile. God, but she was a beautiful woman.

She said, "*Touché*, Bonney. *Touché.*"

She drove away just as Hank's bus stopped to deliver Slat and the Flynn boys.

"Who was that in that long car?" Slat asked. Elaine Farley's Continental was topping the rise in front of Rose-Mama's.

"That was Mrs. Junior Farley," Bonney said, still standing there smiling.

"What'd *she* want?"

"Just visiting."

"In the café?"

"Nope, in the house."

"The house! My law, Bonney, this mornin's the first time I *ever* went off to school without picking up that house and look who comes. I didn't even make up your bed."

"Don't worry about it."

Slat went on inside and Bonney asked me, "What'd you think of her?" He was still looking up the slope where the Continental had disappeared.

"If you mean Mrs. Farley, I think she's something else."

"Yessir, she is. She really is something else."

He stayed in a high humor all the rest of the evening, while I sat wondering whether he'd been trying to tell me something he didn't want to come right out and say. Something about Elaine Farley. "She knows me, all right. But she won't let on." What did that mean? Then during the visit he had tried to make her uncomfortable. First the remark about having me, as a chaperone, in the house. And then the one about his room. Then that "I've seen your tree." It seemed to mean more than it said. True, Mrs. Farley had ignored it all. Yes, but she ignored it a little too smoothly, maybe. And finally, just before she left, evidently her guard had come down when she smiled and called him Bonney instead of Mr. McCamey. That wasn't any

125

cool smile. And the way she said Bonney, I'd bet it wasn't the first time she'd ever called him by his first name.

That night, after closing time when Bonney and I were having our customary game, the swinging door to the kitchen squeaked and there was Turnip standing in the dim night light over the back bar.

"How come you're not in bed?" Bonney asked him.

"I wanted to ask you . . . Mister Bonney, you ain't gonna make me go off to the school, are you?"

"Why, hell no, boy, whatta you talkin' about? Now you forget all that and hit the sack. I was just messin' round with you a little."

All the same, it took the boy about a week to recover from the injury. Just the idea that Bonney would kid him about such a thing cut him deep.

"Mister Bonney really had me worried," he told me, when I rode to the pasture with him to feed.

"Well, he kids a lot. But about schooling, don't you agree with Mrs. Farley? Wouldn't you like to finish school?"

"I don't want no more school. Mister Bonney done taught me ever'thing I need to know."

"That may be, right now. But suppose Bonney wasn't here."

"He don't stay gone but just a day or two."

"I don't mean just Corpus Christi. I mean what if he went off and didn't come back, for a long time?"

He almost stopped the truck. The idea of that had never occurred to him. "Where's he gonna go?"

"I just said what if. What if he moved?"

"He'd take me along."

"But maybe he couldn't."

Turnip shook his head. "Mister Bonney ain't gonna move off nowhere he can't take me."

"All right, but suppose he got real sick, all laid up. People do get sick sometimes, and even die."

He laughed at that notion. "Mister Bonney don't ever get sick. What's *he* gonna get sick from?"

"How long have you known Bonney, Turnip?"

"I don't know. Long time."

126

"Do you remember the first time you ever saw him?"

"Right when he come here. He come down in the Chicken-hawk Bottom one time where we was hoein' corn. He come down there tryin' to buy some creek bottom. He had candy, and he give me a piece, and I went home with him."

"He took you home?"

"Well, I reckon I followed him."

"He took you back home."

Turnip nodded. "He taken me back home five, six times."

"Then you mean you kept running off, going to Bonney's."

"I reckon that's it."

"Why?"

"I just did."

"Was it because you just liked him?" *And because he was the first man who ever gave you a piece of candy? To treat you like a human? To smile at you? To laugh with you? To love you?*

"I reckon," he said. "I reckon I just liked it here."

"But when you finally stayed, why didn't your folks come and get you?"

"Because they taken the money for me."

"What money?"

"The money Mister Bonney bought me with."

I suppose I shouted. *"Bought you!"*

The reaction startled him and he seemed a bit scared for a second.

"Turnip, for god's sake, boy, people don't go around buying and selling each other. That couldn't be so."

"I reckon it is. I reckon I stood right there and saw Mister Bonney give my daddy a hundred dollars for me."

I had to ask somebody. J. R. Wetzel was the one to ask. He seemed to know quite a lot about the people in the Blackjack and along the Chickenhawk, and he'd understand why I, why anybody, would want to ask about such an incredible idea.

But he was gone, to a meeting somewhere. So I decided to ask Rose-Mama. And I did, before we drove down to the tavern that night.

"Who told you that?" she countered.

"Turnip told me. Told me he saw Bonney pay for him."

127

"Well, then maybe it's so, but if it is it's none of *my* do, or anything to get your bowels in an uproar about. It wouldn't be the first time it's been done."

"You mean it's a common thing?"

"Oh, I don't know it's so common. Hard to tell, really, because nobody says much about it."

"But Rose-Mama, *my Lord,* buying and selling human beings, just like slavery times."

"Oh, hell's jingle bells, Johnny, it's not that way. Not really. It's been goin' on up and down the Chickenhawk forever. These darky families will have eight, ten kids or more, and can't feed 'em all, and they'll just send one of 'em to stay somewhere else, and he doesn't ever come home. What it amounts to, most of the time, is just *givin'* 'em away. Once in a while some money might change hands. Like if a family needs a young colored boy or girl to work, on a farm or around the house, why they'll pay its daddy a little something, kind of like wages. It's not often that happens. More likely it'll be a matter of swappin'. The colored folks, especially those way back there in the woods, they sometimes swap children, among themselves, I mean. One family will be heavy on boys, and another on girls, and maybe they'll even things up a little."

"That's hard for me to believe, right here in the twentieth century."

"Well, it's not hard for *me* to believe. Truth is that like as not the ones gettin' swapped or given away or sold or however you want to say it are better off for it. You know that old Calladium woman, that Bonney likes so. She told me one time if she hadn't been swapped off for a big strong boy when she was a girl, she'd likely starved to death. Said she got swapped into a family that leastways had somethin' to eat and a bed to sleep in. I don't see anything so bad about that."

"Well, I don't know. I wonder what happened to that big strong boy who went to live in Calladium's place. Maybe *he* went hungry, and if so then I can damn well see something bad about it."

"But he wouldn't starve because he was big and strong. He'd make it, where a skinny little weak girl wouldn't."

"All right, so maybe the swapping is not so bad. But this

128

business of money changing hands, that chills me. I don't care what you call it. Just the idea of a person handing over money and then going off with a child, Rose-Mama, that's not civilized. And it's always Negroes, right? You don't find *whites* swapping children or farming them out."

"Don't be too sure about that. I'll say this, I know some white kids be hell of a lot better off if they did get swapped. We got a little sample of that right here under our nose."

"Slat?"

"Yes."

"But she ran off, away from home."

"So did Turnip, more times than one. His daddy could see the boy wasn't about to stay home anyway. A man sees he's gonna lose a hoe hand no matter what, he might as well take a hundred dollars if it gets offered."

"Then you *do* know Bonney paid that money to Turnip's father."

"No such thing, I *don't* know it. You're the one said that."

"But to me, the taking of the money may not be so bad as the offering of it. The man offering it is saying to the parent, 'All right, you're losing something of value here, and so I'm reimbursing you for it.' That's what people say when they *buy* something."

She grunted. "You're splittin' splinters now, Johnny. Anyway, what's it matter? If Turnip thinks Bonney bought him, he's mighty likely proud of it, and nobody else cares. Unless it's you. Why *do* you care?" She threw me her stern stare over the evening's vase of flowers she was arranging.

"Why, because Turnip is one of my fellow human beings, that's why."

She kept staring. "Would you take him into your house, the way Bonney did?"

Touché, Mrs. Whitaker, touché. "I don't know," I said. "Maybe I wouldn't. I don't deny the prejudice taught me from the cradle. I struggle with it, all the time. Maybe it's part of the struggle, that I resent that it's black kids getting traded or paid for or whatever, just like when they were slaves. How about this? What would you think, what would Slat think, if Bonney went to her father tonight and said, 'Your daughter's staying now at my place and so I'll just buy her from you, here's a hundred dollars.'"

Rose-Mama grunted again and said, "I don't know what Slat would think but if Bonney did offer Joe Rankin a hundred dollars, I'll bet you a paint horse he'd take it." She latched the back screen door. "Now come on, let's go. And bring the whiskey."

Dear Pop:

Hey, what's happened to you? No word from you for a month. I'm fine. Arch is back on the job now and he drives up every weekend. Pop, he's started arguing to get married Christmas! I've managed to put him off until at least early spring. I know, I've always said I wouldn't get married until I could carry my diploma down the aisle with me, but to tell the truth I'm sort of worried about all those love-starved secretaries in Arch's office who don't snore and probably don't have to wear girdles. But I've told Arch we absolutely cannot get married until you're home to walk me down the aisle. I'll keep you posted, and you let me hear from you. How's the detective work going? Love,

Midge

Dear Midge:

You and Arch plan that wedding and let me know and I'll be there. Sorry about not writing. I've gotten lazy, I guess. And I'm so healthy it's sinful. I've gained seven pounds since I came here. (Your mother would hate every pound of it, after all those years she tried to put weight on me.) The detective work, as you call it, is somewhat disorganized. Without really meaning to, I've somehow become involved in the lives of the local people around

130

here. The most curious thing is that they accept me, ask no questions of me, and a few of them even depend on me for certain small services. I find myself liking it. I suppose you know what an awful emptiness was left inside me when we lost your mother. It may be that these people here have helped to fill it. I've come to realize that since your mother died, I've had no one other than you and Arch and a handful of friends that I really cared anything about. And all of them are so self-sufficient (including you) that I never worried about them. Now suddenly I'm surrounded by people who seem to need me. It's very strange. I'm reasonably certain I've found our man but getting him on the hook is not as easy as I thought it would be. Well, I have to go now because (I wonder if you'll believe this) it's time for me to milk the cow.

Love from your
Pop

The detective work. She asked how it was going and you didn't really tell her.

Sure I did. I said it was disorganized.

Disorganized isn't the word. Nonexistent is more like it. You've quit, that's what you've done. In the last six weeks you haven't made an ounce of progress.

How can you say that? If I were still keeping the ledger, there'd be plenty to write in it.

Yes, and most of it would show Bonney to be a two-bit crook. He shortchanges Norman Akers. Steals Akers' cow. Cheats on income tax. He practically stole an expensive place of real estate from a lonely widow merely by hopping in bed with her. *Bribed* her, is what he did, just like he bribes that sorry deputy. Then he wins the deer contest with an illegal buck and——

Yes, but look what he did with the buck—gave it away to the Negroes. Gave the rifles away too. And with Akers' cow, he fed all those people.

All right, but how about this latest piece of intelligence? Him buying that Negro boy just like a loaf of bread.

Hold on, now, that's not so. It wasn't quite like that. Rose-Mama said——

131

Rose-Mama! Why, hell's jingle bells, man, that woman would think it wasn't anything but exactly right if Bonney robbed the Farley State Bank.

I know, I know, but what does it all prove? It doesn't prove he stole the money from the Old Man.

No, but it damn sure proves he's the kind of man who would. And do you really think he bought that land with money he won playing eight-ball? Do you imagine he hustled twelve thousand dollars out of a bunch of sailors playing pool? And he's already admitted he spent time around Beaumont.

He hasn't said he knew the Old Man, though.

Well, then, ask him. My god, man, all you have to do is to ask him. Ask him anything, and he'll spill his guts. He's a compulsive talker. He's one of these guys who's got to tell everything, to confess all his sins trying to convince himself what he does is not really wrong. Ask him!

No. Not just yet. It's too much like—well, it's too much like asking a man to testify against himself.

Ah, so that's it. You're afraid of what he'll say. You don't *want* him to be the man who stole that money.

Quit putting words in my mouth. Besides, it's not just Bonney. It's all these people around here. It's Turnip and Rose-Mama and Slat and Barney and the Regulars. I like them, and they like me.

Yeah, they depend on you.

Yes, they do, and I enjoy it. I like helping Slat with her homework. And I like helping Rose-Mama. She wouldn't take my rent last month. What do you think of that? I like talking to J.R., and I like helping Barney clean up the kitchen. And then when Uncle Batey came to me last week, to get me to write a letter for him, I liked that. Nobody else has really needed me, not since Eva died.

Even Bonney needs you, right?

Well, yes, in a way.

Sure he does. He needs you to follow him around and be his rooting section. You're something he hasn't had before. These cowboys and mill hands don't quite understand what an operator he is, but you do, and he likes that. He's a performer, and you're his audience. That's why he doesn't ask *you* any questions. He doesn't want to run you off. He likes to have a guy ten years older than he is, from the outside world, to argue with him about what's right and what's wrong. Nobody else ever questions what he does. You're the only one he's got to listen to him defend himself. You know what I think? I think he's mired in *guilt*, up to his armpits.

Well, maybe so. I'm not sure. Let's not discuss it now. I've got to go milk.

9.

The last Friday in November. A stiff norther rattling the tavern windows, the bare limbs of the cottonwood by the front door scraping across the roof. A light crowd for Friday night. Northers aren't good for the beer business.

Rose-Mama and I sat at the bar. Bonney behind it, his long body leaning across the iceboxes. And Maudie close beside him, her thigh touching his, pretending that's where she just happened to be standing.

"No way, Jo-Boy," Bonney was saying, shaking his head. Two husky youngsters had approached him, a little cautiously, experimentally, talking quietly.

"Just a six-pack? Just one," the larger boy was saying.

"Nope," Bonney said. "You know better'n that. You're what, eighteen now? You ought not to come in here asking me to sell you beer. There's a law, you know. Get us both in trouble."

"How about if I pay you," the boy said, "and go on out, and somebody bring it to the car. That way we—"

"Nothin' doin'. Look, Jo-Boy, what the hell you want to drink beer for? Hell, son, it's not gonna do anything but hurt you. You got the world by the tail on a downhill drag, and you want to screw it up. Anyway, what you think your daddy would say, he finds out I sold you beer. Man, he'd come out here after me with that deer gun of his."

The boys grinned. "Well, we'll just hang around, wait for the pool table. Shoot a game or two." They turned and Bonney reached out.

"Listen, fellows," he said, his tone almost pleading, "why don't you boys go on. Go on to the show. Go to the drive-in. You don't need to be hanging around a beer joint. Sooner or later one of your daddy's friends will come in here and see you, and by the time they get back with the story they'll have both of you drunk, even if you don't take a sip."

The boys said nothing but they wandered on out.

"That's Junior Farley's nephew," Maudie said, "that tallest one."

"Yeah," Bonney said. "Beats hell out of me why they come out here. They think just because I'm out in the country we don't have beer laws."

"How did you know he's only eighteen?" I asked.

"He played fullback on the football team this year. Made all-district. Hell of a good athlete. He's not any twenty-one years old, playing on a high school football team."

Rose-Mama offered a little testimony. "Bonney here does more to keep beer away from these kids than their own mamas and papas do."

Which may have been true. Actually, few minors passed through Bonney's door. When they came, it was almost always to buy beer, or try to. Bonney was a master at spotting them.

He ducked, to get a better view out a window. "Well, here comes Sam, poor ol' devil. Looks like he's really carryin' him a cargo tonight."

Sam came in singing, already down to the fourth or fifth stanza of "O'Riley's Daughter."

Came a knock upon my door,
Who should it be but her goddamn father,
Two horse pistols in his hand,
Lookin' for the man that had shagged his daughter . . .

"Hey, Sam!" It was Ben Ashley, with the Regulars at the long table. "How many verses that song got?"

"Forty-two and a chorus," Sam answered grandly, "at the top of the Hit Parade."

"Sam, come on over here and sit yourself down. What you need is a nice cool one, to wet your gizzard a little bit."

"Naw, man, I don't want no beer. Beer is a *mornin'* drink."

They all laughed.

"How much whiskey you had tonight, Sam?"

"Why, I had me just a couple."

"Couple of what? Couple of *quarts?*"

More laughter, louder, as if that was the cleverest thing to say. When the Regulars had put away a few rounds on Friday nights and developed their customary glow, they often enjoyed teasing Sam. It got a little crude sometimes. Slat always resented it, and I knew she held it against Bonney that he let it go on. "Hell, they're just havin' a little fun."

Slat stopped at the table. "Sam, have you had any supper tonight?"

He faced her, apparently trying to remember.

"*You* haven't had any supper," she said, in her motherly tone. "I'm gonna get Barney to fix you some nice poached eggs, and some milk, all right?"

"Why, all right."

Slat glided toward the kitchen, past Colonel Ralls sitting alone against the wall, watching for her, hoping for a crumb of attention. Slat reached out and patted him on the cheek as she went by.

"I tell you," the Colonel said, "by god, that girl's gettin' a *real chest* on 'er. Gonna be like Maudie, she keeps on."

"Sam," Buck Thornton said, from the end of the long table, "tell us about that time you sang on the radio, you know, in Houston."

"Why," Sam said, "that was when that radio station had them contests on, and they ast me to come in there to that studio and sing, so I taken my guitar and——"

"Hey, Sam, did you tell 'em when you went in not to have no open flames, that might catch your breath afire?"

Laughter. Laughter. Big joke.

"——so I taken my guitar and went in there, and——"

"What did you sing, Sam? Did you sing 'O'Riley's Daughter'?"

Laughter, laughter. Thigh-slapping laughter.

"——no, I sang my 'Red-Bird Song' and——"

135

"You mean the red *nose* song, Sam?"

Oh, haw haw haw.

So finally Sam stopped his story and sat quiet. He loved attention, the same as Colonel Ralls, but he wasn't drunk enough to take all that.

"Say, Sam, how long you been drinkin', anyway? When did you start? In the cradle?"

He decided to go along. It was better than being ignored. "I reckon I started when I was twelve, or about that, on the mustang wine my daddy made."

"Good god, Sam, you been drunk now for forty years. Do you count on it to kill you, one of these days?"

"Well, if it does, I'll just go quiet, and I won't complain."

"Looks to me like, Sam, you oughta make you a will. Anybody's been drunk forty years oughta make 'em a will."

That was Carlos Freeman, who had the idea about the will. It struck a responsive chord among the Regulars.

"Yeah, how about that, Sam, hadn't you ought to make a will?" That was Ben.

"I hadn't ever thought about it," Sam said.

"Well, we'll *help* you think about it," Ben said. "Why, we'll *write* you one, all proper and legal as a lawbook. Hey, Slat, bring us a pencil here, and some paper. We got us a little lawyerin' to do on Sam's will."

At times like these, the Regulars became strangers to me. They weren't the same people I knew on Tuesdays and Wednesdays.

Slat wouldn't bring the pencil and paper. Instead she brought the eggs and milk Barney had fixed, and tried to get Sam to move over in the corner and eat. He wouldn't move. Slat left the plate and the glass before him. He never did touch it.

And Bonney, although he paced about and viewed the proceedings with an indulgent smile and didn't take part, he did bring the pencil and paper.

"Now then," Ben said, licking the pencil, "I know myself a little somethin' about wills. Sam, we got to have your full name, that your mama and daddy gave you."

And so Ben, with a silly smile, wrote it out as Sam gave it to him. Samuel Wilkerson Hobbs, Jr.

"Don't forget, Ben," Buck instructed, "you got to say he's sound. Sound in his body and his mind."

"That's a fact," Ben said. "Do you reckon we ought to say he's drunk too?"

"Oh hell no, don't say he's drunk. It might not stand up if you say he's drunk."

"Are you *very* drunk, Sam?"

Sam grinned. "Not too."

"Put that down, Ben. Say he's not too drunk."

Carlos stood. "I heard a little poem one time, you might want to put it in.

> *He is not drunk who from the floor*
> *Can rise again, and drink once more.*
> *But he is drunk who prostate lies,*
> *And cannot drink, and cannot rise.*

"Whyn't you put *that* in, Ben?"

"Damn right I'll put it in. Ain't many wills got poetry that way. Say it one more time, Carlos, real slow."

So Carlos recited the verses again, and again, and Ben scrawled on the paper. "How you spell that prostate?"

"Hell, I don't know," Carlos answered.

Charlotte Ord intervened. "It's not prostate, you idiot. It's pros*trate*."

"What difference does that make?"

"A prostate is a gland, that a man has."

Buck said, "She's got you there, Carlos. If you hadn't ever been to the doctor and got your prostate rubbed, man, you done missed a real little thrill."

"All right, we'll make it prostrate then," Ben said. "Now then, Sam, how about your kinfolks? Have you got any kin that you want to leave your belongin's to?"

"No, I got no kinfolks."

"Not even a mother?"

"Nope. I never had no mother. She died before I was born."

Laughter, laughter, and Sam didn't understand why they laughed.

"He's like ol' Calladium," Rose-Mama said. "He was laid by the buzzards and hatched by the sun."

"Yeah, put *that* in, Ben. Put it in the will."

"All right." And he did. "Now then, Sam, we got to list all your belongin's, and say who's gonna get 'em. What's first? How about your money?"

Laughter.

Sam dug in his pocket and came up with seventeen cents.

"Who you gonna leave that seventeen cents to?" Ben asked.

"I reckon Bonney," Sam said. "I owe him ten dollars."

"Ten dollars, hell. More like two thousand, I bet," Rose-Mama said.

"Anyway, we'll leave all your cash to Bonney," Ben went on. "What's the most expensive thing you've got, Sam?"

"I expect my overcoat. My new overcoat. That goes to Bonney too, seein' that's where it come from."

"Bonney don't need no overcoat. Anyhow you can't leave all you got to Bonney."

"To Slat, then," Sam said. "Leave the coat to Slat."

"Slat! Jeescries, Sam, you ain't takin' this serious enough. You put Slat in that overcoat and she'll have enough room left over in there for a big red barn."

"Turnip, then. Give it to Turnip."

"All right, coat goes to Turnip. What else?"

"Well, I got a cot in my room. I reckon I'll let Charlotte have that cot."

"Thanks a lot," Charlotte said.

"Then my straight razor, and my shavin' mug."

"Give that to Carlos," Ben said. "Maybe he'd start shavin'."

"All right. Then I got a Bible. Brother Luther give me the Bible, when I went to church that time. Slat. The Bible goes to Slat."

Sam appeared to be sobering a bit, taking more interest in the will. He needed no more prompting.

"Let's see, I reckon one of the nicest things I got is that bourbon bottle that it had the twelve-year-old whiskey in it last Christmas. It's on my shelf."

"Hell, it ain't nothin' but an empty bottle, Sam," Ben said.

"It's nice, though." He looked around. "I'll let Johnny there have my bottle. He's a bourbon man."

Every one of the Regulars was named in the will. Maudie

got the two army blankets on Sam's cot. Ben got Sam's wallet and its contents, which included a six-year-old ticket stub from a major league baseball game. Colonel Ralls got a picture that hung on Sam's wall, a picture of a field of bluebonnets. Buck got Sam's other pair of shoes, after a long discussion and comparison of feet sizes. J. W. Bradley "seein' he's a cowman" got a Mexican spur Sam kept on his shelf alongside the empty bourbon bottle. Barney got a straight chair, which Sam said was the only piece of furniture that really belonged to him, other than the cot. Sam also named J. R. Wetzel, Hank Mills, Wiley Scott, even Norman Akers, who got a good-luck horseshoe nailed above Sam's door.

And toward the end of the bequests, when he ran out of possessions before he exhausted his list of recipients, he said, "Now I don't want to forget Millie. I just want to leave her . . . well, I'll just leave her a message, and tell her to go to hell."

Millie. I hadn't heard her mentioned in weeks. She was the woman who'd been in Bonney's the first day I walked in.

I confess that as it progressed that ridiculous will fascinated me. A sort of depressing fascination. I mean here was a fellow in his fifties, a gentle-natured man, a man of good will, reduced to a nothing, naming off every material thing he'd accumulated in this world and the most valuable item on his list was the overcoat given him not a month before. As the list grew the Regulars became not quite so loud. Didn't laugh as much. Sam was taking the will very, very seriously. It had become important to him.

"Sam," Ben said, "I just about run out of paper. Now if you'll just put your John Henry at the bottom here, it'll be all finished."

"I'm not through," Sam objected.

"Well, I got no more paper."

Bonney was standing behind Ben now. "All right now, Ben, Carlos, yawl started this thing. So let him finish."

"OK, OK," Ben said, and took up his pencil.

"What was it you wanted to add, Sam?" asked Bonney.

"I forgot my bench."

"Hell, Sam," objected Ben, "that bench don't belong to you. It goes with the place here. It's Bonney's."

139

"It's Sam's bench," Bonney said.

So Sam said, "I want that bench put by my grave, so people can come there, and sit."

Ben didn't make a move with his pencil.

"Write it down, Ben," Bonney said quietly.

Sam was slumped in his chair, his eyes toward the ceiling. At that moment he seemed perfectly sober. "I want to get buried in Rose-Mama's yard, among them rose bushes and flowers."

Ben slapped his pencil down. "Aw, come on, Sam, ain't nobody wants a person buried in their front yard."

"Then across the blacktop," Sam said, "in front of the house where them pines are, on the ridge. Right there in them pines, be a good place."

Ben searched for an objection. "That's Brad's land, right along in there. You'd have to ask Brad about that."

"He won't care," Sam said.

"Write it, Ben," Bonney ordered. And Ben wrote it.

"Then I want Rose-Mama to plant some flowers, all around there. Roses, and all them other kinds, around the grave."

"I hadn't got any more paper," Ben said.

"Slat, get him some more paper," Bonney said. "We got plenty of paper, Ben."

This time Slat brought the paper.

"Brad's cows graze there along that ridge," Ben muttered, while he wrote. "Ain't no flowers gonna grow there with cows grazin'."

"Well, I thought maybe yawl could fix me a little fence, just bob wire be all right, to keep the cows out."

Ben looked at Bonney and Bonney nodded and Ben wrote.

"Then I want a nice little sermon said, and a prayer at the end, and everbody standin' around, bareheaded and all."

Ben was writing dutifully, because Bonney was standing beside Sam's chair just across the table and watching. "I reckon," Ben said to Sam, "we'll put it down that Brother Luther comes out to do the sermon."

"No," Sam said, "I want Bonney to do that."

Ben, exasperated, threw the pencil down again. "Well, my

140

busted butt, Sam, I ain't never heard such a lot of crap. Bonney ain't no *preacher!*"

"Don't matter," Sam said. "That's how I want it."

Ben wrote, and looked up at Bonney with a grin in his eye. *Now by god I guess you'll tell me to keep writing.*

"And I want a tombstone with my name on it."

"A tombstone," Ben growled, but he wrote. "Who you think's gonna buy you a tombstone? Them things cost money."

"Don't have to be a fancy one," Sam said. "Just one of them ol' flat rocks from back yonder on Bonney's creek."

"I don't have no doubt," Ben said, "you'll want a bunch of fine words on the stone, that it'll take a monument tall as a tree to get 'em all on."

"No," Sam said, "it don't matter what's put on the stone just so long as my name's there, so people'll know who it is when they come by."

"All right, what else?" Ben asked.

"That's all."

"Why, you mean you don't want Congress to come down, and vote in a holiday?"

"All right, Ben," Bonney said.

So Ben finished writing and shoved the will over to Sam and he took a long time signing it. The signature was shaky but bold and dark. *Samuel Wilkerson Hobbs Junior.* With the Junior all spelled out. Then he got up and asked Slat to thumbtack the will to the wall, at a place where the light was good. When it was posted he stood there a long time, reading and rereading it. Once he found a spot where he wanted a change made, and Bonney called Ben over to make it. Sam had forgotten Rose-Mama, so he took the chair away from Barney and gave it to Rose-Mama, and instead of the chair Barney got the good-luck horseshoe originally left to Norman Akers. Sam said he wouldn't leave Akers a damn thing. He said leaving Akers the horseshoe was a mistake anyway. But finally he thought he'd just leave Akers the message, the same one he left Millie, if Bonney thought that'd be all right, and Bonney said that'd be just fine, Sam, just fine.

Gradually the Friday night racket built back up. The Regulars

141

forgot the will and ignored Sam the way they generally did. By eleven o'clock, when Sam was normally passed out on his bench, he was still standing around near the spot where the will was posted. A late bunch of customers came in, and there was a very, very busy period during which I went back and helped pull beer.

While the rush was peaking I felt Slat nudge my arm with an elbow and nod toward the front door. There went Sam, walking out, walking straighter, looking closer to sober than I'd ever seen him. The force of his habit made him pause at the jukebox and crook his index finger into the coin return. Nothing there. Slat and I watched him look all around the tavern and raise his hand, not high, but just above his belt buckle, and wave a little and he said something. I couldn't hear him over the noise.

"What did he say?" Slat asked.

"I don't know."

He went on out and he never did come back to his bench that night.

Not that night, or any other. When he didn't show up by noon the next day, which was a Saturday, Bonney sent Turnip to look for him. Turnip found him in the culvert where he kept his jug. "He's stiff as a post, Mister Bonney. He's dead. Mister Sam's gone. He froze, look to me like."

Wiley Scott, the deputy, drove out in answer to Bonney's telephone call. He brought Judge Horton, justice of the peace, to fulfill his role as coroner according to Texas law. The judge had tobacco juice in the corners of his mouth.

"You hadn't ought to have moved 'im," he told Bonney.

Bonney had picked Sam up and carried him in the house and put him on his own bed. And covered the body with a sheet.

"Well, I did, anyway. I couldn't let him lay out yonder in that culvert."

"I reckon it don't matter much in this case," Horton said. "But you take a fellow that dies without benefit of a doctor, it's law that he ain't supposed to be moved until the coroner comes."

142

"Well, he's moved, all the same," Bonney said.

Horton grunted and went to the bed and raised the sheet and pinched Sam sharply on the arm.

"What the hell you think you're doin'?" Bonney snapped.

"I got to see if he's dead," Horton said, wiping his mouth. "If I'm gonna say a man's dead in my report, I got to see if he'll jump."

"Well, he's dead, all right."

Horton nodded. "I reckon we'll just put it down that it's death from natural causes."

"From squirrel whiskey, be more like," Wiley Scott said.

Leaving, Horton stopped by the front door and said to Bonney, "I reckon the county will have to bury him."

Bonney shook his head. "No, Sam's not gonna cost the county a cent. We'll take care of him."

Horton nodded and clodded out.

"Hey, Judge, wait a minute," Wiley said, stopping at the tavern's back door. "You don't expect we gonna drive all the way out here to Bonney's without we get us a cool one."

Horton grinned. "Are you buyin', Wiley?"

"Why sure, Judge." He laughed, and winked at Bonney.

The two were still in the tavern drinking beer when the funeral home in town sent an ambulance for Sam's body. Bonney followed the ambulance in and picked out a casket. When he got back about three o'clock, the justice of the peace and the deputy sheriff were getting in the patrol car to leave, both of them a bit droopy-eyed.

"Bonney," Wiley said, "I got that little girl to make me a ticket on them beers we had. I don't happen to have none of my personal checks with me. All right?"

"All right." They drove off, and Bonney spat in the sand behind them.

Rose-Mama had to put Slat to bed shortly after Bonney got back from town. Sam was almost more than she could bear. She tried to work, but we'd find her in the kitchen on Barney's Couch, curled up and crying.

Barney stood at the back door and stomped and snorted and muttered. He was a great big stick of dynamite, about to explode.

"It's not so much Sam dyin'," Rose-Mama said. "With Barney, it's seein' Slat cry that way. He can't stand for her to cry."

When Barney had to take some kind of action he took the only course he knew. He quit. He threw his apron on the refrigerator and stormed out, saying a man was a goddamn fool to work in a screwed-up place like Bonney's and he went roaring off in his car.

"What's the trouble?" whined Colonel Ralls, when Maudie and Rose-Mama took Slat out to the house. "What's the trouble with that girl?"

"It's Sam, Colonel," I told him. "Sam's gone."

"Where's he gone?"

"He's dead, Colonel."

He turned and went back to his chair. "Oh well, hell, I seen plenty of 'em die at Santiago. I seen a fella die at Santiago one time with his belly swelled up so big you——"

"Colonel!" Bonney called. "Colonel, you go on home now. It's time for you to go home."

He didn't go, but he sat down and kept quiet.

About four-thirty a couple of cowboys I hadn't seen before came in for a beer and fed the jukebox and punched a fast rock-a-billy number that seemed a dozen times louder than usual. It played about a minute before Bonney went over and put his foot against the juke and shoved it away from the wall and jerked the plug out.

"Hey," one of the cowboys said, "I put a quarter in that thing."

Bonney went to the cash register and flipped a quarter to the cowboy. He offered no explanation.

The usual Saturday crowd grew, but Bonney didn't plug the jukebox back in. The customers would come in and they'd ask the old question they always asked when things were quiet around the tavern.

"Who died?"

"Sam Hobbs."

"No joke?"

"No joke."

"Well, I'll be damned. Ol' Sam."

144

It was a mighty slow Saturday night. Plenty of business, but no racket. No eight-ball. No music.

Ben Ashley seemed particularly affected by Sam's death. I watched him sit for an hour at the long table, exactly where he sat the night before when he wrote the will. He sat there just staring at the door.

When he moved he walked slowly to the jukebox and fished in his pocket and dropped a quarter in the coin return.

"What you doin' that for?" Buck asked.

"I don't know," Ben said. "It's just for ol' Sam, I reckon."

Buck nodded, and seemed to understand. Presently he went to the juke and did the same, put money in that coin return where Sam always fished for forgotten change.

It got under my hide a little, before it was over. Gradually they all came, one by one, parading, not saying anything, digging in their pockets and their purses, to put money in the coin return for Sam. Soon the small receptacle was spilling silver on the floor and Bonney got Turnip to bring a bucket and put it there by the jukebox on the floor, and they fed it all night. Some made two, three trips. Dollar bills, even a few fives showed up in the bucket.

I was sitting at the bar when Turnip came to Bonney and said quietly, "Mister Bonney, the men in the Dark Room, they wanta know it's all right if they make up a little pot and give it to you, for Mister Sam. I reckon it's all right?"

"Why sure."

Turnip started off but Bonney grabbed him.

"No, wait. Tell 'em to come on in. Tell 'em to come through here and put the money in the bucket, the same as the rest."

Turnip was doubtful. "I don't 'spect they'll want to come in here."

"They'll come. You tell 'em I said to come."

And they did, after a long delay. Lincoln Hill's face appeared in the Dark Room door and Bonney beckoned to him and said, "Yawl come on, Lincoln. Right on through the kitchen. That'll be just fine."

Lincoln walked straight and dignified across the dance floor and dropped some coins in the bucket. The others followed him,

145

not so confident as their leader. They were ill at ease, self-conscious, trespassing on White Territory.

Bonney stopped them all as they returned to the kitchen door to go back to the Dark Room. They huddled in a small group there, looking uncomfortable.

"All right, now listen to this," Bonney said. "Everybody listen a minute. This money there at the juke, I don't know how much it is, but we'll count it and I'll put it up and it'll go toward Sam's stone that he wanted for his grave. I'll let you know, tomorrow, how much it is. But that's not what I wanted to say. I just wanted to let everybody know that this place is gonna be closed tomorrow, until after Sam's funeral, and I want all yawl to come to the service."

"When's the funeral gonna be?" Carlos asked.

"Tomorrow, up yonder on the slope, in the pines where Sam said. At two o'clock. In the morning, I wish everybody'd spread the word around. I want a crowd there. Carlos, you and Ben can tell everybody in town that knows Sam. Buck, you get the word around over there in your neighborhood." He turned to Lincoln Hill. "Lincoln, I wish you'd tell all your folks. Be sure and get word to Calladium, and tell her I said I want all the folks in the Blackjack to be here."

"All right, Mister Bonney," Lincoln nodded, "we'll get word around."

"Brad?" Bonney searched the crowd. "Where'd Brad go?"

"Right here."

"Brad, you been buildin' fence. I wonder could you bring us about half a dozen posts and some wire and staples, for the fence."

"I'll take care of it."

"Fine. That's good."

Lincoln Hill spoke again. "Mister Bonney, you want us to, I'll get some men in here first thing tomorra and we'll dig Mister Sam's hole for him. We could do that."

"Good, that's good, Lincoln. I'll meet you up there around eight o'clock and show you where. Rose-Mama? You take care of the flowers, all right?"

"All right, but it's gonna rush me, havin' that funeral to-morrow."

146

"Can't help it. The will says flowers."

"That will ain't legal," Ben said.

"Far as I'm concerned it is," Bonney said. He walked over to the wall where Sam's will was still posted and he rapped on it with a knuckle. "We're gonna do everything just the way it says in this will."

Ben grinned. "Well, it says you're gonna preach the funeral. Are you gonna do that?"

Bonney didn't grin back. "We're gonna do everything just the way the will says."

He came back to the bar and looked at the clock. "Now I think I'll close her up. Let's all hit the sack, because we got us a busy day tomorrow."

Rose-Mama and I drove home in a light winter drizzle.

"I'd sure hate to get buried in weather like this," she said.

"Maybe it'll clear up tomorrow. Do you suppose Bonney really means to preach Sam's funeral?"

The weather did clear. Sunday came bright and crisp and fresh. When I got in from milking Elizabeth I looked out my window and saw Bonney and Lincoln, standing on the slope across the road, overseeing the digging of Sam's grave.

I went to see if I could help.

"Naw, we about got things under control. Well, wait, there is something. I wish you'd go get on Rose-Mama's phone and call Warren, at the undertaker's, Farley Funeral Home, and tell him I said to put Sam in that biggest hearse he's got. That Cadillac. I don't want him wheelin' Sam out here in that little old gimcrack panel truck. Tell him the ground's all right in here, didn't rain much, so he's not gonna get stuck."

I went to make the phone call. When I delivered the message Warren said, "Bonney's taking this mighty serious, isn't he?" He laughed. "You ought to see this casket he picked out, for an old drunk like Sam Hobbs."

I told him I thought it'd be wise if he didn't make any such remark to Bonney, and Warren said he knew what I meant.

Before noon I helped Rose-Mama take the flowers across the road to the site. She had half a pickup full of roses. Brad

147

showed up with two of his ranch hands and half a dozen others pitched in to help and within an hour they dug holes and set posts and strung barbed wire around the plot.

"We'll just leave a gap here right now," Brad told Bonney, "so they'll have room to bring the casket in. Later on, if you want, we'll put a gate in. And we'll have to brace our corners, too."

Bonney nodded. Rose-Mama fished out the roses with the longest stems and attached them some way to the wire in the fence and sent me back across the road for a raft of her big fern-looking plants that grew in the winter, and you never saw a prettier barbed-wire fence when she got through with it. Bonney was pleased, and patted her, and her expression said she'd decorate an outhouse if it would please him more.

Two men from the funeral home came out and fixed the trappings over the grave to hold the casket, and not until that was done did Bonney go back to the house.

They began coming an hour before the service was scheduled. Cars from Farley lined the blacktop and had to park far down the slope, halfway to the tavern. I stood on Rose-Mama's front porch and watched the black people come across the fields and pastures and woods, just the same way they came to the stew supper. Except this time they were in their Sunday clothes. I could see white shirt fronts contrasting against dark faces for more than a mile away. At a quarter to two, I made a rough count of almost five hundred people.

There was no gate in the fence along the road, but Brad cut his barbed wire to let the ambulance through, and the people. Hank Mills came up with his arm around Slat, looking pale and hollow-eyed. Turnip drove Bonney up the slope in the pickup. They both wore suits, the only time I'd seen either of them with a necktie on. When Turnip parked, he stepped to the bed of the truck and wrestled out Sam's bench and carried it inside the enclosure and sat it down by the grave.

I was at the fence when Warren arrived in the big black ambulance and nursed it across the borrow ditch and through the gap that Brad cut. "Man," he said to me out the window, "I don't think I've seen more people at a graveside service since we buried Old Man Farley."

148

All the Regulars were there, of course. And a few of the nesters and at least two hundred blacks. The mill hands and the cowboys and the ranchers all came, with their wives. Most of them were just nameless faces I'd seen in the tavern on Saturday nights.

I felt sorry for Bonney. He was nervous. The tight collar bothered him. He kept sticking an index finger behind the knot of his tie and yanking, wiggling his neck, trying to loosen things up. When the casket—a beautiful thing, dark metal, almost black but with gray and brown tones showing in the sun—when it was over the grave Warren nodded and Bonney stepped inside the little enclosure. He stood there, being uncomfortable, with all those hundreds of eyes on him. For a panicky few seconds I was afraid he wasn't going to go through with it. But then he turned to Rose-Mama, outside the little fence, and beckoned to her and she came and stood beside him. Then he took two steps and put his hand on Hank's arm and whispered, and Hank and Slat came inside. And then Turnip. He drew them in close to him. *His family.* He didn't seem quite satisfied. His eyes searched the crowd, looking for somebody. For Barney? For Maudie? *For me?* I stayed back, and stood on an old anthill by the fence. Finally Bonney coughed and spoke. Talked his native rural Texas tongue, the language of the cowboys and the mill hands.

"Well—" he began, "well, I reckon we can start." Clearing his throat, coughing when he didn't need to cough. "Ben here— Ben Ashley—he said I ain't no preacher and that's sure right. But Sam, you might say he give me this job, one of the last things he did, and I'm gonna do it the best I can." He stopped again for maybe ten seconds and it seemed an eternity. *Come on, Bonney, come on, boy.* He had his finger inside his collar, yanking.

"All yawl know," he started again, jerking his head toward the casket, "this here's Sam Hobbs in that coffin. First off I want to say it's not my idea to come up here on this ridge and put on a big funeral show. I always figured havin' a big preachin' over a dead fella's not gonna get his score changed any. It wouldn't matter any if it was me in that box, but to Sam it's important and that's why we're here. If a man can't get his final wants—well, I always figured he might not rest so easy. . . ."

Final wants. The Old Man's letter came rising into my mind. *Remember this is your Dads last request before going onto glory.*

"Now then, it's not any use in me tryin' to stand up here and say Sam wasn't just an old drunk, because that's what he was. I don't know what preachers and Bible folks would have to say, about an old drunk that died. All I can think of, I'd just like to say Sam wasn't *born* no drunk. He wasn't *always* a drunk. He was *made* one. I guess some of us would say, well, Sam had woman trouble and took to drinkin' rotgut. But I don't guess it'd be proper to go into all that, not now. Sam Hobbs did himself a bunch of hurtin' in his life, and I don't figure he ought to get blamed for all that whiskey he drank. I know this—I know there's a bunch of us standin' up here right now that didn't do much to help *stop* his hurtin', when he needed us—so I expect you might say we did our little share on puttin' him in this casket. I asked everybody to come out here because I just want you to hear this: before he got down in that bottle, Sam Hobbs was just about the best ol' boy I ever knew. . . ."

Another awkward moment then, while Bonney suffered. He wanted to say more, but it wouldn't come. At last he asked for help.

"Ben? Where's Ben Ashley? In that will, what else is there to do?"

"The prayer," Ben said. "He wanted the prayer."

Bonney's finger went back in the collar, yanking. "Can anybody here give a prayer?"

Silence. A few heads turned toward Deacon Buck Thornton, but he had his eyes down. He wanted no part of it.

"Well," Bonney said, "I guess I'll have to give it a turn myself."

As if in great relief that he hadn't been called on, almost every man in the crowd immediately bowed his head.

At that moment a cattle truck came roaring down the blacktop. Bonney waited until its noise was a distant hum. One of Brad's cows bawled down in the creek bottom. A sudden breeze whipped the pinetops and produced a whistling, a swishing chord that built to a high pitch, faded, and died.

150

"Lord?" he began. Then nothing.

What are you waiting for, man? For the Lord to answer?

"Lord? I know You've kept up with Sam Hobbs, that's in this casket, so I'm not gonna stand up here and try to pass him off as any kind of a Sunday school teacher. . . . I don't know, exactly, how the game goes after a man dies, but I expect Sam's gone already, one way or the other, and I want to say I always thought it was a waste to pray over a dead man. My mama used to say a man ought to pray at funerals for the ones that's still livin' . . . so that's what I'm doin'. . . . You've got yourself a bunch of mavericks standin' here on this ridge. We're not the worst folks but we're not the best, by a long way. If anybody needs forgivin', it ain't Sam Hobbs . . . it's us, for the way we treated him sometimes. . . . Now then, I'd like to tell You we're gonna reorganize, and start out new, and be better folks . . . but I know we won't. . . . We'd like to, but we just haven't got what it takes to do it. Just as quick as this funeral's over, I know I'll go right back down that slope and open up that beer joint and I expect about half this crowd will go along too. I got me a bottle of eight-year-old bourbon in the kitchen and I expect I'll crack it and get a little drunk because I had me a hard time these last two, three days . . . so we'll just have to depend on whatever mercy You can spare us. I reckon that's it. Amen."

He did open the tavern, just after the funeral, and fully 90 per cent of the crowd followed him down the slope and produced one of his biggest Sunday nights of business. Bonney and I sat on Barney's Couch and almost killed the eight-year-old bourbon. At eleven-thirty, when the place was still crowded, Bonney grabbed Maudie by the arm and, without a word, took her out to the house and, I presume, to bed. I can still see Carlos Freeman's face. He was standing at the kitchen door, looking through the round window, watching Bonney disappear into the darkness with his wife. He stood there a few seconds before he turned slowly and went back to sit down in the tavern.

Then Tuesday, after the funeral. Bonney asked me to drive into Houston and order Sam's gravestone. He handed me the

151

jukebox collection, which came to a hundred and twenty dollars. He gave me a signed blank check to pay for the difference.

"They'll need to know what you want on the stone," I told him. "The inscription."

"You think up something," he said. "Think up something Sam would like."

Carlos was hanging around the front door of the tavern as I walked out. "You want some company, Johnny? I wouldn't mind goin' in with you."

I said sure, but I wasn't enthusiastic about it. I'd never liked Carlos very much. It's not easy to develop an admiration for a man who sits around in beer joints while his wife is in bed with another man not thirty steps away. Besides that, Carlos had an unwashed, dissipated look about him all the time. He looked not quite clean. Not really dirty but not clean.

"Pretty nice day," he said, before we hit Sullivan and turned onto the Interstate.

It was a nice day. Beautiful. Clear and windless. Not the kind of day, I thought, to be going after a tombstone.

Have you thought of this? Here are you going to order a tombstone for Samuel Wilkerson Hobbs, Junior, a man you didn't know until last September. And you didn't even order one for your own father. What do you suppose Midge put on the Old Man's stone? What kind of inscription?

"Lotta traffic, for Tuesday." He made another attempt to start conversation.

If I could duck Carlos, get him into a beer bar somewhere, I'd call Midge at school. Suddenly I missed her a great deal. Wanted to see her and hear her say "Hi'ya Pop" and feel her place her cool cheek against mine for just that little instant, the way she always did. She smelled like Eva. The only thing left in this world of Eva.

Then Carlos again. "Whatta you reckon a piece of tail cost now, in one of them motels in Houston?"

For just a second I resented the question, I suppose because it arrived while I was thinking of Eva.

"I don't know," I said.

Carlos grinned when I looked at him. "I wouldn't mind buyin' me a little piece of strange, if we got time. How about you?"

152

"Not today."

"You used to could get it, pretty good stuff too, for around five bucks. Then it got to goin' up, goin' up. Last time I was down here I had to pay twelve bucks, for an old fat-gutted gal had a big scar on her belly, look like somebody stuck a cane knife in her. Twelve bucks is too much to pay for tail."

"I agree."

A peculiar business. Here was Carlos, married to one of the sexiest women in creation, talking about paying twelve dollars to go to bed with a fat-gutted girl with a scar on her belly.

"I don't know about you"—he wasn't going to let the matter die—"but me, man, I got to get off once in a while and get me a little strange."

He let the subject ride for a mile or two but came back to it.

"Way I look at it," he said, "a man's got a right to slip it to anything he wants, if his wife's messin' around on 'im."

Then it hit me. *My god, he wants to talk about Maudie and Bonney.*

All right, so I let him talk. "I suppose you're right."

He took the bait and went. "Well, me and Maudie, we never was able to do much good at it. She claims she's always too tired, generally, and then when she's not I can't ever do her no good."

Well, for crying out loud, he wants to make a sex confession. OK, Carlos, just proceed. "You mean you're impotent? You can't get it up?"

"Not at home I can't. Not in two, three years. That's why Maudie horses around with Bonney. You stayin' there so much, I figured you knew that."

It wasn't exactly a question so I pretended to take special care in passing a truck and didn't answer.

He plowed ahead. "Bonney's been takin' care of Maudie now for about two years."

"But doesn't it bother you?"

"Not any more. At first it did. But it didn't after Bonney come and talked to me about it."

"He *told* you about it?"

"Sure."

"That's the damnedest thing I ever heard."

153

"Well, it was the damnedest thing I ever heard too, when he first told me. But when he explained it to me and all, it wasn't so bad."

This I've got to hear. "How did he explain it?"

"Aw, he just said Maudie was a mighty sexy girl, and needed to be made love to awful bad, and she wasn't gettin' taken care of at home. Said she was goin' to waste. Said a woman like Maudie'll get mean, if she's not kept bred. Told me if she wasn't taken care of, first thing I knew she'd be hoppin' into one of these lumber trucks with some big ol' boy and goin' off to god knows where and then look where I'd be. You got a match?"

I lighted his cigarette and waited for the rest. There had to be more.

"No, Bonney come around to me, I think it was the third weekend Maudie went to work out there at his place. I was still workin' then, at the Mills. He come around one day about quittin' time, and waited for me there at the gate. Said he'd come to let me whip his butt. I told him *I* didn't want to whip nobody, and he said, 'Well, you'll want to whip *me*, when I tell you what I come to tell you.' So I said what was that, and he told me he taken Maudie to bed just the night before. He said some sumbitchin' gossip would tell me about it sooner or later, so he just thought he'd tell me before I heard it from somewhere's else."

Hello, Carlos. Oh say, Carlos, by the way, I slept with your wife last night and I just wanted you to be the first to know. Did you ever hear anything to beat that? Hod-oh-mighty damn.

Carlos was stretched out now, on the story, just like Buck Thornton telling how he shot the spotted dog that time. "Well, hell fire, I didn't know what to make of it. I guess if he *hadn't* told me, why I'da heard about it like he said and I'da gone out there and I *would'a* whipped his butt, or tried to. He stood right out there by that gate, with the whole damn payroll walkin' by us, stickin' his chin out and tellin' me to go ahead and hit 'im. Said he wasn't goin' to hit back. I didn't know what to do. Told 'im I'd have to think about it a while. Then he told me *how* to think about it. Said he'd promise, if I wanted him to, said he'd promise not ever to lay a hand on Maudie

154

again. But he said somethin' had to be done about Maudie, because her pants was so hot you could pretty near see the smoke. He told me I had a choice to make. Said I could get back to satisfyin' Maudie or else he'd do it himself. I told him I'd let him know. I had to get rid of the bastard, some way. I couldn't tell what to do about him. He said he'd see me tomorrow. Well, I went on home, and I cleaned up, and I drank me about a six-pack, and when Maudie come in I throwed her in the bed and I done my damnedest, I really did. But I couldn't do no good. I don't know why exactly. One time I went to the doctor about it, when it first begun to happen to me. He said there wasn't nothin' wrong with me. Said it was in my mind. Anyway, I seen Bonney was damn sure right. So I went out there to see him and I told him to go ahead, because I wasn't able to cut the mustard. You know what that bastard said?"

"No, what? What did he say?"

"Well, he said he'd do it but he wasn't interested in breakin' up no homes. Said he'd had a go at that once and didn't want no more of it. He told me he'd do the best he could by Maudie if it'd be any help to me, and if I ever wanted her back to just let him know and he wouldn't touch her again. So that's the way it's been, for two years now, and I've about got used to it. Say, how about let's stop and get us a beer?"

I pulled off the Interstate and stopped at what tavern operators in the Southwest have become fond of calling a lounge. The main difference between a highway lounge and a beer joint like Bonney's Place, the lounge may have a place to wipe your feet at the door, and the beer costs a nickel a bottle more, and the light is dimmer.

"No," Carlos said, when we groped in and found a booth and he'd wrapped his hand around a cool one, "the trouble with that bastard, Bonney, the women all just love 'im. I reckon you've noticed that."

I said I had.

"Maudie says he's hung like a Shetland pony."

"You don't mean that Maudie *tells* you about sleeping with Bonney."

"Hell yes, she tells me. She gets a charge out of tellin' it, some way. Me and Maudie's got a understandin' now. She can be a real sweet girl, she wants to be. She's good to me, I tell you that. And I like it, havin' her for my wife. Sometimes I take her into Spearman's when she's all dressed up and got them nylons on, and one of them low-cut dresses. You can see them ol' boys mouth waterin' all over the place. You might say I'm proud of her, I guess. I don't know if you know, what I mean."

I know, Carlos, I know. You should have seen Eva. "I think I know what you mean."

"Well, I figure I got Bonney, to thank. For havin' Maudie. Because he's right. Hadn't been for him, takin' care of her like that, she'da been long gone from me and I know it. But it don't seem to be no strain on 'im. That sumbitch is a *stud*, man. Maudie ain't the only one he takes care of."

"Charlotte."

"Charlotte, sure. And that Lucille what's-her-name, that big-titted one down at the bank. Bonney used to ease *her* pain a lot, and might do it still. Then Elsie Smith, the one in the office at Mrs. Farley's school? Hell, I've seen Bonney take her to the woods plenty of times. Her husband, I don't know if you've seen him, he's the one drives that meat truck for the locker plant. Call him Smitty."

"He was at Bonney's once," I said.

"Well, Smitty's got the same trouble I got. Can't get it up."

"It seems to me Bonney's drawn to women who . . . well, what would you say? Women who aren't getting loved?"

Carlos nodded. "That's about it. He's always been that way, even when he was young."

Carlos went off to the men's room—he'd gotten around two quick beers while I was on a cup of coffee—and it struck me that my feeling toward him had changed now, a little. It couldn't be easy for a man to live with the situation he had.

"Carlos," I asked him when he returned, "what did Bonney mean when he told you he didn't want to break up a home? Said he'd had some of that before and didn't want any more of it."

"I ain't real sure. It had somethin' to do with Millie. Millie don't stay around Farley much any more, and I don't reckon you've seen her. But it had somethin' to do with Millie, and with Sam Hobbs, a good long while ago. Bonney don't ever talk about it, at least not to me." He slapped the table. "I reckon you're ready. Let me get me a cold can, to take."

I let him out at a small motel just off the Interstate on the edge of town. He seemed to know the place. Told me to pick him up there on the way back.

I stopped at a drive-in grocery with a phone booth and called the office. Dan was out of town, and I was glad. He has a way of getting me to talk, tell everything I know, without asking me one question. I wasn't sure I wanted to tell him anything at all right now, and he'd want to know when I was coming back and I didn't want to tell him that either.

I got back in the car and spent half an hour deciding what to put on Sam's tombstone. It took another hour to find a monument company and order the stone. The cost came to nearly three hundred dollars. The woman in the office smiled thinly about the way I paid for it, but she didn't say anything. I gave her the jukebox money, most of it in quarters and nickels and dimes. Then I filled in Bonney's signed check for half the difference, something like sixty-four dollars. And I put the balance on my own bank credit card. I don't know why.

Then I went by the house. That was a mistake. "You ought to rent that house, if you think you'll be gone a year," Dan had said. "Nothing's harder on a house than not being lived in."

Yes, but I didn't rent it. I didn't want to think about other people, strangers, moving around in there among Eva's things, walking on her rugs, sleeping in our bed. But Dan was right. The house had already died. I walked through it and right back out the front door and drove away. I used to think I could feel a little bit of Eva in that house, but it wasn't there any longer.

I went back to the same phone booth and called Midge at school. She wasn't in her room. It was five o'clock so I drove back out the Interstate and Carlos was waiting, standing out front of the motel, all slumped over, his cigarette hanging in the corner of his mouth.

"*Twenty friggin' bucks!*" he moaned. "Why, gee-zus pee-zus,

I never brought but twenty-two with me. Didn't even have enough left to buy a beer. Twenty bucks is too much to pay, Johnny, for tail."

We drove on back to Farley in silence.

10.

Tuesday night, December sixth. I'll not ever look at a calendar and see December sixth without visualizing the date printed in red, and shimmering, to attract attention to itself. When I see it I get that burning sensation down inside me. Or is it a chill? I can't tell. I can feel it even now. It begins down in my intestines and burns or chills its way up into my chest. For a long time it would wake me at night and I'd sit up in bed and rub myself to make it go away.

I've thought about what happened, gone over it carefully I suppose a thousand times and it always astonishes me that I can recall the smallest details, every sight and every sound there in the tavern, just *before* it happened. Then comes the blank, an interval of what—one minute? two?—when I can remember nothing at all. Trailing along behind the blank interval is a sort of mixture, a semiawareness of the thing that happened. A crazy, incredible thing, which changed my entire existence. It changed my situation around Bonney's Place. Changed my reason for being there.

Looking back on it, trying to analyze it, I'm amazed at the unique circumstance that led to it all: Not one woman came to Bonney's that night. Even Uncle Batey was there, without Aunt Kate. Slat was off on a date with Hank. So it was a small all-male group in the tavern: Ben, Brad, Buck, Turnip, Colonel Ralls, Uncle Batey, Carlos, Bonney, and me.

And Norman Akers.

Normally Akers went home on Sunday nights. He didn't go the night of Sunday, December fourth. We all knew why. He'd bragged about it. His grandson had a birthday coming up Wednesday and Akers was giving the boy an Appaloosa colt. So on Monday he drove way over into Louisiana and bought the colt. He brought it back to his ranch on Tuesday and that's why he was in Bonney's that night.

It was cold. A norther had blown in about noon. Akers was standing with his backside to the gas heater near the pool table. I was playing eight-ball with Brad. Bonney was behind the bar. Barney was in the kitchen, looking out of the serving window, his chin resting on his thick hairy forearms. Turnip was leaning against the east wall, listening. At the long table sat Uncle Batey and Carlos and Buck and Ben. Colonel Ralls was asleep in his chair, near the end of the bar.

And Ben was talking about the time he hitchhiked to Florida when he was twenty-two years old and got picked up by a blonde in a Buick. Everybody was listening, carefully. You get ten men in a bunch with nothing to do and sooner or later they're going to start telling sex stories, most of them lies. But there's this understanding, this unwritten agreement, that you listen.

Even Norman Akers was attentive and quiet. He had his hands behind him, the backs of them against his fat broad buttocks and the palms turned toward the fire. The smallest hands, and plumpest fingers, for such a big man.

Well, Ben said, the way it was, he was standing out on the highway on the other side of New Orleans and it was around the middle of the afternoon and he had just exactly eighty-five cents left in his pocket because he'd spent all his money in them strip joints on Bourbon Street. And he was sort of thinkin' about turnin' around and goin' on back home, seein' he hadn't got started, hardly, to Florida before his money run out. Then this Buick pulled up and stopped and this woman leaned over and cracked the window a little and asked him how far he was goin' and Ben said he was goin' all the way to the Atlantic Ocean if he could make it. Woman wanted to know if he could drive. Hell yes he could. Did he have a driver's license? Sure, had it right here. Well, she said, how about if Ben just come around on her side and drove a while, because she'd come all the way from Dallas and sure was tired.

159

So he got behind that wheel and herded that Buick. Pretty damn good-lookin' ol' gal. Old'ern Ben, by a good ways. Maybe thirty, or might be more. She had on this short skirt and she'd lean back and close her eyes and that skirt commenced crawlin' up her legs and by god it was all Ben could do, to keep his eyes on the road.

Well, they got on over to some little burg that Ben couldn't remember the name of it, back this side of Mobile a way, and the woman she said how about somethin' to eat. Ben said hell, he was broke, but she said that's all right, she had plenty. So they went in a café and sat down in a booth and Ben sat on the other side of the table and she said, listen, wasn't no use in him sittin' way over there, and patted the seat beside her, so Ben moved over there with her and sat right up close, her leg touchin' his, you know. And while they was eatin', why ever now and then she'd reach for somethin' and she'd rub one of them boobs on 'im, and goddamn, it like to run him crazy.

Well, about fifty miles on down the road she said she was just gonna have to get her some sleep, been on the move so long, so how about pullin' in to a motel somewhere. Ben said, hell, *he* didn't have no money to rent a room, guess he'd just have to sleep in the car. And she said No, he could just come in *her* room, if he'd behave himself, so that's what he done. When they was in the room that ol' gal went to the toilet and when she come out, why, kiss your tail if that babe didn't have a goddamn thing on 'cept a brassiere and some little ol' pants wasn't big enough to wrap up a pound of liver. And she got in the bed and pulled the sheet up about halfway and then you know what that ol' gal said? By god she said, *Well whatta you waitin' for, big boy, whyn't you come on to bed?*

Man, Ben has seen some horny women in his time but he hadn't *never* seen anything to beat that gal in that Buick. They stayed in that motel room two days and two nights and in all that time Ben never did put his pants on. If they wanted somethin' to eat or drink why she'd just send for it. And he stayed with her all the way to Florida. She couldn't get enough of that stuff. Hell, they'd stop and do it on the *road*, by god. Once they hit Florida they taken that beach highway, and over in there at a place named Caraboo, or Carabelle, or somethin'

160

like that, it was night, and she said she wanted to go swimmin'
and get it in the water. Said she hadn't ever had it in the water
and wanted to try it. So they went out there in the friggin'
Gulf of Mexico and knocked off a little in the water, just naked
as dressed quail, which it wasn't bad stuff in the water, either,
but it was a hell of a lot better up on the sand.

Well, it turned out she lived at Orlando, and Ben he drove
her all the way there, and she, by god, took him right to her
house, a big brick house with trees and flowers all around. Her
husband come out and met 'em, a bald-headed ol' boy musta
been twenty years old'ern her, and she said to him, now listen to
this, by god, she told her husband, *Honey this here young
man's Mister Ben Ashley, from Texas, and he's done me a big
favor by drivin' me all the way from New Orleans and I think
you oughta do somethin' nice for him.* You know what that ol'
sumbitch did? Took Ben in the house and give 'im a pair of good
slacks and two sport shirts and one of his spare suitcases and
fifty bucks in cash and then taken him downtown and bought
him a bus ticket to Daytona Beach, where they have them car
races you see on TV sometimes.

No comment, for just a few seconds, and then Carlos said,
"Ben, that's one of the best damn lies I've heard today. I got to
give you credit."

"It ain't no lie, I'll guarantee you that," Ben said, not a bit
disturbed by Carlos' remark.

I decided it wasn't a bad story either, and classed it to be
only three-quarters false, which is a low percentage for such
stories, told by men everywhere in this world.

Then it happened.

"Well, Ben," Norman Akers said, "I'll say this for you, you
went in the right direction, looking for women. I've been in all
fifty states and a number of foreign countries and my opinion
is that if a man's looking for women to take to bed, the best
place to go is southern Louisiana, over in that bayou country.
It seems to me they breed for it over in there, breed women
who're put together perfectly, in mind and body both, for
sex. . . ."

Brad and I were back at the eight-ball game. We'd stopped
for Ben's story but it was customary among the Regulars that

161

we paid as little attention as possible to what Akers had to say. He droned ahead, in that stuff-shirt manner of his, and I paid no attention until the first time he mentioned the name.

". . . Terrell, his name is, which isn't a Cajun name, of course. His father is Irish, a giant of a man who married a Cajun woman. This Terrell is a lawyer, in Baton Rouge. I had occasion to use him in a personal injury suit that came out of an accident there in our Baton Rouge store. . . ."

Terrell. A lawyer. At Baton Rouge. *Wait a minute, what the hell's going on here? He's talking about Sid, about Eva's brother Sid.*

". . . and the first time I ever saw the girl I suppose she was about nineteen, just out of high school. She was absolutely the most beautiful woman I ever met. A large girl. She must have stood five-eight or nine, but perfectly proportioned. Jet-black hair, you know, and skin like milk. . . ."

What the goddamn hell does he think he's saying? Who's he talking about?

". . . so I took her to dinner, two nights in succession. I think the thing that overwhelmed me about the girl was that she was so much the perfect lady, and yet she had a way of hinting to you that if you happened to be the one she chose, she'd be a tigress in the bed. And she had a voice so full of melody, low and musical, and . . ."

Listen, you son of a bitch, are you talking about Eva?

". . . so the second night, I propositioned her outright. I had the feeling the direct approach might appeal to her. She just laughed, and smiled, and said she'd have to think about it. The next night when I went to Terrell's house I was a little nervous, I admit. I certainly didn't want that big bastard mad at me, and I was afraid I'd have him mad if he found out I'd propositioned his sister. . . ."

Why, you are, you queasy bastard! You are! You're talking about Eva!

". . . and this is the most amazing thing. Terrell and his wife didn't come into the living room to talk, when I went to pick her up. I was sitting alone and she walked in wearing this short skirt and a sweater outfit that must have been tailored to her breasts. She had these magnificent breasts. I asked her

162

where she'd like to go and she stood up there for just a few seconds and posed a bit, turned a shoulder and an ankle and then she said, 'I thought maybe you'd like to take me to a motel.' Well, I . . ."

I felt something burning my leg. It didn't hurt but I could feel it and I remember looking down to see that I was standing up against the butane heater, right behind Akers. I couldn't seem to see him very well. But I remember things. I even remember Brad tugging at me and saying it was my shot, that he'd missed the eight and left it sitting in the hole. And Akers was still talking.

". . . it was like going to bed with some kind of goddess. I never expect to experience anything like it again. That perfect girl, so goddamned beautiful, and here she was giving herself up, completely, to lust. I've seen erotic behavior in women but nothing like that girl. It seemed she got the most pleasure out of *giving* pleasure. Any way I wanted it, she gave it. The first time——"

That's when I hit him.
Hit Norman Akers.
Hit him hard, in the back of the head.
With the butt of my pool cue.

The blank space, the empty time when I don't remember anything, came just after I watched him go down. I don't remember any thud or any feeling on the small end of the cue, but I can see him going down, curling to one side with his neck twisted and ending up in a big fat heap on Bonney's floor. He didn't move.

After that, Bonney said I stepped back to the west wall and put the cue in the rack and sat down in a chair. I don't know how long the empty time lasted but Colonel Ralls was standing in front of me when I began to see again. He was standing there asking what happened, and saying one time in Santiago he saw a fellow from Mississippi stick a bayonet plum through his best friend in a fight over a whore.

And then Bonney. "Colonel, get away. Go on. You need to get home. You go over there and call and tell 'em to come get you. Johnny? Johnny, hod-oh-mighty damn, what'd you want to hit Akers for? I'm afraid you've killed the bastard."

I got up and looked and Akers was still lying there in a curled-up heap. Blood was coming out of one ear and he certainly looked dead. I walked over and sat down on a bar stool in front of the flower vase Rose-Mama had sent down that night. She'd told me what flowers to cut and how to arrange them. A dozen roses. I sat there and counted them. Six red ones and four whites and two buds just beginning to open, so you couldn't tell for sure yet what color they were going to be.

I could hear Bonney. "Listen, you guys, we got to do somethin'. We got to get Akers to the hospital. Ben? Get on that phone and call Warren. Call him at home. Not likely he'll be at the parlor now. Tell him there's been an accident out here. Get that? An *accident*, and don't tell him anything else, except just get his butt out here in a hurry in that ambulance."

I could hear every word Bonney said but it didn't seem to have anything to do with me so I just kept sitting there looking at the flowers.

"Turnip? Get Colonel Ralls in the truck and take him home. Buck? Come here a minute, you and Carlos. Yawl get hold of Akers and move him over, just a little bit, out of the way. Brad, give me a hand here, will you? Bring a chair."

I swiveled the bar stool to watch all the activity. It seemed a long, long way off but I could see everything clearly. Bonney and Brad brought chairs and set one on each side of the spot where Akers fell. A little circle of blood was on the floor there. Then Bonney and Brad were standing in the chairs and Bonney had his hands up over the blades of the old ceiling fan, the one that hung by loose bolts and wobbled all the time when it ran. Bonney was instructing Brad. "I want this fan pulled loose, by the roots. It oughtn't to be hard. Damn thing's about to fall anyhow. When it comes loose, we want to jump back, out of these chairs, and let it hit the floor just right in front of the stove. All right?"

Brad nodded. "All right."

"Ready?" Bonney said. "All right, *pull*." He and Brad were bent forward at the waist, an awkward position for pulling down, but it took only one yank and the fan came down between the chairs and thudded into the floor and two of the blades broke. They put the chairs back and Bonney examined the broken fan and looked up at the ceiling where the wires were hanging down. "That's not bad. That'll be all right."

Carlos and Ben were squatted down beside Akers. Somebody had taken off a jacket and rolled it up and stuck it under Akers' head. They had him straightened out a little, not so curled up.

"He's breathin'," Ben said. "Ain't he breathin', Carlos?"

"Looks like. He ain't dead, yet."

Bonney wiped his hands on his jeans and looked around. Then he took a deep breath and said to Barney, "Come on, Barney. Come on, all you guys. Carlos? Ben? Come over here a minute. We got to do somethin'. Where's Turnip?"

"You sent him home, to take the Colonel."

"That's right. Ben, you look in the Dark Room and see if anybody's in there."

Ben was back in five seconds. "Naw. Ain't nobody."

Bonney looked at the bar clock. "All right, now this has got to be decided in a hurry. I want to ask all yawl to agree on something. I don't know if everybody saw what happened. I reckon you did. I don't know what it's all about but I know this—Johnny here's gonna be in a bunch of bad trouble if we don't give him a hand. Now then, let me tell you what *really* happened, and see what you think about it."

He turned and pointed to the ceiling where the fan had hung. "You see that old fan. It's been hanging up there mostly by one bolt for two years, and I kept meaning to fix it. Well, I never got around to it and tonight the damn thing decided to come down and it was just bad luck that Norman happened to be standing under there when she fell. I don't know what made it pick just that time to fall. You can't ever tell about things like that. Maybe Norman stomped, with those big boots. Maybe that north wind got to shaking the rafters. It's a pretty strong wind. Anyway she came down and he was right under it. He took a pretty damn good lick, on the head. That'd be plenty lick enough to cold-cock a man. That fan's heavy." He paused and drew the deep breath again. "Well, how about it? Is that what happened?"

Silence. Faces in the little audience all absolutely blank.

And I was sitting over there listening carefully and wondering why Bonney wanted to think up a ridiculous story like that.

It was Brad who started it. "Sounds all right to me, Bonney."

"You think it'll work? You think a ceiling fan like that could fall and lay a man plum out?"

"Hell yes," Brad said. "That brother of mine got hit in the head one time by a hay hook, just a little hay hook fallin' out of the loft and it damn near killed him. Hook part didn't even hit him, just the handle."

Bonney studied the faces of the others. "Ben? How about you?"

"That's fine with me, Bonney," Ben said, and he walked back over to Akers and squatted down. "He's breathin' little better. Maybe he ain't gonna die. You reckon there's anything we oughta do for him? I can't tell if he's got a hole in his head or a knot on top, with that blood in his hair. But he don't seem to be bleedin' much now."

"Buck? How about you?"

"All right. Fine. The fan fell on 'im. I been lookin' for the damn thing to fall any night."

"Barney?"

"OK. Sure. If you say the fan fell on 'im, then it's——"

"No, now wait, dammit, it's not me just *saying* the fan hit him. I want you to *see* it hit him. Swear to it. Hell, I don't know where this thing'll end. Maybe in court, all I know."

"All right," Barney nodded, "I *seen* it hit 'im."

"You can damn well bet *I* seen it." That was Uncle Batey casting his vote. "I seen it fall and heard it hit 'im, and it's a mighty damn bad accident, too."

"Carlos?"

"Sure. Hell yes. Man have to be blind, be sittin' in a beer joint and a fan hits a guy and he don't see it."

"OK. Good." Bonney seemed a little bit relieved. "That's all of us. But remember this—I don't care if the district attorney and the high sheriff and the whole damn U. S. Army comes out here asking questions, we're not gonna change this story, you hear? We may have to answer a few questions right here tonight. Warren's gonna be here pretty quick now, and I know damn well the law's gonna be right behind him, maybe

166

with him, maybe ahead of him. They get all these ambulance calls."

"Say, Bonney, how about Turnip?" Brad asked. "He's gonna be comin' back in here pretty soon."

"Don't worry about him. I'll check him out. He won't say anything. Now the Colonel, he may be something else. I don't know if he was awake or not when that fan fell. I'll have to feel him out on it in the morning."

"Here comes headlights," Ben said, at the window. "Must not be Warren, though. He'd have that siren goin' and the cherry flashin'."

Bonney opened the front door when the car stopped out front. He turned to me and said, "Hey, Johnny, looks like we might have us a little luck. It's Wiley. Wiley Scott. And he's all by himself."

The deputy came in humped over, rubbing his hands. He always reminded me of a turtle in winter, because he wore a heavy Mackinaw with the big collar turned up and his long neck poking forward—a turtle, with a badge and a pistol.

"Hey, Bonney," he said, "I done heard you had yourself a accident out here." His eyes found Akers on the floor and he said, "Well, by god, you did, didn't you? Who is that? Is that Akers?"

"Yeah, it's Norman Akers. I'm afraid he's hurt pretty bad. I was afraid to move 'im."

"He ain't dead, is he?"

"No, he's breathin' pretty good."

"What in hell happened? He ain't shot, is he?"

"Naw, hell no, he ain't shot." I was still sitting on the bar stool, seeing and hearing everything, and yet I don't remember being scared or nervous or especially concerned. I just sat there like a fool, watching and listening to Bonney as usual, hearing him switch over to his seediest grammar when Wiley came in, adjusting down a notch or two, to communicate with Wiley.

". . . and that's all there was to it, Wiley," he was saying. "One minute Norman's standin' up there talkin' pussy and next I know, why, that ol' fan come down and I mean it clobbered him one. Beats the sandstone hell out of me, how it happened."

167

"Well, I'll be damn," Wiley said, bending over Akers.

"Where's Warren? What's takin' 'im so long?"

"He's comin'," Wiley said. "Oughta be toppin' that rise up yonder right now." Wiley stayed beside Akers, watching him, inspecting his head. He said to Bonney, "You sure wasn't nobody just *slugged* ol' Norman."

"Hell yes, I'm sure," Bonney said. "Whatta you think my fan's doin' smashed all over this floor?"

"Yeah, that's right. Well, ol' Norman don't look too good, does he? He sure ain't makin' none of his speeches right now." Wiley produced a false shudder. "Man, sure is a *cold* sumbitch out there tonight. Whyn't we have us a beer, Bonney, while we wait for Warren?"

Bonney moved quickly toward the bar. "Maybe you'd like somethin' with a bite to it, cold night like this." He produced a pint of bourbon, the seal intact.

"Well now," Wiley said, and grinned. Bonney cracked the seal and handed the pint over and Wiley held it up and said, "I reckon I ought to drink to ol' Norman's health. Looks like he needs it." He turned up the bottle and took a long pull. And then another quick one. "Hah! Hoo *wee*, that's good. How can anything tastes so bad be so good?"

"I'm gonna call Warren again," Bonney said. "Looks to me like he oughta been here already."

"He's comin'," Wiley said. And took another pull.

Bonney was right, I thought. Something needed to be done, and soon, about Akers. *He's just going to lie there and die.*

Warren was alone when he came. Bonney helped him with the stretcher. Warren was all business. Asked only necessary questions, short, quick ones, and Bonney answered the same way.

"Wiley," Warren snapped, "call the hospital and tell 'em to get Doc Bartlett over there in a hurry. Tell 'em I'll be there in six, seven minutes, and I need somebody at that door to help me."

He and Bonney carried Akers out and loaded him. The ambulance went screaming up the blacktop.

Wiley had the hospital on the phone. "Hello, who's speakin'? . . . Alice May? Howdy, Alice May. Listen, you gonna have to call Doc Bartlett away from his TV. I'm out at Bonney McCamey's and Warren has just left here with Norman Akers in his meat wagon and Norman shore ain't feelin' too well. Warren said get somebody at the door to help him."

He listened to the phone a few seconds.

"Naw, he ain't havin' no heart attack. He's done been hit over the head with a ceilin' fan. . . . Naw, a *ceilin'* fan, one of these ol' overhead fans out here at Bonney's. . . . Naw, didn't nobody hit him with it, it just fell on 'im. . . . Well, how do you *reckon* I know? I know because I'm out here where it happened, that's how. You better tell Doc to hustle his bustle. Looks to me like ol' Norman might be tryin' to haul off and die on us."

He hung up and took another pull on the bottle and handed it to Bonney. About a third of the pint was gone. "Much obliged," Wiley said. "That sure went good."

"Why don't you just keep it, you want to," Bonney said, holding the bottle out. "I got more."

"Why, all right, thanks. Well, I better get on to the hospital and see what happens." With a loose grin and an exaggerated motion, Wiley pulled one of the huge Mackinaw pockets open and dropped the pint in it. He patted the flap down and went out, dragging the heels of his boots.

When the noise of the patrol car faded, Bonney said, "Let's everybody go on home. I'm closing up."

They were all gone by the time Turnip returned. The boy came in quietly and fell immediately into the routine of helping Bonney close up. He said nothing. He didn't even look at me.

"Did you see anybody? Talk to anybody?" Bonney asked him.

"Naw, I didn't talk to nobody."

"Well, when you get through there, go on out to the house. I got somethin' to talk to you about."

"All right."

Bonney came and stood in front of me. "We get closed up, and Slat comes in, think it'd be a good idea if we went in to the hospital and checked on Norman. Maybe you ought to go too. Be more natural."

I nodded. Yes, it would be more natural. Bonney and I,

going around together, to the feed store, to the auction barn, to the hardware store. . . . It *had* become a natural thing for me to go about with this man, this man I'd come to judge and condemn and— What was that I was going to do?

Put him behind bars, is what you told Midge. And now do you see what he's trying to do? Yes, yes, I see, but it doesn't make sense. It's too crazy. This couldn't be me, here in this place. It's somebody else.

Slat didn't come in the tavern when Hank brought her home. Bonney waited for them to finish their prolonged good night at the door. He told me to sit there and wait. He stayed out in the house maybe five minutes.

"Well, I explained everything to 'em," he said when he got back, "so we haven't got anything to worry about there. And Turnip says the Colonel didn't even mention Norman after he left here. We might be lucky. Colonel's the main one I was worried about. No way to shut that old poot up. You ready? Let's go on in. Are you all right?"

"I suppose."

We got in the truck. Passing Rose-Mama's, Bonney's headlights fell on Elizabeth, Rose-Mama's cow, grazing in the borrow ditch.

"That cow's got out again," I said. "We better stop and get her in."

"Not now," he said. "Later."

"Truck's liable to hit her."

"Hell with that. We got to get on in. Listen, Johnny, I don't know if you realize it, we got ourselves in a little spot here. Do you remember what you did, back there in the place? Do you remember how you hit Norman?"

"I know. I remember."

"Well, you got to get hold of yourself, and go along with that fan falling on him. If he heard those calls, the high sheriff may be at the hospital when we get there."

"There's not any use in making up that story. It won't work."

"It *will* work, dammit, if you'll help me a little. Wiley's on our side. I'm betting he'll stand flat-footed and say he *saw* that fan fall on Norman."

170

"It's stupid. I might just as well tell the truth."

He slowed the truck and turned and looked straight at me.

"Johnny, here's what the truth is—the truth is that damn fan fell and hit Norman on the head. Now I want to hear you say that."

"I can't say that. I don't care. I don't care what happens. Hearing Akers talk back there, what he said, after that I don't care about anything."

He shifted into second and we sailed on toward town. "Hell, I don't even know *what* he said. I wasn't listening. I reckon you had a good reason to do what you did. There's not half a dozen people in this county cares whether Norman gets his skull laid open. But if he doesn't make it, if he dies, hod-oh-mighty, Johnny, you might end up doing time. If he doesn't die, if he pulls through and finds out what happened, the bastard'll stick charges on you."

"That's all right. It doesn't make any difference. I don't care. I hit the son of a bitch and I don't care what happens. What he said back there just about finished everything off for me anyway. When I came here I didn't have much left, not much I cared about, and now I don't have a thing. Nothing makes any sense. The reason I *came* here doesn't even matter now. You don't know, Bonney, why I came here."

"Hell," he said, "why you came here doesn't make a damn. I don't care, and nobody else does. But, man you keep quiet about you not having anything. That's a lot of crap, Johnny. You got *friends* here. *Friends,* you hear? Now, by damn, you listen to me. You've come in here and you've got so you fit, you know? We like you around here. Everybody does. Rose-Mama, she was telling me last night what it's meant to her to have you staying there at her place. And Slat, she likes you, and Barney, and Turnip. All of 'em. They tell me about all those things you do for 'em. Writing those letters for Buck, and helpin' Maudie get her Social Security straight, and going after that medicine for Aunt Kate, and making those phone calls about the Colonel's pension, and doing all that work around Rose-Mama's house. Hell, Johnny, we *need* you around here. You've helped us, and now you got to let us help you."

"But it won't work, Bonney. Even if it did, it wouldn't be right."

"Aw, *come on*, Johnny, don't give me that holy business again. Don't start that scoutmaster crap about what's right and what's wrong. You tell me this—if Norman's all right, if he gets well, you tell me what difference it makes whether somebody hit him with a pool cue or a ceiling fan fell on him or a streak of lightning got him or a horse threw him. What's the difference?"

"Well, the law. The law says there's a difference."

"The law's ass. Law's not always right."

"But standing up there and looking the law in the face and telling a lie. . . . I can't do that."

He almost laughed. "Well, blister my butt, Johnny, you're all mixed up. I never did see such a mixture. Here a mile back you sat there saying nothing makes any difference any more and you don't care what happens, and now here you are saying you can't tell a little old lie, about a fan falling on a friggin' drugstore cowman."

Well, what do you say to that, Mister Scoutmaster?

I said, "All the same, I won't do it."

He stopped arguing for a while. We approached Farley's one traffic light, which quit turning from red to green at ten o'clock every night and began flashing amber. Bonney didn't slow down. He went speeding right on across the Kirby County Courthouse Square, its buildings all dark and lonely except for Spearman's Restaurant which was still showing lights.

"Johnny," he said, "we'll be there in a minute. I want to ask you this—if you won't do it for yourself, how about doing it for me? And for Rose-Mama and Slat and Turnip and the rest. Think about it. If Norman's a goner and you go and spill your guts to the sheriff, there's not but one thing they can call it and that's just plain murder. It'll be a mess. They might close my place. Least it'll do is hurt me, bad."

He turned into the hospital entrance and eased the pickup into neutral and coasted, looking at me for an answer.

"I don't know," I said.

"Then promise me this much. Say you'll keep your mouth shut, at least tonight. Will you do that?"

172

"All right."

"Good. That's fine. We're gonna whip this business. You'll see."

Kirby County Memorial Hospital, a flat-roofed, one-story structure. Twenty beds and a staff of two doctors and oxygen piped to every room and Miss Alice May Vaughn on night duty at the desk.

"Hey, Alice May," Bonney greeted her. "How in the world's my ol' sweetheart doin'?" He leaned across the desk, stretching a full yard, and gave her a loud smack right on the mouth, north and south.

"Bonney McCamey, you idiot," she said. But she grinned.

"Alice May," he said, with his best smile, "I'm fixin' to run off to Kansas City and see the sights and I come to get you and take you along, because I want me a pure woman and I figure you're the only one left in Kirby County. So if you'll just——"

"Bonney McCamey, you shut your mouth, you idiot." She was still grinning, though. A thin, pinch-faced woman. About Bonney's age, I guessed.

"Say, Alice May," bending close to her, "you 'member that time when we was in high school and I had 'at ol' blue Ford and I picked you up walkin' home from the football game and we went out on Buttermilk Road? You 'member that?"

She turned beet-red and reached across the desk and slapped him. But not very hard. He didn't even flinch.

"You talk too much, Bonney McCamey. Now you state your business here or go on back to your beer joint."

"Why, we've come to see how Norman Akers is doin'. He got a little lick on his head out at my place a while ago."

"Yes, he certainly did," Alice May said. I searched her face for a clue. *Is he dead or alive?*

"Could we talk to him just a minute?" Bonney asked.

"*Talk* to him!" she exclaimed. "Do you imagine it's afternoon visiting hours? Even if it was, you'd do mighty well getting any conversation out of Mr. Akers now."

Does that mean he's dead?

"Then how about us just lookin' in on him a second," Bonney

173

said, making a move to walk down the hall. "Ol' Norman's a good friend of ours. We're real worried about him."

Alice May came curving out from behind the desk and grabbed him by the arm. "You're not supposed to go in any of the rooms this time of night."

"What room's Norman in?" Bonney asked.

"Sixteen, but you're not going in there."

Bonney's long right arm wrapped itself around Alice May's waist and, without much choice, she began walking with him down the hall. "Alice May," he said, "you know what I always used to tell all them ol' boys? I always told 'em you had the prettiest pair of legs in Farley High School"—he leaned backward and looked down behind her—"and damn if I don't believe you *still* do."

"Shut up, you fool," she said, and giggled a little, and kept walking with him down the hall. Bonney's left hand trailed behind him and beckoned. That was for me. It said, "Come on. Let's have a look at Norman."

I followed and joined Bonney standing in the door of Room Sixteen. Alice May was fussing with the covers on the bed. Akers was a long lumpy mountain range under the blanket. His big stomach rose and fell steadily. His head was a round ball of white bandaging.

We stood silently and looked at him for half a minute and then Alice May pushed Bonney on the chest and said, "Now go. He's not supposed to have visitors."

We all went back up the hall.

"Ol' Norman looks all right," Bonney said. "He looks pretty good to me."

"I guess he's doing well enough," Alice May said, "considering he's got a fresh haircut and six hemstitches in his scalp and a severe concussion and a possible skull fracture."

"Is Doc Bartlett still here?"

"No."

"What'd he say about Norman?"

"He said Mr. Akers wasn't going to be chasing around after those Hereford cows for a good long while."

"But he ain't gonna die, I don't reckon."

"I don't think so."

174

Back at the desk Alice May gave Bonney a suspicious little grin and said, "Bonney, you're a fraud. Norman Akers is not your friend. He's not *any*body's friend around here. I know why you're so concerned about him. He got hurt out there in that beer joint of yours and you're afraid you'll get the pants sued off you."

Now it was Bonney grinning. "Alice May, you ain't only got pretty legs, you're a smart girl to boot. Listen, tomorrow when Norman comes around and joins the world, you tell him I was here, will you? Tell him me and Johnny Lancaster was here, late at night, to check on him, and we'll be back pretty soon."

She nodded. And Bonney gave her another loud smack on the mouth and this time she didn't slap him.

We were already outside, on the walk, when Alice May pushed the door open and called, "Say, I meant to tell you, if you see your friend the deputy you better tell him his boss man's looking for him. Sheriff's been calling here, trying to find him."

Bonney seemed concerned. "How long since he left here?"

"Maybe an hour."

"He didn't act drunk, did he?"

"He didn't act sober."

"All right, thanks, Alice May. And listen, next time you get a night off, why you come out to see me. Buy you a beer." Then to me. "Come on, let's hustle. We got to find Wiley before the sheriff does." He peeled out of the hospital parking lot.

He knew exactly where to look. "Wiley gets too much to drink, he'll generally park back behind the Mills and sleep." Bonney whipped the pickup across a set of railroad sidings and bounced down between two strings of boxcars. Presently Wiley's patrol car was in the headlights of the truck. The car was parked with the right front fender jammed almost up under a boxcar.

"That sorry bastard," Bonney said. "He musta tried to chug-a-lug that whole bottle. I shoulda given him just half a pint."

Then Bonney had Wiley by the lapels of that big Mackinaw and I thought the deputy's long neck would surely break, from

175

the shaking he got. "Wake up, you sorry drunk son of a bitch," Bonney muttered. "Where's that bottle?"

Wiley's answer was to bend over a fender of the patrol car and vomit. Bonney fished under the front seat and found the pint. He held it up, then flipped in into the darkness, and it shattered against the side of a boxcar.

When Wiley straightened up, coughing and spitting, Bonney grabbed him again. "Now listen to me, you sorry bastard, you've got to get on that radio and call in to the sheriff, you hear? And you damn well better talk sober and say the right things. Now, tell me, what do you remember about what happened out there at my place tonight?"

Wiley rubbed his mouth. His neck seemed to protrude a full foot forward, from the collar of his Mackinaw. The turtle. "You mean 'bout Norman, gettin' hurt."

"Gettin' hurt how?"

"Hit . . . ol' fan fell, and hit 'im."

"How do you know?"

Wiley spat. "You tol' me, I reckon."

"I told you no such a damn thing."

"Then I musta seen it . . . I was there?"

"Don't ask me, *tell* me. I don't know whether you were there or not, you sorry-ass drunk excuse of a lawman."

"Well . . . sure I was there . . . damn right . . . and I seen the fan fall, too."

Bonney pushed the deputy toward the patrol car door. "Now you get in there and call in, and for the rest of the night you stay awake and look sharp and keep that radio on, and if you take one more drink of *any*thing tonight I swear I'll beat your bowels out."

We got in the truck and waited for Wiley to call. Then Bonney followed him to the square. He seemed to be driving all right, so we headed back toward home.

"That was close," he told me. "We needed ol' Wiley a *little* bit drunk but he almost went too far. He gets *too* drunk and the sheriff finds him, all Wiley knows to do is tell the truth. But I think now he's mixed up just about right. He thinks he saw that fan fall. He *knows* he saw it, and I'll bet all the lawyers in hell and Philadelphia can't make him say

176

he didn't see it." He whistled, on the way home. "We got the law on our side, Johnny."

It was long past midnight when he stopped at Rose-Mama's. He cut the engine and we sat and looked down the slope. The norther had swept the clouds south and the wind had laid and the moon, almost full, hung over the tavern.

"Man, that moon's bright," he said. "Bet you could stand out there without a light and read the want-ads in Harvey's paper."

He pointed down the slope. "See that sort of light-colored spot, way over yonder other side of the branch on the hill? That's Eddie bull. He's standin' up there pawin' at the moon. He likes moonlight. Makes his peter hard. Then look back down yonder on the road, just this side of the culvert. See something movin' there, real slow? That's Elizabeth. She's found her some grazin' down there in that ditch. Reminds me, we got to get her back up here before we turn in." He whistled. "O'Riley's Daughter." Hummed a bit. "It's real pretty, Johnny, don't you think? In the moonlight?"

The scene, he meant. It was. I hadn't thought of it before, but it was. The tavern, squatting low and comfortable down there among the trees. Then Bonney's little house, and the barn, and the rolling hills beyond, blanketed in that soft glow.

How he loves this place, this little piece of the earth that he commands, which seems so secure in the moonlight and the shadows. Is it possible? Can it be true that this very night I heard Norman Akers say those awful things right down there under that tavern roof beneath those trees?

"Well," I said, "I've really screwed everything up."

"Don't let it bother you. We got it whipped, I think. Norman's gonna be all right, looks like. Don't worry."

"Yeah, *you* can say don't worry. It wasn't you that hit Akers."

"Hell, Johnny, remember you're the guy doesn't care what happens any longer. Man like that oughtn't to worry about anything."

A stray cloud, a small one, trailed across the face of the moon. We watched, and waited for the shadows to pass.

"You ever been in love, Bonney?"

177

He laughed. "Damn right. Ever Saturday night, and sometimes Wednesdays."

"No, I mean really. Like when a woman is all that matters to you. Where everything you ever thought was good is wrapped up in one female human being, and it doesn't even have much to do with sex, because all that's important is just lying beside her, and touching her hand, and knowing that she's beautiful and good and that she loves you, and feels the same way. It's a miracle, when it's that way. It's almost *too* good, so good you wake up at night and you want to turn on the light so you can look at her, to see if it's really true. Have you ever had it that way?"

The question bothered him. He didn't answer it. He twisted his body there behind the wheel of the pickup and lit a cigarette, in that sweeping, smooth motion of his, the pack coming out of his shirt pocket and the thumb and forefinger bringing out the lighter and then everything going back in its place, all so smooth. "You're saying *you* had it that way."

"Yes."

"Your wife."

"Yes."

"She's dead."

"Yes."

"How?"

"A sick stomach." I said it that way, to myself sometimes, when I felt especially bitter about Eva's death. "She got one of these virus things, and got to vomiting, and she hemorrhaged. Blood vessels in her brain. It killed her. One day she was alive and the next she was dead and I was in New Mexico when it happened."

He took a long, deep drag on his cigarette and exhaled and said quietly, "Jesus." He spoke the word almost reverently, as if he wasn't cursing but actually calling the name of the Lord.

"Except for Midge, that woman was the only thing I cared about. Then afterward, what mattered to me was remembering her, and how it all was. And now . . . Akers . . . he's even taken that away from me."

"How do you mean?"

"That story he was telling . . . before I hit him."

178

"I wasn't paying much attention. He was just talking pussy."

"He was talking about Eva. About my wife."

I could feel him staring at me. "How do you know? Did he call her name?"

"No, he didn't have to. He knew Eva, all right, and he knew her brother in Baton Rouge. He did call her brother's name."

"Well, you know those stories. They're all lies. You take that yarn Ben told, about the woman in the Buick, and going to Florida. If I had to bet that story I'd say she picked him up, all right, and he drove for her, and the rest of it wasn't anything but what Ben *wished*."

"Akers knew my wife. He said too many things about her that were right."

"When's all this supposed to happened?"

"Long time ago."

"Right after you got married?"

"Before we got married. Even before I met her."

"Before you met her? Well, hell's afire, Johnny, you don't hold against her what she did before you *met* her, do you?"

"I guess I do. I hold it against Akers, anyway."

"That doesn't make any sense to me."

"No, I guess it doesn't make sense. But that doesn't change it."

His cigarette went cartwheeling out of the truck window onto the blacktop and he said, "Well, let's get Miss Elizabeth back up here and then hit the quilts."

It took us thirty minutes to herd the cow back up the slope and get her in the lot. A light came on at the back of the house and Rose-Mama appeared on the porch in her outing gown. "What in hell you boys doin' up so early?"

"It ain't early, Rose-Mama," Bonney said. "It's late. Me and Johnny been out chasin' females all night and the only one we caught was Elizabeth, grazin' down yonder at the culvert. Now you owe us half an hour's labor."

"Charge it to the dust," she said sleepily, "and let the rain settle it." And went back to bed.

When the sun drew its first shadows from the pines across Sam's grave, I was still sitting at the window looking over the

179

hills. I'd tried to sleep a time or two but I'd keep seeing Eva in a motel room with Norman Akers and my guts would take turns freezing and burning and I'd have to sit up to get my breath.

Come on now, man, you're making too much out of this. Norman Akers is a liar. All men are liars when they talk about women.

Yes, but he knew too much. He described Eva, almost perfectly. He *knew* her, I tell you.

All right, so he knew her. That doesn't mean he took her to bed. Him saying it doesn't make it true.

I know, I know, but the way he described her. Her hair and her skin and the way he said she stood there, and what she said. *I thought maybe you'd like to take me to a motel.* Almost exactly the same words she said to me, that night at home, not a week before she died. *Eva, Eva, how could you?*

Aw, come off it, will you? So what if it's true? What if she did go to bed with him? That was before she ever saw you.

But not long. He said she was nineteen. It wasn't but a year before I met her.

So what? You're not making sense, man. Eva's gone and you're jealous of her, even jealous of her being dead, and now you're trying to be jealous of what she did before you ever heard of her.

But Norman Akers! That sleazy, fat-butted bastard with his big belly and his hand-tooled boots and fat old lips. I wish I'd hit the son of a bitch harder. I wish I'd killed him.

Oh, sure. That'd be nice. Then you could have yourself a *banquet* of self-pity, spending the rest of your life writing letters to Midge from behind those red brick walls at Huntsville. You've caused a big enough mess now. Akers may die yet, you know. Or he might never completely recover. Or if he does, he'll probably find out what really happened. Then you'll have everybody drawn into it. Bonney and Turnip and Slat and Brad, all of them, because they're going to lie for you and save your hide. What you ought to do, right now, before it goes too far, you ought to go tell Bonney it's no deal, that you're going on into town and see the sheriff and tell him what happened.

Maybe I will. I might do that.

180

No you won't. You're going to let it ride, just because Bonney wants to do it his way. Seems to me you're doing everything Bonney's way now.

Aw, go to hell. Lay off me.

You're a real winner, man. You come in here all full of wrath and vengeance to nail a thief and you end up sleeping in the same barn with him.

But Bonney's not guilty. *He* didn't take that money from the Old Man.

You say he didn't. I say he did.

Well, what do you want me to do? Ruin the only man who's trying to help me?

Then Thursday. The Farley *Weekly Rocket*. And the news according to Harvey Wilks. The story was on Page One, with a two-column headline:

AKERS GETS FANNED

Last Tuesday Night Norman Akers that has his Akers Acres Ranch east of town and raises fancy Hereford cows was standing in a bad place out at Bonney McCamey's. A fan fell and hit him on the head and he is still in the hospital in bed with a special nurse. He suffered concussion and six stitches. I was by the hospital to see Lee Ann's new baby weighing 8 lbs and 2 oz, Lee Ann's husband Roscoe delivers the *Rocket*, and I never saw as many people in one hospital room, Norman Akers room, I mean. His wife Mrs. Norman Akers was there and three grand children and his daughter Mrs. Sanders from West Texas, and his boy Mr. Winton Akers that's a lawyer but runs one of Mr. Akers furniture stores in Shreveport. Mr. Winton Akers told me he is making a investigation into how his daddy was hurt because it seems funny to him that a fan will fall on you without any reason for it. The sheriff sent Wiley Scott out to Bonney's to ask questions with Mr. Winton Akers. Wiley was out there when it happened and said he was sober and saw the fan fall. Plus Wiley, nine more witnesses saw it fall and hit Norman and nobody knows why. These were Buck Thornton, Brad Bradley, Ben Ashley,

Carlos Freeman, Barney Teague, Bonney, Turnip the colored boy that works for Bonney, Uncle Batey Hall and Johnny Lancaster that lives with my old friend Jim Whitaker's widow Grace. It doesn't sound like any funny business to me, because of so many witnesses that saw it all. Mr. Peters that ran the *Rocket* for 42 yrs use to say if you can get 2 people to see one thing alike your lucky, and here you have 10. Norman has been around Farley about 4 years and spent a lot of money. He never did advertise his cows in the *Rocket* but thats his own business. He looks all right to me. He said his head hurts some and is dizzy when he gets up to go to the toilet but his worse trouble is he cant remember even going out to Bonney's on Tuesday night or anything except bringing a Apaloosa colt to his place about 4 o'clock, which was a birthday present for his grand son. I asked Dr. Bartlett and he said sometimes when a person gets a lick on their head like that they dont remember anything for a good while after or before. Wiley said the investigation is closed already. Accidents of all kinds happen in Kirby County ever day, last week you know Everet Shaw got his finger cut off at the Mills, he is back at work already.

11.

Before Christmas, the rain came. It fell lightly but steadily for two days and three nights. Bonney's hardware-store rain gauge on the corral cornerpost measured seven inches in one forty-eight hour period. The little branch by the tavern overloaded the culvert and filled the ditch and put water a foot deep over the blacktop.

When the weather was wet and cold the Regulars were always in faithful attendance at Bonney's. On unpleasant nights the tavern represented warmth and comfort and security and friendship. I felt at home there. I'd stand near the pool table and lean on my cue stick and watch the Regulars huddled close around their long table. With all their faults, there wasn't anything to do about them but to love them. What else could you do with this assortment of strange humans, who had perjured themselves, lied to keep me out of trouble? And evidently not a one of them had an ounce of doubt that they'd done anything but exactly the right thing. It was wrong, all wrong. But it was done.

When it became clear to the Regulars that Slat and Hank were in love, they all fell in love with the idea. I confess I did too. A young couple in love is a beautiful thing. I'd forgotten how beautiful. It had happened to Midge and Arch almost under my nose, but with them it seemed to be a gradual thing that grew over a period of two or three years. With Slat and Hank it was lightning.

Hank came to the tavern almost every night. He sat on a stool at the open end of the bar while Slat worked and he waited for her to pass by and smile at him and reach out and pat his arm. Sometimes when there was a lull in Slat's duties, she and Hank danced. Somebody would feed the jukebox and punch a slow number and one of the Regulars would call, "Hey, Slat, how 'bout you and Hank dancin' one for us?"

No other couple would go on the floor. Slat and Hank would dance slow and dreamy, and the Regulars would watch and smile and you could tell they were proud, just as if they had arranged this beautiful match, as if they were all parents, ever so pleased.

"By god," Ben said once, after Hank and Slat had danced, "the way they're stuck on one another, if I could bottle that stuff and put it on the market, inside a week I'd be rich as Junior Farley."

A week before school was to dismiss for Christmas, I wandered back in the kitchen and found Slat on Barney's Couch, on her knees, staring out at the rain.

"Hey. Where's Hank tonight?"

She turned and slipped down in a sitting position and smiled, a little sadly, I thought. "He's at a meeting, in Austin. I just hope he's not caught out in all this rain."

"Well, you know Hank, the world's best driver. He'll be OK."
She nodded. "Johnny?"

"Yes."

"We want to get married."

"Of course you do. Everybody knows that."

The sad smile again. "But I'm worried . . . about Bonney."

"You think he'll object?"

"I'm not sure. What do you think?"

"I don't think he'll try to stop you."

She looked down at her hands in her lap and rubbed her ring finger. Bonney had bought her a big costume ring and she had worn it for several weeks on her third finger left. Now she had moved it over to the right hand. It had made a visible white circle around her ring finger.

"No," she said, "I don't think he'll try to stop us, either. But I don't know. I'm all mixed up. Do you know, Johnny, that too *many* good things can happen to a person, and they happen so quick that it's almost more than the person can stand? And it's more than the person can keep, too, because all of a sudden the person finds out she's got to make a choice and can't keep all the good things, and law, it hurts. It just hurts to think about it."

"Nothing's happened to you, Slat, that you don't deserve. What are you worried about giving up?"

"Why," she said, "living here, with Bonney and Turnip. And you and Maudie and Rose-Mama. For a while, living here was the only really nice thing that ever happened to me and I thought, well, I wouldn't ever want anything else except just being here with people I love. And then Hank . . . I love him so much, Johnny, I just ache about it all over. But if we get married, I can't keep living here."

"No, I wouldn't think that would be a very satisfactory arrangement. But then you're not going to move to Alaska, for crying out loud. You'll be close."

"Hank doesn't want me to keep working here. I want to keep working."

"Well, I'd say that's a reasonable attitude, on Hank's part, I mean. A man's usually not too keen on having his bride work in a beer joint."

"But Maudie does, and she's married."

184

Yes, but you're not going to be married the way Maudie is,
child. I didn't say anything.

"I want to get married awful bad," she went on, "but I don't
want to leave here and not come back. I don't think I could.
I don't think I ought to. It wouldn't be right."

"Well, things'll work out. You'll see."

"Nobody can know, Johnny, what me living here means.
And having a room? I never had a room before, or clothes.
Won't anybody ever know how I lived before I came here.
I lived in hell, just plain hell, and I won't ever tell a soul how
awful it was."

"Why did you come here to Bonney's, when you left home?"
She stood and turned back to the window.

"The first time I saw Bonney," she said quietly, "I was about
eleven, maybe twelve years old. He came to our house over
yonder in the Blackjack. That day I thought he was the nicest
person I ever met. He smiled at me. I mean a real smile, friendly
and kind. He came back to our kitchen. I was back there making
hot-water cornbread. He rubbed my head, like you see him
rub Turnip's head now sometimes, just sort of tousling up your
hair a little, you know. And he said, 'Hello, little girl. What's
for supper?' And I told him hot-water cornbread. He said,
'What else?' I told him that was all, because there wasn't anything else. He stayed there in the kitchen a few minutes, watching me, and then he said, 'Well, pretty girl, there's not anything
the matter with hot-water cornbread, but it's just not enough
for supper. You hold off, now, and I'll be back in about an
hour.' You know what I did? When he drove off I got my
pencil and I wrote what he said, all his words, on a paper sack.
Because he called me pretty. *Pretty!* I kept that piece of paper
for a long time and I'd get it out and read the words sometimes. . . ." She fished a tissue out of her pocket and blew her
nose.

"Did he come back?" I asked. "Did he come back that night?"
She nodded. "He came back with a carload of groceries.
Chickens and ham and potatoes and turnips and greens and
flour. . . . I can't remember what all. Bacon, eggs, milk. And
candy, too. He brought all that stuff in there to our house and
when he set it down he tousled my hair again and smiled and he

185

said, 'Listen, pretty girl, if you ever need any help, if you ever need a friend, you go over yonder on the county road to Mrs. Whitaker's house and you tell her to find Bonney McCamey, you hear?' He made me say his name, out loud, just like I might not remember it. He left then. He came back a few times and then he didn't come any more and I didn't see or hear about him for a long time, several years, until he came back here and built this place and went in business. Anyhow, you asked me why I came here when I left home. Well, that's why, because he *told* me to come, except I don't reckon he remembers it."

"Where was your father then, when Bonney was coming to your house?"

"Oh, he was in and out, here and there. He'd go off sometimes for a week, ten days sometimes. I don't know where."

"But why was Bonney coming to your house?" I thought of Turnip's story, in some ways very similar to Slat's. "Was he coming there trying to buy land?"

She fixed those big eyes on my face and without any sadness or embarrassment she said, "Why, no. He wasn't trying to buy land. He was coming to see my mother, to sleep with her."

She turned back to the window and I got up and kneeled on Barney's Couch beside her and we watched the rain.

"Where is your mother now?"

"I don't know." She shrugged. "She shows up now and then. Last I heard she was in Houston."

At the sound of the front door she pushed off the couch and went to serve a couple of customers. I stayed in the kitchen and presently she returned and said, "Johnny, will you do me a favor?"

"I'll try."

"Talk to Bonney about Hank and me. Will you?"

"Talk to him about you and Hank getting married?"

"Yes. Will you?"

"Hold on, now. Seems to me if anybody's going to talk to Bonney it ought to be Hank and you."

"Yes, but Bonney puts a lot of weight on what you think. I've heard him say so. Even if you're just there, with Hank and me, when we talk to him, it'll help us. Will you do that?"

"Well, if it's all right with Hank."

"It's all right with him. I've already asked him."

So we hatched a plot, to spring it on him the next day.

"Get married?" he said, when the three of us cornered him out in the barn. He said it just as if the possibility hadn't occurred to him.

"Yes, we wanted to tell you," Hank said. "To ask you . . ."

"You mean *some*time. Later on."

"No," Slat said firmly. "Pretty soon."

He was sitting on a bale of hay, trying to break loose some rusted bolts on an old trailer hitch, using a couple of wrenches. "You mean like in the spring? After school's out?"

"No," Slat said, hanging in there tough. "Right away. Before Christmas."

"Christmas! Hodamighty, that's not two weeks off. That's a pretty big rush, you ask me."

It seemed to me he was acting strange about it. He was bound to have known it was coming. Everybody knew. It was hanging on the air. You could feel it. Everybody around the tavern was talking about it.

For what seemed a full minute he tinkered with the hitch, kept his eyes down and said nothing.

Then at last, "Well, I don't reckon it's any of my business to say Yes or No. You're both over twenty-one and anyway I ain't your old man."

Hank tried again. "Well, we just didn't want to do anything, plan anything, without telling you."

Bonney looked up and tore into Hank with one of his cold-eyed stares and he said, "Well, hell, you want me to give you some kind of written permission?" Why, he was really angry. Suddenly he flung one of the wrenches, apparently just out of frustration or anger. Flung it with that backhanded, wrist-flipping motion. He threw it harder than he meant to. It bounced off the tool chest and ricocheted toward Slat and missed her ankle maybe an inch. Even if it had hit her it wouldn't have hurt very much. But I saw the horror in his eyes when he watched that wrench sail by her foot.

And she understood, at that second.

187

I suppose Slat always understood him better than any of us. Suddenly she sprawled on him, her thin arms wrapped around his chest and her dark head buried inside his jacket. Bonney gathered her to him with those long arms and sat there patting her and rocking back and forth. They didn't say a word, because they couldn't, but you knew they were getting everything understood right there on that bale of hay.

While Hank and I watched, I dismissed the final trace of doubt I had about what sort of relationship Bonney and Slat had, living together in that house. You have to understand there was a lot of talk about that after Harvey Wilks wrote in the *Rocket* that Bonney built a room onto his house for Slat. What else, the human mind being what it is, were people going to think when a man in his middle thirties brought a twenty-two-year-old woman into his home? Other than Charlotte Ord, not a one of the Regulars had ever mentioned it or provided any hint that they even thought about it. But it had been pretty clear what Mrs. Junior Farley thought. I wished she could have seen them sitting on that bale of hay. Slat had her legs drawn up in his lap like a baby and he hung his chin over her head and held her close and rubbed her hair.

"Now listen . . ." He cleared his throat and started over. "Now you listen to me, baby. Of course you're gonna get married. It's just exactly the right thing, I know that. I knew when I put you on that school bus, some old boy was gonna spot you and stick a ring on your finger. Hank here did it just a little bit quickern I thought, is all. It's all right. It's fine. I'm not such an old fool that I thought you were gonna be staying here with me and Turnip the rest of your life. Now you hush. Everything's gonna be fine. You can get all hitched up and you and Hank'll have you a little place to yourselves, and your room, it'll still be here, and when Hank goes off to those school teacher meetings of his, why you can come back and spend the night with us and . . ."

Hank interrupted. "And I was just thinking, Bonney, I'll still be driving the bus and she can ride out here with me every day and I can leave her off to see you, and visit, and then pick her up on the way back." He talked eagerly, like

190

a schoolboy, and he looked so young standing there saying that.

"There you are, you listen to Hank," Bonney said. "You're not gonna be far away."

When she could talk she said, "But I want to keep working. Hank doesn't want me to work any more."

"Well, of course he doesn't," Bonney said. "Of course he doesn't want you working in a beer joint. But that won't mean you can't come to see us. And listen, we're gonna toss you a wedding, hoo boy, it'll make those Farley women bust their corsets. We'll get the Methodist Church and rent the whole damn Farley Country Club and . . ."

"I want to get married here," she said, nodding back at the tavern. "Right in yonder, in Bonney's Place, in that beer joint."

He laughed. "Why, hodamighty, girl, you can't get married in a beer joint. Hell, no."

"The hell I can't."

"Now don't say hell. You need to get married in a church."

"It's a woman's choice where she gets married." She was sitting up on his knees now, mopping at her nose with his handkerchief. "I say right here in this beer joint."

He laughed again. I think it pleased him. "Well, now, Hank might holler calf rope on that. Hank?"

"I don't care," he said. "Anywhere. And the sooner the better."

"Next Saturday," Slat said.

"All right, by damn, we'll do it. We'll hire us a string band and——"

"No, I want it just the way it is now. We can put 'Here Comes the Bride' on the jukebox and we'll get Rose-Mama to fix us some flowers and that's all we'll need."

"Whatever you say, but we'll throw us a feed, a celebration. We'll make this bunch of tight-pockets around here cough up a flock of presents for you." He put back his head and laughed, and Slat laughed, and Hank did, and so did I. "Come on, let's go in and tell the bunch we're gonna have us a wedding. Hell, we'll call Harvey and he'll put it in the paper for us."

191

He grabbed Slat and swung her over his shoulder, like he was carrying a sack of feed. He popped her a hard one right on her fanny, which must have hurt twice as bad as the wrench would have if it had hit her. He put his arm around Hank, and they walked toward the back door of the tavern.

And so that's where we had the wedding—in the beer joint. Maudie, an excellent seamstress, made Slat's wedding dress. White satin, and long. With a veil, as Buck Thornton said, "so damn big you could seine enough crawdads with it to bait ever trotline on the Chickenhawk."

The wedding dress was Bonney's idea. "Ain't nobody gettin' married in *my* beer joint without they wear a long white dress."

All the Regulars considered the long dress to be just exactly right. But not Charlotte: "My god, a formal wedding in a beer joint. And that white dress, it kills me. Who ever heard of a virgin coming out of the Blackjack? There's no such animal." She was careful not to let Bonney hear her saying that.

Slat made the announcement that both Rose-Mama and Maudie would "stand up with me."

"Two matrons of honor?" said Charlotte, and laughed. "You can't have two matrons of honor."

"I damn sure can," Slat said.

"Don't say damn, Slat," Bonney corrected her, and then turned to Charlotte. "She damn sure *can* have two. She can have six if that's how many she wants."

Most of the Regulars came forward with offers to loan things for the ceremony. Buck offered the use of his "Baptist Bible."

"Slat, it'd look mighty grand for the weddin'," he said. "It's biggern the Book of Knowledge. Weighs fourteen pounds. My daddy weighed it on cotton scales one time."

"You don't need no Bible to get married," Ben said.

And Carlos: "Well, it'd make things more revrent, seems like, to have a Bible that way."

Then Ben: "If you get that red-nose justice of the peace out here to do the marryin', he won't know what a Bible's for. He'll likely figure it's a wish book from Montgomery and

Ward's. You better get the preacher if you're gonna have Bibles."

The question of preacher versus justice of the peace hadn't been settled. There was a lot of discussion about it.

Uncle Batey had an opinion. "I don't see no reason to ring in a judge, or a preacher, either, to tie the knot. Bonney, why'nt *you* just do the marryin'? You done a good job on Sam's funeral and there's mighty little difference between buryin' and marryin'."

A cackle from Ben. "Why, jeescries, Uncle Batey, Bonney can't marry nobody. You got to have a license for work like that. If Bonney did it, Slat and Hank wouldn't be married legal."

"Then Sam Hobbs ain't buried legal," Uncle Batey said.

"Hell, Uncle Batey, the law don't care nothin' about people dyin'. A damn ape from Africa could preach at a funeral and the victim wouldn't be no more dead and buried if he had a Catholic pope doin' his talkin'. But a weddin', now that's a different thing. The law wants a record of it, and a license, all signed by a preacher or a legal judge."

"Well, I don't reckon that's true, not for a minute," Uncle Batey said. "When me and Kate was sixteen, her daddy didn't take us to no judge to get married, or a preacher either. He just taken us over to Tatum Bentley's gristmill. Tatum wasn't no judge, and he wasn't much closer to a preacher than that ape of yours. But he taught Sunday school in Tennessee before he come to Texas, and prayed a good bit, and he only just said a few words while me and Kate stood up by the side of each other under a chinaberry tree and that's all there was to it."

"Then you ain't married, and never was," Ben said. "Not legal."

"Well, I expect I'd like to hear you tell that to Kate."

"All the same you ain't married."

Carlos laughed. "How about that, Uncle Batey? You and Aunt Kate's been livin' in sin, all this time."

"Well, we ain't lived in very much of it lately."

Bonney and I played pool and kept quiet and spent a lot of time back in the pasture bouncing around in the pickup and looking at his cattle. He never tired of driving pastures, jumping stumps, looking at those cows.

"How about going with me to Norman's?" he said, two days before the ceremony. "I think it'd be a good idea if we invited him to the wedding."

I went, but it wasn't pleasant. I didn't suppose I'd ever meet Akers again without seeing him in a motel room with Eva.

We'd gone to see him twice when he was in the hospital. Bonney had stayed an hour both times, being extra friendly and accommodating. He almost groveled before Akers. I hated to see it but he said it was just the smart thing to do. And it was working. Akers thrived on all that attention from Bonney. He didn't remember anything about That Night, and he was recovering. If he meant to sue, to make trouble of any kind, he was hiding it well.

Akers Acres. The words were painted a foot tall on the sign over the entrance to Akers' ranch. "That's got to be the crappiest name for a place I ever heard," Bonney said, driving under the sign and up the winding road to the house. A two-story red brick, with four white columns in front. Akers' "country place." I guessed it cost him at least a hundred thousand.

Neither of us had met Akers' wife. She never came to the tavern and in fact seldom accompanied Akers to the ranch. And we'd missed her on both visits to the hospital.

She met us at the door. A large, round-faced woman. About fifty-five, I figured. A little overweight and fighting it hard. The loose flesh on her neck said she was dieting but the seat of her oriental pant suit said she had a long way to go yet. And her face said she wasn't glad to see us.

But Bonney conquered her. He did it in two minutes, using his grin and his backwoodsiest tongue.

"Miz Akers, it sure is nice to finely meet you. Bless your heart, I been *tellin'* ol' Norman I wished he'd bring you by my place when he comes. I told him I just bleeved he was hidin' you *out* all the time, and me needin' somethin' over there at my place to help the scenery, and give it some class. Well, now I got to give him credit. I don't *blame* ol' Norman for not lettin' all these other fellas get a look at you, because——"

It was enough to make you vomit. *Look out Bonney the syrup is dripping off your chin.*

But it worked. It always did. Not so much that silly speech, which no intelligent person would swallow. It was his god-damned sensuous style that got them, his wholehearted dedication of himself, for the moment, to the person before him. He swallowed the person up, with that ever-loving whatever-it-was. He could do it to a six-year-old child or a seventy-five-year-old woman. He did it to Rose-Mama, to Maude, to Charlotte, to every woman he needed or wanted to conquer. *He even did it to Mrs. Junior Farley and that must have been a real challenge.*

"Norman's doing fairly well. He's up and around now, but the doctor won't let him drive yet. He has dizzy spells occasionally. . . ." She was answering Bonney's question but talking . . . well, a little vague, and distant, because she was studying Bonney's face. She was reaching way back inside herself, back about twenty years and bringing forth a little soft-eyed smile that must have been very nice to see when she was younger. She ignored me. I could trace the route of her eyes as they moved from Bonney's hairline, down his forehead to the white scar in his brow, lingered along his jaw and then on down the length of him to his flat-heeled rough-out boots he wore in cold weather. "What an interesting man," her eyes said, but then she caught herself and her face stiffened. "Norman's in the den. He'll be glad to see you."

He was. He looked healthy enough to me. He brought out a bottle, flashing the label to show it was expensive Tennessee sour mash, and fixed us a drink, himself.

"Man, Norman, now that's real *sippin'* whiskey," Bonney said, and leaned back and stretched his long legs out and added, "I wonder what the *poor* folks are drinkin'." And of course that pleased Akers.

"The reason we're here," Bonney went on, "plus checkin' on Norman, we're gonna have us a weddin' at my place and we want both yawl to come. It's Saturday, at eleven o'clock in the mornin'. Our little girl, Slat, she's gonna marry that school teacher of hers and we'll have plenty to eat and a real big celebration. We won't have no black-label Jack like this, but we'll have plenty of nice cold beer, all on the house, and we'll sure be lookin' for you to come."

"Why, that's nice of you, Mr. McCamey," Mrs. Akers said. "And we thank you, but I'm not sure Norman will feel up to a wedding."

We didn't stay long. Mrs. Akers followed us—followed Bonney—all the way out to the truck. He stood by the cab and took her hand and held it and gave her his parting shot. "Now Miz Akers, you listen here, whether Norman can come or not, I want *you* to come. I'll come over here, personal, and get you. I'll clean all the dog hair out of this truck and wash it off and you and me'll walk into that weddin' party all armed up, how about that?"

She flushed like a high school girl, and I swear to God I bet Bonney could have reached out and zipped that oriental blouse down over her big bosom and unhooked her brassiere and she would have just stood there loving it, his victory over Mrs. Norman Akers was that complete.

It embarrased me a little because he was doing it for me, because we had to have Mr. and Mrs. Norman Akers on our side.

On the day of the wedding, I bet myself a dollar that Mrs. Akers was deeply disappointed when her husband felt fine and accompanied her to Bonney's Place for the ceremony.

We never did know how many guests came. Uncle Batey fired six washpots of his stew. Rose-Mama harvested every bloom and every bud in her yard and half the winter greenery. The bar was a solid bank of roses. The pool table became a garden of chrysanthemums. Two or more dozen potted poinsettias stood on the beer tables, which were pushed back against the walls to make room. Buck Thornton's big Baptist Bible was spread open on a card table draped with white linen, in front of the bar. It got in the way during the ceremony and had to be moved, but everybody commented on how nice it looked. "Damn ol' beer joint looks holy as a church house," Ben said.

There was no rehearsal. That was the only decision Bonney was allowed to make. He decided he couldn't wreck a Friday night business rehearsing a wedding. "Anyhow, gettin' married's just the same as parachute jumpin'. No use practicin' somethin' you got to do perfect on the first try."

The guests began coming at ten o'clock. All the Dark Room customers came with their families and stood out back, again with their spoons and tin plates. Harvey Wilks came, looking important with a wad of notepaper in his hand and four pencils poking out of his shirt pocket. *Make way for the press, gentlemen.* The Regulars came dressed exactly the same way they'd dressed for Sam Hobbs' funeral.

Wiley Scott came, and even the high sheriff. Henry Mac-Leash, the tough old cowman who'd been drunk in the tavern that day I arrived, he was there and sat out in the car until time for the ceremony. A woman was with him. I didn't get a look at her until after the wedding, but the woman was Millie. J. R. Wetzel was alone, round and healthy and jocular, carrying a can of Vienna sausages and showing it around as a trophy bought out of Bonney's Place. The two little Flynn boys wore new jeans which I know Bonney bought. Before the ceremony they sat out on the corral fence, quiet and subdued, and I also know they had orders from Slat to stay clean. They would do anything Slat told them. Each held a new airgun across his lap. The guns were rewards, promised and given by Slat, for not missing a day of school for six weeks.

The wedding crowd was made up generally of the same people who came to Sam's funeral. The cowboys, the mill hands, the pulpwood men, the cattle people. Bonney's customers.

And a few, as they say, notable exceptions.

Such as the handsome middle-aged couple I spotted, half an hour before the ceremony. They were walking up to the live oak tree. I guessed them to be Hank's parents. So I alerted Bonney.

He went striding through the crowd toward Mr. and Mrs. Mills. He looked nice. He really did. He'd bought a new suit, dark blue with a pale vertical stripe and it made him look taller and straighter. He'd bought new shoes too, and Maudie

197

had picked out a shirt for him, and a tie, and she'd tied it on him and told him if he went round tugging at the collar and getting his tie all crooked she was going to give him a swift kick in the butt.

I came within a breath of saying to him as we walked toward Hank's parents, "Listen here, dammit, the kind of impression you make on Mr. and Mrs. Mills is important. Important to Hank, and to Slat. So for god's sake, don't be giving Mrs. Mills that I'd-like-to-take-your-pants-off look of yours."

But he did everything exactly right. He didn't even grab her hand and hold it and pat it the way he usually did. He was just folksy and rural enough to seem honest, and proper enough to show he wasn't a barbarian. I was relieved when he delivered Mrs. Mills his now-that-you've-come-we-can-begin smile. Instead of that other one.

And he made them a nice little speech. "Listen, Mrs. Mills, I know you haven't ever been to a wedding at a country café, or eaten stew at a reception, but it's just the way we do things out here and I sure hope you'll understand it. We've got a bunch of real good folks in this bunch, black ones and white ones both. They're my friends, and they're Hank's, and they'll be yours, too, you'll see. I want you to know I'm real proud of Hank. He's a fine young fellow. From the first day I met him, it sure wasn't hard to figure out that he came from good people."

Rose-Mama bellowed at Bonney from one of the tavern windows.

"Well," he grinned, "I see the boss lady's calling. Mrs. Mills, Mr. Mills, if you want anything you don't see, why you just ask Johnny here and he'll get it."

Mrs. Mills followed him with her eyes until he disappeared around the corner of the tavern.

"So that's Bonney," she said.

"Yes, ma'am, that's him."

You could say for Slat and Hank's wedding that it was at least different. And it was a happy wedding, full of smiles and occasional explosions of laughter that seemed to bother nobody other than the minister, Brother Luther. He seemed miserable, and I expect that night he prayed forgiveness for performing a sacred rite while standing in front of a bar. Poor fellow, I felt for him.

Slat was just beautiful, of course, and perfectly calm and smiling. Bonney gave her away. When those two took their first step inside the tavern, I saw Bonney's eyes lock onto something for a moment. He seemed surprised and pleased with what he saw. I searched and found the person he was looking at. Another notable exception in the crowd. It was Mrs. Junior Farley. Now who would have invited Elaine Farley?

The ceremony was so brief, it seemed ridiculous to me that there'd been so much preparation. Brother Luther said the magic words, "husband and wife," and suddenly there was a shout and about half the crowd charged outside to the six kegs of cold beer lined up beneath the live oak. The others remained to join in the laughing and the shouting, the hugging and the kissing of the bride. Almost immediately, a party started. Pints appeared out of coat pockets. Dancing began over in one corner. By the time Slat and Hank were cutting the first slice of the huge wedding cake that Barney made, a dice game was going hot and heavy on the pool table.

Bonney puzzled me. He kept apart from the celebrating. He smiled his tolerant smile and let them play. I thought he looked tired. He broke out the great supply of bonded bourbon he'd bought for the wedding, and personally mixed drinks, but he drank almost nothing himself. I overheard him say to Elaine Farley, ". . . so if you don't want to eat stew, Barney will fix us a steak. I don't like stew myself." And she answered with that absolutely exquisite smile of hers and said, "I certainly intend to eat stew. It smells delicious. . . ."

Mrs. Farley didn't leave until after the riotous departure of the bride and groom. She stood laughing beside Bonney and read the signs the cowboys soaped onto Hank's car.

TONIGHT WE LOVE

CONTENTS OF THIS CAR IN HEAT

IN LIKE A LION, OUT LIKE A LAMB

What is this beautiful, expensive woman doing here at this beer joint? Why did she come?

Before she drove away, Bonney stood with his head hanging in the window of her car and talked with her for fifteen minutes.

"Hell's jingle *bells* but I'm tired," Rose-Mama complained when I took her home at midnight. "My feet feel like I been ironin' all day in flat-heel shoes."

I went back down the slope to help Bonney close up. It was after one when we got everybody out. The place was a mess. Bonney had reopened the tavern about four o'clock when the free wedding beer played out, and he'd done a huge Sunday night's business. He slumped into a chair and gazed around. "Hod-oh-mighty. What a day." The silence following his comment was thick. It almost roared, punctuated by the occasional knock-knock of Turnip's broom. He was back in the Dark Room, sweeping.

"Turnip?" Bonney called quietly. "Why don't you quit? Go ahead and hit the sack. We'll clean up this mess tomorrow." The boy came out of the Dark Room and Bonney told him, "You did a good job today, old son. You did fine. Thanks."

A tired grin spread over the black face. *A kind word from the master. How he does worship the master.*

"Feel like a game?" I asked.

"I don't believe," he answered. The first time he'd ever turned down a game with me. "Man, I'm bushed. These damn new shoes like to killed my feet." He crossed a long leg over a knee and pulled off a shoe and massaged his foot.

"That Elaine Farley," I said, "she's one more good-looking woman, mister."

He nodded slowly and took off the other shoe. "Yeah, she really is."

"I didn't know you invited her."

He didn't look at me to answer. "I didn't invite her. She just showed up."

I decided to let that matter drop.

"Well, your old friend Henry seemed to have a good time. I notice he had that Millie with him. First time I've seen her in here since the day I came."

200

"I expect that's because I told her not to come around here any more."

"Oh? Then I wonder why she came to the wedding?"

He got up, carrying his new shoes, and walked behind the bar to switch off the lights. "I reckon the main reason she came is, she's Slat's mother."

12.

After the wedding, Bonney McCamey was not the same man.

Something changed him. Something that happened at the wedding. Not the wedding itself, I was sure. Not Slat's departure from his house. He wasn't pleased with the romance in the beginning but after the scene on the bale of hay in the barn, he was satisfied and he was all for it. He'd gone full ahead to see that Slat had everything she wanted at the wedding.

So it wasn't Slat.

Thinking about it, every track I took led to the same conclusion: The instant he changed could be traced back to his first step down the aisle with Slat on his arm, when he looked to his right and saw Mrs. Junior Farley in the crowd. And apparently she came without being asked. Came because she wanted to come.

Then on Sunday, the day after the wedding, he drew me aside in the tavern.

"Johnny, when are you leaving?"

I didn't quite understand him at first.

"What I mean," he hurried on, "you said you were figuring on spending Christmas with your girl, with your daughter. I just wondered when you were going to leave."

"Oh. Well, I don't know. No plans. Before Christmas, I guess. Just enough time to buy a couple of presents."

He nodded. "Yeah, well, that's me. I got to get presents too.

I thought I'd kill two birds. I need to go see Mama before Christmas and I could do my shopping while I'm gone. But it'd take me three, maybe four days. If you aren't fixing to leave right away, I was going to see if you'd kind of look after things, while I'm gone. Turnip can take care of the cattle but that cash register, it needs attention."

"All right, sure."

He thanked me and went off in the truck, alone, and stayed two hours. And when he left the next morning, a man half-blind could have seen that he wasn't going on any routine trip to Corpus Christi. He wore the suit he bought for the wedding. And the new shoes that hurt his feet. And he didn't take his truck—he borrowed Barney's car.

On Tuesday I was cleaning out the cash register at closing time and Rose-Mama phoned. She hadn't come to the tavern that night.

"Johnny?" she bellowed. She always yelled into the phone. "By god, guess what? I was sittin' right here on my tailbone while ago listenin' to TV and heard a car pull away and I just now checked and somebody has lifted your window cooler. Swiped it, while I was right here in the livin' room."

That was fine, just great. I'd paid a hundred and fifty bucks for that little unit. But it wasn't any mystery to me how it could be stolen with Rose-Mama there in the house. She kept the TV volume turned up so high she couldn't hear thunder.

Early the next morning I reported the theft to the sheriff's office. Just before noon Wiley Scott came out and stayed ten minutes at the house and then drove on down to the tavern. "I can't find no clues up there," he said. "Where's Bonney?"

"Bonney's not here."

Wiley drank three beers and left without paying. I ached, ached all over to call after him, "Come back here, you sorry bastard, and pay for what you drank." *You can't do that, though. Wiley probably knows Norman Akers wasn't hit by any fan. You're in cahoots with a sorry bastard like Wiley.*

Then in midafternoon I made my phone calls. I waited until about three o'clock, when Ada Hicks was taking her daily nap in the slow part of the day and when she'd have one of her young substitutes handling the telephone switchboard. I'd learned long ago that a phone call on Farley's one-horse system was often a conference proposition, with Ada listening in.

Elsie Smith answered at the Farley School for Boys. I told her I was with the Department of Health, Education and Welfare, and needed to speak to Mrs. Farley about a "funding matter." Elsie said Mrs. Farley was out of town, that she was in Houston shopping and wouldn't be back for perhaps two more days. I thought for a second Elsie was going to tell me where I could locate Mrs. Farley in Houston, but she caught herself. "No, I don't have that information."

No matter. I found out what I needed to know: Elaine Farley was out of town. Then I called the executive offices of Farley Lumber Mills and was informed that Junior Farley was in New York City and wouldn't be back until Saturday.

Well, well, well.

"Barney, did you know that Millie was Slat's mother?"

"Yeah, I knew it. Why?"

"Oh, no reason," I said. "It's just a little strange to me that it never is mentioned around here. I didn't know it until the wedding."

"Well, she ain't *much* of a mother."

"What kind of woman is she?"

Barney's puffy eyes leveled on me. "She's a bitch."

"Is she a whore?"

"That's what I call her."

"But does she really go sleeping around, and charging?"

"She charges, one way or other."

"Well, I wish you'd tell me this. Where in the hell did Slat get her sweet disposition? From what I've heard about her father, it didn't come from him."

"From her grandmother," Barney said, "is what I figure."

"You knew her grandmother?"

"Yeah. She was a good friend of my mama's. She used to come to our house. Real nice ol' lady, too." Which was just about as many words as I'd ever gotten Barney to say in a row. He was in a good humor. The reason was that we'd just had a visit from Slat. She and Hank were already home from a wedding trip of three days and nights. They stayed an hour with us and it was like the doors and windows had been opened to let in fresh air, having her back. When she and Hank left, Barney loaded them down with enough food to last a week. Slat took hold of his ear and pulled him down and kissed him three times on his red old jowl and told him she loved him. It's a good thing she didn't ask for his right arm because he'd have taken the cleaver and cut it off and wrapped it up for her.

And right now, doing what for Barney was a lot of talking, he was still flushed from the delight that girl's visit gave him.

"Slat's grandmother was a friend of Miz McCamey, too," Barney said. Why, look there, a volunteer statement coming out of Barney. How about that?

"Mrs. McCamey. Bonney's mother?"

"Yeah. Now there's a nice lady for you, you want nice ladies. Bonney's mama is about the nicest lady I ever did know. She saved my life."

"Really?"

"Damn right really. Me and my mama both was sick. I had the dipthera, and like to choked, and Miz McCamey came over to our house and stuck her finger down my throat and got all that flem out and got me to breathin' and she taken me and Mama both to her house and nursed us till we got well. She nursed a lot of folks around here."

"How old was Bonney then, when you stayed in his house?"

"I don't know. Just a little ol' shirttail kid."

"You knew his father, then, I guess."

"Yeah, I knew him."

"What sort of man was he? What did he look like?"

"Like Bonney, sort of, I guess. Tall. Nice-*lookin'* fella, but he was sorry-ass. Gambled a lot. Boozed around. Went sniffin' after anything had a skirt on it. He had a mean streak, some way. He used to give Bonney a hard time."

"What about, mostly?"

"Oh, sometimes about his mama, but mostly I guess about Suzie. His little sister, Suzie. Bonney's old man wouldn't let her go to school."

Another surprise. Bonney had never mentioned he had a younger sister. "Why?"

204

"She was a cripple," Barney said. "Got sick when she was little, and it shriveled up her leg and her arm, here."

"Polio, I guess. Infantile paralysis?"

Barney nodded. "Yeah, that's it. Bonney used to put Suzie in her wheel chair and push her to school and his old man would come up there about the middle of the morning and get her and take her home. And then when he got hold of Bonney he'd just beat hell out of him. He had a mean streak that way."

"Why do you suppose Bonney's father didn't want Suzie to go to school?"

Barney just shook his head.

"Maybe," I said, "he was ashamed of Suzie, her being a cripple."

He nodded slowly. "Maybe. I reckon that was it."

"What happened to Suzie?"

"She died. When she was about fifteen, I think, or sixteen. Bonney always said she died from being sad. Just sad, all the time."

The noise of the front door brought me up. It was Uncle Batey and Aunt Kate coming in.

"Barney," I said to him, before leaving the kitchen, "do you know who Slat is?"

I didn't ask the question right and he didn't understand.

"I mean, do you know who Slat is, as far as Bonney is concerned? She's Suzie. You know what I mean? Him taking her in his house. Treating her like she's sixteen. Putting her in school when she's twenty-two. Protecting her from everything. To Bonney, Slat is a healthy, happy Suzie, a little sister. Sort of funny, wouldn't you say? Because half the people around Farley figured he brought Slat in his house to sleep with her."

Barney nodded. "That could be. But that ain't all of it. It's just part."

A yell from out in the tavern, from Aunt Kate. "Hey! How come nobody's mindin' the store? Who died, anyhow?"

I went out and pulled a couple of beers and delivered them to the long table. "Be right back with you, folks. Here, have a waltz on me." I fed the juke a quarter and the old couple got up to do their daily waltz and I stepped back in the kitchen.

"What do you mean," I asked Barney, "it's just part of it?"

205

"Well, about Bonney bein' so good to Slat and all. What you said about Suzie, that may be part right, I don't know. But you don't need to think you're gonna figure out everything Bonney does. He's all a jumble. He's the best friend I ever will have in this world, I know that. But he's all mixed, you know? He's a crossbreed. He's got a lot of his mama in him, but he's got too much of his daddy to keep him straight. You know who it was made a whore out of Millie? Well, it was Bonney. That's his daddy, doin' that. And him bein' so good to Slat, that's his mama. But there's other things, you b'lieve me. Listen, I been tryin' to figure Bonney out for a long time, and it ain't a easy riddle."

By eight o'clock that night, nobody was coming in and asking who died. We had a fine Thursday night. I kept looking for Bonney to walk in the back door, but he didn't.

A lot of Bonney's customers came out only occasionally, but they all showed up this Thursday. It was nine o'clock before I realized that they'd come because they knew Slat and Hank had returned from their short honeymoon. They'd all attended the wedding, and they knew.

A fat powder-faced woman grabbed me by the arm and said, "You mean that little girl won't be working here any longer?"

"No, ma'am, I'm afraid not."

"Well, foot."

Rose-Mama folded up on us about eleven and Carlos volunteered to drive her home. He didn't come back. By closing time I was dragging. Maudie found Bonney's bourbon bottle in the kitchen and fixed us a highball and we sat down by the gas heater to relax.

"I sort of looked for Bonney back tonight," she said.

"Yeah. Tomorrow, I guess. Not likely he'll leave it with us over the weekend. I sure hope not."

"I didn't think he'd stay gone this long."

"Well, he's shopping. And seeing his mother in Corpus."

"He never has stayed gone this long, though."

"Maybe he just needed to get away. This gets pretty steady, running this place seven days a week." *There you go, defending him again.*

"Well, Bonney never has been afraid to work, I'll say that

much for him. He's always horsed around a lot but he's always tended to business."

"Did you grow up around here, Maudie? Did you know Bonney in school?"

"Yeah, sure. We lived in a little old shotgun house two miles the other side of town, by the railroad track. Hancock Crossing. The Belle of Hancock Crossing, that's me, and didn't have an extra pair of drawers until my sixteenth birthday." She laughed.

"You must have been a few years behind Bonney, in school."

"Just a couple," she said. "When he was a senior at dear old Farley High, I was a sophomore. I had a class with him that year. Typing class. Don't ask me why he took typing, but I think maybe it was because he liked the teacher. Miss Guthrie. Miss Angela Guthrie. She wasn't but about twenty-four. Boy, what a snow job he gave her. He had to make forty words a minute to pass typing and graduate, and about a month before school was out he was making about ten or twelve. You know what he got in that course? She gave him a B. Made a B in typing and he didn't hardly know how to put a piece of paper in the machine. Bonney could have made good grades. He had plenty of sense, but he snowed his way through school."

"Too bad he didn't go on to college."

"He joined the Marines, two days after graduation. Him and Joe Whitaker, Rose-Mama's boy. They went off down there to Houston and joined up and within six months they were both in Korea."

"What's the story on Joe getting killed, Maudie? Rose-Mama doesn't talk about it."

"He was killed, all right, but not in a battle or anything like that. Joe, or Bonney either, they didn't do any fighting. All the fighting was finished, a good long time, when they got over there. Joe was killed in a car wreck. A Jeep." She paused. "And Bonney was driving it."

Ah, another little piece of the puzzle.

"They got all boozed up one night and Bonney plowed that Jeep into a tree. Joe never did know what hit him. Killed him instantly." She crossed her arms over her plump chest, shuddered a little, and inched closer to the stove.

"Pretty hard on Bonney," I said.

She nodded. "When he came back, Joe's dad wouldn't even let Bonney in the house when he came to see them. Mr. Whitaker just never did get over it, losing Joe that way. He had a couple of heart attacks, and then finally another one that killed him and after that Bonney moved in there with Rose-Mama. Stayed several months. He even worked at the Mills for a while, and worked like a dog too, and spent every nickel he made on Rose-Mama. Trying to make it up to her, you know, about Joe."

"Do you think that's why he finally came back here, and opened the tavern, to be near Rose-Mama, and help her?"

Maudie stared thoughtfully at the stove's butane flame. "I think that's one reason. The other is named Flora Wellman."

"Who?"

"Flora Wellman, or anyway that's who she *used* to be. She's Mrs. Junior Farley."

Well, I'll be damned. She knows. Maudie knows. "But Mrs. Farley's first name is Elaine."

"It damn sure isn't, either. Or it isn't unless she went to court and changed it. She was just plain Flora Wellman until she got up in high school, and then all of a sudden she started calling herself that Elaine."

"You mean she grew up here? I sort of figured she was an imported product."

Maudie grunted at that. "Yeah, that's what she acted like, too, from the time she was old enough to fill up a sweater. You know where she was raised? In one of those company houses, just a block and a half from the Mills. Her dad was payroll clerk for Old Man Farley. Still works there, in Junior's office now. Flora's mother always worked in Swale's, that women's clothing shop on the north side of the square. And I happen to know this for a fact, that nearly every dollar she made there went onto Flora Baby's back. Clothes? Boy, that girl had clothes, and she knew how to wear 'em, too. And she got sent to Houston for dancing lessons, ballet, you know, and she got courses in make-up and manners and all that crap. And you know why?"

"I could guess. Junior Farley."

"Right. Flora's mama planned that little match, I bet, from

208

the day Flora was born. And mister, she did a damn good job of it. Old Junior never knew what hit him."

Wait a minute now, Maudie, let's back up. "But what about Bonney? You said Mrs. Farley was one reason he came back here. You mean Bonney and Elaine Farley used to have something going between them?"

Maudie shifted her chair, leaned forward and spread her fingers to the fire. "Flora Wellman was the only girl I ever saw Bonney chase after, just really chase after. And she wouldn't let him catch her. It used to make me sick, watching it. I don't guess you can understand it, being a man and all, but there's just something about him, I don't know what it is. There wasn't half a dozen girls in Farley High School that didn't want to take Bonney McCamey back behind the gym and zip his britches down. And a good many of them did, too. But all he wanted was Flora. We'd have a dance, and when he couldn't get a date with Flora he'd go get the ugliest girl in town and take *her*. It was like he was saying, 'Well, if I can't have Flora I'll just take anything, because it doesn't matter.' Oh, she'd string him along, you know. She *liked* him, don't think she didn't. It was impossible not to. But she'd torture him, break it off in him when she got the chance. I can remember the first date he ever had with her. He——"

"*You* remember it?"

She smiled and nodded. "Listen, Johnny, I've been chasing Bonney McCamey since I was fifteen years old. I used to follow him around. I can tell you every woman in this county he's ever been out with. I know more about him than he knows about himself. And he *knows* I know, and when he gets a little tight, he talks to me . . ." She hesitated just a second. "Oh, what the hell, you know I go to bed with Bonney. Carlos knows it. Everybody knows it. I don't give a damn. I'll take him any way I can get him and right now this is the only way. But I know this—he's still got the old fire burning for Flora Wellman. He can't help how he feels, any more than I can. He gets tight, he'll lay there in bed and look at the ceiling and he'll talk about her."

Poor Maudie.

I said, "I'm a little surprised to hear they were ever very friendly. When she came out here, about Turnip, they called each other Mrs. Farley and Mr. McCamey."

Maudie leaned away from the fire and ran her hands through her hair and sighed. "Yeah, well, that goes back to one of their big fights. They were always having fights. They couldn't ever get along, for very long at a time. Always trying to hurt each other." She grinned, almost laughed. "In high school, they were like that. When they were about seventeen, one time he kept pestering her, wanting a date. And she made one with him, to go to the show. When he went to get her she looked out front and asked him where the car was. Said she certainly wasn't going on any date unless he had a car to go in. Well, shoot, Bonney didn't have any car. My god, the picture show wasn't but two blocks from her front door. He was just gonna walk her to the show. But she wouldn't go because he didn't have a car. Mad? Boy, was he ever mad. She slammed the door in his face. And he stuck his foot through the screen. Kicked it, he was so mad, and his foot went through it. Well, the next time he had a date with her, he had him a car, all right. An Olds Ninety-Eight."

"Where in the world did he get that?"

She smiled. "Borrowed it, I guess you'd say. Without telling anybody. Right after she slammed the door in his face that time he started hanging out down there at the Buick and Olds place, just stayed there, warting everybody, until they gave him a job washing cars and sweeping floors and cleaning up and moving cars around the lot, things like that. It was easy. One night he just put the keys to that Ninety-Eight in his pocket and after dark he went back down there and drove it off and went over to Flora's house and parked out front and honked. Didn't even go to the door, just honked. Well, that car was just a little bit bigger and longer and fancier than the one Junior Farley happened to be driving around here at the time, so he knew she'd fall right in it. And she did, too. Flounced out there and hopped in, and he drove her way out south of town nearly to the bridge on the creek and then he turned around and stopped and got out and went around on her side and yanked her out of there, right on her behind, and told her a big girl like her oughta learn how to walk a little bit and maybe if she walked all the

210

way back to town then it might not be such a strain on her next time to walk two blocks to the show."

"Did he leave her? Really?"

"Damn right he did. Peeled off and left her right out there on the road, and didn't go back for her either. She walked all the way home, and he took the car back to the lot and they never did know it'd been gone."

"Beautiful," I said. Well, it was. I don't suppose there's a young man in creation who didn't want to do something just like that to a conceited, good-looking girl, but not many of them have the guts. "She didn't squeal on him, or get her parents after him for leaving her out there like that?"

"Why, no, wasn't any danger of that, and he knew it. *She* wasn't going to tell anybody what happened. She was too stuck-up. Didn't want anybody to know she'd been suckered, you know. All she did, she just sat back and waited her chance, to get even."

"And she did, I suppose."

Maudie nodded. "Yeah, she sure did, finally, the night they graduated from high school. She was going steady with Junior Farley by then. Junior's mother used to give these parties, lawn parties, in the back yard of that big house. You've seen it. I don't guess you've been in it. Out back it's real pretty. Must be three or four acres in the back yard, and a great big live oak tree and flower gardens and shrubs and tall bushes and a patio thing, where we used to dance. Well, about a week before graduation she started making up to Bonney, flirting with him a lot, you know, and then she stopped him in the hall at school one day and baited her trap. Said she was eighteen years old and about to graduate from high school and she was still a virgin and she was tired of being a virgin and she wanted him to do something about it and——"

"Aw, come on, you don't really think she said that."

"Oh, she said it, all right. Listen, you don't *know* that woman. She told him she'd always wanted to lose her cherry under that big live oak tree in Old Man Farley's back yard and if Bonney would meet her there at two-thirty in the morning after graduation, why they'd see what could be done about it."

"That's hard to believe."

211

"Not for me, it isn't."

"And did he go? Did he show up?"

Maudie threw a look at me. "Of course he did. He's a male, isn't he? He went in the yard the back way. It's a jungle, back in there. They've got benches, for picnics, built around the live oak and when Bonney got there she was sitting on a bench, waiting for him. She had on a coat, just a light coat, and when he walked up close to her she stood up and opened up her coat and she didn't have a thing on, underneath. I can just see her, standing up there showing herself. Oh, she had a figure, and still does. Well, Bonney, poor thing, you know what that did to him, her standing up there naked. It runs a man crazy, especially one that age. He grabbed her and she let him give her one big long kiss and then she backed off and wound up and just slapped hell out of him." Maudie got out of her chair and stood with her back to the stove. "Just think. For a whole week he'd been going round thinking about it, waiting for the time. Poor thing."

"So she didn't let him . . . touch her again."

"No. But she gave him a few words. Said she was going to lose her cherry, all right, but it wasn't going to be *him* that got it, it was going to be Junior Farley. Said she was going to marry Junior, inside of a month. And she said that house, and that tree, and the Mills and everything that Old Man Farley had his brand on in Kirby County was going to be *hers*, because Junior wasn't anything but a top-crop and his mother and daddy were old and wouldn't live another ten years and she was going to be Mrs. Junior Farley and own the whole county and if Bonney ever spoke to her again he would have to call her *Mrs. Farley*. Oh, she's a bitch, Johnny."

"But how do you know that's all true? Bonney wouldn't tell all that."

"He tells it, all right. I've heard it three, four times. Bonney's got to talk, you know. He's got to tell things. It's the way he is."

"So that's when he left town, ran off."

"Yeah, just as soon as he could get Joe Whitaker to go with him. Two days later. What burns me though is that she was right, about everything. Junior's folks didn't live five years after Flora and Junior got married and she got everything, just the way she said."

212

"Well, you know, Maudie, there's no justice in this world."

"No, I guess not."

"Did Bonney have any—what would you say, contact?—with Elaine Farley after he came back?"

"If you mean did he sleep with her, no. He got invited to a couple of those big shindigs Flora gave, back there in that jungle, and she let him hang around just long enough to hear him call her Mrs. Farley. But he hasn't touched her"—she hesitated just a second, before she said it—"not until now. I suppose you know, Johnny, where he is now."

"In Houston. With her."

"Yeah. Bedded down, finally, with Flora Wellman."

"But why? Why would she do that, now?"

"Simple. Because she's always been crazy about him, that's why. And because being married to Junior Farley is about like . . . well, I'd just about as soon make love to Colonel Ralls."

He came back the next day about noon. And he was a stranger. Dark-faced and ill-tempered. When he found out about the missing air conditioner, he called Wiley and told him to get off his lazy ass and find that unit. He tore into Turnip about the house being "filthy" and he snapped at Barney about "rancid grease on the grill." And Barney quit. Said he wasn't *ever* coming back.

But the worst thing Bonney did, when he came home he didn't go up the slope to see Rose-Mama, and he didn't hug her when she came down to the tavern. That hurt her, and it made me angry.

Slat almost thawed him out when she and Hank came out and got him to talking a little. But I noticed her studying his face.

"What's the matter with him?" she asked, when she caught me in the kitchen.

"Beats me."

"Well, we ought to find out. Something's the matter. I can tell."

"I'll talk to him."

But he beat me to it.

When we got everybody out at midnight he locked the front

door and kicked it a couple of times and nearly rattled it off the
hinges and he rubbed his hands and said, "OK, Johnny, rack 'em
up. I'm gonna beat your tail, three straight." It was a noble
effort but it came out just a fair imitation of Bonney McCamey
at midnight Friday.

*Go ahead and break. Let's see what happens. He's about to
tell you something.*

The trey fell on the break and I sank three more spots and
then missed the six and didn't get another shot. He poked the
tip of his stick at the corner pocket, to call the eight-ball, and
rolled it in and scratched. "Well I'm be damn. Up jumped the
devil. Hodamighty I haven't touched a stick in so long I can't
shoot a buzzard." But the scratch was intentional. It was an insult, trying to get me to believe he scratched by accident.

All right, here it comes. Listen now.

"Johnny?" He was racking the balls. "How'd you like to own
this beer joint?"

"What do you mean?"

"Just what I said. Own this place."

Just go along. See what's coming. "I don't know. Why?"

"Because I'd like to sell it to you."

"Like hell you would."

"Like hell I wouldn't. I wouldn't sell it to just anybody, but
I'd sell it to you."

"I wouldn't have the damn thing. Now get out of the way and
I'll break."

"No, wait a minute. I'm serious. Will you buy it?"

"I haven't got anything to use for money."

"Don't need any. Just take it over. I'll carry the paper myself
and you can pay it out any way you want."

"No, thanks." *Hang on, let's see what comes next.*

"Come on now, Johnny. I'm not kidding. I want to sell this
place. I'm selling everything. Tomorrow morning, first thing,
I'm selling my cows and my land. To Brad."

My god, he means it. "Why?"

"Because I'm leaving here."

"I don't believe it."

"You *better* believe it because I am."

"Why?"

214

"Because I've got what I came here to get."

All right, let's see if he'll tell us what that is. "What is it you've got?"

"Mrs. Junior Farley."

The way he said it nettled me. He said it smarty-pants, grinning, like a kid who'd put a snake in the teacher's desk and was proud of it.

"Well," I said, "I know you've been sacked out with her down there for four nights, if that's what you're trying to brag about. I know it and Maudie knows it. But if you came back here and went into business and bought land and cattle just to get one piece of tail, well, you've finally got it, so what's all this crap about selling out?"

"No, not just one piece of tail," he said. "I'm selling out because I need the money. I'm leaving, and she's going with me."

Well I'll be damned. "You can't mean that."

"It's a fact. She's going with me."

What he was saying, and all it meant, I resented it.

"If that's true, if you do that, it's a pretty goddamned ugly thing to do."

"Why, hell, Johnny, that woman, she's the only thing I ever wanted in my life. It's been like that the whole time, ever since we were in school. And it's been the same with her, too, I know it. All that Mrs. Junior Farley crap, that wasn't *her* idea. That was all the doing of that old bitch of a mother of hers. . . ."

"You mean she's ready to go off with you and quit being Mrs. Farley Lumber Mills and Mrs. Kirby County?"

"You damn right she is. Now that's got to prove *some*thing."

"Are you going to marry her?"

"Damn right, some time. But we're not going to wait. We're just going."

"And you want me to buy this place. Why?"

"Because you fit in around here, and my folks here, they like you."

"You want me to take your place, right?"

"Well . . ."

"I suppose you want me to tell Rose-Mama you're leaving, and Turnip, and Slat."

He twisted a little, and looked down, because the question bothered him. But he shook his head. "No, I'll do that."

"What'll you do about Turnip? You better take Mrs. Farley a long way, and lay low, or Turnip will find you. He'll damn sure follow you, you know that."

"Well, she says the school. We could put him in the school."

"I agree he ought to be in school but he wouldn't stay in her school and you know it."

"I don't know. He might."

"You could lock him up in there and he might stay, at least as long as it took his heart to break. And how about Rose-Mama? I want to be around to hear, when you tell her."

No response to that one.

We talked about it, argued, I suppose for the better part of an hour. There was plenty that worried him about the situation but I didn't shake him loose. He was going. We ended up just standing around by the stove, not saying a damn thing.

He went back to the pool table finally and said, "Johnny, you're a kind of gambler. I tell you what I'll do. I'll shoot you one game, for this beer joint."

Now what's this? What's he trying to do now? "You mean if I win, the place is mine?"

"That's right."

"Free and clear?"

"Well, I got a little note against it still, but it hasn't got much balance on it. Maybe two thousand. You'd have to pay that. You could make a living and pay that off, oh, in a year, maybe less."

"What kind of gambling is that? If I win I get the tavern. If I lose, I haven't lost anything but a game of eight-ball. Why don't you just *give* me the tavern?"

"No, you got to put up something, against the place."

Now it comes. "What?"

"You got to make me a promise."

"What kind of promise?"

"You got to promise me, if you lose, you'll stay around here from now on and sort of watch after things. Keep living up there at Rose-Mama's, until . . . just until you know it's all right to leave. Until she dies, or until she's . . . well, you know."

Just until she gets over your leaving is what you mean.

". . . and keep Turnip straight. Send him to school, if you

want. I know, you're right, he ought to be in school, I guess. And Slat. Keep in touch with her, you know. She'll be all right but keep in touch. And Barney, he needs somebody to . . . oh hell, Johnny, *you* know. You know how it is around here."

"Let's see, now. If I lose, there still won't be anybody to run this place. All I'll have to do is take care of your neighborhood responsibilities."

"Well, I'll turn the tavern over to Barney, in that case."

Ho ho ho. Barney, I doubt he can even add a column of figures. He doesn't even know how to cheat on income tax.

I faked it a while and considered the bet. A ridiculous wager in all ways, and completely one-sided. He couldn't lose. In the first place he didn't intend to let me win, and even if I did win I'd own the tavern and I'd still be around, to take his place. *To be his conscience, is what he wants me to be.*

I decided to play. I got up and chalked my cue. "It's my break."

"All right. Let 'er flicker."

I got the heavy break ball, which Bonney and I never used. I hauled back and really socked 'em one, gave 'em the old whorehouse roll, just the way those strong-armed cowboys did when they were showing off. The five fell and so did the twelve, and before the balls stopped rolling I could see that Bonney wasn't going to get a shot, and so did he. "Well, I'll be damn," he said, and put his cue in the rack and sat down. Every one of the stripes was sitting around the holes, crippled, and there wasn't a really tough shot for me on the whole table. Even so, by the time I sank all the stripes and called the eight-ball shot in the side pocket, I was trembling. And I shot a little too hard and damn near scratched in the far corner.

When the cue ball stopped an inch short of the hole I looked up at him and said, "Bonney, you're sitting in my beer joint."

He nodded and grinned, but not a very wide grin. "Real nice place you got here, Johnny."

So that's how I came into ownership of Bonney's Place, three days before Christmas.

Rose-Mama's light was still on when I went up the slope. She came in her outing nightgown and stood in the door of my bedroom and she looked very old.

"Johnny, can you tell me what the hell's the matter with Bonney?"

"I don't know. He's in a sour mood, seems like."

"Well, somethin's happened. I think he's in some kind of trouble. It's about to worry me sick."

I never did hear her snoring the rest of the night.

By seven o'clock the next morning I was back down at the tavern. I got the back-door key Bonney kept under the rear step and let myself in. And slammed the door.

The noise brought him out of the house.

"Well, well," he said. "Look at the new proprietor. Already up and got his milking done and on the job, eh?"

"By damn," snapping my fingers, "I flat forgot about that old cow. I think we'll have to get somebody else to fool with that cow, from now on. After you leave and I move on down here to the house I——"

"Down here? You figuring on staying here in my house? Hell, you didn't win the house, Johnny."

"I know, but I thought you'd rent it to me. Somebody ought to be staying in it, here close to the business. You've said that yourself."

"Yeah, but Turnip, he'll be here."

"I'm not too sure about that. When you take off, I look for him to take off right behind you, go looking for you."

He laughed. "Shoot. That boy wouldn't leave those cow dogs."

"He would if he thought you weren't coming back."

He swung up on Barney's sturdy old cook table by the stove and let his legs hang and he hunched over and stared out the window toward the barn. He didn't look too good. Eyes red. Must not have gotten any sleep. His hair was all tousled and his T-shirt was droopy and a little patch of stubble on his chin was showing gray, almost white. He didn't much look like a hot-shot lover man.

"I'll talk to Turnip," he said, still gazing out at the barn. "I'll just have to tell him not to do anything dumb, like try to follow me."

"But you haven't told him yet."

"No. Not yet."

I went through the swinging door and inspected the wall between the ladies' rest room and the bar. I rapped on it, and he came out of the kitchen and asked what was the matter.

"Nothing's the matter. I was just looking at this section of wall here. Last night, I was thinking I could tear it out and make a big wide door here and open things up a little. Give me some extra space."

"Why'd you want to do that? I tell you, Johnny, you got to have that colored business or you won't make it."

"Oh, I want it, all right, but I just thought I'd eliminate the Dark Room."

He was shaking his head, putting his hand on the wall, as if he wanted to protect it. "Lincoln and them, they wouldn't have any place to come if you did that."

"Well, I never have thought it was right, making them stay back in there to themselves that way."

"But they *like* it. They *want* to be back there. You ask Lincoln. You'll lose the colored business without that Dark Room."

"No, I thought I'd just serve them right in here with everybody else. That's how it's done most other places now."

"But dammit, Johnny, Lincoln and his folks don't care anything about that. *They* don't want to come in here. They wouldn't come."

"I think they would if I invited them."

Shaking his head again, pacing, walking in little half-circles with his hands in the back pockets of his jeans. "No, they wouldn't either. And even if they did it'd be a mistake. My regular customers——" I threw him the old raised eyebrow. "All right, *your* regular customers, they wouldn't like it. They'll leave you, right flat on your butt. It'll wreck your business."

I tried to sound all smug and confident. "It'll hurt at first, maybe, but it'll work out, I think."

He turned away and those long arms flapped once and slapped against his thighs. "Well, it's your beer joint."

"Listen," I said. *Watch it now. Don't overdo it. Don't carry it too far.* "Do you think the Colonel's granddaughter—what's her name?—do you think she'd understand if we asked her to keep him at home a little more?"

His cold-eyed stare. "Why?"

"Because he's not helping business around here. Underfoot all the time. Warting people about Cuba. Going to the ladies' rest room. The other night when you were gone some woman went in the rest room and the old bastard was in there alseep, on the ladies' john."

He kicked the swinging door and went through it growling, "Well, *you* talk to somebody about him. It's not any of my worry, now."

By hustling, I stopped him before he got in the house. "Say, I wanted to ask you, when are you leaving?"

"Aw . . . I don't know, quite yet." He put out a foot and made little circles in the dirt with his toe and then he looked out toward the barn at the sound of laughter. It was Turnip, having his morning romp with the dogs. He was rolling and giggling in the door of the barn, his body almost hidden by a wiggling mass of tails and ears and rumps. Bonney watched that scene for more than a minute, before he spoke to me again. "We haven't decided, definite. I've got to see Brad and get this land thing settled. It might take him three, four days to get my money, with the holidays and all. It'll be after Christmas. Maybe a week. And she—" Mrs. Farley, he meant. Elaine. He never once referred to Elaine Farley by her first name when speaking to me. "She's got things to straighten out. Said she'd let me know."

Then he straightened up and faced me and brightened a little and said, "But say, how about you? You still figuring on going to see your girl for Christmas? You know tomorrow's Christmas Eve?"

"Yeah, that's what I wanted to ask you. I thought I'd go on, this afternoon. I mean you'll be here, won't you?"

"Sure. Hell yes. I'll be around. Take your time. Take several days, you want to."

I had to laugh. "Sounds funny, huh? Me asking you to stay around here and look after things?"

"Yeah," he said, "it sure does sound funny. Well, I got to get cleaned up and go see Brad."

220

"Will you stop by Rose-Mama's on the way?"

"Thought I would."

"Are you figuring on telling her, about leaving?"

"I don't know. I guess."

"Well, it might be a good idea to wait. I'm a little concerned about her. She's not feeling very well. I know she didn't get a lick of sleep last night. Might be a good idea to wait until I get back. So somebody'd be with her, you know?"

"OK. Right. Good idea. I'll just wait then."

I drove over to Sullivan and used the phone at the Kingfish Inn, a restaurant on the Interstate run by one of Bonney's friends, Thelma Evans. I finally located Midge at the home of Arch's parents and I sure wasn't any hero when I told her I wouldn't see her Christmas. Had to give her the old something's-come-up thing.

"Is it about the man who took the money?" she wanted to know.

"Yes, and it's coming to a head right now. So I'll see you pretty soon. Maybe New Year's. We'll celebrate."

Then I called Eva's brother, Sid Terrell in Baton Rouge. Told him I'd be there the next morning and needed to see him. He didn't ask why. Just said, "I'll be at the office until noon."

So I spent the remainder of the day and part of the night driving to Baton Rouge, and checked into a motel outside town. God, but it was lonesome. I was waiting for Sid the next morning when he got to the office.

"Hey, man, you look good," he said. "You've put on weight. You must have found you a widow woman who can cook."

I grinned. *As a matter of fact, Sid, you're right, but you ought to see her, hell's jingle bells.* "I've come for some legal advice. Free."

"Shoot."

"Nearly four years ago, a guy at Beaumont took fifteen thousand dollars from my father, when he was in that rest home. It was supposed to be some kind of a business deal. The guy told the Old Man—my father—that he was going to use the money to set up some kind of business, and they'd be

221

partners. But he just went south with it. Took off and didn't come back. There wasn't any kind of written agreement or anything. The Old Man evidently just handed him the money and trusted him. What I want to know is, what can I do about it, now?"

Sid leaned back in his chair. "Do you know where this man is? Can you find him?"

"Yes, I know."

"Are you certain he's the one who took the money?"

"Yes."

"Any evidence?"

"He'll admit it."

"He *will* admit it? But he hasn't yet?"

"That's it. But what I want to know is, what can I charge him with. Theft? Embezzlement? And how do I go about it?"

He grinned at me. "Well, first, you go about it in Texas, not in Louisiana. Go talk to the district attorney in the county where it happened and give him your evidence and see if he'll accept a complaint. I don't know. The statute of limitations may get in your way on that. Your man might claim the money was just a loan, a personal debt."

"So I ought to begin back there where he took the money," I said.

There was the funny little grin again. "Come on, pal, you're giving me the old finger. *You* didn't drive all the way over here to ask me something any country lawyer in Texas could tell you. Why did you come, all the way over here at Christmas?"

It wasn't pleasant for me, but I had to ask.

"All right," I said, "I want to know if you remember a guy named Norman Akers."

"If you mean the Norman Akers who has that string of furniture stores, sure, I know the son of a bitch. He's got a store here in town. I did some work for him, represented him one time. What about him?"

"When Eva was staying with you and Stella, back there before I met her, did she ever know Akers?"

He frowned. "Hell, I don't know. Why?"

222

"Did Akers ever meet her? Did you take him out to the house, when he was your client?"

"Great god, I don't know. You're talking about twenty years or more, man. Maybe I did. I've taken a hell of a lot of clients to the house. What difference does it make?"

So then I just came on out with it. "I heard him say he had dates with Eva. That he slept with her. He said some awful things. Said he took her to a motel, and . . ."

Well, it made him mad. I'd never seen Sid Terrell mad and it was frightening. There for a minute I thought he was going to hit me. He did give me a cussing out. I mean he really laid me low. Said he ought to beat the goddamned hell out of me. Called me a sorry bastard, coming in there at Christmastime with a sleazy story like that, trying to make Eva out some kind of whore. When I saw he wasn't really going to hit me, I sat back and let him rave until he ran down. Finally he slumped in his chair, breathing heavy.

So I said quietly, "Now you know how I felt when I heard Akers say those things."

He got up and went to the window and looked out at the dull gray sky.

"Not Eva," he said. "Eva wouldn't do that. Not with *that* fat slob. My god."

I searched for doubt in his voice. I couldn't tell whether I heard any or not.

"You can see, though," I said, "why it's important to me, to know it's not true?"

"Yeah. That son of a bitch. If I'd heard him say that, I'd have killed him."

"I damn near did."

He wheeled, some of the shadows gone from his face. "Did you hit him?"

"Yes."

"Hard?"

"Damn right."

"What with, your fist?"

"No, with a cue. A pool cue."

"With the heavy end?"

"Yes."

"Great! Good! Nice going!" He was grinning. But the grin disappeared and he said, "You're in trouble about it."

"No, he doesn't even know I hit him. Concussion. He can't remember what happened. Thinks he had an accident."

"Beautiful," Sid said. "But listen, if he ever does remember, if you ever get in trouble over it, you call me, you hear? We'll nail that bastard. He's not any more than a dope peddler anyhow. He's screwed everybody he's done business with in two states. Screws his employees. Screws his customers. Screws the government on taxes. And he's a liar. That I *know*, because I saw him sit flat on his ass in a witness chair and lie under oath. If that son of a bitch ever gives us any trouble, we'll nail his butt to the wall of one of those furniture stores. It wouldn't be easy but we'd do it, if it took from now on."

It wasn't much after ten o'clock but Sid said I wasn't going to leave until I had a Christmas drink with him. We went around the corner and down an alley and he beat on a narrow door until a bald-headed man with a mustache opened it. "Cal, we need a drink."

We sat in the rear booth of the dark bar, not even opened yet, and downed two huge Bloody Marys and when we left I was feeling a lot better. Back at the office Sid called a lawyer he knew in Beaumont, an Albert Sutton, who agreed to see me on Christmas Day if I'd come out to his house.

Just before I left Sid told me, "Listen, I want you to do something. I want you to let Eva rest easy. You've got to quit acting like she's still alive. Quit worrying about her. Quit getting your bowels in an uproar about what she did or didn't do. I know, I know, I'm the same way about her, I guess, but it's no good. Hell, you're not old. You need to get out and make some kind of life for yourself. You're gonna be around for a long time. You ought to start chasing widows, or get married or something. Let Eva lie. She's dead and gone."

So there were the words that used to hurt me. But now they weren't so bad. Sid was right. *Eva's dead.* I could even say it myself now. I'd done the right thing, going to Baton Rouge. I needed to hear Sid say Akers was a liar. Of course I don't know, even now, whether Akers was telling the truth about Eva, but I had to talk to somebody who knew her and loved her and hear him say the words were lies.

224

I drove to Beaumont and checked into a motel. Christmas Eve. The place was almost deserted. I sat in the lobby and talked to the lonesome woman on duty at the desk. She had a black tooth and wasn't very pretty but she was friendly and seemed to have a good heart and she was in favor of economy in the federal government. She was also nice and bouncy. I went out and got a bottle and we went back in the office. She said she had two grown sons so I expect she was over forty. At midnight when she got off duty I'd had four bourbons and she wasn't but about thirty-two by then. So I took her to bed. What the hell. She seemed to appreciate it.

"It wouldn't be theft," Albert Sutton said. "It wouldn't be embezzlement, either. Swindle, maybe, except you haven't got any evidence."

We sat out in my car, in front of his house. Early Christmas afternoon, and he had a houseful of company. I liked him. He had a good homely face.

"This"—he flicked the Old Man's wrinkled going-on-to-glory letter lying on the seat between us—"it's not any good. Wouldn't be admissible. It doesn't say a thing, really. Hasn't even got your man's name in it."

"But what if he'll admit taking the money?" I said.

"In court?" He sounded doubtful. "All he'd have to do is claim the money was a loan. A personal debt. Statute of limitations on a personal debt is two years. You're late."

"You mean a guy can just take fifteen thousand dollars off an old man and run off with it and I can't do anything about it?"

"You've got to have evidence. I don't see that you have a shred. You'd have to convince the district attorney you've got a case before he'd accept a complaint. Well, I don't think you've got one. No partnership agreement. No witnesses. No nothing."

"There's not anything we could do, just to scare him? Is there any way we could hit him with something, something legal and threatening, that would keep him from running off? Keep him from leaving town, or the state?"

Sutton shook his head slowly. "I don't know what it'd be, since you're in a hurry."

225

"What if I wasn't in a hurry?"

"Well, only thing I can think of is income tax. Maybe this Bonney didn't report the fifteen thousand as income. You could stick him on that but it'd take time. You'd have to have some evidence on that, too, to get Internal Revenue to run a check on him. But you're talking about time. Weeks, maybe."

Because I'd invited Bailey to go to hell the last time I saw him, I walked into Lakecrest Home with my hat in my hand, ready to apologize. When the woman in the front office told me Bailey was no longer manager of the home, I confess I was relieved to hear it. The new manager was a Mr. Callendar, a grinning young fellow surely not much older than thirty.

"You bet," he said. "I sure did know your dad. We used to joke about being in the same class. I came to work here, as assistant manager, the same week he moved in. Great old fellow. We sure miss him around here. These old folks still talk about him. Talk about him nearly every night when they're in there around the color TV set. Your dad gave us that TV, you know. Gave it to the guests, I mean, after he got sick and couldn't watch it."

I asked Callendar if he knew where the Old Man got that television.

"Yes, sir. Friend of his gave it to him. A fellow he met, oh, just right after he came here."

The name. Did he remember the name?

He tapped on a desk lighter with a pencil, trying to remember. "Bonney something. Can't recall. We'd have his last name around here somewhere, I guess. Everybody called him Bonney."

Did he mean Bonney used to come there, to the home?

"Sure. Yes, sir, he sure did. Lots of times. Came to see your dad two, sometimes three times a week, for several months. Sort of a strange guy. Unusual, I mean. He seemed to love these old folks. That's not very common, you know, in younger people. That guy could come out here and hang around a couple hours and do more for morale than Mr. Bailey and I could do in a month. . . ."

Well I'll be damned.

". . . and he had an old rattletrap station wagon and he'd come get your dad and three or four more of the guests and he'd tour 'em around, down to the docks to watch the ships, down to Sabine to the beach, things like that. Once or twice he took your dad and one or two of the other old gents to Houston, to the Astrodome, to see a ball game and . . ."

Well I'll just be goddamned.

". . . these old gals around here, man, they *loved* him. He'd circulate around out there and pat 'em and call 'em honey and tell 'em they were beautiful and they'd eat it up. I used to tell Mr. Bailey we ought to hire the guy."

I said, "That's all very strange to hear. Mr. Bailey told me my father never *had* any visitors while he was here."

Callendar's grin faded and he picked up the desk lighter and flicked it on and off a couple of times. "Well," he said, "let's just say Mr. Bailey had some problems. That's why he's not here any longer."

"I see." *Let it go. It doesn't matter now.* "Would you have any idea where my father met this Bonney?"

The grin came back. "Yeah, yes, sir, I know." The grin getting wider. "Are you ready?"

"Go ahead. Hit me."

"Isabella's Recreation Lounge."

Isabella Medina, Mexican-American. Five feet three, two hundred pounds, fifty years old (just my guesses). I found her sitting on a stool behind her cash register like some kind of little round brown queen on a throne, telling a joke to three sailors.

When the joke was over I introduced myself as a friend of Bonney McCamey and it worked just the way I guessed it would. I was afraid for a second she was going to come off the stool and hug my neck.

"Son of a gun," she said. "That son of a gun. Tell about him. Where is he? Son of a gun."

I leveled with her. Told her the truth about as much as I wanted her to know, at least.

"Son of a gun," she said. "Bonney got his own place? I

227

wouldn't ever think he'd stay put so long." She swiveled the stool and screeched toward the rear. "Fleep? *Fleep!*" No response from Fleep. Then the screech again, louder. "*Fay-LEE-pay!* Come guess what. Here's a man from Bonney and he's got his own place now, that son of a gun."

Felipe appeared in a doorway at the back, behind the line of six pool tables. "Son of a gun," he said, then retreated and closed the door and I didn't see him again.

Did Isabella remember the Old Man?

Why, I guess she did, son of a gun. Came there every day, for five, six, seven, no, wait, maybe eight months. No, a year. Two years? *Fleep! Was it a year?* Came with Bonney, yes, all the time with Bonney. Like son and father, that pair. Going here, going there. Laugh. Talk. Drink. All the time one with the other. And *then!* When Bonney left. Swish! Swoop! He is gone, and no trace. Who knows where? And the Old Gentleman, every day he came, came to this place and sat and waited for Bonney. For weeks? For months? *Fleep! How long?* And always asking has Bonney come, where is Bonney? And who can know? Our Lord knows, and the Blessed Mother knows, and the saints and prophets and angels and the police, perhaps, son of a gun. The Old Gentleman, where did he go?

"He died, Isabella."

"Dead!" She grasped her round self with her short arms, and shuddered, as if she'd never before known a person who died. "And your own *father*. How sad, even for old men with a stroke. Son of a gun."

And yet, she told me a great deal.

Before I left, I went to the rear pool table in Isabella's Recreation Lounge and for almost an hour I practiced the eight-ball shot I'd seen Bonney make, that first day I walked into his beer joint back in September. And I got it down pat.

Ninety miles from Beaumont to Houston. I had to go home to get the keys and then I went to the office. I wonder if there's a more lifeless place than a business office at night. Rows of desks, clear, sterile. Little ships, abandoned, on a lonely sea.

228

I stopped at Cassy Ballinger's desk, with its sign: Cassy At Home. And her phone number beneath. When she answered I said, "I'll make a deal with you. I won't ask what a good-looking divorcee is doing at home at ten o'clock on Christmas night, if you won't ask me what a guy on leave of absence is doing at the office."

She laughed. "It's a deal. What do you need?"

"I need a phony letter typed on an Internal Revenue Service letterhead, and an IRS envelope to put it in. Can you do it?"

"I might, if it doesn't have to fool experts."

"It doesn't. I guess you know when I need it."

A fake groan. "Be there in half an hour."

I hunted-and-pecked out the letter to Bonham J. McCamey, and by the time I finished I could hear Cassy's heels clicking down the hall. She zipped in, grinned, asked if this was the department of forgery, and went to work. Within thirty minutes she had produced, on the office copying machine, a presentable IRS letterhead off some correspondence she took out of her files. In Dan's desk drawer she located a ripped-open IRS envelope. She patched it up beautifully, typed Bonney's address on a white paper tag and pasted it on the envelope. "They use these paste-on addresses, anyway," she said. Then when she sat down to type the letter: "I'm going to bet you a great big scotch and water that you don't want this letter done in triplicate."

"Right, just the original. And don't worry about being an accomplice in this crime, because I'm not going to mail the letter. Now then, one more favor. I've written out here the wording on a wire that I want you to send, in the next few days. But don't send it until I call and say so. And I want it signed with this phony name, this Arthur J. Foster."

"OK. What else?"

"Merry Christmas," I said.

13.

It was 3 A.M. by the time I got back to my room at Rose-Mama's. But I couldn't sleep. Eyes just wouldn't stay shut. So I turned on the bed lamp and read three newspapers from front to back. Two were dailies I'd picked up in Houston. The third was the *Weekly Rocket.*

I'd gotten somewhat out of touch with the news of the world. There in Joe Whitaker's bed I studied the front pages of the two dailies. Stories about:

The record level of shoplifting during the Christmas rush just ended: offshore wells leaking in the Gulf and spreading a huge oil slick toward a wildlife refuge on the Louisiana coast; the vice-president of a bank indicted on a charge of misappropriation of funds; a hassel over chemical plants polluting streams; two dead in a shoot-out at the scene of a liquor store robbery; a doctor, charged with income tax evasion; and the box score on the number of people dying violent deaths in the state, compared to the total predicted for the holidays by the department of public safety (thirty-six down, and forty to go).

Happy Holidays, folks.

So it was a relief to pick up Harvey's *Weekly Rocket.* I studied every item in his regular dot-and-dash front-page column about the doings around Kirby County. After I read it I went back and counted and of the twenty-four people he mentioned in the column, eighteen of them had become my friends or at least acquaintances.

THIS WEEK . . .

I went around a little while with Louise Madison and her sophomore class from Farley High while they sung Christmas carols all over town . . . I saw Bro. Luther of First Baptist and his Deacons delivering food baskets to poor families, the baskets looked better than what we're eating at my house . . . I talked with Mr. Junior Farley in Spearman's, he and I are getting along better these days, I guess it's Christmas that does that . . . I went with Audie Mahon to the Chickenhawk Bridge south of town to run his throw lines and he caught a yellow cat of 12 lbs using chicken gut as bait . . . Monday I was up in the North Part of the County with Sheriff Overton where we stopped at the Bluff, still a pretty spot like when I was a boy. In 1936 I shot 8 squirrels in one day out of that big pecan at the foot of the Bluff and Tatum Bentley says his grand son shot 6 out of it last week. Happy Birthday to Mr. Bentley who was 92 Friday . . . Ada Hicks tells me she won't know what to do when we get the new dial phone system, she has been phone operator now for 32 yrs. Keep up the good work Ada but dont listen in so much, ha ha . . . You ought to ask Uncle Batey Foster how come he doesnt like his new thick glasses he got in Houston, I cant print it . . .

And on and on, for a full column. Childish, some of it, and yet it was real, and human, and personal. I liked it. And I made a note to ask Uncle Batey what was wrong with the glasses. He'd had eye trouble for a long time. Cataracts. And if Ben Ashley hadn't decided to go at the last minute, I'd have been the one who drove Uncle Batey to Houston to get his new specs.

At dawn, still sleepless and in a rotten humor, I went out to milk. The prospect of leaving Farley and Bonney's Place didn't improve my mood. Elizabeth's frame of mind was a lot better than mine. She was loose as a goose and let me foam the milk bucket over the sides in ten minutes.

"Hey," Rose-Mama called from the back porch. "I didn't hear you come in. Did you have a merry Christmas?"

"Yeah. Sure. How about you?"

She came on out and stood at the fence in her nightgown and her old bathrobe with the little tassels around the bottom. "All right, I guess."

"How's everything down at our favorite beer joint?"

231

"All right." She sounded like an undertaker saying business was satisfactory.

"Bonney have a crowd last night?"

"Yeah," she said, "but he didn't take care of it. He got drunk. I mean skunked. Not like him, doin' that. He's still got something eatin' on him. I don't expect he'll be very bushy tail this mornin'. He had problems last night."

"What kind?"

"He had four women around there wantin' to get in his bed."

"Four? That's a couple more than usual. Charlotte and Maudie and who else?"

"Well, Alice May."

"Alice who?"

"Alice May Vaughn, that nurse at the hospital. She came out."

"That makes three."

"Then Big Belly Akers' wife."

"Mrs. Akers? Really? My god."

"Yeah. That witch not much younger than me. But she wasn't feelin' very old last night. She put Norman to bed with one of his dizzy spells and showed up down there about 'leven o'clock. Tight as a tick. Pretty near made me throw up."

Elizabeth looked back and told me, in a good-natured way, that I ought to leave at least enough milk in her bag for seed, so I quit and Rose-Mama followed me in the house. She sat at the kitchen table and watched me pour the milk through the strainer, just as if she hadn't ever seen it done before.

"You want to churn this or put it in the refrigerator?" I asked.

"Churn it, I guess."

So I poured it up in two big crocks and left it sitting on the drainboard.

"Well," I asked her, "did you see which one he picked?" Meaning Bonney, and she knew exactly what I meant.

She laughed a little. "Not any of 'em. He got drunk and went to bed and left all four of 'em high and dry and horny as high school girls."

232

He's saving up, I guess, for Elaine Farley. "Well, he's not himself, like you say."

"I wonder what's gnawin' at him. I wish I knew. I might help him."

You ought to tell her something. The old girl's going to worry herself into bed.

The coffee in the percolator was showing dark brown in the top so I poured us each a big mug and sat down across the kitchen table from her. "I wasn't going to tell anybody, but I'll tell you if you'll swear to keep it under your hat."

She was suddenly alert. "Cross my heart," she said, and zigzagged a forefinger over her chest.

"That beer joint down there doesn't belong to Bonney any longer."

"How *come* it doesn't?"

"Because it belongs to me, that's why."

"The hell it does."

"The hell it doesn't. It's mine."

"Why? He didn't *sell* it to you."

"No, I won it, playing eight-ball."

"I don't believe that."

"It's true."

Her eyes were bright now. They drilled me, searching my face.

She said, "I'll be switched. It *is* true."

"Yes."

"Well, I'll be damn. What do you want with that beer joint? Are you gonna run it?"

"No, I'm going to give it back to Bonney. But he doesn't know it and I don't *want* him to know it, yet. You crossed your heart, remember."

Then she began laughing. She started slow and built up and finally raised her feet and slapped her legs and her knees hit the table and overturned both the coffee mugs onto the oilcloth. She found a dish towel and began mopping up the spilled coffee, her shoulders still shaking with laughter.

"Johnny," she said, "you *dawg*. You're just a damn city slicker. You *slickered* 'im, didn't you?"

I grinned.

"You never *did* fool *me*. I knew, from the day you came here, all you wanted was to beat Bonney playin' pool. You're just like a damn gunslinger from times past. You hear about somebody that's a stick and you got to come here and beat 'im, isn't that right?"

I kept grinning.

"That smart britches. That Bonney. I swear, I wish I coulda seen his face when you whipped 'im for the place. You been hustlin' that boy, all this time. Hell's jingle *bells* but that's good. No *wonder* that smart-ass been feelin' bad."

She stomped off to her bedroom to get dressed. She was a new woman. Totally revived. I felt good about that much.

At eight o'clock I went out on the front porch and waited for the mail carrier.

"Son . . . of . . . a . . . *bitch*," he said, when he read the letter. He came out from behind the bar and began pacing around in tight circles on the dance floor.

"Those *bas*tards!" Pacing, circling, slapping the letter.

It was easy. It worked fine. When the mail carrier passed Rose-Mama's house I got in the car and rolled down the slope right behind him, so nobody could get to Bonney's mailbox before I did. Bringing in the mail was a habit of mine, anyway. When I went down in the morning I'd stop at the box and take the mail out and go on in and toss it on the bar. So this time when I opened the box, I just slipped the phony IRS letter in with the other mail.

I thought he'd never get around to reading it. He had a hangover. He came in the kitchen and got a cup of coffee down and then he stretched out on Barney's Couch for half an hour.

When he stirred I held up the almost-empty bourbon bottle that he stuck under the bar when he went to bed the night before. "Look, I found the dog that bit you. Little of his hair left if you want to try it."

He shook his head and frowned. "Ugh. Don't think I could get it down."

Finally he went to the bar and opened the coldest can of beer he could find and sipped, experimentally. It seemed to help him. He got about half the beer down before he began going through the mail. In a few seconds he was out there on the dance floor, pacing and cussing.

"What's the trouble?" I asked him.

"Those *bas*tards! Look at this, will you? From the hod-dammed sons-a-bitchin' *in*come tax office. Internal Revenue. They wanta *check* me! On the tenth, of all the stinkin' pieces of crummy luck. *Look* at this."

I thought the letter was pretty good. The reproduced letterhead was a little pale and fuzzy, but then who looks at letterheads? The envelope with the pasted-on address was a masterpiece. Cassy had to repair it where Dan had torn it with an opener. She did a good job. But it wasn't important now because Bonney ripped the envelope up when he opened it. I didn't have a guide about how to word the letter, except for the vague details I remembered from five years earlier when I'd gotten one of those friendly notices to come visit the boys in the office for a tax audit. I made the letter to Bonney read a little more menacing. It instructed him to show up at the Houston office of the IRS on the tenth day of January with all the receipts and invoices and canceled checks and accounting records necessary to justify his income tax returns over the past five years.

"Five years. Hod-oh-mighty damn. Ain't *that* a pretty kettle of guts? Five friggin' years."

"Tough break," I said. "Comes at a bad time, huh?"

"Yeah. Bad time."

"Well, you'll just have to change some plans, I guess, and hold off a while on leaving."

He quit pacing and walked over to the west windows and sat on the pool table. He always raised hell when anybody else did that. He didn't like people sitting on the table, mashing down the cushions.

"Well," he said, "things are *really* screwed up, now."

I let him sit there and simmer for a while.

"Maybe it won't be so bad," I said. "The way your books are, maybe they'll just put it all down to bad accounting. They might not stick you much. Just make you pay up, maybe."

235

He shook his head. "Those books, they're not what I'm thinking about. There's another little thing or two."

"Oh?"

He had the letter in his hand and he thumped it. "They're talking about canceled checks here. Well, I got a canceled check back there somewhere for twelve thousand dollars that I wrote to Mrs. Covington for my land here."

"So?"

"So I expect they'll be real interested in that check. And a few others I wrote back about three years ago or so, along about that time."

"You mean that money you won playing pool, like you told Brad?"

"Yeah. Except I didn't win it playing pool, and I didn't put it down on any income return, either."

"My god, Bonney, you had twelve thousand dollars and didn't report it as income? Man, that's asking for it. That's pretty stupid."

"More than twelve. Fif*teen*, is more like it."

Well, here it comes at last. He's going to tell me. "Man, that may be pretty tough. Robbing your own cash register is one thing. But that fifteen grand, hoo boy, I don't know about that."

"Hell you don't," he said. "You know well as I do. They give a guy a little college education for things like that. Put him in school up there at Seagoville. If he's *lucky* he goes to Seagoville."

"Why in the hell did you want to do such a dumb thing?"

He swung off the pool table and went to the bar and got his can of beer, drained it, and opened another. I pretended I needed the rest room and I went in and stayed five minutes. *Just let him stew, see what he says.*

When I came out he was in front of the stove, with his back to it, his hands behind him as if he needed to warm them. The stove wasn't even burning. He had his chin tucked and his eyes down, not focused on anything. His thoughtful pose. I'd seen it before, when he considered things he didn't like to consider.

"Johnny?"

"Yes."

236

"Why will a man screw up the only things he cares a damn about?"

"Because the things he cares about are the easiest to screw up, I guess."

He looked at me quickly and nodded. I doubt he'd ever thought of that ancient truth.

"I'm just a damn wonder at it. Sometimes I figure I hold the championship. Been that way—oh, hell, ever since me and Joe Whitaker were running around here, chasing tail. Joe, he was the best friend I ever had. You know what I did to him? I killed him off. What do you think of that?"

"Maudie told me a little about that. She said it was an accident."

"Well, it wasn't any accident that I got him to run off and get in the Marines with me, when he didn't even want to go. I *made* him go, and then damn if I didn't put him in a Jeep and run him into a tree and kill him. One minute he's sitting there with me singing a song and the next I know he's laying up there on the hood of that Jeep, with his head all smashed. . . ."

It's confession day, folks. He needs to tell it all. So just sit back and let him go.

". . . and Sam Hobbs. Same way. Sam was the best old boy. I *swear* he was good to me, way back there. So I got *him* all screwed up, too, with that bitch of a woman. . . ."

"Millie?"

"Yeah. Sam, he wasn't ever very good with the girls. Afraid of 'em, sort of. Well, I figured all he needed was a good piece of tail. So one night I took Millie over there and just threw her in Sam's bed. Hell, she wasn't any kind of a prize by then, I guarantee you. Me and anybody else around here with five bucks and a bottle been banging her for a long time. Fact is, you want the truth, I'm the reason she went bad. I used to go over in the Blackjack when Slat wasn't anything but a little skinny-ass girl and crawl in the sack with Millie. Slat right there in the house, and her daddy out horsing around somewhere. I'd leave a little something over there. Like groceries, or a couple of bucks. I'd *pay* her, is what Millie thought. So she wasn't much better than a whore when I stuck her in Sam's bed that time. But poor old Sam, damn if he didn't fall in love with her. Couldn't

237

help himself. And she drained him. Took every damn nickel he had and got him in that bottle and flat finished him off, and it was me that put her in his bed. That little honor, that's mine. . . ."

He had a foot up in one of the chairs near the stove and he was leaning forward with his elbows crossed on his knee, his third can of beer hanging loosely between a thumb and a forefinger.

". . . a nice old fellow like Sam. It beats the very hell out of me. You'd think I'd do it to somebody like Norman Akers, a son of a bitch that *deserves* to get screwed. Even Rose-Mama, and my own mother, too, I've managed to hit them some hard licks. Killing Joe that way, in that Jeep. That really hurt them. And Joe's dad, it killed him the same as it did Joe. . . ."

"Aw, come on, now. You're taking credit for too much."

"No, hell no. It's the truth. My own mama, I couldn't even be what *she* wanted me to be. It hurts her, right now, because I'm here running this place, and she doesn't even know it's a beer joint. Thinks it's a café and a grocery store. And she didn't ask much. She didn't want me to be a judge or a preacher or anything impossible like that. Just wanted me to be something except what my old man was, and damn if I didn't take my chip right off the old man's block. Like it runs in the blood, you know, the same as Eddie bull having that pinch-ass and all his calves got one too, just like his. But Mama—I wish you could know her, Johnny, because she's the sweetest little old woman that ever was—she always needed somebody to . . . to be *proud* of, you know? That old man of mine, hoda*mighty* he led that little woman a hell of a life. I don't really know why. At first, when I was a kid, things seemed all right. I mean I thought the old man was really something when I was little. He was a big tall fellow, nice-looking and all. Worked at the hardware store, back when Arty Baker's daddy had it, and, hell, I thought he was the most important man in the whole world. When I was four, maybe five, he'd take me downtown with him on holidays, like the Fourth of July, to put the flag out. The store'd be closed, you know, but he had a key to the front door and he'd open it and get a broom and sweep off the sidewalk out front and then he'd get the flag and stick it in that brass slot they always had out front of all the stores. Then we'd stand there a minute, looking at the flag waving in the wind, and then we'd go walking around the square and telling people howdy. Mister, right then I was proud of him, because he was so tall and important. One day after we put the flag out—I was about six years old, I think—we went walking around the square and we met some people, just strangers, I didn't even know who they were, and I was so proud of walking around that square with the old man I just busted right out loud and *told* those strangers about it, right there on the street. I told 'em he was my daddy and he worked at the hardware store and had a key to the front door and he swept the sidewalk and put out the flag on the Fourth of July. I just had to tell it, you know. Well, when we got around the corner, that bastard grabbed me and just slapped the living *hell* out of me, about six times, right across the mouth, and he told me if I ever said anything like that again I wouldn't have any tongue in my head to talk *with* and . . ."

Father in heaven, did You ever hear anything to beat that? Why, it's a marvel he didn't grow up in a lunatic asylum after that.

". . . it took, I guess years, for me to realize why he did it, that he was ashamed, you know, to be a clerk in a hardware store. And then when Suzie got sick—Suzie was my little sister, I don't guess I've ever told you about her—she had polio when she was little and ended up crippled and it seemed like the old man blamed Mama for it some way. After that he turned just flat bad, and chased around after women a lot. Wouldn't even sleep with Mama. Never did, after Suzie. I don't know, Johnny, if you've ever known a good woman who needs to be loved and nobody's loving her. It's the saddest thing can happen to a woman. They just sit there and die, from the inside out. Mama, she ended up without anything left, except me. And now this," jerking a thumb at the bar, where he left the IRS letter, "this'll just finish her off, I expect, when they stick me on that money."

He took his foot off the chair and drank the rest of his beer and looked over his shoulder and flipped the can, fully twenty feet across the bar. It clanged and rattled and bounced down into the empty garbage can he kept back there. A direct hit. But he didn't snap his fingers.

I went behind the bar and got him another beer. *Just keep quiet, now. Don't say anything. He's not through. He'll tell the rest of it, and then you'll know it all. There's not much more.* He took the can of beer without a word.

"That money? The fifteen thousand? Johnny, you really won't believe this."

Here it comes.

He was almost grinning. "Hoddamn, I'm telling you, it's the damnedest thing. I was over there at Beaumont, hustling those fuzzy-faced sailors in the parlors, taking their pay. Making pretty good money. But you can't make *big* money playing eight-ball. *You* know that. You make some, sure, but it's like any kind of gambling money. It's not worth a damn. It won't stay with you. I got to staying in a place over there, a fat little Mexican woman ran it. Real sweet woman, and just crazy as hell. I liked her. She was real good to me. . . ."

He shook his head, really grinning now, at some private memory.

". . . and there was this old guy, I guess he was seventy-five, maybe more, got to coming in there and sweating my games. Some reason, he took to sort of following me around. Nice old guy. Name was Keller—Edward B. Keller. Well, he'd come in there and—"

Keller. Almost a shock to hear him call the Old Man's name. Yes, and my name too. It sounds foreign, doesn't it, as if it belongs now to somebody else.

"—finally we got to eating dinner together and walking around the streets late in the afternoons and telling jokes and just horsing around. I got to where I really liked that old devil. We went fishing a few times. Old fart really loved that fishing, and he was pretty good at it too. Then he kept pestering me to come out and see where he lived. It was one of these old folks homes, out on the edge of town. I went out there and fooled around a good bit. Place just full of lonesome old guys, and gals too, prettiest old gals you ever saw. Why, hell, it didn't take a damn *thing* to make 'em smile. You could say hello and pat one on the hand and she'd just purr. Made you feel like a hero. I liked that place. Bunch of real sweet old folks. (His face bright now, and happy, as if he were there again, spreading cheer, making them smile.)

And that old guy, that Mr. Keller, we got to be regular buddies. I messed around with him, oh, I guess six months, maybe more. We went to ball games a time or two, into Houston, and we'd go to the beach, a lot of places. He was a lonesome old bird. Didn't have anybody cared a damn about him. But it got to where it seemed like we sort of be*longed* together, you know? Strange as hell, tell the truth. But it was a little bit the way I used to feel when I was a kid, way back yonder, and going round the square with my old man before I found out what a *son* of a bitch he was. . . ."

He walked out on the dance floor so he could look through the serving window and through the kitchen toward the barn. A racket was coming from out there. But it was just Turnip, romping with his dogs.

When he turned back to me, his face was dark again. "We had a thing going, that old gent and me. And then you know what I did? Old Bonney, he's got to screw it up. That old guy used to talk to me a lot about opening some kind of a place. He always wanted to go into a business. Like a pool hall. I'd keep telling him it took money to open a place. Finally he said he *had* some money. Said if I'd go partners with him we'd open us a hall. At first I just kidded along with him. I'd say, sure, sure, we'd go partners. Hell, I thought he was just whistlin' Dixie. Then one day by damn he walked into that Mexican woman's place and called me to the back and tossed a package on one of the tables and kiss your tail if it wasn't fifteen thousand dollars, cash. I told him to go put it back where it came from, before one of those winos or jitterbugs knocked him in the head and took it off him. But no, hell no. He kept saying take it, take it, open a place, we'll go partners. Finally he just walked away and left me standing there, looking at that money on the table. I bundled it up and took it home with me, to the hotel room I was staying in. Man, I didn't sleep all night, laying there with that wad of money in my pillow case, poking into the back of my neck. . . ."

He paced a little on the dance floor, remembering, running his hand over his scalp and down his neck.

". . . I don't know, Johnny, if you ever wanted fifteen thousand bucks, as bad as I did that night. All my life, I'd been

241

daydreaming about just one good payday like that, so I could get the hell away from towns, and buy me a little piece of ground and get a few cows where there's trees and creeks and all. So finally before sunup I just took off. Put that money in my suitcase and cut out. And I never did go back."

He grabbed one of the chairs by its back and twisted it around and sat down on it, straddling the seat backward. And gave a sarcastic little laugh. "Wasn't that a real Boy Scout stunt? Hodamighty. I used to keep saying, well, one of these times I'll go look that old fellow up and start paying the money back. But I'd keep putting it off, you know. And now it's too late."

Well, there it is, finally, all of it. What are you going to say now?

"Poor old Mama," he said, "she hears about this income tax thing, it'll pretty near kill her."

I was glad when Turnip came in, and Barney just behind him.

Before noon I walked up the slope. Not along the blacktop but through the low-growing brush and up on the ridge to the pines and Sam's grave.

A bright, calm day. I could see Turnip burning trash in the oil drum behind the barn. The smoke from his fire rose straight up and then flattened out and formed a wispy umbrella over the tavern and the house down there beneath the trees. From across the blacktop I could hear Rose-Mama singing in her kitchen . . . "When the roll is called up yonder I'll be there. . . ."

Far down the west side of the slope, Brad's cows grazed on a winter oat crop, a carpet of deep blue-green contrasting in an almost violent way with the summer grasses laid low and brown by the frost.

Well, it's just about all over, isn't it? Almost time to go. Not quite, though. Just a little more unfinished business. Mrs. Junior Farley.

Yes.

Do you think it's going to work?

I think so. It'll work, just as soon as she finds out about that tax rap he's got coming to him. She won't be throwing any sexy smiles when she hears he's not going off on any wife-stealing honeymoon, that instead he'll very likely be going to that federal college up at Seagoville.

But he's not going to Seagoville, you know that.

Yes, but *she* won't know it.

You think that'll cool her britches down?

Mrs. Junior Farley? You damn right it will. Can you see that woman pledging her undying love, promising to wait for him, when she knows he'd come out of a federal prison without a dime, without enough money to buy a bus ticket to Houston?

I don't know. It's not pat. It may not work.

It's *got* to work. It's the only thing I have.

Do you think he'll tell her about the letter?

I'll ask him, tonight. If he won't, I'll go tell her myself.

Somehow it didn't occur to me that he might just pick up and run off. But he did, that night, before I had the chance to talk to him again. Turnip came running up the slope about dark, his face glistening tears. "Mr. Bonney's gone," he sobbed. "Gone . . . and I know . . . he ain't comin' back."

Barney had his old scowl on when Turnip and I got to the tavern. He had a good many beer drinkers and no help and I could tell he was about to take off his apron and quit.

I got him back in the kitchen. "What's this about Bonney leaving?"

"He sure left," Barney said. "Didn't say a word. Just come in here a while ago and opened the lockbox and cleaned it out. He damn near cleaned the register out too. Didn't hardly leave enough in there to make change. He's damn sure going somewhere. Beats me, I don't know. Didn't even say kiss my butt, just took off, wearin' that goddamn suit, too."

That suit! Elaine Farley!

"How long? How long's he been gone?"

"Twenty minutes, half hour, maybe."

He could be halfway to Houston, because he'd be driving with a heavy foot. No way to catch him.

Buddy, you've screwed everything up now, real pretty, with that income tax letter. Hell, they may go to Mexico.

I was standing in the kitchen trying to think when Maudie

came in the back door. Her face said she knew something. She beckoned and I went out the door with her.

"Bonney's gone," I told her.

"I know. And I know why. She called him."

"Elaine Farley."

"That's right. She called him and told him to meet her."

"How do you know?"

"Ada Hicks. Bonney didn't lay it all out for me but I could tell something was up. So I got Ada to listen for me. Flora called him from the house about five-thirty. Told him to meet her in Houston at eight o'clock tonight. At the Stanwick Hotel."

The Stanwick, my god. No wonder he cleaned out the cash register.

I went back in and got Barney and Turnip together. "Listen, I need your help. I'm going to Houston and try to catch Bonney. He's about to make him a big mistake and I'll try to stop him. If you want to help Bonney, both of you stay right here and take care of business. Take care of it just like nothing's happened. Don't tell anybody Bonney took off. Turnip, in about fifteen minutes you take Barney's car and go up and get Rose-Mama. And listen, you keep your face straight, you hear? Tell her we had a bottle, that we're drinking, horsing around. But don't you get any notions in your head about going off and trying to find Bonney yourself. And Barney, for God's sake, don't quit on me, not now. Place'll fall apart if you do. If either one of you ever want to see Bonney again, you stay put."

They stared at me, blank-faced. But they nodded.

I walked quickly through Bonney's house, just to check. Every item of clothing that might be considered dress-up was gone. And his toilet articles were gone from the bathroom. I almost missed the envelope on top of the television set. It wasn't sealed. A single sheet of paper inside. And Bonney's handwriting:

To Who It May Concern
Johnny Lancaster is owner of the Highway Cafe & Gro. at Farley, Tex. This house too, if he does what I told him.

Bonham J. McCamey

244

That smart bastard. He knew that note wasn't worth its ink. But he also knew me, knew I'd take it seriously, knew I'd stay around and try to carry out the duties of Bonney McCamey's conscience. I crammed the note in my hip pocket.

Within fifteen minutes I was roaring down the Interstate at ninety, trying to watch for Highway Patrol and thinking what I'd told Barney and Turnip and Maudie. "I'm going to look for Bonney."

That's exactly what you told Midge, four months ago.

I got to the hotel at fifteen minutes past eight and I was walking through the front door when it hit me what I looked like, going into the most exclusive hotel in town. I had on what I wore when I milked Elizabeth. Khaki pants and a lumberjack shirt. I bet I smelled bad.

So I didn't get the time of day out of the gentlemen on the desk. Oh, they were polite. Just as polite as you can expect clerks in fancy hotels to be, toward a guy in khaki pants who probably smells bad. No, they had no one named McCamey registered. No one named Farley, either. And, no, they hadn't seen a tall brown-haired man wearing a blue suit.

I spent about twenty minutes sitting in my car, watching the hotel, looking for Bonney's pickup, for Elaine Farley's Continental.

Then I called Cassy and drove out to her house. She laughed when I walked in.

"Well, Farmer Brown," she said. I looked down at my shoes. They had dried cow manure on them. My God, standing on Cassy's living room carpet, with cow manure on my shoes.

She stayed on the telephone for two hours. She called most of the airlines and half a dozen travel agencies. She checked small-plane charter flights. She even called a woman she knew at the bus station. By eleven o'clock—nothing. No luck. "They could be in Mexico by now," Cassy said.

Yes, or helling it down some highway in that Continental, who knows what direction.

Before I left she asked, "What about the telegram? Will you want me to send it?"

"No point in it, now. I guess I better retire from the forgery game. I haven't managed to do anything but foul up the works, really proper."

"I'm sorry."

"Yeah, so am I. Well, Cass, thank you. You've helped a lot. Above and beyond the call."

She stood in the door as I left and asked, "Will you be coming back soon? To the office?"

"I don't know. Tell Dan I'll call him in a couple of days."

I loafed back across town and hit the Interstate. Just to keep from going on back, to report, I stopped at the airport and walked through both terminals and searched faces. Suddenly I just ran out of gas, so damned tired I couldn't walk, so I collapsed in a chair and sat there an hour or more, hoping a miracle would occur and Bonney would come gliding around a corner. I knew he wouldn't, though.

Well, what do you do now?

Go on back to Farley, I guess, and tell Turnip and Rose-Mama and Barney and Maudie. Tell 'em he's gone.

And then what? Settle down? And run that beer joint?

I suppose so. What else can I do?

Well, you might as well get going then. They don't like for beer-joint operators with cow dung on their shoes to sleep all night in fancy airports.

It must have been two o'clock in the morning, maybe two-thirty, when I swung off the Interstate to hit the blacktop to Farley. I almost didn't glance over at Thelma Evans' Kingfish Inn, darkened and closed on the service road along the highway.

But when I did, I hit the brakes.

Well I'll be damned.

Sitting out front, easily recognizable in the parking lot light, was Bonney's pickup.

Well I'll just be goddamned.

I whipped off the blacktop and stopped at the side and looked in a window. Nothing. Just the night lights over the bar. I went to the rear where Thelma and her husband had living quarters. I bammed on the door until Thelma opened up.

"Thelma? Johnny Lancaster, from over at Farley."

"Oh, yeah."

"Sorry to wake you up but . . ."

"I wasn't asleep. What's the trouble?"

"I see Bonney's pickup out front. I need to know. What time did he leave it here?"

"He didn't leave it. He's still here."

Well I'll be damned.

"Still here? Who's with him?"

"Nobody. He's sitting in yonder in the front, in a booth. Been there since nine o'clock."

"And nobody's with him?"

"Nope."

"Is he drunk?"

"No. I thought he was at first, but he's not. He's been sitting in there all this time not saying a thing. When I closed up he didn't want to go, so I just left him."

"Can I talk to him?"

"I wish you would. Something's eating on him. Come on in."

He was in one of the front booths, sitting in almost total darkness. I slipped into the seat across the table. "Hey."

"Hi, Johnny."

Thelma was right. He wasn't drunk. He had a fifth on the table but it was almost full.

"You all right?" I asked him.

"Sure. In the pink. You?"

"OK."

He didn't seem to be sulking. He wasn't slumped down in the seat. Just sitting there, straight and still.

"I've been looking for you," I said. "I was afraid you'd cut out on me."

He nodded, his head a vague shape in the gloom.

"Turnip and Barney, they got all uptight when they saw you leave, with your clothes and all," I said.

"Yeah, that was crappy, I guess."

"I thought maybe you and Mrs. Farley had left, like you planned."

"Yeah. She called me to meet her. In Houston."

"You didn't go?"

"Sure, I went."

"Change your mind, at the last minute?"

A little mirthless laugh. Then he said, "She didn't show up."
Well, I'll just be goddamned.

"She stood me up, Johnny, like a tall tree."

His cigarette lighter flicked on and he shoved a piece of paper across the table.

"A bellhop," he said, "met me at the door of the hotel and gave me this." He held the lighter so I could read it.

> Bonney McCamey: You can go to hell or
> anywhere else you care to go because I'm
> not going with you and I never will.
>   Mrs. Junior Farley

That bitch. So it was all a setup, just so she could shoot him down, the same way he did it to her that day she came to see Turnip, the same way they'd always tried to cut one another. But man, *what* a setup! Her coming to Slat's wedding was part of it; her spending four days in bed with him was part of it too. My, my.

"Pretty rough," I said.

"I'd say she sort of told me off, wouldn't you?"

He flicked the lighter again to smoke and maybe there was a hint of a crooked grin on his mouth, maybe a little gleam of admiration in his eyes.

"That woman," I said, "she's really something."

"Yes, sir," he said, "she really is."

My eyes gradually adjusted to the darkness and I could see the outline of his hands, the fingers revolving the lighter, over and over, end over end, slow and smooth.

I said, "Then you won't be leaving now."

The fingers stopped fiddling with the lighter. He slapped it down, flat, on the table, like a man setting out a stack of chips. "I've just been sitting here thinking about it all, trying to decide whether I ought to go on home or not. I don't believe I will. Think I'll just go back to Houston. I won't be staying a lot longer anyhow. When this tax business comes up, I'll just have to go through a lot of good-by crap. I don't think I could stand it. Just like tonight. Hell, I didn't have the guts to go and tell 'em I was leaving. So I think what I'll do, I'll just call Brad in the morning and sell him my land over the phone. He can get the papers fixed up and meet me in Houston and bring me my money. Then I've got till the tenth of January before that tax thing. Before that, I'm going back to Beaumont and find Mr. Keller and give him his money back. I know that won't keep 'em from sticking me on the tax thing but——"

"That old man may be dead, by now," I said. *Careful, now, careful.*

"Well, if he is, then he's bound to have folks somewhere. I'll find 'em. If he's got folks, they'll damn sure be wondering where that money went."

"You said he was lonesome, that Mr. Keller. Where were his folks when *you* were going round with him, fooling with him, showing him a good time?"

"I don't know."

"Seems to me, by god, *they* were the ones should have been seeing the old man wasn't lonesome. How long did you pal around with him? Six months, did you say?"

"Six, maybe seven. I don't know."

"Was the old gent happy, during that time?"

"I guess he was. Well, sure, hell yes he was. What are you getting at?"

"Did his folks ever come to see him? Did they do a damn thing for him?"

"Beats me. I don't know. He never mentioned 'em."

"So if the old guy's dead, and he very likely is, by now, you want to look up his folks and give *them* the money, when they didn't care a damn about him?"

"Well, it's theirs, by rights."

"I say it's not."

He fired the lighter again and I watched his pupils grow suddenly smaller, reacting to the flame. "You trying to say I *earned* that money?"

"Well, didn't you? How many guys, guys your age, would spend six, seven months fooling around with a lonesome old man, making life mean something to him?"

"Hell's afire, Johnny, I stole that money from him."

"No, you didn't. Not from what you told me. He practically forced it on you. Listen, I bet that old guy wouldn't *trade* those seven months for fifteen thousand dollars."

249

"I don't know. Anyhow, it wasn't any trouble for me to mess around with him." Then he said it. I didn't think he could say it, but he did. "I loved that old guy, Johnny."

That's all I want to hear. That's plenty.

"Then you don't owe anybody a thing," I told him. "If I were you, I wouldn't go back looking for the old man because he's dead and . . ." *Watch out, you stupid bastard!* ". . . at least it's a good *bet* he's dead, and I sure as hell wouldn't go selling off any land to pay back money to the old guy's family, not when they didn't do as much to earn it as you did."

But he came back at me again. "You say *you* wouldn't do it. That's a lot of crap. I know you. You'd go and do it because you'd think it was the right thing to do."

"No, I wouldn't. Not on a deal like that I wouldn't."

"Well, anyhow, that wouldn't change anything. I still got the tax business on me. I'll pretty likely have to sell the land anyway when they get to digging in *my* little doings, on taxes."

Take it easy, now. Go slow. Think. Do it right. He's down on himself right now and you have to be careful.

"Are you saving this bottle for New Year's?" I asked him.

He shoved it across the table to me, along with one of Thelma's little glasses. I poured about a double shot and sipped on it.

"That tax thing?" I said. "It's just a routine audit. It could be fixed." Trying to say it casual, you know, and patting my pockets. "I'm out of cigarettes."

He passed me a cigarette. When he thumbed the lighter I tried to make him see a different face, one he hadn't seen on me, sort of half-smiling and wicked and knowing.

"Fix Internal Revenue?" He chuckled. "Shoot."

"On a little thing like this," I said, "it could be done."

"Who's gonna do it? You?"

"Sure."

Then he laughed right out loud. "That's the best joke I've heard this week. You! Johnny, you couldn't fix a friggin' parking ticket. Or you *would*n't, if you could."

"That's just what you think. You don't know a damn thing about me. All you know about me is, I just walked into your

250

place and rented a room up the hill. You never have *cared* what I am. I may have more money than Norman Akers, and be a big shot."

He laughed again. "Sure. And I might be Howard Hughes. Hell, Johnny, you haven't ever been any mystery to me. You're not anybody. You're just a guy that had a pretty wife, and she died, and you're out running around trying to forget things. You're not even a pool player, like Rose-Mama thinks. You couldn't make room rent playing pool."

"I beat *your* tail. Won me a beer joint, too."

"Yeah, and you did it with a whorehouse break and shit-stick pool. Just luck. Anyway, you wouldn't fix that tax business if you *owned* the government, because it'd be against the law."

"The law's ass," I said. "Law's not always right. You said that yourself, the night I hit Akers and damn near killed him."

"That was different."

"No it wasn't, not a bit. But get back on the subject. I'll bet you a hundred bucks I can fix that tax audit."

Maybe I said it right because he quit laughing. "Internal Revenue? Johnny, you're talking about a big coon up a terrible tall tree when you say fix Internal Revenue."

"Well, hell, we're not talking about fixing the whole damn federal government. We're just talking about a tax examination on a country beer-joint operator in Kirby County, Texas. But you're right, it's a fact I couldn't fix it myself but I have people who owe me. They could do it for us."

"How?"

"Hell with how."

"How much it cost?"

"Not a cent. Like I said, I have people who owe me."

He put both hands on the bottle and rolled it back and forth across the table. Thinking. Considering.

"You're not kidding," he said.

"I'm not kidding."

"What would it take? I mean, what would I have to do?"
There!

"You'd have to get your ass out of this booth and get in that truck and go on home and act like nothing's happened. Tell Turnip and Barney and Rose-Mama and Maudie and anybody else who's still awake and waiting for you that you and I have just been out screwing around, that everything's all right, that there's nothing to worry about. Tell 'em to go to bed and forget it. Tell Turnip—if he's still there, because by this time he may have taken Barney's car and gone looking for you—tell him the world hasn't come to an end. If Rose-Mama's found out something's wrong, tell her *nothing* is wrong. If Brad's around there —hell, they might have called him in by now—tell him your land is not for sale. Don't try to explain anything to anybody. Just tell 'em everything's all right. Now come on, let's go. You told me the night I hit Akers that I ought to let somebody help me. All right, I did let you. Now you let somebody help you. All right?"

"All right," he said. "Let's go."

When we got to the back door, Thelma came to let us out. Without a word, Bonney hugged her and kissed her square on the mouth.

Well, maybe things are getting back to normal.

"You go ahead," I told him, outside. "I got a phone call to make."

"This time of night?"

"Just go on, will you?"

"OK. OK."

When the taillights of his pickup disappeared I went in the phone booth in Thelma's parking lot and dialed Cassy. Heaven knows what time it was.

"Cass? The next time I see you, I'll bring a gun and you can shoot me, for waking you up. But I have to know . . . do you still have the telegram, to Bonney, that I wrote out for you? I mean you didn't tear it up or anything."

"No, I still have it."

"Great. Send it, in the morning, will you? I'm about to go to sleep. I'm dead. I haven't slept in two nights and I'm afraid I won't wake up until noon. Send it about nine o'clock. And just sign it with the phony name, like I said. Don't let IRS get on it anywhere. You know?"

"I know. Arthur J. Foster."

252

"That's right. Bless you, Cass. And tell Dan I'll be back to work January second."

It would have been fun to watch his face when the telegram came. But I was asleep. I was so tired I barely remember driving those last ten miles from Sullivan to Rose-Mama's. I fell in the bed and didn't regain consciousness until almost eleven o'clock the next morning.

The first noise I heard was the screech of tires, braking on the blacktop in front of the house. Then car doors slamming. Shouts. Laughter. Dogs barking.

"Hey! Johnny!"

Then the thud of his boots hitting the steps.

"Rose-Mama? Johnny! Hey, where in the hell *is* everybody?" Stomping through the house. Turnip's dogs happily yelping on the porch, their claws tick-tick-ticking on the boards.

Then he was in the room and beating on me, giving me an awful pummeling through Rose-Mama's quilts.

"Johnny, you son of a bitch! You *bas*tard! I didn't think you could do it! Looka *here*, will you?" And he jerked the yellow paper out of his shirt pocket and fanned it in my face and then he fell back in a chair, laughing, all doubled up and shaking, laughing out of control, his face deep dark-red and the veins in his temples so distended I was afraid he'd pop one.

Turnip was in the door of my bedroom, grinning happily. His eyes said he didn't know exactly what it was all about, but it was bound to be good and that was enough.

And now Rose-Mama came in from out back somewhere in her old blue suspender overalls and rubber boots, asking what in the everlasting *hell* was going *on* and Bonney leaped out of the chair and hugged her and kissed her and then began to dance about, swinging her. Stomping. Singing. . . .

> *Chickens in the horse trough, apeckin' up grain,*
> *Papa's at the depot, awaitin' on the train,*
> *Mama's in the smokehouse, afetchin' up a ham.*
> *Where's ol' Bessie? Akissin' ol' Sam!*

Turnip, his grin growing, patting a foot, clapping out the beat, and suddenly Bonney grabbed him and drew him close

253

and hugged him with his free arm and there they were, all in a bunch, hugging and laughing and Turnip and Rose-Mama not even knowing why, and not caring.

I got out of bed and shoved them out in the hall, where they nearly fell into a heap. I said, "Get out of my room and let me sleep." I shut the door. For a long time I could hear them in the kitchen, talking and laughing and making big plans for a New Year's Eve celebration that was "pretty near goin' to cause earthquakes."

I found the telegram down in the covers:

> BONHAM J. MCCAMEY
> HIGHWAY CAFE & GRO
> ROUTE 2—FARLEY, TEX
> REGARDING NOTICE DATED 23 DEC INSTRUCTING YOU
> REPORT MY OFFICE 10 JAN, PLEASE DISREGARD—
> MY APOLOGIES—NOTICE SENT IN ERROR.
> > ARTHUR J. FOSTER

I went down to the tavern around three o'clock. Brad was getting in his Jeep to leave as I rolled up.

"Did you make a deal with him?" I asked.

"Nope."

"Why not?"

"Price of land around here," he said, "still goin' up."

"Then he's not going to sell it?"

"I'd say that's pretty close to the mark."

Bonney stuck his head out the front door. "Brad? I've changed my mind. I'll sell all my ground. For eight hundred an acre."

"You better go sell it to Norman," Brad said, driving off.

Bonney stood in the door laughing and watched him go. Then to me, "Come on, Johnny, I got to bounce down yonder in the creek and check my cows. And we got a little business to talk over."

We got in the truck and he wound up the hill behind the tavern, past the cattle pens, along the fence where we killed the doe that night. And down into the creek.

"Topsoil along this little creek here, Johnny, it's I bet forty

254

foot deep. It's real good dirt, man. No telling *what* Norman would pay for this bottom here. I might sell a little of it, sometime, and get all that tax thing squared away. Just walk in down there and tell 'em I made me a mistake a few years back and now I want to straighten it out. Just pay 'em. How about that?"

"Do you think you'd really do that?"

"I don't know," he laughed. "I might. I been thinking about it."

I devoted a few seconds to guessing whether he'd ever do it or not. I doubted he would. What was it he said, up there on the ridge at Sam's funeral that day? *We'd all like to reorganize, and be better folks, but we just don't have what it takes.*

"Tell you what, Johnny, I owe you, now, you taking me off the hook and all. Whyn't we——"

"Call it even," I said. "You saved my bacon when I hit Akers. Now I saved yours. Even-steven."

"Naw, man. What I was about to say, whyn't you and me just go partners here? That beer joint is yours now anyway, and the land and cattle, they're mine. We could join up, make a partnership. *You* haven't got anywhere you need to be, besides here. We couldn't make any money, but we'd have a hell of a lot of fun. We could make enough to eat, and drink a little whiskey, and play a lot of pool, and chase women, and stay out of jail."

"No, I don't want to run any beer joint. It's not my game. I got a taste of it when you left it with me those few days."

He stopped the truck. "Well, you want to sell it back?"

"No, but I'll play you a game for it."

His wicked little grin. "Charity, Johnny. I'd win it back. You can't beat me two straight."

"I've done it before."

"Luck. Just luck."

"Maybe so, but I could get lucky again. I *feel* lucky today."

"Naw, I'm not gonna do that," he said.

"You're afraid," I challenged him. "You're afraid I'll luck

255

out again, because you know damn well I'm going to make you put up something against my beer joint."

"All right, what?"

"Same thing you made *me* promise, when we played before."

He frowned. "You mean if I lose again, all I got to do is stick around here and take care of my folks? Shoot, I'd do that anyhow. You know that. I'm not going anywhere, not now."

"I'm not sure about that. I figure if Elaine Farley comes wiggling out here you're liable to go chasing off after her again."

A vigorous shake of his head. "No *way*. You don't need to worry about that."

"But that's not all you have to put up. If you lose, you'll run the place, for me. We'll work out a percentage, or a lease, whatever's fair. And if you run my beer joint, by god I want it run right. Quit screwing off on income tax. Quit shortchanging people just because they have a lot of money. And I wouldn't want you running my place if you're going to spotlight doe deer, and kill bucks out of season. And quit banging women on Barney's Couch, or there in the house when their husbands are sitting around not fifteen steps away. You're goint to get shot."

"You mean Maudie? Aw, me and Carlos, we got a deal on that."

"I know, but you don't have any deal with Charlotte's husband. He's going to walk in there one of these nights and blow your guts out."

"Well . . ."

"Are you ready to play?"

"Sure, smart-ass. If I win, I get my beer joint back."

Which was the most important thing to him. I knew that. The other stuff, the little sermon, he wasn't worried about that, but then I thought maybe he'd get the message even when he won. Because I wasn't figuring on winning.

Several beer drinkers were in the tavern when we got back but the pool table wasn't busy.

"We lag for break," Bonney said.

256

"We do like hell," I said. "I don't expect you've forgotten who won the last game. It's my break."

"All right, break."

I gave 'em the old cat-house roll again but the balls didn't set up crippled as before. And nothing fell.

He was all business. He studied the table for a full minute. He wasn't whistling or humming. Finally he chose the spots and sank the trey and the five. Then on his third shot I saw he was nervous. And he made a bad pool shot. When a guy gets nervous he'll shoot too hard sometimes. I'd never seen Bonney do it but he did it now. He cracked the six and it danced back and forth across the mouth of a corner pocket and popped out. But the worst thing was that his cue ball went banking around the table, moving balls, boxing corners. It looked like a shot one of the cowboys might make, just shooting hard and hoping nothing bad happened.

"Hod*damn!*" He turned away and sat down.

I think I could have won again. His cue ball had broken up a nest of the stripes and scattered them about, and I might have won, shooting smart pool. He saw it too. When he did, his face showed what I hadn't seen on it since the first day I walked into that tavern. He was scared. Winning the tavern back was so goddamned important to him that he was actually scared. It was written on him as clear as that telegram. The stiff upper lip and the little areas of white around the corners of his mouth.

So I went ahead and got it over with. His bad shot had moved the eight-ball near the side pocket. I put the draw on the cue ball off the ten to the corner pocket. The ten fell and the cue ball came skittering, curving backward and kissed the eight on the cheek and moved it just enough. Just barely enough. I didn't think it was going to fall. Bonney's table wasn't quite as fast as the one in Isabella's place in Beaumont where I'd practiced the shot probably a hundred times. The eight hung, even wobbled back toward the center of the table a little, before it dropped. It might not have fallen if I hadn't performed my little act and stomped the floor in disgust when the eight went rolling slowly toward that hole.

"Johnny," he said, "I never saw a prettier pool shot. I tell you what. Seeing you're a guest here, in my beer joint, I'll treat you to a cool one."

"I'd rather have whiskey," I said.

He laughed, and glided in that smooth way to the bar and fished the bottle out from under the bar.

We didn't have time to get the drink fixed before a fat fellow in khakis wandered in.

"I'm looking for a Mr. McCamey?" he said.

"You've found him," Bonney said.

"I got a stone on my truck. They said look for you."

"A stone?"

"A gravestone. A tombstone. For Mr. Hobbs? We'll set it if you'll tell us where."

The sun was slipping down through the pines and the little group of us sat on Sam's Bench and watched Rose-Mama wipe off the face of the gravestone. It was a private ceremony. Bonney and Turnip and Rose-Mama and Slat and Hank and me. And Brad, who just happened by, and told Bonney how he planned to put a gap, maybe even a cattle guard in his fence right along there, so people could stop and come in.

We stayed a long time, standing there reading the words sunk into the pale gray Texas granite:

SAMUEL WILKERSON HOBBS JUNIOR
COME SIT ON MY BENCH, AND REST

Bonney was pleased.

"Hoddamn, Johnny, that's good. That's just right. I wish ol' Sam could see it."

"Maybe he can," Slat said.

They all came to the tavern that night. All the Regulars, plus dozens of the Occasionals. A good night's business. I sat at the bar by Rose-Mama's flower vase.

Bonney was back in the saddle again. Being The Man, The Overseer. Slat and Hank were there and they danced the waltz along with Uncle Batey and Aunt Kate and said it was a good idea, dancing together that way every day. They said they were going to do it, the same way Uncle Batey and Aunt Kate had done it for fifty years.

Maudie—I'd never seen her looking so seductive—Maudie did her floor show. Picked up the salt shaker, both east and west, and got a fine ovation.

About ten o'clock I decided to go.

Just before I left, Norman Akers came in. He did his cowboy act and ordered up drinks for the house. I didn't see the denomination of the bill he gave Bonney. But I watched Akers stuff his change in his pocket without counting it and I decided not to ask Bonney whether he'd shortchanged ol' Norman. Because if I did ask, he'd tell me, and I didn't want to know.

When I went through the swinging door into the kitchen, Bonney was saying, loud, standing out in the middle of the dance floor, "Trouble with you folks, weather gets a little cool you don't drink enough suds. Me and Barney, we been thinkin' 'bout putting in couple more stoves, heat you up a little, give you some thirst in the wintertime."

Barney was busy frying leftover potatoes when I walked through the kitchen and out the back door. He didn't even notice me. I circled the tavern, past Charlotte's car parked under the longleaf pine, and drove up to Rose-Mama's.

It took less than fifteen minutes to gather up my things and get them in the car. The house was like a tomb, without Rose-Mama in it.

Well, do you think you've done the right things?

I don't know. Let's not get into that now.

You don't want to leave, do you?

No, I don't. I could stay here the rest of my life. What Bonney said? He was right. There's not really anywhere else I need to be.

I doubt that. You wouldn't ever really fit in around here. You'd always be an Outsider. You need to go back to the office, to your own people.

Back to a Better World?

Well, *isn't* it better? Surely you don't want to spend the rest of your life around here just playing pool and drinking a little whiskey and chasing women and staying out of jail?

You say I wouldn't like to. I say I would. Your Better World isn't so hot. Don't you read the papers?

But if you stay, sooner or later he'll find out who you are and that will undo everything you've done. Besides that, staying around here might not be so healthy, you know? The first time you cross somebody up—Wiley Scott, for example—his memory is likely to improve about what really happened to Norman Akers that night.

Well, that much is right. Wiley might be a problem. But the others, the Regulars, they wouldn't let me down. I know that. Don't you see? That's the good part. That's what makes me want to stay, here among people who could hang me if they wanted to but they wouldn't. And you know why? Just because I seem to be a pretty nice sort of a guy. No other reason. It's not much of a requirement, is it?

No, it's not. I'd think, in fact, that you'd want to live where the standards are a little higher.

Higher! Man, that's a laugh.

Well, are you going?

Yes, I'm going. Don't rush me.

What are you going to do about Rose-Mama? She hasn't taken your rent now in a long while.

Well, let's see, what kind of balance I've got in the Farley State Bank. Two hundred. I'll just write her a check for that amount and leave it on the kitchen table. That'll close out the account.

Are you going to stop at the tavern before you leave? Tell them all good-by?

No, I don't think so. No need for that. They'd ask a lot of questions about why I'm going. And where. As it is, they have a phony name and they won't know where to find me. I'll just go.

And besides, if you went in to say good-by, they'd talk you into staying, right?

Yes, they might. They might at that.

I did stop at the tavern, though. I didn't go in. I parked out in the darkness and walked around in front and felt the bottle caps crunch under my feet.

I stopped at a good time. Or a bad one, maybe.

"Uncle Batey!"

That was Bonney. I could see him standing out in the middle of everything, not only calling Uncle Batey but getting everybody's attention.

"Uncle Batey? Listen, these folks all been readin' in Harvey Wilks' paper about your new specs. Now you get up and tell us, how come you don't like them new glasses of yours."

Scattered applause. "Yeah, Uncle Batey, how about it?"

Then there was Uncle Batey getting up and Aunt Kate smiling at him and holding his hand and patting it and the customers shushing their neighbors, so they could hear.

"Well, it seems like I got somethin' the matter with my eyes, they call 'em cat-tracks. It makes you so you can't see so good and they always want to operate on you. Well, they give me these here new specs, which they're thick as clabber and do you funny. What I mean, you look at somethin' and sometimes you see double that way. All right, ever since I's a kid, I had this habit of goin' out on moonlight nights before I went to bed and takin' me a leak off the back porch. So just right after I got these specs I asseled outside in the moonlight and hauled out to tap my kidney and I looked down and I'll be damn if I didn't see *two* of them things ahangin' out. Well, one of 'em was little. But the other one, why, it was *big!* Size of a wagon tongue. I wanted to call Katey here, so she could see it. But while I was standin' there admirin' that big one, why that *little* one, it *pee'd all over my leg!*"

Oh, laughter. Boot stompings. Shouts. Whistles. Applause. "Uncle Batey, you won't *do!*"

I could still hear the racket when I pulled out on the blacktop and left Bonney's Place behind me.

14.

"Pop? Why is this empty whiskey bottle sitting here on the mantel?"

We were home. Midge and Arch and me. They were in the living room, waiting for me to get dressed so we could all go out and celebrate. New Year's Eve.

You may as well know this too: I came home a hero. Why?

261

Well, because of the money, of course. I brought them a cashier's check for fifteen thousand dollars and they were in there right now, both of them wedged into one chair, looking at the check, thinking of everything it would do for them.

Sure, I told them it was the Old Man's money. I told them Bonney finally just paid up, in full, and there it was. Take it, I said, it's yours, just like your granddad always said. Just like I promised when I left.

Before I ever called Midge and told her I was home I went down to the bank and took a close look at my little estate. My savings and my bonds and a few shares of stock all added up to something more than twenty thousand. Not much to show, I guess, for nearly twenty-five years of work. But it was more than most guys accumulate. I cashed out fifteen of it and brought them the check. I didn't need it. Hell's jingle bells.

"That bottle," I answered from the bedroom, "was left to me. In a will. By Sam Hobbs."

"Who?"

"Samuel Wilkerson Hobbs, Junior," I said.

She didn't ask anything more for a while but I could hear them whispering.

"Pop?"

"Yes?"

"That man, who took Granddad's money. Was he really a very bad kind of person?"

I was trying to knot one of the neckties she gave me for Christmas. The narrow end kept coming out longer than the wide one and I had to retie it three times to get it right.

"I'm not sure," I said.

262